RIPPLES IN TIME

THE SEVEN PORTALS SERIES

ANDRE JONES

ALIEN
PRESS

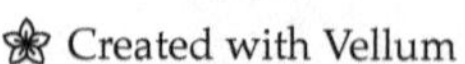 Created with Vellum

AUTHOR'S NOTE

Does anyone read this?

I thank you all for your patience! I will endeavour to be more punctual.

I'm still getting used to this writing gig – it's only my third book after all ... but there's really no excuse for the delay.

Actually, just the one. Thanks to my intrepid beta-readers and editor, several changes were made requiring a bit of culling and rewriting ...

One more thing, stay tuned for a new urban fantasy series coming up in the near future!

<u>Please consider leaving a Review</u>

Help other readers find this epic fantasy series by leaving a review on Amazon, Goodreads, or any other website. Even simple ones like a star-rating really help with a book – and an author's – success.

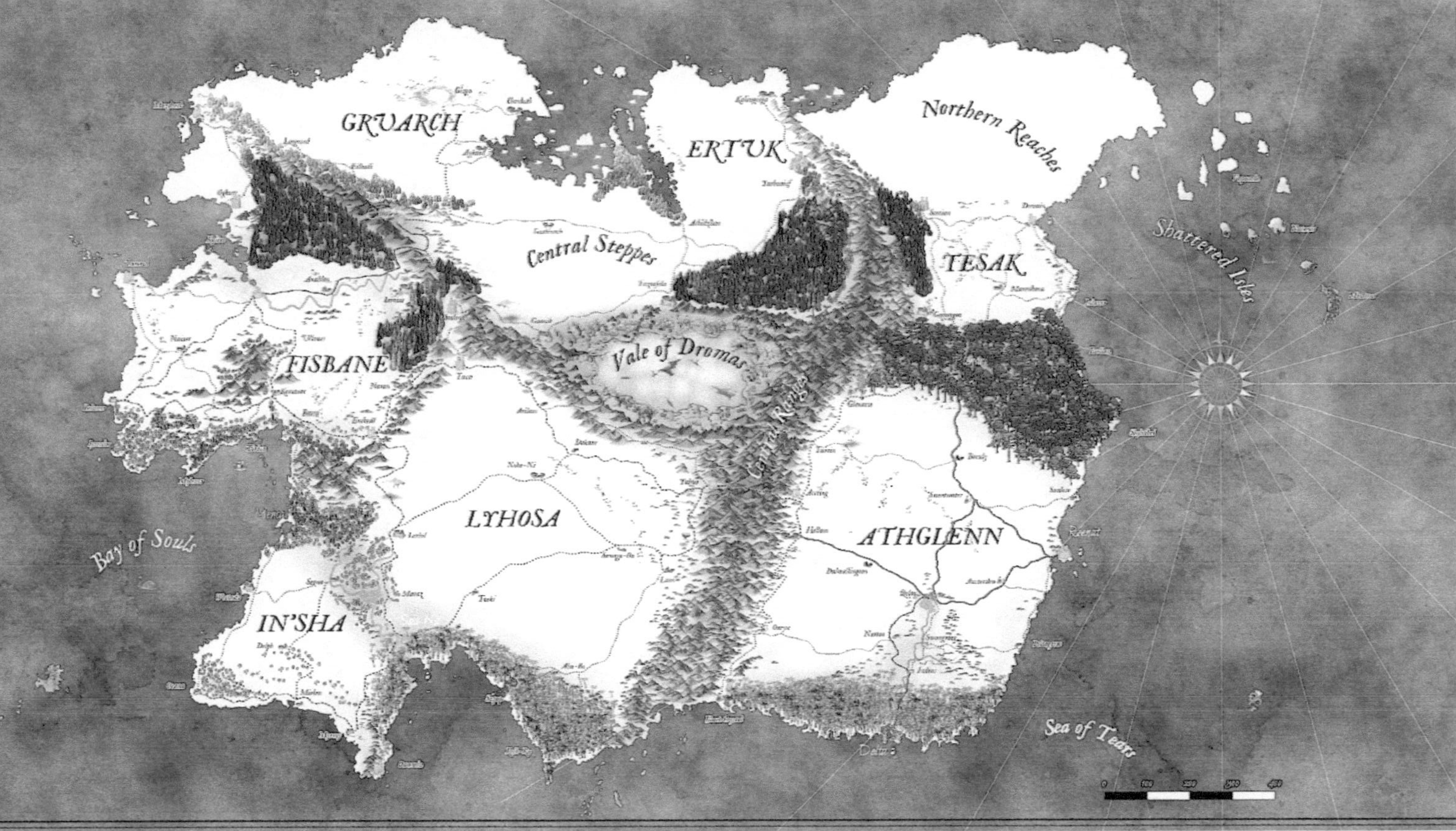
GRUARCH
ERTUK
Northern Reaches
Central Steppes
TESAK
Shattered Isles
Vale of Dromas
Central Range
FISBANE
LYHOSA
ATHGLENN
Bay of Souls
IN'SHA
Sea of Tears

1

AFTERMATH

Leonie understood why she had to leave David up there alone. Alex needed to steal the time-machine and it had to be a successful outcome. Without it, Alex, Dianah and Brendon would never arrive on Yarnik. Delta would never happen. She would never happen. David would never happen.

A rogue flyer trying to land on the SciCorps landing pad was a mistake, but to convince others, the theft couldn't look too easy. Failing to respond with the correct identity codes, the SciCorps lasers took it out.

"My way's quieter," Leonie muttered into the comlink. She flew a few hundred metres away from the tower base to avoid the falling fuselage, then returned to her concealed position after putting out the spot fires from the wreckage and waited in anticipation.

When she heard the shots over the link, she feared the worst. As soon as he came into view, she activated the timer. *Frack, if that's David, I hope he's okay!*

"Let me know when you're at five hundred," Leonie called into her link, raising her voice over the wind she could hear through the earbuds. "Frack it!" she cursed after several repeated calls elicited no response, concerned about the sudden silence.

Allowing them to steal the *Skydancer* needed to be done, but there was no guarantee what would happen beyond that point. After seeing David – or his clone – die with the assassination of Nicholai Zodaich, it was obvious that Alex would not leave any loose ends.

She kept a close eye on the body as it fell. He wasn't moving as a conscious faller would; there was no attempt to level out or try to become stable. The body fell like a rag doll.

Leonie didn't like it, but David had strongly suggested to let him fall for as long as possible before slowing him in case someone was watching from above. She wasn't supposed to approach him for a few minutes.

Finally, she saw enough detail to confirm it was David. The body was five hundred metres up before Leonie gauged she could still safely slow him down. She released her stored power and focused on reducing his speed.

David's body fell to the ground. He lay there unmoving.

She quickly scanned him. He was alive but unconscious, and after detecting an injury, completely disregarded the earlier instruction for her to wait, went invisible and raced to where he lay unmoving. His right temple was slick with blood, with streaks of it down his shoulder and sleeve. Looking closely, she saw a gouge on his scalp and noted a bit of the mesh implant.

"Was that the shot I heard?" She rolled him over. "That's going to hurt." There were no other wounds – no bullet holes at least – and she was certain his landing wasn't hard enough to do more than a bit of light bruising.

After a few gentle shakes, he opened his eyes. "Some things I would rather forget. I don't want to have to do that again."

"Me neither. Who shot you?"

"Alex. He wanted me to jump – which I would have obliged with after the appropriate dramatic pause – but there was a disturbance in the corridor." David sat up with assistance. "He panicked. I realised time was running out and as he raised the gun, I ducked and rolled over the edge. It was a near thing." He checked his com. "And I believe I damaged the link. My actions weren't fast enough." David then tentatively touched his head.

"You're breathing, that's the main thing. Your medicomp will deal with what's left once I get you back up there."

"True, but we should wait a few minutes for whatever is happening to sort itself out. Remember, we actually want them to succeed."

"Fair enough. Have a drink at least." Leonie passed him her flask.

"It must take a lot of courage to knowingly fly at great heights," he said after he took a swig. "I was petrified just thinking about jumping off. Bravado aside, if it wasn't for the fact Alex was about to shoot, I may not have willingly jumped at all."

"It isn't as if I learnt to fly immediately from a few thousand metres. I started at ground level. Nothing courageous about it. One step at a time. I guess one just has to trust the magic as much as you trust the technology; like putting something weighing several tonnes in the air."

David took a breath.

She put her paws up. "And no, I don't need to hear the technobabble on aerodynamics – the point is, you trust the science as much as I trust the magic. You get used to it." Leonie collected the flask, had a drink herself and clipped it back on her utility belt. "Ready to go? I'll rise slowly." Leonie lifted David towards the dock, two-thousand metres above them.

Just before rising above the pad, she slowed and moved closer to the side of the tower, scanning the interior. "There are still people inside. But not Alex, or anyone I recognise."

"I assume there's another way inside we could attempt," David asked. "From your experiences, I mean?"

"None that either of us would care to try. Can you hang on to this?" She pointed to the lip around the edge of the dock. It was barely wide enough to balance on, as long as one had a good hand-hold.

"If you can turn around, we'll see," he suggested, sounding dubious.

Leonie pivoted so David could squirm his backside onto it, reaching up, but the angle was too awkward to maintain a good hold. "No," he said simply. "Pretty sure when you move away, I'll slip off." He closed his eyes for a moment after he looked down at the long drop below his feet.

"Ok." She repositioned herself, taking his full weight again. "Give me a moment." She scanned the minds of the people inside SciCorps for more details. "You might be in luck. Nicholai Zodaich is up there now."

"Is he? Not dead then. That's a surprise."

"Looks like you weren't the only clone. How about this? I'll help support you, but all they will see from their angle is you clambering over the edge."

"And I can tell them I was injured and managed to hide on this ledge?" He shrugged. "May as well. How could they doubt it? It isn't as if I can fly or anything."

"Exactly. And I'll wait underneath and come out when the coast is clear."

He nodded.

It was awkward getting him into position, but with her assistance, he slowly and carefully clambered over the lip.

"I'm so glad to see you!" he gasped as he knelt on the floor, feigning shock and exhaustion.

Stunned, the group inside the docking area turned as one, staring as the scientist climbed up.

"Where the crud have you been?" Nicholai stepped forward, stopping warily a few metres from the edge.

David slowly stood and retold his version of the attack and how he managed to crawl onto the ledge in the confusion. "I believe Alexander was too rushed to check, hence why I'm still alive. I was an easy target otherwise." As expected, no one was willing to peer over the sheer drop to confirm the validity of his story.

"Well, that's amazing. And extremely fortunate for all concerned," Nicholai said.

"Desperate times; desperate measures. Did you apprehend Alex?" David asked, looking around as he walked inside, noting any damage or items missing.

"No. The sergeant here tells me he left in a space yacht which was docked *inside* SciCorps. Can you shed any light on this?"

"Ah, yes. I can, but may I strongly suggest it is for *your* ears only? We can talk securely in here." David indicated the lab.

"After you," the Prime invited.

As the two men walked to the lab Nicholai motioned for a TowerPol officer to stand by the door.

"Prime," the sergeant said. "Considering the recent attempt on your life by this man, I advise against going in unaccompanied."

"Sergeant, that was a clone, but I understand your concern." Nicholai nodded. "This *man* obviously had little to do with that unfortunate incident."

"Very good, sir." The sergeant nodded, not risking going against the tower's highest-ranking member.

"So then, Osbourne," Nick asked once inside. "What's the story?"

David closed the door and stepped further in. "Prime, sir—"

"David, since we 'died' together, Nick is fine." He followed the scientist.

"Thank you. This room held one of my special projects with the *jotnarium* SciCorps was tasked to research."

"I heard about your request for a larger quantity. This is the material that has enabled stealth ability?"

"Yes and no – but that's still undergoing thorough research, which is what led to yet another discovery."

"One which you were going to reveal ... when?"

"As soon as I knew exactly what I was dealing with, how to make sure it was safe, and couldn't be exploited." *Though I am guilty of it myself.*

"And what is it that you were dealing with?"

"With in-depth experimentation and examination, the material produced surprising and unforeseen temporal anomalies the likes of which we've not encountered before—"

"Osbourne, there's an old phrase my father used to say: 'Don't bullshit a bullshitter'. Spell it out."

"I've discovered time-travel."

Nick stared for a moment. "David, I know you're a very accomplished genius, and have gone through a traumatic experience – and I see you have a head injury. Maybe we should continue this debrief after you've been medically examined?" he suggested.

"Believe me, Nick. All my faculties are intact. I know this is hard to believe—"

"Even to this old bullshitter that's an understatement." Nick shook his head in bemusement.

Expecting disbelief, David walked over to a locked drawer. "I have this as evidence of one of my recent experimental trips." A retinal scan gave access to the secured drawer. He brought out one of two flat metal cases, unlocking it with a thumb-scan. David showed the contents to Nick.

The Prime's eyes went wide in surprise. "Is that real paper?"

"A newspaper, yes. One of the last remaining tabloid newspapers in Sydney."

"This is amazing! It must be over 300 years old!"

"This one is the evening edition of 20 August 2030."

"Surely it's too fragile to handle?" Nick said as David withdrew it from the case.

"If found after all this time, most assuredly, however, the paper is less than a month old. You will note there is no mention of the meteor. I looked through three of them. Not a word."

"How long have you had this?" Nick caressed the paper.

"I've had this newspaper for two weeks, but I've been testing the ship for thirty-four days."

Nicholai perused the paper, fascinated by the contents. "And this is all you brought back?"

"Of course," David replied quickly. "Bringing objects from the past to the future could be catastrophic."

"How so?"

"What was the function of the hypothetical item? Removing something that may have previously been insignificant could potentially stop a past event from occurring, thereby creating a new outcome. A different timeline. This is why, until it can be somehow policed, no one must ever be in a position to exploit it for their advantage."

"Yet someone has just done that! Three murderous criminals," Nicholai stated. "I think this is something we should have known about earlier. I'm sure there's some clause in your contract regarding sharing information."

"Forgive me, Nick. It's *time-travel!* If word got out too soon, what safeguards would there be? Everyone would be wanting to use it, try it. Even *steal* it. I needed to ensure what its true capabilities were."

"Then how on earth did Alex find out?"

"I did not knowingly divulge any information. I believe Dianah's new partner has telepathic abilities."

"Telepathy?" The Prime screwed up his face like it was a dirty word. "Are you talking about her new partner, Brendon? Is he a mutant? Is that how they managed to enter this otherwise highly-secure area?"

"It's the only way. I believe he must have become privy to the passwords, and since they are involved with cloning, it's a natural assumption they had an ability to bypass the hand and retinal scans."

Nicholai nodded. "We found an eyeball and a hand by the door. I assume it's *yours.*"

"From the clone of me. Yes, it would have to be identical to get through the scanners." He chose not to reveal the previous vid he'd seen of them using the full-fledged David-clone to enter several days earlier – the clone just used in an assassination attempt. His foreknowledge of the breach and *not* preventing it would raise too many questions.

Nick perused the paper for a few minutes. "Fascinating," he muttered. "If I ask how time-travel is possible, would I understand it?"

"The easiest way to explain what has to be done would be time and space must both be considered. The time axis alone will not move you through space. For example, if I wanted to go forward without considering the location in space, I would simply reappear at the prescribed time, but not moved physically. The ground – the surface of the planet – would have moved on. I'd be in the void."

"And when you travelled back to Sydney in 2030, you had plotted where the Earth would be in space, at that time."

"Correct."

"And if you made a mistake?"

"It's why I adapted the space yacht. The initial jump had a safety margin of ten thousand kilometres."

"And the potential of arriving inside a planet?"

"Problematic, at best, but I don't believe it would occur. Two solid masses cannot merge within one another, unless by pure chance it was in a large empty area like a cavern. The phasing into real-time wouldn't happen. As I said, the initial jumps are calculated to be thousands of kilometres away. I then move in closer, recalibrate the device and repeat. The next jump is exactly on target."

"Where could they have gone to?" Nicholai strolled around the large room, curious about the variety of equipment.

"*When* would they have gone to? They are on the run for several heinous crimes – all of which would result in immediate Recyc." Following him around the room, David continued. "You'd know your son's mind better than me. Would he go to the past or the future?"

"It's apparent I may not know his mind as well as you think. Maybe back in time – is that possible – to stop or warn himself from his mistakes?"

"Part of my testing has shown I can't phase-in within my own timeline – I can't meet myself," David explained. "Or, more accurately, to occupy the time-space where I already exist, the energy requirements go off the scale the closer I get to phasing."

Nicholai considered. "Possibly the future then, but not too far in case technology advances so much he can't catch up – assuming we're still around. Either way, I'm guessing."

"And, ironically, *this* is precisely my dilemma, and why I haven't released any of this information. I feel it best to know how time-travel can be managed before others start trying to manipulate history, or possibly affect the future."

"Like a time-police?"

"How about 'Galactic Authority Temporal Enforcement'?" David suggested with a grin.

"A bit pretentious, don't you think?"

"Possibly," the scientist sighed. "I'm considering AI-controlled sensors to remove the human element; this will greatly increase speed, efficiency, and reduce inaccuracies. I'd need to determine parameters – what time they would be looking for; how it could be detected; and at what range? How many sensors would be needed to cover the solar system, or even the galaxy?"

"I'll leave that up to geniuses like you. This is a remarkable achievement, but now that I know about it, I expect to be kept informed of any progress."

"You have my word. In fact, even my earlier research indicated the prototype, the *Skydancer*, was not the ideal design. I've already arranged for one of our facilities on the L5 orbital to lay the hull of a new design. This newer version, far removed from adverse gravitational influences, is tailor-made to the *nth* degree specifically for time-travel."

"Do you need anything from me?"

"Financially, no. Only the approval of the extra *jotnarium* shipment. Perhaps security and papers, cutting through red tape if and when the need arises."

"Always tricky dealing with those orbitals, but not insurmountable."

"You have my thanks."

Nicholai nodded. "I'd prefer regular updates."

"Progress reports will be securely sent; you can be sure on that. Please accept the paper as a paltry apology for my lapse. I have another one."

Nicholai returned the precious item to the metal case and David reset the security to Nicholai's thumb print. Once he and his TowerPol detail left, David secured the cabinet and donned a replacement comlink.

"All clear," he called as he headed to the medicomp.

"I thought they'd never leave." Leonie floated inside. "What would happen if I flew very fast through that?" She hooked her thumb over her shoulder, indicating the kinetic field.

"You'd be spending more time on the medicomp. The moment you enter the field at speed, it will slow you very drastically. Assuming a head-first trajectory, you'd more than likely incur spinal damage as the rest of your body came to a very sudden stop. Compressed discs would be the least injury."

"Best to not do that then. What news with his lordship?"

"He wants to be kept abreast of progress."

"That's all? His thoughts were saying differently."

"I'm sure more will be asked later." David set the comp controls and relaxed.

2

SKYHOME

WHEN SHE FLEW OVER A ROW OF INFLATABLE DOMES INTO THE MAIN area, Leonie saw the ruined buildings had either been repaired or pulled down to utilise the stonework for other construction. Most of the wood, too weathered to be considered structural, had been set aside for fires.

"I love what you've done to the place," she called out to no one in particular.

Leonie's arrival surprised everyone. Many of the wilders who knew her came over to greet her with hugs or a friendly slap on the back.

"Good to see you," Bern called out, making his way through the crowd. "Welcome to Skyhome. We're about to have lunch. Interested?"

"Always," she replied with a smile, nodding to people as she waded through the group.

"Leonie!" Sussah raced up, throwing her arms around her neck. Not far behind, Harrond and Lerry strolled up, laughing.

"Help!" Leonie feigned choking.

"What are you doing here?" Sussah asked. "Where's David? It's been too long!"

"I'm here to stay, more or less." Leonie answered the rapid

questions. "Busy. Three weeks isn't too long. It's good to see you too. All of you," she said to the other agtechs. Turning back to Sussah who looked disappointed, she said "David's doing what David does best. Researching and inventing. He does send his love though."

Slightly mollified, Sussah found an extra seat for Leonie and they all sat for lunch.

They spent the afternoon catching up on the news from the tower. Not that it had much to do with the wilders, but the agtechs and Sussah were shocked to hear about the assassination attempt, and the death of Veronica Zodaich.

"My David would never do that!" Sussah said.

"They know it was a clone and they know exactly who did it," Leonie informed them.

"Have they been arrested?" Lerry asked her.

"They're working on it."

"How could that be? Where can they hide in the tower?"

"Alex has many high-ranking friends, but I'm sure everything will work out." Leonie dodged the truth. "The good news is, David is no longer under suspicion."

After a myriad more questions, she was offered a tour of Skyhome, the new wilder community, with Bern, Sussah and both agtechs. Veggie gardens had been established, and with the aid of some equipment and agtech knowledge, some varieties of vegetables were almost ready for harvesting.

"We've adapted some of the bio-domes for aquaponics," Harrond stated proudly.

"We do have one concern though," Lerry said as they were nearing the spare powerpac storage. He pointed to each pac's charge level.

"They've dropped?"

"Considerably so for pacs that haven't been hooked up to anything."

"What's draining them? Are they damaged?"

"It isn't my area of expertise, but pacs I've worked with before remained charged far longer."

"Solar charging not working?"

"We can only charge a few at a time, but it can't keep up." Lerry scratched his head. "At the rate of discharge, we have about one month left before things like food storage and the medicomp will be useless."

"Aren't these pacs supposed to last a decade?" Leonie asked.

"That's a decade of average use," Harrond added. "These aren't being used at all."

"Okay, I'll see what can be done. With David working from the orbital, it might take time."

"Will you be staying with us now?" Harrond asked.

"That's the plan, but I guess I'll need to go back a couple of times for more pacs."

"The portal isn't losing charge?"

"Not from the tower end; it's plugged in to the tower supply. This draining is something local."

"So, maybe store more pacs near the tower portal, and we'll only swap them when these are spent, and put them on charge in the tower."

"I'll arrange for that to happen," Leonie said. "Problem solved then?"

"For the interim," he said as they all headed back to the eating area. "I'd still like to know what's draining them."

Rhiannon was waiting for her. "It's such a pleasure to have you join us. Why the change of heart?"

"David being so busy for one, and something's bugging me."

The pair wandered away from the main group as they talked.

"Admittedly, it's not something that I've been able to work on until recently, but I have a random dream with Styx in my head, and this prophecy they're determined to involve me in. I recall hearing something about it back in Jenolan when we first arrived. As their seer, can you tell me more about it?"

Rhiannon quoted "'From a distant land another of our kind will appear. A pure one, to give birth to a new hope. With her will be a guardian to bring all the peoples together and to their origins'."

"So, Sussah's 'another of our kind'. Is David the new hope?"

Rhiannon smiled. "As you'd expect from a *seer*, I've given this much consideration – especially since your arrival."

"But for you, Earth is *your* true home. How does that work out if you're now here?"

"I am unsure. We are here now, that's what's important. Maybe a way will be paved for a safer return?"

"And all the 'peoples to their true homes' means finding the seven portals for the seven races of *this* world."

"Only six to go. Seems like the other skylands you mention are possible sites. Have you ever been to this Vale of Dromas? Maybe they are there?"

"And lots of l'ith. It could be very difficult."

"Difficult? Look where we are, Leonie. You made it possible for the wilders to travel to another world. I think you'll manage somehow."

"I thought you'd say that," Leonie growled, kicking a tuft of grass. "Hey, I've a question I keep forgetting to ask. Do you know a wilder named Brendon? He's about David's age."

"I do. He was a Runner, like Bern. He went missing a few months back, presumed dead. It happens, and it is a sad thing, especially if it happens quickly. We don't get any telepathic feedback. We're never sure if it's the howlers or patrols or they're simply too far away. Why do you ask?"

"He's in the tower. When did he go missing?"

"It would be over eight months now."

"Don't you find it coincidental that they knew exactly where Jenolan was after all this time, and they took only *you* captive? It doesn't look like Brendon has been suffering either."

"You've seen him? You think he informed?"

"You mean did he betray you? Knowing what I know of the future Brendon and Dianah, I wouldn't be surprised in the least. Dianah is trying to improve her psionics. He has some ability, though maybe not enough. You might have been the bargaining chip to make him look good."

They found themselves near the portal. Leonie jogged closer

and picked up the torc. She put it on her neck, feeling the constant vibration. She undid the zipper and slipped it under the front of her top.

"So, tell me all the gossip," she said. "How are the Ivanas and Redmonds working out."

"For starters, they've been given proper names – and are no longer addressed as a collective noun."

––––––

Two weeks after Leonie's return, she heard a commotion outside her window.

Like the other elders, she had been accommodated in one of the more solid buildings. Her protests for what she considered favouritism fell on deaf ears. The wilder community insisted it was the least they could do for all she had done for them.

While she wouldn't admit it, she did feel much relieved at not having to camp constantly. *And much more comfortable.*

I heard that.

Morning, Rhiannon. She got up from her bed and sauntered downstairs to see what was going on.

Following to where some of the wilders were pointing, she saw a dozen glins'ool approaching on foot.

"What are they?" Lerry asked, jogging up beside her. Like Harrond, he had been allocated a room in the building next door, along with the other male elders. They both had pulse rifles.

"Who are they, is more correct. They are glins'ool, and these in particular are warriors, but if they remember me from last time, they're no threat to us."

"That was over twenty years ago." Lerry said as they both slung their rifles.

"True. One way to find out." She walked out to greet them, meeting them in the open, halfway across the green.

"May the winds sustain you," she said.

The group stopped, looking at each other before one stepped forward.

"That is normally used as a farewell. But greetings, nonetheless. I am Talon Flin si Sloor, at your service. How is it you know something of our ways?"

"Forgive me. I met with another Talon here twenty years ago. I cannot recall the commander's full name, I'm sure it was ... Gruy. He had several warriors with him, Wyth and Sera helped me a great deal."

One of the warriors at the rear squawked.

Flin paused. "Please forgive the hatchling; he is from Wyth's brood, second generation."

Second generation? "Is that like his grandmother?"

Again Flin paused, considering. "I believe in some groundling terms, yes, Wyth would be his *grandmother.* She was from nest Snarr."

Leonie remembered the wilders behind her, waiting and watching. "Allow me to make some introductions." Leonie went through the more prominent friends with her, and Rhiannon fed her some names when she forgot.

"We would be honoured if you would come and meet the others," Rhiannon suggested. "We can share food, and talk."

"The honour is ours." The Talon dipped his head. "I will be interested to hear how it is you came to meet Wyth," he warbled to Leonie as they made their way to the eating area.

Leonie was saddened to hear of Wyth's passing, two seasons earlier.

"She tells a story where you fought and killed a l'ith by yourself with fire?" Flin continued. "Is this true?"

"I didn't fight a l'ith alone. They both assisted greatly. I couldn't have succeeded without them. Have you seen a l'ith up close? The shell is still here, in those trees."

"I have not, but I have only been a Talon for a short period, having flown up from southern In'sha. It is a complex inter-nest custom," he explained to her curious look. "The l'ith are more frequently found closer to the Vale area."

After their meal Leonie, the agtechs and Rhiannon, along

with the talon and a retinue of wilders, walked to the wooded area where the l'ith remains could still be seen.

"This young lady, Sussah, and I were here when Talon Gruy arrived with his warriors over twenty years ago. Wyth and her friend Sera remained for protection until the others returned with food and healing assistance. This l'ith – believed to be a scout – arrived. It was damn tough, too. We fought as best we could. Wyth injured her arm, and Sera her shoulder."

The glins'ool walked around it, cooing and warbling at its size, pointing to the fire damaged eye socket. There was a raucous warbling between two of the younger looking flyers.

The Talon squawked tersely. The noise abated immediately. "Forgive these *jurida* for their outburst. You must be a strong powershaper to do this."

"She *is*," Sussah added, nodding.

"Hardly. Wyth and Sera wounded the creature a great deal already, but I guess I'd better show you otherwise you'll think they were exaggerating." Leonie beckoned, walking into the clearing where she conjured a small fireball.

The talon gasped as one.

Leonie's control had increased over the years, so she made the fireball larger, holding it in her paws for all to see before sending it skywards. She was surprised at the strength of her fireball, remembering very weak results on her first visit. An idea dawned on her; something to discuss with Lerry later.

Even those who had seen her magic before were surprised at her control. At their enthusing, she created another one, and the glins'ool craned their long necks in for a closer look. She finished off by conjuring a short stream of electricity between her paws before reabsorbing it.

Some of the group started applauding and most of the wilders headed back home to continue with their chores.

Your eyes are glowing, Rhiannon informed her.

They are? Leonie cleared her throat, feeling embarrassed at the attention. "I have no idea where we are at the moment. Where is your nest? Is that the right word?" she said as the group strolled to the edge. "Where does this talon go to when not on patrol?"

"While many of the group are from this region, *we* are based at Tana Keep," he chirped. "It is a small fortification on the eastern side of Mount Tana behind us."

"I guess we are close, for you to be here?"

Flin nodded. "This skyland is passing through our patrol area. We saw the smoke and came to investigate. We are very surprised to see groundlings up here."

"We're not planning an invasion." Leonie smiled to reassure him. "I hope we aren't intruding."

"No laws have been breached." Flin continued, "This skyland is now about halfway between Naran and Soolind, heading south."

"I think I visited Irinius a while back. These skylands drift and rotate, it's hard to keep track. You reckon we're heading south now?"

"Yes. When it meets the coastline, it will slow and then return more or less along this path."

"I remember. I was on a skyland many years ago over Athglenn. When it reached the coastline, it shuddered and swayed. I thought it was going to break apart."

"It is the way it is. One of my distant nestlings knows of a ranger. Having studied the skylands for years, she has mapped out the paths of many skylands – there are hundreds of them – though maybe only two dozen of this size."

"And this skyland, it follows the mountain range?"

"I believe so," Flin replied.

They walked along the edge before heading back inland.

"I hope you do not think it impertinent of me – and as a Talon I should ask – how is it you are all here?" He looked over the community as they approached. "And how you brought all this *nesting* material with you."

"Have you heard of portals?"

Flin ruffled his feathers. "I know of the stories they tell nestlings."

"I expected as much. Please, let me show you something else."

With the talon softly trilling in curiosity to each other, the group headed towards the portal.

"I have seen this on previous patrols when passing overhead. But this glow is different. How is this so?"

"It's charged now. I reckon when you saw it before, it had no charge."

"Charged?"

"Containing power, magic."

"And this *portal* enables you to travel up here?"

Leonie considered what to tell him, not out of secrecy, but she didn't want to sound crazy to him. "More or less, but from a very distant land, where there's another portal. It acts like a gateway."

"I ... see. Do you mean Ghalena?"

Leonie didn't want to lie. "No. Much, *much* further."

"Are there glins'ool there? I hear some of us have traversed the oceans."

"I've never seen any, not where we come from."

"Still, this is truly remarkable."

Before the question of using it came up, Leonie offered to show them the community. She let Lerry take over this part, but stayed with the group, answering the occasional question.

"Again, forgive my impertinence. You said earlier you visited Irinius? How is this so?" Flin asked. "If this portal only allows travel to your distant homeland?"

She grinned. "You're not the only ones that can fly."

The avians stayed overnight, enjoying the unusual food from the wilders, and in turn, sharing theirs. There was also a promise to bring local seeds next time they were in the area. Many wilders were present to say their farewells.

"One more thing before we go." Flin turned to Leonie and

Rhiannon. "There have been sightings of a wyvern in the area. It hasn't caused any trouble yet, but these creatures are fickle."

"Is he green, with amber eyes?" Leonie asked.

"You have seen him already?" Flin chirped in surprise. "I can confirm the reports are of a large green wyvern."

"His name is Noldor. I don't believe he would trouble those that don't trouble him. Could you tell me where he was last seen?"

The flock of glins'ool chirruped to each other at the name.

Flin cleared his throat, silencing them. "It was over a month ago, but other patrols have seen him around the woodlands at the foothills near Mount Chark to the north."

"Thank you. Perhaps I should pay him a visit. See how he's settling in."

"Visit? Settling in?" he clucked in wonder. "I see what Wyth has said about you is true. You are a very strange person."

"She gets that a lot," Lerry said, laughing along with the others.

"And it is now I say to you on behalf of my talon, and Tana Keep, 'may the winds always sustain you,' Leonie and friends."

The wilders and agtechs waved and in a flurry of feathers and wingbeats, the glins'ool took off. The children collected discarded feathers and wove them into their hair. One young boy handed one to Rhiannon.

"Thank you, Symon." Holding the feather by the quill, she ran her fingers along the tips of the fine vanes. "They were fascinating," Rhiannon said, trailing behind the group as they returned to the community.

"There are so many great things about this world ... but that's not to say Earth hasn't any wonders—"

"It's okay Leonie," Rhiannon laughed. "Earth doesn't need you defending it. I'm sure you're glad to be here."

Leonie took a deep breath. "You know I am."

"So, you're going to see the wyvern?" Lerry called over his shoulder.

"Soon. We have a few things to do here first. I'll need to get back to the tower and find some more powerpacs. Maybe we can swap the discharged ones first, and store any spares closer to the portal. I'll need to show you and Harrond around SciCorps – David's labs – so if you need to go there while I'm away, you won't get lost."

"It can't hurt. I'd like to see what he's managed for himself," Lerry agreed.

"It's wonderful what he's achieved." Sussah said proudly. "I might even sneak in a bath."

"Lerry, I have a theory where your power might be going," Leonie said.

"A theory? You've been with David too long."

She laughed, then told them of her thoughts, why her power was stronger now. "When I'm on or near solid ground, I have no trouble drawing power. Last time I was here, it was difficult and tiring. And you saw how much easier it was this time."

"Easy for some," Harrond whispered to Sussah.

"I heard that," Leonie laughed.

"You're saying the skyland is absorbing the power from the pacs?"

She nodded.

"Any way to stop it?" Lerry asked. "They're quite important, at least until we can get the crops growing properly."

"Not that I'm aware." She adjusted her comlink. "I didn't notice it at the time, but I reckon we are lower." She showed him the altimeter.

"Lower?"

Leonie shrugged. "I thought the altitude changed with the hills; they rise, we rise ... and Skyhome still might do that, but ..."

"But what?"

"During the Powershaper Wars, they say these skylands were drained of power so quickly, the surrounding crystal repelled them."

"And, by absorbing power, the skyland is dropping."

"It's a guess. Maybe over the next few weeks we can study it." She shrugged. "It could simply be an aspect of the type of terrain we're travelling over. I'll need you guys to help work out what equipment we'll need."

"You got it. May as well start sooner than later," Lerry said.

"How about now?" she asked.

"Why not. I've nothing better to do, and it is only a few steps away."

"Can't argue with that logic." She turned to Sussah. "Looks like you get your bath."

3

SCICORPS

Part of the SciCorps labs had been sectioned off from the rest of the manufacturing floor. Robots and many forms of automated machinery were tirelessly and efficiently churning out products. As long as no one entered the red-striped areas on the floor, they were safe. After unloading the powerpacs Leonie then moved them to the recharging station against the wall and swapped them out with charged ones.

"I must say, I'm impressed with everything he's achieved," Lerry looked around in awe when Leonie gave them the tour afterwards. "And all accomplished in a few years?"

"Less. You could call this the back end of SciCorps, several sections away from any possible prying eyes," Leonie informed them.

"Is that likely?"

"I very much doubt it. Knowing he was going to be away for prolonged periods, David has revamped the security. Anyone not on his AI's check-list gets zapped. TowerPol will be informed of breaches, droids will then move the intruders to the front door. No one gains access."

"Am I still able to have a bath?" Sussah looked disappointed. "Or were you teasing?"

"No. You don't think he'd forget his mother, do you?"

"David forget? Pfft."

"What's he up to again? You say he's on an orbital?"

"Special research that needed to be done with as little gravitational influence as possible."

"You know what it is, don't you?" Sussah accused. "You'd think he'd tell his *mother*."

"You remember when we thought he was joking about a time-machine?"

"Of course. I thought it was unkind too, teasing his mother."

"He wasn't," Leonie assured her.

"Wasn't what?" Sussah frowned.

"Teasing."

"Now you're—"

"C'mon. I'll show you all something." She led them out. "I'll have to add your faces to the security program first."

"Why didn't it detect us when we came though the portal?"

"He has different systems; one for out there, and one for in here. He's made sure no one not on this list comes through, at least until he comes back." She showed them a list of registered people. It was short as it only listed them.

Bypassing the security took time, as did making their way through the SciCorps facility. The group sat around the dining table afterwards.

"Before you have your bath, have a look at this." The vid showed them where the *Skydancer* had been stored before it was stolen. While they watched, she turned the coffee machine on.

They saw three figures run in and board the craft. A couple of minutes behind them the armed TowerPol team followed, then the two-minute warning sounded. The *Skydancer* vanished.

"Where did it go?" Sussah asked.

"Not where – *when*. Keep watching." Leonie readied the mugs.

The vid continued. Leonie fast forwarded until more figures appeared. "Recognise him?"

"Isn't that Nicholai Zodaich?" Sussah asked.

"It is. Remember when I joined you guys on Skyhome I told you about the assassination attempt?"

"You said a clone did it. I know my David couldn't have."

"A clone that also *died* in the attempt. Recognise any of those people who got on the *Skydancer*?" Leonie continued at the shake of heads. "They were Alexander Zodaich, Dianah Felton and Brendon."

"Felton? The daughter of the geneticist?" Lerry queried.

"And the Prime's son!" Harrond exclaimed.

"So, it was all true?" Sussah asked.

"Them travelling back to Delta? Yes, all true." Leonie brought the coffee over on a tray. "I know it's hard to take in, but seeing is believing. I wanted you to see this first, which is why I didn't really answer the 'why they hadn't been arrested' question. You wouldn't have believed me."

"And David knew how to get to Delta because of the orb?"

"He knew how to get to Yarnik, not sure about Delta."

"And he didn't tell us?" Sussah frowned.

"I only found out recently and now I'm letting you know. He also told me the *Skydancer* was a prototype, having discovered some problems. He didn't want to risk anyone's safety. I bet there's lots of things David hasn't told us. I'm sure he will, in time. Now, you go enjoy your bath."

"This is great," Lerry said, looking around. He pointed to a large door, noting the higher ceilings. "Is that a loading dock?"

"Yes. There's a landing pad outside, but since he's away for long periods, he's sealed the place up tight. No one in or out – except the portal." She pointed to the sensors and unusual weaponry in the ceiling. "The new security."

"How long will he be away do you suppose?"

"No idea." Leonie shook her head. "It could be a week, month, or he could return before Sussah gets out of the bath." She moved to the desk. "How's Skyhome for supplies? David's granted access and allowed us to order stuff if needed." She displayed the current supply inventory on the screen. "But I'm sure you've more experience with these things."

Lerry sat down and studied the display, making a few entries. "How do these get past security protocols?"

"There is a fully automated and highly-secure lift. The droids collect from below at a designated area, then bring it onto the elevator. David made some modifications; the elevator will not allow biologicals in; no heat signatures and the like. Once sealed, it is depressurised. The shaft has sensors with back-ups and redundancies, and is weaponised. Even I wouldn't try it."

"Sounds elaborate."

"He's got a lot of stuff here people would be dying to get hold of."

———

'*Blue Six*, welcome to Tranquillity Orbital. Blue Mountains Tower registration confirmed. We have you on auto, berthing at Bay 43. ETA five mins.'

"Affirmative, Tranquillity. Out." David released control and watched out the viewport as the ship was drawn in closer under the orbital's AI control. Manual docking onto any station was deemed too risky, not only for the number of lives put at risk, but the cost of repairs and loss of production if there was even the slightest mishap.

As Blue Mountains Tower helped fund the project, it had a couple of dedicated facilities to use for specific projects. With his current project – also partially funded by the tower and SciCorps – he had the use of one of them for six months.

He could see the new hull on the gantry from a distance. The conversion from a diagram to 3D model to the full-size ship now before him was amazing, even though he designed it himself. Progress reports from his crew were reassuring, with everything on schedule.

"Good to see you again," David greeted Sally and Paul as he

disembarked. "The reports are looking good. I hope you've both been well?"

"Well enough," Paul replied. "New ship?"

"Something like that. I'll tell you about it later." Not for the first time, David marvelled at how well they'd adjusted to their new life – so vastly removed from anything they were familiar with. In his enthusiasm and arrogance, David had been keen to test the *Skydancer*. After the many preliminary trials proved accurate, he took a leap of faith to test his time-machine. In so doing, he tested – and failed – his ethical standards; putting his life above science.

He had gone back in time to 2030, three hours before the destruction of Sydney, to witness what happened, and had experienced more than he bargained for. Parking the ship in Hyde Park, invisible as always, he had obtained the newspapers he'd showed to Nick, then had been mugged mere metres away from the vessel. Paul and Sally intervened, Sally got shot and with scant minutes to spare David coaxed them into the *Skydancer* to escape the city's destruction.

With the *Skydancer* hovering in geostationary orbit above Sydney, David played back recordings taken by drones he'd released before landing. While Sally's wounds were being repaired by the medicomp, Paul watched the devastation in fascination, seeing the world he knew vanish beneath the melted Antarctic. Shortly after, three hundred years into their future, David landed the ship in his workshop, showed them his implant and together, they stepped into a future they could never have imagined.

They saved my life. It was the least I could do.

"Would you like a tour?" Paul broke into his thoughts.

"Hmm?"

"You've not seen inside for real." Paul pointed out.

"Considering there was no *inside* previously ... yes, I'd like that. Virtual tours are great, but the mind still knows it isn't real."

. . .

Decked out in EV-suits, the two men walked out onto the gantry once the airlock cycled. David paused, leaning back to look up at the curved hull looming over them. While his scientific mind knew it was pointless, he raised his gloved hand to 'feel' it.

The hull sat between two long arms. Along these arms was the standard array of attachments and connectors providing essential services for the designated tasks.

Moving on, they arrived at the entrance midway between two of the four landing struts. Paul led the way in.

"We'll have to use the stairs as the elevator isn't rigged up yet."

"That's fine." David adjusted the volume of his helmet, admiring the workmanship of the interior ... if the programmed tasks of droids could be regarded as workmanship.

"Obviously, the ballast tanks are empty, but the conduits are in place and tested," Paul said as they climbed the stairs spiralling around the large central column.

Not all the panelling was in place as some sizeable equipment still needed to be installed, so David popped his head inside.

"That's going to be one big gyroscope," Paul said over his shoulder.

"It'll need to be to keep the ship correctly positioned."

"To what?"

"It will provide an inertial reference point in space that TAU can use if it needs to change the ship's orientation. Because of where and when the ship will be travelling, this will be relative to the galactic plane. Otherwise, jumping through time could be problematic."

"I think I need another upgrade," Paul joked.

"Just name it." David pulled his head out as Paul continued up the stairs.

"When's the computer being installed?" he called down."

"I estimate TAU will be ready in two days, and once calibrated, should be at optimal functionality within a week."

"Will you be here for that time?"

"I'll be installing it and running the diagnostics. You and Sally deserve some time off if you'd like. By the time you get back, the ship should be running."

"That's great!"

4

NOLDOR

After a few trips back and forth, Lerry was satisfied Skyhome was well-provisioned for the foreseeable future.

"Just remember that entry list and who's on it. Make sure no one else enters. It could be disastrous," Leonie cautioned.

"The wilders have learnt a long time ago to be cautious; no one will come near if the elders warn them off. We'll put up signs just in case."

"Good. I'll see you when I see you." She waved. With enough supplies for a few days' flying, Leonie headed north, studying the expanse of the woodlands ahead and below. There was the infrequent split with a canyon or river. And to the south on the horizon the terrain changed to plains or farmland. To the north was a low mountain range angling to the west.

She'd been flying for several hours and had a quick rest. Not long after taking flight a flock of glins'ool flew up from the edge of the woodland to intercept her. They looked like warriors, but she didn't recognise anyone from Flin's talon.

"What is your business here?" the lead warrior asked as they swooped around her. "How is it a rrell is flying?" he clucked suspiciously.

"I have some powershaping abilities. Why is it your concern?" She disliked the arrogant and abrupt manner.

"There is a wyvern ahead. We're keeping people at a safe distance. You should go back until the threat is nullified?"

"Threat? Nullified? What's happened?"

"I am not at liberty to tell you anything. Once again, I suggest you head back."

"How about we land and talk about this? I've no intentions of going back just yet." Leonie started to descend.

"Halt! You do not have permission to land."

"I don't recall asking. Look, I don't want trouble. I know Talon Flin si Sloor from Tana Keep. He seemed far more agreeable. Just let him know Leonie has come through; he will assure you I'm no threat."

"How do you know him?" The warrior manoeuvred in front of her, brandishing his javelin, as did three other warriors. The others gathered behind her, bows drawn and aimed.

"We met recently. Unlike you, he was very friendly and certainly had no concerns. I'd appreciate it if you moved aside so I could land."

"You are not permitted—"

She dropped like a stone until she was a few hundred metres below them, then shot to the north. As it was magical in nature, her flying wasn't limited to manoeuvring like they were. The arrows fell far behind. The glins'ool gave chase, but quickly disappeared in the distance.

"Frack it," she cursed. "And I was starting to like the glins'ool."

Closer to what she believed was Mount Chark – as it was the most prominent peak along the ranges – she slowed. She saw another flock of glins'ool – mere specks at this distance – circling above a ridgeline. The scene reminded her of gulls circling fishing boats coming into the harbour after a day's trawling. Knowing the avians had eyesight almost as good as hers, she descended to tree-top level before they noticed her and made her way closer.

Noldor, are you around?

Ah, Leonie. So nice of you to visit. I was wondering when you would be back.

Are these glins'ool giving you trouble?

Hardly. More of a nuisance really. At the moment they are taking turns to see who can get the closest to me before darting away.

Yes. If they're anything like the ones I just left, they aren't as welcoming as some others I've known.

It is to be expected; fear of the things they don't know. Stay where you are. I will come to you.

Leonie landed in an area where she could keep the avians and mountain in view. The circling glins'ool suddenly scattered as the great green wyvern took flight, but they followed in his wake as he flew to the woodland. When Noldor landed, he brought down a few branches in the process.

"Good to see you again."

Likewise, Noldor replied.

She watched as the avians finally caught up. The bulk of the talon circled just above the forest canopy while three slowly flapped to the ground, landing at a distance.

"I'm surprised you're still here," she said. "I thought you'd be off to find more of your own kind, or even visit Dorn."

The three grounded warriors ventured closer, warily.

I was going soon. I thought it polite to wait and see if you returned as you planned. All is well?

"The wilders are settled in. Thanks." She turned to the approaching warriors.

"Who are you, and what is your business here?" the closest ordered, brandishing his javelin.

"I should ask you the same thing." Leonie's hackles rose. "Are you here in any official capacity? I don't see any coat of arms or uniforms?"

"We are a patrol from Ullvaes," the warrior answered.

"Well, I'm here to visit a friend."

"This creature is your friend?" He eyed the wyvern suspiciously.

"Well, I'm not talking to myself," she laughed.

"Your *friend* has been causing chaos with the local farmers. Eating their cattle."

Two cows only. I stunned them, so no stampeding. I was not aware of any chaos.

Stunning them was very considerate of you, she replied to Noldor, then answered the warrior. "Well, he *is* a wyvern," she said. "What's he supposed to eat? People? But he *does* apologise."

I do?

Shhh. "If it makes you feel better, he would be happy to leave," Leonie added.

"Leaving would be a good thing," the warrior said. "Compensation would be better."

Compensation? Noldor barked a laugh.

"Compensation? From a wyvern?" Leonie shared Noldor's mirth. "How about he doesn't eat any of you?"

Yuck. Those feathers.

"Seriously?" she responded to the warrior, trying not to laugh in the avian's beak. "For the inconvenience of a farmer losing a couple of cows, I'd think you'd be relieved to see the back of him." *I'm really not in the mood to fight two dozen glins'ool.*

The warrior noticed the other talon arrive, doubling their numbers. "How about we skewer you instead?" he replied.

Our friend is feeling quite brave now.

More fool him. "You know, out of all the talons I've met, you lot are the rudest I've come across. Talon Gruy si Ferik, of the Nest of Snarr, and Flin si Sloor would be most disappointed."

Name-dropper, Noldor snorted again.

Leonie smiled.

The Talon of the new arrivals strutted into the clearing. "This is good, well done." He bobbed his head to the other warrior. "We can bring this one in for trespassing."

"Pfft. Guys, we're trying to be nice here," Leonie scoffed. *I've had enough of this.*

Me too.

"You can keep your pleas for later at your hearing," the warrior stated puffing out his chest.

"Oh, my apologies," she said sarcastically, bowing. "What I meant to say was, could you get the rest of your nestlings on the ground so they're not too injured when we depart?"

"You do not tell us what to do." The Talon now stepped forward, brandishing his javelin. The others moved closer.

"Fair enough." *Noldor, would you, please?*

Mind-blast?

If you would be so kind. She nodded encouragement.

And you—

Will be fine.

Why didn't you say so in the first instance?

The avians on the ground, being the closest and getting the full blast, crumpled when Noldor roared. Those in flight spiralled down, some crashing into the upper branches of the trees and getting stuck. One of the warriors hit a limb and started tumbling. Leonie caught her and lowered her to the ground.

"That's a relief. I didn't want them to be too injured," she said.

Seems their wings lock in place as a reflex action. Interesting.

"Very handy. It's a shame though. Up until now, I quite liked the glins'ool. I guess every race has its arseholes."

Noldor snorted.

Leonie went around to check on their condition, even those caught in the branches, which she brought down to ground level. No severe injuries were found; cuts and bruises mostly.

Leonie unzipped her top. "Is it warm here or what?"

I have nothing to compare it to. It could be summer.

"Must be. I think we should go." Leonie sighed afterwards. "Better for all if we're clear of the area before they come around."

Their squawking did grate the nerves. I thought Evlin was bad.

"You had to go and spoil a fine day." Leonie lifted off the ground. "Coming?"

Noldor unfurled his wings and leapt from the ground, pushing upwards with great sweeps of his wings. *How did you know of the mind-blast?*

"Dorn," Leonie replied

Ah. Yes. She was quite adept at that. She even gave me a headache.

Leonie winced at the memory. "She didn't need to roar quite so loudly though."

We have our reputation to uphold, you know.

Leonie purred. A couple of thousand metres above the ground was nice and cool.

The skyland came into view as the sun was setting. With his permission, Leonie was now astride Noldor. She had covered a fair bit of distance getting to Noldor, and was finding the return leg wearisome.

I better go ahead and warn them. They'll panic seeing you arrive unannounced. They have weapons from Earth which might actually hurt you.

I should get some food first.

Leonie hopped off while Noldor reduced speed. *Why do you eat? I thought you were dead.*

It is what we do. I gain no sustenance, but it is good for my mental health.

Maybe consider a wild animal this time. She raced ahead, sending Noldor the all clear once the wilder community was forewarned.

As expected, the community were in equal amounts of fear and awe when the wyvern landed on the green. Some of the Jenolan wilders had encountered Noldor when he first appeared on Earth, but the others needed more time to adjust to seeing a creature so large.

"Noldor, if you remember, this is Rhiannon and Bern. You met them briefly when we finally dealt with Evlin."

Bern nodded a hello.

It's so wonderful to see you again, Noldor, Rhiannon sent. *As I've told Leonie many times already, this is such a fascinating world.*

Your Earth was interesting too, though after the years I did find it … empty.

It was a different story centuries ago. "Allow me to introduce you to the others." The seer turned to the crowd.

Pleased to meet you all, he sent after the many introductions, making them gasp. *Welcome to my world.*

"I have a task." After breakfast Leonie strolled up to Noldor as he lay on the grass, swishing his tail in the dewy grass. "If we're both going the same direction, perhaps you could assist?"

I have nothing better to do.

"There might be l'ith involved," Leonie cautioned.

All the better.

"Let me guess. Fighting l'ith is good for your mental health too?"

It is the best. We have been doing it for millennia. What is this task of yours?

"Finding more portals. I'm guessing there's at least six more."

Six?

"To equal the number of exotic species here on Yarnik. Am I correct in saying you and the l'ith are native to this world?"

We were here long before any of the new arrivals.

"Apparently my *destiny* is to bring all the people back to their worlds, or some such."

Destiny is a powerful thing. A good motivator.

"Perhaps, but I'm here, and like it or not, circumstances indicate there might be something to it. May as well see where it goes."

Perhaps, as I am not quite dead yet, I too have a role in this prophecy of yours?

"Who knows? Time will tell." *Glad to have your company though. I'll just grab my gear.*

. . .

From Skyhome, the pair of unusual travellers flew east over a small mountain range, before crossing the northern corner of Lyhosa. It was a monotonous expanse of dry grassland. Other than watching herds of unknown animals foraging, they regaled each other with their previous experiences to kill time. To save energy Leonie rode Noldor, much like the way she rode Slana. She reminisced at length about her time at Hell's Maw until, on the afternoon of the second day, Noldor spied movement.

Look ahead, the wyvern said.

Leonie glanced down and ahead. *Your eyesight's better than mine. You mean that town?* In the distance there was what looked like a walled settlement surrounded by farmhouses and the mosaic pattern of tilled fields.

I see l'ith in numbers approaching, the wyvern informed her. *And there are five hunters coming in from the east.*

They flying ones? Do l'ith use tactics, coming in from two directions? Leonie turned her head, looking down slightly.

No. I believe in this case it is simply two lots of l'ith arriving at the same time; not coordinated. They have never used tactics before.

So, there are two types?

Three, actually. Drones and hunters, yes. And the breeders, but they do not surface.

You reckon we can assist? she asked.

I was hoping you would concur.

I was getting bored anyway. Leonie noted his enthusiasm. *What's your plan, does mind-blast work on them?*

For the drones, it is their one weakness – they are very susceptible to it. The hunters are more resistant. I suggest we deal with them first. For the walled fortifications, they are the biggest threat. Not as large as the drones, but are faster and more agile.

Interesting to know. After you, good sir. Leonie hopped off and let Noldor do what wyverns did best. *I'll watch and learn.*

Firstly, we come in from above. If you have wondered why wyverns choose to fly at such high altitudes all the time, this is it. It is instinctive to us, so we are always above them, and they dislike the cooler air.

Noldor spiralled sharply down until he was almost upon a l'ith hunter on the flank. He then tucked his wings in momentarily and dropped like a stone onto the hunter's back. At the same time, he swished his tail to the side, damaging the nearest l'ith with the barbed end. The wyvern's claws found purchase in the segmented joints. In a matter of moments, he ripped it apart. His momentum put him below the other l'ith. Letting the two halves fall, Noldor arced sharply to the west, avoiding the l'ith that dove at him.

Leonie went for the injured one. Whether it disregarded her as a threat, or was too preoccupied by the wyvern and its own injuries, it didn't react to her. She knew from experience how tough the shell was, and she definitely didn't have the strength to pull it apart.

As she flew in, she considered any weaknesses. The only l'ith she'd fought were on the ground. "So, let's put him on the ground. Those wings look a bit delicate." Concentrating, she closed in between the rapidly beating wings. Careful not to touch, she summoned a fireball directly to the joint. The discharge blew the wing off, but also blew Leonie back and numbed her paw.

She dropped several metres as she spun while the hunter, mandibles clacking uselessly, twirled out of control with only one wing working. The other l'ith noticed her now and moved in, giving her no time to watch her first prey hit the ground. Rolling onto her back, she let gravity take her briefly while she summoned the energy for a bolt. It was then she noticed the many joints for the legs on their underside.

Like an insect's underbelly. I think I found another weak spot. Using her left paw, she cast her electric bolt, hitting the nearest directly under the neck – the joint between the thorax and the head. Because of its fall, the airstream caused the liquid gore to flow in streaks over the smooth shell before forming a greenish spray in its wake.

"That's three," she exalted, twisting away to avoid the spray.

The three remaining hunters turned to follow.

One-and-a-half each, Noldor sent.

Are you counting?

It is a game I used to play many, many years ago. This reminds me of my youth.

I thought it would be harder, she said.

To those without adequate talents, they are truly formidable.

I can't believe I thought that! One almost killed three of us years ago.

Noldor flew in and swung his tail, the barbed end cracking the carapace of another hunter. When he flicked his tail free, part of the shell came with it. *It seems now you have the adequate talents.*

Seems so. To the north was another string of low mountains. Scuttling over the rugged, rocky terrain – perhaps avoiding the pass due to its openness – more than thirty l'ithnamagri approached. *The drones on the ground are getting closer to the township. How about you leave me with these?*

Enjoy. Noldor circled around to avoid the town as much as possible so as not to distract the folk who were in preparation for the confrontation.

Gaining altitude, Leonie tried to repeat her first attack, but the hunter was too agile and flittered back and forth erratically.

"Fair enough," she muttered. A quick lightning-bolt, and she twisted away. The screeching of the l'ith faded as it fell. The damage inflicted wasn't sufficient to kill it, but the impact with the ground would take it out.

She also noticed the hunter crumple on the road near the front gate. They were now almost directly over the town; a large manor house in the middle surrounded by many other buildings, encircled by the wall. At first it looked like the town was in turmoil, but after a few moments of observation, the flurry of movement was well-coordinated.

"One to go." She glanced around for the other l'ith, which was coming in from her right. It mirrored every movement she made; she veered left, it veered left; she dropped, it dropped.

"Not bad. I bet I can fly faster though." She darted to her right to draw it away, then increased speed. Unable to catch her, it quickly gave up and returned to its prime goal, which was to attack the town.

As quickly as she left, Leonie returned, taking the hunter by surprise. As it zoomed down to attack, she hit it from behind, forcing it into the hard paving of the courtyard, then twisted and rolled to the side. Several townsfolk screamed and ran.

She stood up, slightly dazed and bruised. The l'ith's legs were cracked and useless, but its mandibles still snapped as she stepped in close.

"No doubt they'd rip me in two," she said as she raised her paw. The concentrated electricity blasted through its eye and fried the brain.

I think these townsfolk have done this before, she sent to Noldor as she watched the controlled reactions of the people – despite the shattered and smoking l'ith in the courtyard.

This close to the Vale, it is unsurprising, he responded.

I can't understand why they'd risk being here.

I cannot fathom why people do many things.

Wiping her fur matted from sweat, Leonie noticed several men on the wall calling out a warning and pointing towards the wyvern. She flew up, landing near them. "It's okay. The wyvern's here to help," she called out to them.

Some people turned to her with surprised looks; many continued on with their tasks, deeming the approaching drones more of a threat. They ran up the stairs two steps at a time to the ramparts of the surrounding walls. At the top, they started loading large weapons, looking much like a crossbow, but several feet wide. The crossbow bolts were as long as her leg and as thick as her arm. Two men at the back of each weapon turned a ratchet device to tension the bow. Along the wall, she counted ten of these weapons on swivels.

How's it looking out there? she asked Noldor.

We will know shortly.

Leonie moved to the far side of the ramparts, away from the activity to get a look at the approach, but also to see how the weapons dealt with the l'ith. She saw Noldor swoop in from the north-west.

"Wait for the signal, men." She heard someone call out. Leonie looked along the wall to a burly fellow with long hair, obviously in charge.

Towards the l'ith, she heard Noldor's roar. It was difficult to tell from this low angle, but she estimated twelve l'ith toppled from his mind-blast. Most of the affected collapsed, unmoving; others crawled feebly in random directions as if they'd lost their faculties.

The warriors on the ramparts cheered, but the long-haired man gave a sharp rebuke. Everyone concentrated on their tasks again. Some still glanced her way.

More theatrics? Leonie asked.

There is an audience. Noldor gave a mental shrug. He flapped his mighty wings, arcing up and away for another run.

Leonie flicked her gaze between the men and the l'ith. It was then she noticed the series of five shallow trenches paralleling the wall running east-west. She realised they denoted distance; the furthest being around two hundred metres and the closest half that. As the lead l'ith crossed the first trench, the order was given to fire.

There are large arrows coming your way.

Noldor launched himself. *Just in case.*

Like the sound of whips cracking, the bows released. She followed their trajectory. Out of the ten bolts fired, six hit their targets. The l'ith continued forwards, scuttling over or around the fallen.

Immediately, the archers reloaded and began the tensioning of the massive bows.

I reckon you'll only have time for one more run before the weapons fire again, she warned Noldor.

In that case, I will attack the frontline. Be aware though, the mind-

blast rarely kills them outright, but the worst will be stunned for quite a while.

We can deal with them when the time comes, she offered.

Noldor adjusted his approach to assault the front l'ith. His next roar took out another ten, but all of them collapsed, unmoving.

Another cheer; another curt order, but she could see morale was high.

After this volley, how about we finish off those stragglers in the back.

A sound plan. You will have to be quick. The score is currently sixteen to three.

Pffft.

The remaining eight l'ith scuttled onwards, unfazed. They crossed the third trench.

"Fire!" the leader shouted

Again the ten crossbows cracked. One buckled and pitched, knocking two men off the ramparts. They fell back onto the roof of the smithy several metres below.

Six more l'ith went down, leaving two.

Other than death, what stops them?

They have a hive-mind. They do not think for themselves to any great extent, but what their queen, or their leader has ordered.

She wondered how they'd deal with them if they breached the wall. Looking down the face of the wall for the first time, she saw the large down-angled metal spikes. The area was already littered with many l'ith carapace from previous attacks.

As the remaining l'ith pair closed the distance and attempted to climb the wall, the spikes hampered them, giving time for very long spears to come into play. Here two men each worked in unison to try and skewer the creatures, but as she knew from her experience, unless wedged in a joint the spear-heads simply slid off the shell, and hitting a joint from the front was difficult.

Still, the l'ith made no headway. They clacked and snapped at the spears with their mandibles. In one instant, one of the men was pulled off-balance. He toppled over the wall and luckily landed in the softer dirt between the rocks.

Before the l'ith could drop down to finish him off, Leonie leapt out and lifted him up and back over the wall. He was unconscious when she lowered him to the courtyard flagstones.

She looked back to see what Noldor was up to. He had landed and was dealing methodically with each l'ith, starting with the ones still moving. With no range weapons being used, Leonie thought she could finish them off. *I'll be there shortly,* she signalled Noldor. She then flew in close behind one of the creatures.

The men on the wall looked shocked seeing her hovering there.

While she had no authority, she waved them back. They hesitated, looking to their commander. He nodded. "Let's see what she has planned." She heard him say.

Knowing what a fireball could do, she was concerned the blast might injure the men. Hovering directly behind her target, she concentrated and with both paws, sent a bolt of electricity directly into the l'ith's head.

It dropped instantly, cracking when it fell onto the rocks and the other carapaces littering below.

The men cheered their encouragement.

The last l'ith found itself airborne, floating higher and higher above the wall, its legs dangled uselessly. Not satisfied with just dropping it, Leonie body-slammed it onto the rocks.

Who is using theatrics now? Noldor asked.

Pfft. Aren't you finished yet?

Almost.

Leonie returned to the wall, landing near the men, uncertain of their reaction. While she did help, she was still an unknown element to them.

"I hope I didn't interrupt your sport," she called out, addressing the men in general but looking at the one giving the orders. He stepped forward through the gathering men.

"Interruptions like that are most welcome. I'm Castellan

Rodrig Mikanthas, but please call me Rod." He looked her up and down. "We don't get many rrell here, especially females. And never flying warriors."

It would take a bit of getting used to the slower-paced speech. "Pleased to meet you, Rod. I'm Leonie, and my show-off friend out there is Noldor."

She heard a groan. Looking down she saw the two fallen soldiers. She willed them off the roof, lowering them into the arms of those waiting below.

"You have some handy skills there," Rod noted with admiration.

"I get by." Leonie nodded. "I've not seen these before." She pointed to the oversized crossbows.

"We call them ballistae. As you witnessed, they have enough impact to take out a l'ithnamagri if the bolts hit – which reminds me ..." He turned to the men still gawking at Leonie. "Secure the weapons and make sure they're ready. Get the broken one down to the smithy."

"Expecting another attack?" she asked.

"Always expecting, but happy when it doesn't happen. Normally I'd send the men out to dispatch any injured creatures." He turned, watching the wyvern toss another l'ith into the air with its massive jaws. "I gather in this case that won't be a requirement."

"Correct. Noldor hasn't had this much fun in a long time. And I'm sure your men are happy about that too."

"I should ask what brings you out this way. Other than the monthly supply wagons, we rarely get visitors, especially by air and in company with ... Is that a wyvern?"

"He is. As for our visit, it wasn't planned, but when we saw the l'ith approach, thought we could help, but I'm seeing an organised set-up here and I'm certain you could have handled it yourselves. We're heading east, across the Vale and onwards to Tesak. Where are we now, exactly?"

"A long journey, indeed. May I *informally* welcome you to Arilaso. Please, come down for refreshments and to meet the lord and lady of this rural enclave. I'm sure they'd be pleased to thank you for your efforts."

"I'd be honoured. Thank you." *I've been invited for dinner. How are you going?*

I will cope and keep watch.

"My companion will guard the town tonight," Leonie said to the castellan as they made their way down the stairs to the bailey. "Your people can relax. If anything does occur, you'll get plenty of warning."

"I will send out word, but maintain a skeleton watch. How is it you communicate with *him?*"

She touched his tanned arm. *Like this.*

"That's ... fascinating," Rod's step faltered. He looked at her, stunned.

"Never had that before?"

"I can't say I have."

"Lucky you. There's little privacy, and one gets prone to headaches."

"A worthwhile side-effect for all its potential usefulness."

Crossing the courtyard, many people stopped and stared at the gruesome, oozing mass of the last fallen hunter.

"I should apologise for that mess. It got too close and I was too careless." With an effort, she lifted it off the pavers, green fluid dripping on the flagstones before she dropped it over the wall. She swayed on her paws in a fit of dizziness.

The castellan reached out and prevented her from falling. "I think you've done enough for the evening."

"Reckon so, Rod." She took a deep breath and stood straighter. "Thanks. I'm not used to this heat," she panted, unzipping her top in an effort to cool down.

"It is unusually warm, but it has been getting worse for quite a while now."

"Over the months?"

"Over the years," he said. "Even our best winters aren't this warm. This is our second year of drought."

"This is winter?" she asked, incredulous. She was sure it was even hotter here than back on Earth.

Some of the crowd doffed their hats at her, and some saluted the castellan as they passed.

Leonie acknowledged them with a nod, as did Rod. After the castellan sent a runner off to inform their guest's arrival, he stood down half the watch.

"Only half?" Leonie noted.

"Can't let them get too lax," Rod laughed. "I have no doubts there will be extra rations for them afterwards. Besides, the relief there wasn't a full-blown attack tonight is the real bonus."

They soon entered the manor house. There were people moving everywhere.

"Surely it's not normally this busy?" she asked.

"Only when we have a special guest saving us from an attack," he said as she was escorted into a formal reception hall.

A young, well-dressed couple approached.

The castellan bowed. "Leonie, please allow me to introduce the Lady Arulan Simiran and Lord Jesop Simiran."

"A pleasure to meet you both." She shook their offered hands.

"We have just received word of your great and valued assistance. We would be most pleased if you'd join us for dinner. We don't get gifted powershapers here often," Jesop said.

"Or at all," Arulan added. She too looked curiously at Leonie's attire.

"I cannot thank you enough for your hospitality." She ignored the powershaper reference for fear it would only create more questions. Instead, she looked around at the sparse, but good-quality furnishings.

Once the initial formalities were over, Rod excused himself.

The three of them sat and chatted while drinking wine. Sweetmeats and various fruits were laid out quickly by curious young helpers.

"It's the least we can do to thank you for your heroic efforts today," Jesop said. "We welcome you to be our guest and stay for the evening. You must be exhausted. I only saw part of it, but no one here could do what you accomplished. It was amazing."

"Thank you. I did have great assistance—"

"Yes. I understand there's a large creature also," Arulan said. "Is he your pet?"

"Hardly. Noldor's quite free to come and go as he pleases, but at this point in time, we're both heading to Tesak; me to catch up on some friends not seen for many years, and he ... well, because he can, I guess. Who's going to stop a wyvern doing what it wants?"

"Who indeed?" Jesop laughed. "We don't see many rrell in these parts," he continued. "Mainly glins'ool and a few seleth. Your speech is nothing like I've heard before. I understand you were coming from the west. In'sha, perhaps? But it isn't like their speech either."

"And, may I say, your clothing is like nothing I've seen before," Arulan admired. "It looks so ... practical."

Leonie forgot her *alien* jumpsuit would attract attention.

"Oh. I'm originally from Athglenn, by the southern coast." She also hadn't considered how her speech would have changed with the years on Earth too.

"And how is it you came in the company of this *wyvern*?" Arulan asked.

Leonie considered an answer while sipping her wine. "It's a long, convoluted story, but I've met several wyverns in my travels in the Central Ranges. Noldor, by coincidence, also knows these wyverns. I met him while I was exploring a skyland over In'sha."

Arulan gasped in surprise. "You explore skylands? You can fly that high?"

"Actually – and this may sound ludicrous – I'm in search of *portals*. Some sages are of the belief they are gateways to far distant lands allowing instant travel."

"Surely these are folktales? Stories for children?" Jesop poured another wine.

"Perhaps. It's rumoured they were lost during the powershaper wars and the destruction of Dromas. Being so close to the Vale, I was wondering if perhaps you had any knowledge of the area?"

"Decades ago, explorers ventured into the Vale; none have returned, so in that regard we are of no help, other than saying it's a one-way trip. We see several skylands on a regular basis, but not having the gift of flying, again, we can't help. Perhaps the glins'ool would be better suited for this?"

"Are any about?"

"They have nests on some of the lower skylands. There is one due in a week or so."

"It seems obvious they'd nest there, but we will be on our way in the morning. We still have a lot of ground to cover."

"Still, the offer for a longer stay is there. As we said, visitors are rare." Arulan smiled.

"We're not simply a rural community," Jesop said, nibbling on cheese. "Though that helps to feed us. Mind you, things aren't so well at the moment with the drought and all. There are mines nearby connecting cave systems with high-quality crystal." Jesop informed her in detail of why Arilaso came to be and how his great, great grandfather founded the town. "If it wasn't for the caves, this town would have been lost many generations ago. But as for any knowledge of these gateways, we have none."

"Please excuse my brother," Arulan said, then turned to Jesop. "I'm sure Leonie isn't interested in our boring history, dear."

Leonie smiled. "It's fine. My friend and I were curious why the town is here at all, considering the hazards of the location. So, we thank you for that."

"Will we get to meet your *friend*?"

"See how he is in the morning. As you can understand, fortified towns haven't been so welcoming to his kind."

There was a knock at the door. They turned to see the castellan, waiting with several sheets of parchment in his hands.

"So then," Jesop stood up. "The nightly report. If you would like to rest and freshen up after your ordeal, we would be delighted to have your company for dinner in a couple of hours."

"Again, you're too kind." Leonie stood.

"I'll show you to a room," Arulan offered.

5

———

VALE OF DROMAS

After a sumptuous dinner, Leonie fell into a deep sleep. She woke early and refreshed. Wandering downstairs, she was then treated to breakfast of various breads and jams, eggs and fried strips of meat, with Arulan and Jesop telling her about the local produce.

Feeling bloated after all the fine dining, Leonie went for a stroll. They insisted on giving her a tour of the town, even a look at the exquisite jewellery made from the locally mined crystals. The jeweller's, like every other building in town, was all stone and iron.

"Wood is hard to source," Jesop explained. "With all the granite lying around, it makes sense to use it. We've artisans from all over Shak'aran to work the quarry and the mines."

"These fetch a huge price in Saa-Na," Jesop told her proudly showing her a gem.

"Saa-Na?"

"Lyhosa's capital city," Arulan told her.

"I've not seen the like in Delta." Leonie's *thief* mind mentally assessed the jewel's value; it was impressive. *More than I've seen all my years in Delta in this one rock.* "It's truly wonderful," she admitted to them, handing it back with respect. Again, her mind absently took into account the thick bars on the windows and metal-clad doors.

There was a rumble of distant thunder. The weather was closing in and large dark clouds coming from the south-east. Large, flat rain-drops blew in from the nearby storm.

As they moved on, any townsperson she passed either bowed or doffed their hats at the trio, and thanking her for yesterday. "Thanks, but there's no need, really." Feeling uncomfortable with all the gratitude and attention, she looked for a convenient avenue to get out of everyone's way.

She saw Rod on the ramparts just as it was starting to rain. "Ah, if I could have a word with Rod about some ideas I have?" Nice as they were, she hoped Arulan and Jesop would decline going out in the rain. "It might prove very helpful in future attacks."

"By all means. We have a few things to do ourselves, if you'd be so kind to excuse us?"

"Not at all. You have a township to run. You are both too kind." Leonie happily walked out in the rain and made her way up the stairs to Rod. She nodded to a few of the men as they were busy oiling the ballistae.

"Morning. You slept well, I trust?"

"I slept well enough. I was exhausted." She watched as other men covered other ballistae with canvas. "How is it with the fortifications?"

"Just the one damaged ballista. I sent some men out this morning to retrieve what bolts they could find. Not a huge loss, but having more would ease my sleep."

"I can understand. About that ... Yesterday I had a chance to have a look at the underbelly of the l'ith. You no doubt know their joints are the weak spot?"

"I do, but no one wants to crawl under a drone."

"I also saw the difficulty in jabbing them from above with the spears."

"Not a perfect tactic, but the occasional thrust gets an eye and as you've seen already by the dead l'ith outside, we have our successes."

"I don't doubt you for a moment." Leonie looked over the battlements. "See where the downward spikes are located?" She pointed.

"Yes, to prevent them crawling over the wall."

"And the l'ith are there for quite a while."

"They are determined," Rod agreed. "Gives us ample time to jab them."

"These walls are very solid and well built. I assume you have some very fine stonemasons handy."

"Of course, I'm sure you know we're also a mining town and there is a quarry in those hills."

She pointed down the wall. "I'm guessing just over a metre – about three or four feet – below the spikes, would be a good place to have holes so your men can stab the underside of the l'ith."

"Of course, like arrow-slits. Good idea. I'm sure the stone-mason can drill holes of sufficient size."

"And then normal spears can be used. Save any more men being pulled off the wall. How is he, by the way?"

"A broken arm and leg, unfortunately, but alive, thanks to you."

"Maybe the spearmen on the wall can have a restraint. Something easily clipped or unclipped as required."

"You are a treasure trove of ideas."

"Fresh eyes can see clearer. I'm just glad to help." The rain started coming harder. "I reckon I might postpone my departure a bit longer, at least until this storm blows over."

"If the manor house – or the company – gets a bit *stuffy,* there will always be an ale or two for you in the tavern," Rod offered.

"Sounds great." She smiled, purring. "I better see what Noldor is up to. Catch you later."

"Catch me?"

"Sorry, a phrase meaning I'll see you later, or we'll meet again."

"Looking forward to it. I also better attend to the walls before everything rusts."

With a nod, Leonie leapt off and headed north. *Hey, Noldor. Where are you?*

I am about ten minutes north of you. There is an overhang to rest after yesterday's entertainment. What are your plans?

I was thinking to wait out this storm. She blinked hard as rain dripped into her eyes. She wished she remembered to don her goggles before the storm.

That is a sound plan, considering. I am in no rush, but I might cruise ahead and scout the terrain for tomorrow.

You think the storm will last the night?

It has the smell of it and slow moving. Yes.

Ok then. See you in the morning. Let me know if you find anything interesting. She turned around and raced back to a warm fire.

———

"I was hoping we'd get to see your wyvern up close," Jesop said. Standing beside his sister, along with Rod, they gathered on the wall to say their good-byes the following morning.

"I hope you can understand his reluctance," Leonie replied. "Any time he's encountered humans, it didn't go well, and you do have weapons that can do him serious harm. Better for all, this way. Even I can't persuade him to do something he doesn't want to do."

"Well," Jesop hid his disappointment. "Thank him for us anyway."

"And to you, for your hospitality." She shook their hands, then turned to the castellan. "I hope those wall improvements work out, Rod."

"I'm sure they will. I have the artisans working on it as we speak. Maybe the next time you pass this way, you can enjoy a few drinks like we did last night."

"I'd like that very much." She nodded to him, then waved to everyone who had gathered to watch her leave. Leonie quickly put on her goggles, and with much fanfare, she left Arilaso.

"One last show," she muttered. Even though they knew of some of her abilities, she raced off as fast as she could go. Once out of sight she slowed to conserve power.

Welcome back. I can feel something. She received Noldor's message as she continued north.

Another wyvern? Where are you?

No, this feels nothing like another wyvern. I believe it is another portal. The energy is familiar. Keep heading north.

A portal here? Leonie questioned.

You did say you thought they all originated in the Vale.

True, according to the sages. I wasn't expecting to find anything down there other than the ruins of buildings.

There are those too.

Flying at around a thousand metres, Leonie finally spied the wyvern circling ahead.

The ground below was denuded of vegetation like the Badlands on Earth, but without the rad. Many l'ith were out and about; some individuals, some in groups. Their paths seemed random.

"They're just like ants," she muttered to herself. She saw many toppled buildings and collapsed walls, roads covered in detritus, elaborately paved areas, gardens now long dead. *Where is it?* she thought to Noldor.

Down in there.

There was a long shadow below them. *In that crevice?* She estimated the uneven crack in the earth was about twenty metres long, but only five at its widest point.

I believe so. From the amount of activity, I also believe this is an entrance to one their hives? The sense is stronger the closer I get. Strongest when directly over it. As if the crevice itself is somehow amplifying it.

You're sure? I can't feel anything. She moved lower. *How the hell ...?*

Noldor remained silent until she was directly overhead and studied it carefully. While the initial opening was long and wide, it wasn't straight; many obstacles and fallen crystal shards crisscrossed the shaft. *You won't fit down there.*

I noticed.

"Hsss." *No one said it would be easy, but I was sort of hoping they would all be on skylands.*

I can distract them, draw them way. I am certain they would relish the opportunity to get a wyvern again.

I don't like any of this, but can't see any other way, assuming you're right. She circled the crevice a few times, looking for an alternative. *Don't do anything stupid. I have an idea, but don't go too far, just in case I need backup.* Leonie remembered she could go invisible. She had practiced a few times around the unsuspecting wilders. She was unsure the first few times because she could see herself. It was very disconcerting.

Noldor, before you go, can you see me?

I can sense you, but you remain unseen to my eyes. The l'ith may still detect you; they rely on other senses, not just their eyes.

I'll try to keep out of reach, if nothing else.

And no more contact until you get out. They can pick up on that too, especially in confined spaces.

Now you tell me.

Concentrating on remaining invisible – and silent – Leonie slowly descended the cleft, careful to not scrape any of the crystal shards. Most of it was wide enough for her without touching, but it was the l'ith she wanted to avoid. Taking them on in the open air was one thing, but when several dozen can come at you from every direction gave her reason to pause. Once further in, the shaft did straighten, the walls now mostly crystal columns with rock and dirt in between.

Every now and then, she stopped when she heard scuttling or clacking. Slightly turning, a couple of l'ith scuttled into view. If she reached out, she could pull their antennae. She chose not to.

They also paused, possibly *sensing* something. Slowly, she

moved lower. One at a time they crouched briefly, then jumped across the void and continued on their way, disappearing though a vertical crack in the opposite wall. Letting out her breath softly, she continued her descent keeping an eye out for more tunnels.

Looking up, she saw the distant light of the entrance, estimating she had dropped about one hundred metres before seeing a glow about another fifty metres further down.

As she neared, she realised it wasn't the bottom of the shaft. There was a portal, and it rested on a broken crystal column jutting out of the wall. As Noldor had stated, it was quite powerful. Even she could sense it now.

"I'm surprised it didn't crack," she whispered in amazement. After careful examination, she moved some rock debris before deciding it was okay to attempt to lift it without disturbing anything.

Leonie gasped at the strain, wondering why it was so difficult. The one on Earth wasn't this heavy. She paused to examine it more closely, only then noticing where the portal and wall touched it had fused. It reminded her of what she'd seen in the caverns of White Cliffs, and the build-up of mineral deposits over hundreds of years.

She chipped away at it experimentally, zapping it with small bolts of electricity until small cracks appeared along the join. Then lightly applying her will, she attempted to coax it apart. The portal snapped free with a jolt and toppled over the edge. She quickly raced after it and managed to slow it down, then retrieve it. Fearing the worst, Leonie returned to the ledge and let it down gently, leaning it back against the wall before looking around, hoping the disturbance was only loud in her imagination.

Taking the opportunity to recover her composure, she landed beside the portal. Getting down on her knees, she peered through the back side. Much like when she saw a portal for the first time, one side looked clear, but there was a vague image seen through the shimmer on the other side. She realised it was much cooler down here too.

"If it had power, did anything come through? Did the l'ith get to them first?"

Once she felt recuperated, Leonie again began lifting the portal. This time, she remained underneath it and pushed it up. Keeping it upright allowed her to guide it as well as keeping the exit in view.

Near the top, she bumped it against one of the broken crystal columns that crisscrossed the area. Pausing, she heard then saw several inquisitive l'ith heads loom over the exit, silhouetted against bright blue sky.

As one scuttled over the edge with damaged legs, it lost its grip and fell.

She had to decide to try and blast it or dodge, but there was no place to go to avoid it. Before she could cast a bolt of electricity, the l'ith hit the edge of the portal with a crack, then tumbled in and disappeared.

The impact caused the portal to again knock the obstacles, this time harder and louder. Abruptly, the exit was blotted out with many l'ith all scrabbling over the lip and scuttling down the sides. With the portal above her, she couldn't blast them, and staying invisible while flying and carrying the portal was hard enough. She was sure the added effort to do yet another task – to use more power – would undo her.

As secrecy was no longer an issue, and with the creatures closing in, desperate times called for desperate measures. She moved to the narrowest part of the crevice where the portal could fit if she laid it flat, and used it as a shield while she kept rising.

With nowhere to go, the swarming l'ith were scraped off the sides. They either fell past her or tumbled into the portal.

Nearing the top, she put on a burst of speed. Fed entirely by adrenaline, Leonie shot out of the shaft, careening into even more l'ith as they stepped over the edge and knocking them back with her force. A couple held onto the portal edges, their bodies dangling, back legs writhing in the air.

Noldor! her mind screamed. She didn't slow her ascent until she was several hundred metres above the ground.

Yes? He let go the hunter l'ith in his claws. It dropped to the ground, one l'ith drone below unlucky enough to break its fall.

We need to get out of here. Anywhere safe?

Safe? Hardly, but if we head east, it is less infested.

Lead on.

Need me to take that?

Would you? I'm exhausted.

Of course. He pulled off the struggling l'ith with his jaws.

Be careful though. It still may be damaged.

Noldor judiciously gripped the outer rim with his claws, cautiously avoiding the pearl-coloured shimmer.

Later in the afternoon they landed on top of a high cliff face.

We can see a long way from here. Plenty of time to move if need be. I sense you need a rest. With surprising grace, Noldor gently placed the portal upright on the ground.

Leonie landed beside it with a sigh. "Thanks for that." She opened her flask for a long drink. "Many drones fell into it. I wonder where they went." Leonie angled her view, trying to distinguish any landmarks through the iridescence. "I hope wherever this leads, they can deal with them."

The wyvern's neck snaked down so its eye looked directly through it. *Can you see that?*

"What did I miss?" Leonie ducked underneath his bearded jaw, peering intently. "I'm sure that wasn't there before," she said as a number of vague blotches appeared. "Hey, they're getting larger." She stepped away, then decided a better place was even further back, off the edge. Hovering about ten metres out with Noldor standing behind the portal, she cursed when a spiked hroltahg appeared. Its momentum made it roll over the cliff.

"It looks like Styx!" Leonie stopped its fall immediately, and brought it back up to the ledge as others arrived. They were all spiked!

She felt a stabbing pain in her head, bringing darkness, but not before hearing a distant roar from Noldor.

6

―――

QELAY

When Leonie woke, her head felt fuzzy. Gradually the fuzziness faded, turning into many minds talking at once; like in a crowded room with dozens of people talking incessantly.

"Noldor? What the frack happened?"

The noise stopped immediately.

Ah, Leonie, welcome back.

She sat up slowly and looked around. The last thing she remembered was hovering over the edge with a fifty metre drop before the pain.

"How did I get here?" She was now back on the ledge. There were eight spiked rollos surrounding her. "Any of you named Styx?" She noticed the spikes weren't as prominent as on their arrival.

There is no Styx here, Noldor informed her. *We have Afiid, Rutto Jyggr, Werrg, Oueel, Pewwu, Mewwr, and Hassr.*

Her head throbbed again briefly as they greeted her. "Softer, guys." She hissed, clutching her head. "Noldor, can you tell me what happened, but gently. My head's about to split open. There's blood already coming out of my ears!" She showed them her bloodied paws.

As subtly as he could, the wyvern updated Leonie with the happenings in the last couple of hours.

"Hours?" she reached for her flask of water.

As you have no doubt realised by now, we found the portal to Mase-valon, the hroltahg's homeworld. He went on about the first hroltahgs that ventured to this world, centuries earlier. Then everything stopped, and the l'ith started arriving.

The l'ithnamagri killed many of the hroltahg. Did you know the hroltahgs were passivists until a few reverted to the old ways to defend their community? Initially it was a huge disgrace, but when the elders realised there were species out there who would annihilate others given the chance, they made those rogues heroes. Their followers and descendants became wardens of the portal. The portal itself was moved into a secure cavern and warrior-guards were kept on watch constantly.

"For four centuries?" The fuzziness started again. She put her paws out to stop them. "Guys, one at a time," she entreated. She wriggled in an attempt to get comfortable on the hard ground.

Noldor gave Leonie a few minutes to give her head respite before continuing. *They say they're very apologetic for causing you this high level of discomfort. They say several l'ith came through earlier. They thought another attack was imminent, so they sent in these guardians to discover what was happening. We both unfortunately felt the full effect of their 'war-mode'. Even I was dazed for a moment.*

She nodded, sipping again. "So, now there's no imminent attack, what's their plan?"

Realising the portal is free, they want to get word to all their kind to tell them the way home has reopened, thanks to you.

"*You* found it," she protested.

But you risked getting it out. I would not have been able to, as you know.

"We both did it, then." She risked standing up. After the ground stopped spinning, the blood returned to her backside and legs. Shortly, she was ready to walk around to get the circulation back. "When are they planning on starting, considering it's night time now? I feel like crap."

They can start immediately. To save time I have allowed them to scan my mind so they have a comprehensive idea of this land and those that inhabit it.

"Are they aware of White Cliffs, in Qelay?"

No. They only know what I'm familiar with. Is it of import?

"It's like a special hangout for rollos. All I know is there are many hroltahgs there and in Reenat."

May I scan your mind for the precise location?

She sighed. "I'd rather you didn't, but only because of the pain. I take it they now know of Athglenn, Reenat and Hells Maw?" She continued at his nod. "It's almost directly east of the volcano, towards the centre of Athglenn, and halfway to Reenat. White Cliffs is in Qelay, a hilly area on the north side of a lake."

I have relayed this information to them. They are grateful and keen to move on.

"Better let them know their kind, the spikey look, will not be welcomed."

Done. They have their ways to communicate how and why they reverted to the ancient ways.

There was a slight buzz in her head, then they rolled off the edge.

"Wait—!" She watched in surprise as they fell out of sight.

They are okay. Their world has a much higher gravity than here. This fall is nothing to them. See, they are moving away unhindered.

"That's right, Styx told me about that." Leonie walked to the edge, but not too close, still feeling woozy. Sure enough, she could make out the rollos moving off in different directions in pairs. "They've got a hell of a lot of ground to cover." Moving back from the edge, she gingerly sat on a flat crystal shard and dug out some food from her pack. While she ate, she watched the portal, the pulsating glow casting a faint luminescence across the ledge.

"You know, we can take it to Qelay. Why leave it here in the middle of nowhere?"

I thought we were heading to Tesak?

"Change of plans. We didn't have a portal then. It's just a suggestion."

And quite sensible too.

Leonie chewed and swallowed the last of the nutripac. Even after all these years, it still tasted horrible, but very handy on long trips. "I understand if you're in a rush to find Dorn."

Me? No. I'm not in a rush for anything.

"So, tomorrow we'll head to Qelay. Any idea how long it will take?"

I estimate two days. We need to get over these mountains first.

"Perhaps we can visit Hell's Maw? I wonder if anyone's still there?"

We can find out. It would be nice to see somewhere familiar.

Even at night, it was uncomfortably warm. She stripped off her jumpsuit and relished the fresh air, running her hands over her fur. "I need to find more suitable clothes." She rolled it up and used it for a pillow, and fell promptly to sleep.

At dawn, they left. Leonie took it easy, again opting to ride Noldor. It brought back the pleasant memories of riding Slana.

She was thrilled at the prospect of flying over the Central Ranges for the first time. The terrain was so crinkled and rippled, the effect the shadows made as the sun moved across the sky were incredible. Noldor managed to seek out the pair of rollos heading to Qelay and let them know that the portal would be waiting for them, also that they would prepare those rollos at White Cliffs for their arrival.

Leonie sat up. *Can I make a suggestion?*

Of course.

If we're all going to Qelay, why don't they jump through the portal now? By the time we arrive, they can have whatever welcoming party prepared. If memory serves, they always consult their elders, perhaps they can be ready too.

There was a pause before Noldor replied. *They concur. We will land and they will go through.* He spiralled down to a deep ravine.

The spiked rollos appeared and, without pause, jumped through. *Easy. They suggest, on our arrival in White Cliffs, to send them notification.*

Did they say what kind? she inquired.

They did not.

The pair rose again. While on Noldor's back, she learnt to keep herself warm with a modified version of her fire-summoning.

I sense you are now comfortable.

"I am warmer. Better than the previous attempts." She looked down at the singed fur on her forearms. "I don't think I've been this high before. Even breathing is a chore."

Dusk in the Central Ranges was glorious, but the excitement of seeing Hell's Maw turned to disappointment.

"Nice to be here again, but it feels so empty without wyverns wheeling through the thermals."

You say they have all gone to Tesak now? He placed the portal just inside the cavern entrance.

"That was Phil's plan before I left. After twenty years, they could be anywhere."

We shall find out in due course.

Leonie gathered some wood, surprised it hadn't rotted. "I guess the warm dry interior preserved it," she muttered. "Why don't you go and enjoy yourself? There's the heated lake below and the hot thermals above the volcano."

Luxury. Noldor, like she'd seen Dorn and the other wyverns do in the past, leant back and simply dropped off the ledge.

While the fire started to build, Leonie stripped off again and walked around the lair, doing her own reminiscing. Rising up through the levels, she found the old bucket Phil used for his baths – the same one they used to rescue Feiron when he melted.

"Yes!" she hissed with delight. She promptly grabbed it, flew down to the steaming lake and filled it with hot water and used it for a bath. "Not the sort of bath Sussah would like." She chuckled at the thought.

After a good soak, and feeling very much refreshed, she sat

by the fire and dragged dinner out of her pack. When Noldor returned, she regaled him with stories of the enjoyable times she spent here, before eventually dozing off to sleep.

In the morning, after breakfast they made a brief detour to Hellam, the nearest township in the foothills of the ranges, to obtain some food and perhaps clothes. Leonie was glad she had those ales with Rod and his men the night before she left Arilaso, after realising she had no local currency; in fact, no money whatsoever. During the evening of sharing stories and drinking, she'd rectified the situation.

Noldor opted to circle out of sight above the gathering clouds.

Strolling down the street, she saw a couple of massive birds tied to a pole. They had saddles, with a couple of sacks laced to the sides.

"Excuse me," she said to a local, who was looking at her garb as he passed. "Are they gnashers?"

"They be gnashers a'right." He followed her gaze at the seven-foot birds.

"Aren't they supposed to be vicious?"

"In the wild they be, and those two will still give a severe nip if annoyed, but more or less tamed now," he replied. "An' watch out for their feet, they can rip your guts out if they get a chance to."

"Who in their right mind would think to try to tame them?" she muttered.

"Oh, they call him the *gnasher-whisperer*. Huge guy, down in Dalmellington."

"Not heard of it." She shook her head.

He turned his gaze back to her, once again eyeing her clothing. "I gather you be not from around here. Dalmellington is halfway to Qelay, on the East Road. Some are calling it Gnashville now," he said, then added, "Funny thing is, they says the man hi'self can't even speak."

"Thanks," she muttered as the man nodded and continued with his task. Leonie watched the large birds for a bit longer, comparing the sanity of training gnashers to that of training wyverns.

The rain started, prompting her to get on with her supply run. The merchant in the store looked at the Lyhosian coinage and her clothing.

"Don't get much of this here." He turned the coin in his fingers under a lamp.

"Here," she gave him a few more coins. "That should be ample to make up for the exchange rate." *Easy come, easy go.*

The man nodded, though with a dubious look.

Leonie took her pack of goods, including new clothes, waved and left before the merchant started getting greedy. Once outside, she slung the pack over her shoulder and rose, to the startled looks of those in the street.

On my way, she said, heading east.

Did you get supplies? Noldor responded to her call.

I did. I'd like to visit a town after we've finished at Qelay. It might be nothing, but I'm curious about a titbit of information I picked up.

Go on. He glided down beside her, his green wings spread wide, tilting marginally to adjust for the turbulence, keeping him steady.

There's someone in Dalmellington that trains gnashers. They say he's mute, and of very large build. Again, it is a long shot, but I used to know a large mute guy. It's been two decades, and it could be anyone, but my life has been full of coincidences. I'd like to quash this one.

Agreed. Have to follow your instincts.

That's Qelay ahead.

North of the lake glistening in the moonlight, they both looked down on the town.

My presence might be disturbing. Will you be able to take the portal from here?

I reckon so. Leonie concentrated, taking the weight of the crystal gateway. *Let go now.*

As the wyvern slowly released his hold, Leonie adjusted her

mental grip. No way it would survive a fall of a few thousand metres. *Got it.*

She descended towards the lamplight, aiming for the northern hills where White Cliffs was situated. When she was a few hundred metres above the entrance, she sent a message ahead.

By the time she landed, several rollos were waiting at the entrance.

"Hi guys," she waved. "Anyone remember me?"

I do. One of the rollos wobbled forwards. *You were in company of Styx. I am Riff. You say this is the portal to our homeworld?*

She thought she could sense excitement in his thoughts, not something previously experienced. "Hi Riff. Great to see you again." Not that she could tell them apart. "I haven't used it myself," she answered. "But, eight hroltahgs came through. They say they came from Masevalon." *Where else would they have come from?*

The moment she mentioned the homeworld, her mind was full of psycho-babble.

"Where can I put it inside? I'd rather keep it off the streets if possible. I'll tell you everything I know then."

Assuredly. Bring it around the side, the doors to the stables are of sufficient size.

She raised the portal off the ground and followed the directions. After a few minutes, the portal was secured in the back of the stables with a couple of rollo sentries.

It would please us if we could once again have your company. Even now, we still communicate about your previous stay here. Such an eventful time has not yet been repeated.

"That's a good thing, to my thinking?"

We are in agreeance. Now, about this portal ...

"Are you in charge here, Riff? Who's the boss?"

I am the most senior hroltahg here at this point.

"Now that I've arrived here ..." Leonie looked around for something to notify those on the other side. Spotting a horseshoe hanging on a nail, she grabbed it saying, "Watch how this disappears." She tossed it through then stepped back, giving the area in front of the portal clearance.

Fascinating. Did that go to Masevalon.

Leonie had not felt the sensation with his message previously. If she had to guess, she'd say he was in awe.

"If what they tell me is true, yes." While she waited for a response, Leonie recounted the search for the portals, not forgetting Noldor's part in it all. She then told them how eight hroltahgs came out in war-mode, as they were expecting a l'ith attack.

"I just wanted you to be prepared. While Styx going rogue was a disturbing anomaly for you here, it's now accepted at home."

This is indeed serious times. And two are coming here?

"They were talking about getting their elders, but I don't know who will be coming through. I did let them know this is a hroltahg hangout." There was a resounding clang as the horseshoe returned. "How do you contact your elders? Can you do it? Is it difficult?" Leonie asked as she peered into the portal.

I can. It isn't too difficult.

"I suggest you do it now, if not already. Look." Leonie pointed to the shimmering surface. "Sorry, can you sense anything?" She kicked herself, forgetting rollos had no eyes. Like earlier, she saw the blotches within getting larger.

Riff was silent for a moment. *There does appear to be a fluctuation in the portal emanations.*

Leonie hoped they didn't give a war-cry this time.

Four rollos emerged; two studded and two a mottled-grey colour. "No war-cry," she sighed in relief.

Leonie, we meet again. Ruto and Jyggr at your service. You are now in the presence of two of our elders, Mo and Pi.

"Elders? Wow. Welcome to Yarnik. This is Riff, most senior hroltahg on these premises."

If there was any time Leonie thought a rollo could be *speechless*, it was now. Riff was as silent as a dead rock. She felt like she was standing in a stone garden; every hroltahg was motionless – even the guardians. Then she felt an elusive buzzing deep in her head. It went on for several minutes. "Well, I reckon something's happening." She sat on a hay bale, pulled out her flask and waited.

After half-an-hour, with no change and the constant buzzing giving her a headache, she sauntered off in search of the kitchen. By the time she returned with a tray of food and a bottle of wine, there was still no discernible change.

Hi guys. Anyone listening? she asked.

Riff and the others are communicating with the elders in Reenat.

Who's this? She looked around, but no new rollo appeared.

Dwer, at your service.

Hey Dwer! I remember you too.

This conference will take a while. Shall I take you to your room so you can rest and refresh yourself?

Sure thing. She wiped her mouth with the napkin, and strolled out of the stables to the main entrance. In the corridor, another rollo met her with a maid by its side. The maid curtsied and took the tray out of Leonie's paws. Leonie collected the wine before it was returned to the kitchen.

Dwer, is that you? she thought to the hroltahg.

It is. Please follow. As the maid moved in one direction, he rolled off in another. Leonie trailed him through the luxurious foyer. She took the stairs as he ambled up the slightly concaved ramps on the side.

"Dwer, you're all too kind for all this. Thank you."

You forget, you risked your life to save ours. This is not a thing we are likely to forget.

"Styx played a big part in that as well."

That was prior to the changing. At the top of the stairs he moved along a corridor.

Even after her long absence, she recognised the furnishings and paintings, and everything was is in pristine condition.

"Spiked or unspiked, Styx was a loyal friend to all of us," she said. "I hope you can all remember *that*."

Seems you are a loyal friend too. This is pleasing. He stopped by the open door. *And this is your room.*

"Have you heard from him? Any idea where he's at? What he's doing?" She realised it was the very same room she stayed in last visit. A maid had already put another tray on the table and was now warming the water for a bath.

I have no knowledge of his activities or whereabouts, but once the conference with the elders is complete, I will inquire on your behalf because of what you both did for us.

Dwer, I can't thank you enough. She chose to tell him that with her mind, so he'd truly sense her gratitude.

No thanks needed. If this portal is indeed our gateway home as it appears, then our whole species is in your debt. It looks like you are fulfilling the prophecy.

"Styx did mention that. A lot. I'm glad I could help."

It was one of the many prophesied possibilities. We are glad this was the result. The others ... had fewer desirable consequences. Rest now. I will let you know the outcome. Dwer reversed back down the corridor.

"That's two portals down." With a contented sigh, Leonie turned and stepped inside. "And two baths in as many days," she purred.

7

REENAT

Dalmellington was only an hour away from Qelay if she flew fast. She landed quietly behind a barn, then wandered down its side to the main street.

On her approach, she counted almost fifty dwellings; half with adjoining fields with vegetable produce of some sort and two with livestock. Now strolling down the street, she saw several taverns and boarding houses, stores selling many and varied merchandise and warehouses and stables further back along the side streets.

Quite a few people were out and about, not surprising considering the heat of the day. She was glad she changed into more suitable clothes. Now, like in the old days, she wore her new clothes; shorts – she had to slit the back for her tail – and a tight, short-sleeved shirt. After twenty years absence and now in a different town, she doubted anyone would be looking for a rrell-hybrid. "No more hooded cloaks for this cat," she muttered.

Hearing a raucous squawking, she turned and walked in that direction. Down a side lane, was a high-fenced corral, housing another gnasher. Saddle and other riding gear lay on a covered bench nearby. There was a woman oiling some of the tack. She looked up when the gnasher's beak snapped.

"Watch it. You'll lose an arm. Can't you see the sign?" There was large sign very visible: 'Warning. Limbs will be lost if you get too close'.

"I see it fine. I just wanted to ask where you got it from. Do you know this gnasher-whisperer?"

"Yep. He's 'bout an hour north of town. Go to the east end and there's a track. Can't miss it. Don't go calling him the *whisperer* though. Hates it; just call him Rohan."

"Rohan?" Leonie repeated, whiskers quivering in disbelief. *Ro? Could it be?*

"It's what I said, isn't it? Got work to do." She continued rubbing with the oily rag again.

Leonie followed the vague directions. After a short, fast flight, she approached the gate, choosing to walk the last few hundred metres. A flock of gnashers ran in the adjoining field. Any doubts to whether this was the place quashed by the sign above the gate, *'Gnash-ville'*. A young boy met her by the fence.

"Afternoon miss. Are you a rrell? You look different to the others. You after a bird?"

"I'm part rrell," she nodded. "I'm looking for the trainer. Is that your pa?"

"It is, but he's out in the back field." He opened the gate. "My mam's in the house though." He walked back, beckoning Leonie to follow. "You walk all the way? You *do* need a bird."

Reaching the house, she quickly discovered his mam wasn't Netoha. *Mind you, she'd be much older now.*

"How can we help you?" the boy's mother asked.

"I heard some news in town about the trainer. I've been travelling around the country for a long time and lost track of some people I knew. One of them was a large man named Ro, a mute, from Delta to the south."

"My man's name is Rohan, but *his* pa is Ro."

"And is there a Netoha?"

"She is his mother."

"It's been so long." Leonie wiped her eyes. "Any idea where I can find them? Are they here or still in Delta?"

"No. They're visiting the Northern Reaches. How long has it been for you?"

"Nettie was pregnant. Is Rohan her first born, due in the autumn, if I recall?"

"Ro *was* born in autumn, mid-Maniel." She nodded. "I'm Sarrein. Would you like a cup of tea? Other than Auntie Jade I don't know anyone from Ro's previous life."

"I'd love some, thank you." She smiled at hearing 'Auntie Jade'.

So, you will be going to Reenat? Noldor inquired. He was lounging in a field, west of Qelay when she returned.

"I have to go. I mean, yes, I so much want to catch up with Dorn, Slana, Faldo and my friends – assuming they're in Tesak – but Jade was my best friend. If it wasn't for her, I would've been a drowned kitten.

"Sarrein said the last they'd heard of their auntie was of her heading to Reenat. That was a few months ago. She's riding a gnasher, so I'm guessing she shouldn't be too hard to find if she's still there. At the very least, someone will have seen her."

This is a good thing, and I sense you need to do it. I will continue to Tesak and let your friends know you are alive and well. I doubt my presence would be appreciated in a large city.

"You've been such good company." She reached up and stroked his cheek. "I don't know how you're still here, but I am glad for it."

As am I. Farewell, friend Leonie. We will meet again soon.

That's my hope too, Noldor. She stepped back.

The wyvern launched with a leap and flap of massive wings. She watched him soar north, his dark shape rising against the backdrop of stars. The horizon was aglow with the rising of Luminor and Luxor.

With a deep breath, Leonie cruised slowly the few kilometres back to Qelay. The recent message that the hroltahgs had completed their conference surprised her; she thought it would have finished hours earlier.

"I guess catching up on over four centuries of gossip takes time," she muttered.

"What's new, Riff?" she asked when Riff met her at the door.

The elders have decreed that word will be sent out. All hroltahg will make their way here to return to the homeworld.

"That sounds exciting. How long will that take?"

The message is going out now. It should cover the land by morning.

"What? That's incredible."

Perhaps you've forgotten, much of our communication is not on this plane. However, it will take several months for the furthest of our kind to return. Some are on the west coast, and some have travelled to far Ghalena.

"Have you heard from Styx?"

There has been no communication.

"Fair enough." She did sense a change in Riff's attitude towards the rogue rollo since learning how and why many if his kind had done exactly the same thing. "I'll be heading out in the morning. I'm hoping to meet up with a friend in Reenat."

I will ensure you have supplies and an ample breakfast before your departure, with our compliments. Good night, Leonie.

"Night, Riff." Leonie took to the stairs, heading for her room. "Oh, wait." She turned and flew back to the rollo. "Since it's possible for your people to get a message to every habitation, could I ask a favour?"

Of course. What message?

"I'm not entirely sure." Leonie paced up and down the hall, considering. "The thing is, we need to find all the other portals. They could be anywhere, but when we do find them, how will anyone know?"

You wish us to remain to relay this message. We are able to do this.

"You can? Not all of you. I know it's a big thing to ask—"

As you humans say, nonsense. *We are here to help. We always have been, and now in this dire time, we will not leave until everyone is safe. And,* he sensed her thoughts, *there is no need to thank us.* With that, Riff continued on his way

———

She saw Reenat from a long way away. The city was built on and around a set of coastal hills, the royal palace being on the highest point. As she got closer, from the configuration of the rooftops, it looked like the streets spiralled up around the hill. A large wall surrounded the bulk of the city.

Leonie saw flyers rising up to intercept. She recalled Philbert mentioning the Gryphon Riders of Reenat, and she watched them closely. She estimated the gryphons were about the same size as a gnasher. The head, chest, wings and forelegs were bird-like, but the body and rear legs were more mammalian, like a large cat. "Or even the lions from the zoo. Did Dianah's HelixR cloning experiments make it this far?" she muttered to herself.

There were fifteen riders spreading out and surrounding her. Unlike the glins'ool talon, these guys covered all exits. Their armour was a hardened leather breastplate and helmets. Three riders came closer; two flanked her as she slowed. All were armed with loaded crossbows aimed at her. A quick look around revealed no one was going to be caught in a cross-fire.

"What is your business here in Reenat?" the third one asked.

The voice was female. With the armour on, there was little to distinguish men and women. Her tone immediately gave Leonie dark feelings and flashbacks of the guards in Delta. *Is this what they called PTSD back in the tower?* she wondered. Already, this confrontation brought the hard times back.

"My business is mine, thanks," she answered loudly over the flapping wings.

"All powershapers must report to the garrison, so again I ask what your business is."

"I'm not a powershaper," Leonie laughed.

"How is it you are flying, then?"

"Damn. Good point," she hissed to herself. "Okay, you got me. I'm here to catch up with a friend."

"Who is this *friend?*"

Leonie was about to say Jade, but then, considering Jade had been the master of the Takers Guild in a city Reenat didn't recognise, she didn't believe that would go well. Things would have been different if Noldor were around. "Tipp Nul Chor Tukk," she stated.

Some of the riders swore, some chuckled, her questioner one of the laughers. "Oh really. How is it you know of him? Hear his singing in a tavern lately?"

"It was a while ago, but yes."

"Where?"

Damn it again. I can't say Delta. "I forget, I was drunk at the time. Maybe it was Hellam." *The torc, stupid!* "I have this." As she reached for her torc, a shout went out. Excruciating pain hit her in the side, knocking her sideways. As she fell, her mind recalled a similar pain the night she was captured. *Fragging guards!*

Try as she might, she couldn't concentrate to stop her fall. Her last memory was the wind rushing in her ears as she rapidly gained speed. She felt a pair of claws wrap themselves around her in a brutal grip; the air forced out of her lungs.

———

The Reenat Bardic Council was gathering in the foyer. Like every month, the majority headed to the bar to quench their thirst, and pick at the platter of food laid out before the meeting.

"You'd think they'd never had a drink or eaten in their lives," Biell chirruped quietly. She was on the third tier looking down, hidden behind thick drapes. "They screech and whinge like banshees, even the humans. Don't they realise with this drought, the usual delicacies aren't available anymore?"

"Ahh Biell," he tsked. "They're bards. Even *with* delicacies in quantity, they'd whine about some calamity. Haven't you learnt that yet?"

"Apparently not. It's times like this I wish I was still a ranger."

"I wish you were out ranging, too."

"What?"

"Some very lively stints we had, me and you."

"I must admit it's all true." She laughed and stepped away as he reached for her. "When are you going to go down?"

"You have an inkling what I was thinking—"

She hopped away again. "I meant *downstairs* to the council." She slapped at his hands, but not too hard. "You're head councillor, after all."

"Trying to get rid of me?" Tipp craned his neck around as if searching for someone else. "Where is he?"

"Only so you can get it over and done with and return to me. You haven't slept well lately. What ails you?"

"I have this pain, hard to explain."

"I think you've had it for several days now."

"Indeed. You perceived?"

"Every night, ruffling feathers and beak clacking in a dream, how could I not?"

He heard a gong below sounding the five minute notice. With a flustered squawk, Tipp reached for his cape and sash of office and strutted to the mirror. Once donned and positioned as tradition required followed by a final preening, he opened the case holding the accoutrements of his station.

He sensed the gold torc immediately! Reaching for it with a shaking hand, he experienced shock like never before.

"It's vibrating!" he crowed. Forgetting the council completely, three strides took him to the balcony. He launched off the railing into the dusky evening. He gained height with a few beats of his wings and started narrowing down the direction of the source. After completing one circuit of the building, he turned west.

By this stage Biell caught up with him. "What is it, my lovely," she asked, worried.

"Leonie," he stated simply.

Gryphon riders approached, but seeing his cape and sash, veered off with a salute.

Towards the western wall of the city, Tipp zeroed in, landing in front of the garrison. "Hell, this does not bode well." He strutted inside, Biell in his wake, looking for the guard commander.

Seeing the man with a sheaf of papers, he approached. "On your list, you have a torc like this?" He brandished his gold medallion in the surprised man's face.

The background noise of the busy office suddenly went silent.

Looking up from his parchments, squinting at the item. "Ah, yes. It came in a couple of days ago—"

"And after this duration, still no notification! What is the meaning of this?"

Cursing, the commander turned and barked an order at a subordinate, who raced off. The young man quickly returned with the other torc.

Both vibrations ceased the moment Tipp held it.

"We were unaware who its owner was," the commander said. "Don't all you bards have torcs? A message was sent. It was going to be declared at this evening's council meeting."

"Care to make clear how it came to be here?" Tipp clucked.

Another guardsman spoke up when the commander hesitated. "Our patrol found a suspected infiltrator trying to sneak into the city. An unregistered powershaper. She was apprehended."

"A powershaper?" Tipp cocked his head to the guardsman, clearly befuddled.

"She was flying in—"

"Flying you say, by which way? By gryphon? Is she glins'ool? Explain, please do."

"She didn't have wings. A rrell, or a feline of sorts."

The blood drained from Tipp's face. "This cat, where's she at?"

"She's in the infirm—"

"What?" he squawked.

The guard looked troubled. "When we approached her, she reached for a weapon, or it was believed she—"

"A powershaper you say, but uses weapons for melee? Fools!" Tipp bounded over the counter in a flurry of feathers. "If she suffers, there will be a toll. By the scroll, heads will roll!"

"Sir—"

"Not another word. Commander," Biell trilled softly in his ear. "You *do* know who he is, don't you?"

"A bard." He squinted.

"Any particular bard? Wearing *that* particular sash?"

The commander managed to put on his spectacles. His lips made a small circle. "Make way for the First Bard!" he ordered.

"Thank you, commander," Biell clucked, following in Tipp's wake.

Leonie slowly became aware of a softer bed. Her eyes fluttered open. It took a few moments to register the ostentatious furnishings and decorations. *Not a prison cell?* She moved her head, stifling a groan. Hearing a door open and close behind her, she turned the other way. The world swirled. She shut her eyes to let it settle.

Again, the door opened and closed. The light changed as a shadow loomed above. Risking more nausea, she peeked and saw an old bird leaning over her.

"Leonie, it pleases my eyes to see you survive."

Verse? "Tipp? Where am I?" She winced as she tried to sit up. Looking down at the rattling, she saw chains on her wrist. "What crap is this?"

"A condition I abhor, but only to please the law."

"What? Why?" She shook them again. *Where's the lock mechanism?* she wondered at the seamless manacles.

"They're implying you were flying. They say you're a power-shaper with no registration paper."

"Registration?" Her head throbbed.

"All shapers must register their talent. It's something which they will not relent. Banning from the city is the consequence. In this the Bardic Council has little influence."

"That's ridiculous!" she rattled the chain again in frustration.

"I agree alright, but *were* you in flight?" He continued, startled at her nod. "If you were using a device, we could knock this problem in a trice."

"No," she said. "But I have learnt some tricks over the years."

His shoulders slumped. "Powershapers must attend Shaper Hall to assess their level over all."

"For what purpose?"

"To detect any potential royal threat."

"I'm no threat to the king."

"That may be the true, but attend you must do."

Leonie slumped back into the pillows. "Can I have some water?"

"Of course." Tipp poured her a glass.

She lifted her head as he dribbled the cool fluid into her mouth.

"Thanks." She relaxed again.

Tipp settled on a cushion on the floor bringing his head down to her level. "To answer your previous, you are now at my house."

"How long?"

"This is your third night. It was touch and go; you were delirious. Your injury was quite serious."

"What happened?" she asked.

Tipp clucked in surprise. "You don't recall?"

"I remember the Gryphon Riders. I was going to show them your torc, then everything went black."

"A weapon is what they thought you were reaching, the one responsible will be given a teaching."

"No. They're just doing their job," she panted. "Is it hot in here?"

"Possibly, but it's been hotter all over, worse every year. All Shak'aran is in drought I fear." Tipp opened the door, then walked over to open the window and allow fresh air to flow. "Maybe air movement will help with your improvement." He returned to his sitting cushion. "I must ask for your pardon. After a decade of searching here and there, I confess to surrendering to despair."

"You kept looking for ten years?"

"I lost the tune; and gave up too soon. Not long enough as stated. Jade however, will be elated."

"Jade? Is she here?" Leonie tried to sit up, deciding not too with the stabbing pain.

"No, and she is not near, but messages were sent, so do not fear.

"And Styx? What's he doing?"

"Styx may come and go. I'm not-in-the-know. What hroltahg's plan is known by no man."

"Well, from now on, it will be a major exodus of all of them. They're all going home." She emptied the glass.

8

SUNDANCER

David observed the skyland from a hundred metres. He was very happy with the settings and results. The new *Sundancer*, his purpose-built time-machine, was doing everything exactly as it should.

What he was doing now was checking the phase-in sequence to see if the results were anything like his experiments promised. From the lack of reactions from the many wilders below, they were completely oblivious to his presence.

He felt awkward remaining invisible, but he convinced himself it was all for science. After a few adjustments and recalibrations, he was satisfied, then he phased-in completely. The resulting reaction below was more proof of the previous invisibility. David landed the ship on the grassy field near the portal and quickly made his way outside to allay everyone's concerns.

Lerry and Harrond were braced behind the low wall. As soon as David made an appearance, they shouldered their pulse rifles. The wilders then came out from the stone building they had sought for refuge.

"Please forgive my sudden appearance. I apologise for any apprehension or trauma caused." He waved at them.

Lerry walked up and shook his hand. "Stupid as it is, considering where we are, the thought of raiders came straight to our minds." He laughed, shaking his head.

"What is that thing?" Harrond asked, standing beside his father.

Many other wilders were now approaching with looks of bewilderment.

"David!" Sussah came running up, throwing her arms around him. "Where have you been?"

"Here and there, and everywhere in-between. How are you, mum?"

"Better now that you've finally decided to visit. You couldn't have come sooner?" She let him go and stood back.

"Sorry. I'm doing this largely by myself. The research and experiments needed constant analysis and recalibrat—"

"Sounds like nothing has changed."

"Sorry, mum." David dropped his chin, like a scolded child. "Is Leonie about?"

"Oh, no. She left over a week ago, heading east to catch up with some of her old friends, if she can find them."

"Maybe we'll see her when we head that way."

"We?" Sussah asked.

"Of course. Wouldn't you like to visit home?"

"I ... I don't know."

"Well, there's no rush." He saw Rhiannon, who had politely waited to the side with some of the other elders. "Hello, Rhiannon, Lana, Clara. I hope you have all been well."

"Indeed, and you have our thanks. I think I can speak for everyone to say that – apart from your unexpected arrival – we have had the most stress-free time, but it is good to see you again."

"Would anyone like a tour? It's a bit more elaborate than the *Skydancer*."

The agtechs, his mum, and Bern accepted.

"There are a few wilders that I should keep an eye on," Rhiannon said. "They are unwell."

"Nothing too serious I hope?"

"I think it's influenza. We aren't used to this cooler, wet weather." She waved farewell. "We'll see you all at dinner." She left with the others.

"Happy to help if I can," David offered.

Thank you, David, the seer sent.

From the outside, the ship was an imposing fifteen metres high and completely round, except for the four retractable landing struts. Entering via a ramp in the belly, the ship's hull loomed above them.

Much like when touring the *Skydancer* everyone was astounded at the interior. Furnishings and layout were impeccable, following the same blue-white colour scheme of SciCorps.

"Why a sphere?" Lerry was the first to ask the question.

"Think of travelling through time like moving through water. Any shape can do it, but a sphere is the most efficient in any direction. When the ship 'jumps', a pulse of sorts is sent out in all directions and across all dimensions. Call it a ripple. As I found in the *Skydancer*, my prototype, with anything other than a perfect globe that pulse would be distorted. The distortion has an effect on the ship's movement through time and space. I noticed this when comparing the test results of both ships. The *Skydancer* did it, but it used more power and the initial results were far less precise, and if multiple jumps were made in quick succession, it became less accurate.

"Even though the *Sundancer* is three times the mass of the *Skydancer*, it uses one tenth the power." He smiled, then noted their gazes. "Apologies. I better stop."

"So, the *Skydancer* was faulty?" Harrond asked.

"Imperfect, yes. If we use a water analogy – dropping anything into a pond will make ripples, only a spherical object will have evenly distributed ripples. That even distribution makes for more accurate navigation."

He continued with the tour. In the centre was a wide column with an elevator. They entered the lift with enough room to comfortably carry the five of them. "There are five levels," David continued. "Much of the top and bottom level is used for ballast.

The remaining levels are accommodation, dining and recreation, and the control centre."

"Where's engineering? How does the ship propel itself?"

"The control centre is this entire central column. There's a small ion-drive for short trips, but the majority of the travel is by generating the tau-field. The distances the *Sundancer* travels with anything other than the tau-drive would require a far larger vessel just to store enough fuel."

The lift doors opened on level 4 – accommodation. A passageway curved around to left and right. The doors on the outer walls opened up to cubicles. "There are six rooms. I'm not expecting that many guests, but you can never be sure, and it was a convenient number for the area and equitable distribution of mass." They had a brief look into the rooms as they walked around the deck. Everything was pristine.

"And this ballast. What's that?" Harrond asked as they stepped back inside the lift.

"Basically, it's a counterweight to keep the ship on an even keel. Throughout the entire ship, the contents and their place-ment are precisely measured and accounted for. Lightweight items are towards the outer walls, and the heavier mass is towards the centre."

Moments later they were on level 3.

David continued. "The ballast is used to account for passen-gers and their movement. Sensors along the floors are constantly feeding data to TAU. It also calculates and distributes the ballast via a complex system of conduits and valves to counteract any change." He turned to them. "Aaaand your eyes are glazing over again. I must stop." He shook his head. "Put simply, it works, and it's safe."

"How far are we from Earth?" Lerry inquired. "With the ease and convenience of stepping through the portal to another planet, we've completely failed to grasp the significance of where we really are."

"We are 3,211.47 light-years from Earth."

"That's far, isn't it?" Sussah looked from face to face.

"30.3 quadrillion kilometres. Yes, mum, it's quite far."

"And how long did it take you?" Lerry asked.

"Roughly half an hour."

"Thirty minutes!"

"More or less. I was experimenting with energy expenditure. Would anyone like some refreshments?" He guided them to the dining area. The chairs moulded for best fit as they sat along a bench. David went into the galley, on the opposite side. "Coffee everyone?"

Even Bern looked enthusiastic. "I've only had real coffee once, and there's none on Skyhome."

"You mentioned going to Delta? When can we do that?" Sussah asked.

"Whenever you like. But, how have you all settled in Skyhome? Are there any problems? Leonie left a message about the powerpacs draining; perhaps I should take a look at that before we go?"

"Can Harrond and Lerry come too?"

"To Delta? Of course. And Bern as well." David put the first mug under the dispenser. "It would be interesting to see where you came from; what your life was like before you arrived on Earth. You could visit your parents."

Sussah immediately looked uncertain. "It's been so long."

"If I had disappeared, wouldn't you want to see me even after twenty-years?"

"How could you say— Oh, I understand." She nodded. "I will go and see them."

"What's TAU stand for?" Lerry asked. They had finished with the tour, and were back in Skyhome sitting at the communal table for the evening meal. Many of the wilders were gathered around as well.

"Temporal Adaptive Unifier," David said as he selected from a tray of roasted vegetables. "It's what I call the AI running the ship. It calculates the time-space coordinates based on my astronav charts."

"Are they the charts you made with Leonie's orb?"

"They are."

Rhiannon sat down opposite David. "How was the tour?" she asked them.

"Astounding," Lerry replied before anyone could say otherwise.

"I have something for you." David passed over a small case to the seer. "These are vaccines and antibiotics I had in storage. I've set the SciCorps medbay to manufacture more. There should be a batch sufficient enough for everyone by morning."

"That's very generous of you, David."

"Nonsense. I should have thought of it before. There are undoubtedly viruses and bacteria here to which we from Earth have little to no immunity. But I can only work with what we've got now. Keep monitoring, keep me updated and I'll do what I can. The same goes for those who you come into contact with, should that ever eventuate."

"We've already encountered some glins'ool – they're an avian race – several days ago."

"Really? I can only hope they remain well. In our history, many First Nation people, – those indigenous to a continent – were decimated by disease brought in by explorers. In fact, that should be my main priority." He considered for a moment, then turned to his mother. "Before we go, can I get a sample of your blood? You're native to this world, so it's a reasonable assumption your blood may contain what we need."

"Can I have a bath afterwards?" Sussah asked.

"As many as you'd like."

After dinner, in company with his mother and Harrond, they returned to SciCorps labs for the blood sample. The medicomp was quick and efficient, and soon she was off for a bath.

David left them in peace after making sure all their security clearances were in place. "I certainly don't need either of you getting vaporised." He smiled at their nervous looks. "It's ok.

Leonie did well. I'm heading back to Skyhome. See you both later."

On his return, he joined Lerry examining the powerpac issue. The agtech told him all he knew, showing him the readings he'd made ever since the discrepancy was picked up.

"And Leonie thinks the skyland is absorbing it, because of the crystalline structure?"

"She said when she and Su first arrived here her magic was really weak. On her last visit, her fireball was impressive. By that time, we had been here for close to a month draining power constantly."

David nodded in understanding. "And she believes her powers increased because there was now a larger source to draw? Looks like I have some work to do."

"Happy to help if I can but I suspect I'd slow you down."

"Not at all, but it's basically all computer work anyway."

Lerry bid David goodnight, and went to help with any final chores after the dinner.

David watched them for a while, how they interacted and cooperated without regard for inconvenience or discomfort. He was glad – proud even – to be able to contribute in some small way to easing their lives. With a deep breath, he walked back to the *Sundancer* to check a few readings, then portalled back to SciCorps.

By morning, when he strolled over to join them for breakfast, more equipment was laid out on the grass near the portal.

"There are a dozen more solar arrays, as well as the medication I promised you. These two modified droids can do most of the heavier work."

"What's that cable and apparatus?" Lerry pointed.

"A charging point for the powerpacs. It's hooked directly to the SciCorps power supply. It will save the discomfort of portalling back and forth. A temporary fix for the moment."

"Is that the longest cable in the galaxy?"

"In a metaphysical way, yes. Though in reality it's only thirty metres long. I'm surprised it worked."

"You're a marvel," Sussah gave him a hug. "What can I get you to eat?"

"Just a coffee. I've already had breakfast." As he waited for a mug to be poured, he continued. "I believe we're ready to head off to Delta whenever you are."

9

SHAPER HALL

WHILE CONVALESCING, LEONIE SPOKE AS MUCH AS SHE COULD OF what happened since they last saw her, but how can you squeeze two decades living on another planet into a week? The reality of other worlds, while a widely-known theory in sage's books, was a completely different thing.

Her shackles were made from black crystal and therefore immune to any powershaping. Only the Earther monks had the ability to work with it. With persistent requests from the bard, one such monk arrived after a few days and moved the shackles from her wrists to her ankles.

"Things are not well here at the moment. There is drought of the ground, causing torment," he told her. "Coupled with attempts on the lives of the royal lineage, it would not take much to cause more damage. Hence, your arrival was treated so rough, and their belief you needed to be in cuffs." Tipp rang a bell to arrange some food then poured her a drink. "And about the palace when you departed, you've no idea of the damage it started?" he asked.

Leonie shook her head. "Once we were caught inside that spell, Sussah and I were cut off from everything. One minute it was the palace balcony, the next we were on a skyland."

"When we realised you disappeared, Jade and I, the worst we feared. Then an offer to assist, I couldn't resist. Biell was a ranger of great reputation, with much insight on skyland information."

"Was? I heard about the rangers. It would be great to get some information on them; their routes and timetables."

There was a knock and the door opened. A young glins'ool brought in a tray of food. Leonie scowled, seeing the two guards standing by her door.

Tipp chuckled in amusement as the young bard almost dropped the tray, leaving it precariously balanced on the edge of the table before scurrying out. Once alone, Tipp continued with what happened since her departure.

"Biell's no longer a part of the group. I'll see what info she can recoup." He passed over the tray. "While we searched up, Jade searched down. She's been to every corner of the ground. Dedicated as any friend would. Regrettably, council recalled me, but I did what I could."

"It's ok, Tipp, really. It all worked out." Leonie started eating. "I'm sorry to have been the reason for so much angst."

"So, how does this test work?" Leonie asked the bard as he escorted her to Shaper Hall. She was happy to finally have the shackles removed, but two guards followed with crossbows. She still felt a twinge now and then, but tried to push it aside.

"Firstly, it isn't a pass or fail type of test. Only ability and strength will be assessed."

"Is that it? Doesn't sound too bad."

"Grading and registration will come in handy, determining if you meet the royal family."

"If? Why would they not see me? I'm not the threat!"

"The testing is really a formality; everyone now is deemed a jeopardy. To risk the throne, they'll not take that gamble; the resulting chaos would make Athglenn a shamble. Others would then attempt to take advantage. Zander may be after more than he can manage."

"How crazy can one man be?"

"Irrational acts will have a toll, but perhaps Dianah has him under control."

The news stunned Leonie. "Dianah? I killed her and Brendon before I left!" she whispered fiercely so the guards wouldn't overhear.

"Yet somehow they survived. Behold, we've arrived. In here all will be clear."

They were at the base of a series of steps. Looking up, the building was quite impressive; ten huge columns five paces apart lined the wide front portico. The building was constructed of white marble with gold flecks, pink marble tiles lined the floor and stairs.

They climbed the stairs and entered a dark, cool hallway. The far end opened up to the arena. Twelve tiers surrounded the circular area, and they entered mid-level on a wider promenade. The many columns soaring up to the open roof were black as were the walls, contrasting starkly with the white sand covering the arena floor.

Leonie had a closer look at the columns as they passed. "Is that crystal?"

Tipp nodded.

"I've not seen so much black crystal," she said.

"There's a mine way down in the southern range. Black crystal is an anomaly – quite strange. Totally inert to magic attack, absorbing the power is its knack."

As they were ushered to a desk surrounded by officials, she watched the lone person in the centre of the arena. She could hear the young man mutter but it wasn't coherent. As he wiggled his fingers an image appeared a few paces in front of him; it was a tree swaying in the breeze, with leaves falling and swirling in the wind.

"Is that an illusion?"

"I believe so." Tipp glanced down

The young man changed his tone. The image changed to a large flock of gulls on a beach. White waves rushed up the sand before receding.

"He's quite good," she said as he finished.

An older man and woman on the far side clapped. They were the only ones applauding, several other observers quietly talked among themselves and made notes on parchment.

Tipp edged her forward to the desk.

"Name?" one of the officials barked at her impatiently.

"Leonie," she answered.

She began writing. "Leonie what?"

"Just Leonie."

Looking up, she was clearly flustered. "No last name? You have to have something."

"Do I?" Leonie shrugged.

"Of course," the woman rolled her eyes as if addressing an idiot. "Your family name."

"Carter," Leonie said on the spur of the moment.

"Carter. Why didn't you say so in the first place?" she huffed.

"Because I just made it up. I've never needed a last name before."

"Well, child, we do things differently here in the *city*." Some of the other officious fellows chuckled nearby.

"Child!" she hissed under her breath, hackles rising.

Tipp patted her forearm gently, warbling softly to soothe her ire.

"Where are you from?" The woman was unaware of the ire caused.

Crap! Can't say Delta. Her mind raced. "Arilaso."

The woman paused, tapping her stylus. Clearly not having a good day. "Never heard of it."

"It's in Lyhosa. A r i l –"

"I know how to spell it!" the woman snapped, scribbling the name down.

Leonie rolled her eyes and turned her gaze to the contestant in the arena.

"Ability?" the woman asked tersely.

Leonie looked to Tipp for guidance.

"She wants to jot down your talent so they can make sure suitable examiners are present, otherwise we might have to return when they are available."

"Fire," Leonie answered.

The woman made a note then passed the document along. "Now—"

"Is flying an ability?"

The woman frowned. "Of course."

"Flying too."

After a moment's hesitation, she took back the parchment and jotted 'flying'.

"Electricity," Leonie added.

"What's that?"

"E l e c t r i c i t y." Leonie almost smiled at her confusion. "You might know it as lightning."

"Lightning? You can do lightning as well?"

"You asked."

More rapid scribbling. "That it then?" She was about to put her stylus down.

"Levitation."

"You said flying already."

"Yes. Everyone knows levitation is different than flying."

"So, to be clear, you say you can create fire and lightning, fly and levitate. Correct?"

"That seems right." She turned to Tipp. "And creating wind?"

"More Air, I declare," he agreed.

"And invisibility," Leonie said to the growing silence. "I think that's it." Leonie turned to the woman. "Got all that."

"This is ridiculous!" she woman snapped standing, throwing her stylus down. The other officials nearby all stopped and turned at the outburst.

Tipp leant down to her. "Regarding these matters, these

people are very devout. This is not the place to trifle, have no doubt."

"I'm not lying. I wouldn't do that to you. I understand you've probably gone out on a limb for me already."

Tipp looked at her like a stranger. "You ... you insist you can do this?"

She shrugged. "Some things I haven't even got names for."

A dark man stepped away from a nearby gathering. He looked her up and down as he approached, then studied the parchment. He turned his gaze upon Leonie again, appraising her more fully.

"That's Krre'lo. First Magus of the Royal House," Tipp clucked softly.

The silence was broken by a solitary clapping from the benches. The contestant in the arena finished his testing.

"You'll be next," Krre'lo said loudly to her, for all to hear. He turned and motioned to the other group to go. There was a brief argument, but it ended with a terse rebuke from him. A young pompous-looking man and his companions rushed off, glaring at her.

"You're in luck, young lady," Krre'lo said. "Several temples were finished for the day and about to depart." He looked at the list again. "If you can do these things as you claim, now is the best time. Take a few minutes to prepare while the examiners are notified and re-seated." He noted Tipp's sash, and gave a polite nod. "Is Tipp your trainer?"

"Trainer? No, but he's helped."

"Ah." He looked down at the parchment. "Arilaso?" he muttered. "Evidently you are not from this area. It is customary to have your trainer with you for this testing."

"That's okay. I haven't got one."

He frowned as others muttered. Clearly, he was not amused. "We shall proceed, regardless. I hope for your sake you're not wasting our time." He motioned with his hand for them to move along.

Tipp bowed, gently pulling her away. "To the antechamber we go, to prepare before the show. We'll wait for all to find their seats before you're summoned to perform your powershaping feats."

"I don't understand. What's the big deal?" she asked. She could see everyone gawking or pointing. Returning to the entrance hall, they soon turned into another corridor and descended several flights of stairs.

"While there are potentially many powershapers, those with great ability are few and far between," Tipp replied. "Some may accomplish elemental control in two disciplines, but more would be extreme. The list you propose covers four, maybe more." He continued to guide her down another set of stairs. "Do you recollect the last time we met?"

"How could I not? Before the Hunt. You and a balding monk, in the Delta cells—"

"Shhh. Whatever you do, never mention Delta here, *ever*," he admonished softly. "The rrell I saw in that cell was incapable of this," he continued. "Why is it now possible, or was I previously remiss?"

"I haven't the answers for you, Tipp. Maybe Styx did something. All I know is I started doing things and it increased from there over the years."

There were several others in the antechamber. They stopped talking when the newcomers entered.

Tipp nodded to some of them.

There was one small group to the side. Leonie recognised the young pompous man sent away from upstairs. He scowled at her when she walked in, then muttered angrily to his two companions.

Tipp ushered her to a bench to sit. He then fetched her some water.

"You don't need to wait on me, Tipp. I can manage."

"Forsooth, you speak truth," he clucked. "Actually, I'm in anticipation of your evaluation. Origins of bard magic is ambiguous, and many believe it is ridiculous. I would enjoy seeing the smug looks wiped off the face of any who think bards are a disgrace," he crooned softly.

The pompous upstart sauntered closer with his companions, looking at her like trash. "Who do *you* think you are, jumping the queue like that? I've waited weeks for this, and now they have the audacity to delay me yet again."

"Be calm, that's Count Trent." Tipp warbled in her ear. "A boorish but influential malcontent."

Leonie had no idea who Count Trent was. "Do you reckon the evaluators wanted to see real talent, not weak juvenile theatrics?" she asked Tipp calmly, but loudly enough for all to hear.

Red in the face, Trent stepped forward. His companions reached out to hold him back but he shrugged them off.

"I think you need to cool, young fool." Tipp stepped in his way.

"Forgetting who you are talking to, old peacock?" Trent snarled. "I only listen to those with any significance." He turned to his companions. "I wonder if this thing is aware of the farce these bards really are?"

Leonie sat back, still holding her glass. "I've always thought only an imbecile would be ignorant to the talents of high-ranking bards. And now you've just proved it. Thanks."

Once he realised the insult, Trent fumed. As he stepped forward, his legs tangled. He put his hands out, hitting the ground much faster and harder than normal. When he struggled to his feet, he rubbed his wrists.

"Looks like the youngster is only now learning to walk." Leonie spoke to his friends. "Better take him away before he gets himself hurt."

Trent swore and lurched forward, stumbling again. This time he couldn't stand back up, as if a great weight was forcing him down. His friends grabbed his arms and helped him back to a chair.

"What was that one?" she asked Tipp.

"The body-slamming? Air, I believe," the bard clucked. "Same with the tripping, I perceive."

"See, I just make crap up as I need it." She finished her water, watching Trent. A quick scan of his mind told her what she expected. *Looks like I'm not in his good books*, she thought.

After a few terse words, Count Trent stomped out, his friends following. Soon the other contestants left, giving the bard a courteous nod. Tipp and Leonie were now alone.

"Are we it for the day?"

"If you do all you say – and I have no reservation – you will be out there for the duration."

"I better go pee."

Tipp pointed her in the direction for her ablutions.

When she returned, he continued his instruction. "When the gong sounds, it's the start of the round. Those doors will swing open wide, that's your cue to walk outside. Normally, representatives from one temple or another will be here to score, but I dare say for your show there will be more. With you, we might have Earth, Fire, and Air. Life is always present in case things don't go to order; the others are Time, Spirit, Death and Water."

Leonie paced nervously. It wasn't the issue of her ability to do what she said she could, it was the audience factor.

Tipp noticed her nervousness. "All candidates – even with experience – get the jitters before an appearance," Tipp advised. "Easy to say, but imagine you're in isolation, perhaps you can try meditation. Can you do that?"

"I've had some success, though it doesn't come easily." She sat cross-legged and tried to be calm; to concentrate. Tipp started making a soft noise. At first it was more annoying, but strangely, she started to relax as it lulled her.

Her mind was brought back by the shaking. "Looks like the meditation was a success. Now the gong has sounded. Time to impress."

10

———

THE TESTING

WHEN LEONIE walked out, she looked around, certain there were far more people gathered now than the dozen or so earlier. Tipp's last advice was to walk to the centre of the arena. What she did from there was up to her. She might be asked to repeat a particular ability a couple of times.

Another feature not noticed earlier was the four statues situated a few paces in from the wall of the arena. There were also several targets like she'd seen for archery practice.

All was silent; no one said anything.

Leonie turned around, looking at the entire area, taking it all in, noticing Tipp standing just inside the doorway to the antechamber. She was determined not to embarrass him.

Recalling the order of her list, she took a moment to concentrate before creating a ball of fire in her paw, then made it larger before flinging it at a statue.

The black crystal absorbed the energy instantly. That surprised her, but from the non-reaction from the crowd, it was normal.

She conjured three more intense fireballs, juggled them briefly and flung them at the other statues. Hearing murmurs from the tiers, she moved on to the next ability on her mental list. Rising off the ground to about the fifth level, Leonie started going in a widening circle until she was in line with the statues. When she was at one side of the arena, she shot lightning at the targets on the far side, and did this four times before increasing her speed.

Realising this was making her dizzy, she slowed down and returned to the centre, landing when the world stopped spinning.

The crowd's muttering was louder now.

Taking a breath to steady herself, she concentrated on her next task. One of the statues lifted off the ground, as high as the roof. One at a time, the other three joined it. All four did a lap of the roof opening before lowering to their original positions.

As the crowd started cheering, the sand in front of her rose and began moving in a tight circle. It grew in size and strength as it swirled, resembling a miniature whirlwind.

Some people were standing now, pointing. Leonie enlarged the swirl until it covered half the area and enveloped her, blotting out the tiers. When she cut the power, the sand rained down, the grains flowed around her form, but didn't touch her. As the last of the grains settled, she vanished.

The crowd gasped as she suddenly appeared standing on top of a statue. Leonie repeated this, visiting all four statues before returning to the centre.

She sought out Krre'lo in the crowd, gave him a wave and walked back to the antechamber.

"That was truly amazing," Tipp cooed.

"As long as I didn't disappoint you."

"I will never doubt you again."

"Careful, I was a thief and a murderer once." Leonie reached for the ewer of water, sat down and finished it off. "I think I got a bit carried away out there." She yawned. "Reckon it's over?" she asked.

They both looked up at the commotion coming along the passage. From their attire, several were priests representing the various temples, but Krre'lo shouldered his way through.

"Well, looks like you are true to your word. How are you feeling now?" Krre'lo asked.

"I could do with a breather. Would there be a chance for something to eat?"

"That's probably the easiest thing we can manage. Come this way." He turned and walked out. The crowd parted, allowing access for himself, Leonie and Tipp.

The food hall soon had a pair of representatives from each temple except Opsyss. They quietly chatted among themselves while Leonie made her selections. The food was ample if simple fare; sliced fruits, cheeses, cured meats and savoury pastries. She was surprised at the beverage selection.

"Juices?" she asked Krre'lo.

"No alcohol allowed on test days for obvious reasons." He helped himself to the dishes, as did Tipp. Once Leonie was seated, the questions began.

They were the sort of questions she expected; how long had she trained, who was her trainer, how did she learn to splice the various elements together, was there anything else she could do, how far and fast could she fly?

Leonie answered as best she could without mentioning visiting other worlds, but admitted she learnt what she needed as the situation arose when she was battling with the l'ith. "While I haven't a trainer, I guess I should give thanks to the hroltahgs."

The talking became subdued. She looked to Tipp for guidance.

"Krre'lo, I think we need to chat in private," the bard said.

After the supper, the temple priests were ushered away. They requested more testing as they had never experienced such a vast array of abilities from one candidate.

Annoying and frustrating as it all was, Leonie agreed. "What choice have I got," she muttered.

· · ·

They were now in Krre'lo's chambers, several floors up from the meal room. One window overlooked the main street, while double doors opposite opened onto a balcony overlooking the arena. Krre'lo asked Leonie to stand with her right arm out, palm up. As he did this, he made a brief incantation.

"You might feel a tingling," he cautioned.

"What's this for?" Leonie asked.

"You needed to be registered. I'm about to register you. It's an arcane tattoo, but it can only be revealed by those in authority."

She felt a brief drawing of power as his fingers wove sigils in the air. Glowing signs formed, and then disappeared as it touched the skin of her forearm. He did this six times, and each time, there was a slight prickle.

"Six?"

"Hard to believe, but this is what was sensed by the priests."

"What were they?"

"Fire, Air, Earth, Spirit, Time and Life."

"Life?"

"As one expends energy, there is a level of fatigue. While you did show signs of fatigue, you also had an immediate recovery. The Life priestess, from the Mimmis temple, said she saw indications of her element in this self-healing."

"Where does Time fit into it? Sorry for the simple questions, but I've not had the formal training some seem to expect."

"That element is utilised in the speed you accomplish tasks; flying faster for instance. At times it can be quite a subtle blend of elements, other times, like the fireball, are obviously the only element." He stepped away and removed his vest of office, placing it on a hook.

"That formality is done, please have a seat. You too, bard." Krre'lo pointed to the lounges. She sat in the offered padded chairs. Tipp placed a couple of cushions on the rug near the low table and knelt, there being no roost. From a cabinet, Krre'lo brought over some wine and poured the contents into three goblets and sat across from them.

As they got comfortable, Leonie took in the ambience of the old, wood-panelled room. Floor to ceiling bookcases, some with glowing books, lined one long wall. On the opposite wall were several cabinets. She noticed a faint aura enshrouding them.

"What's so special to ward all those cabinets?"

"You can tell they're protected?" The First Magus's eyes widened.

Leonie nodded. "I think it's a racial trait. I've always seen auras of power."

"Interesting." He considered. "As a bona fide magic school, we have a register of every powershaper in Athglenn, and whoever the other countries choose to notify us about. It's a reciprocal arrangement, but sometimes takes weeks to update."

"Impressive." Leonie nodded. "Now I'm part of it?"

"Once we enter your details in the system, yes." He toyed with his drink. "So, what's this you say about the rollos? Are you telepathic too?"

"Is that another powershaper ability?"

"Not entirely," Krre'lo answered. "Possibly connected with Spirit. Either way, some believe telepathy can be very good and others, very bad." He added, "You're aware of the current situation here?"

"The assassinations or the rollos leaving?" Leonie nodded. "Some of one, more, of the other."

"There are those who think this threat to the crown is coming from the inside, and others think it's an outsider. And no, I don't believe it's you, otherwise we wouldn't be sitting here this moment having a chat. So, tell me about your affiliation with the hroltahgs."

"Surely they aren't enemies of the state?" Leonie asked.

"No, not at all. In fact, they have been excellent bodyguards. I have a fondness for them. Actually, I'm quite jealous of you." When he smiled, his white teeth lit his face up. "But there are others who distrust mind-readers."

Leonie smiled. "You have the truth of it."

"Perhaps we could explore a level of your lore?" Tipp suggested.

"By all means. I'm also curious how Leonie has come under the wing of the Reenatian Bards."

"Tell me what you know about prophecies of the rollo?" the bard requested.

"There are several." Krre'lo paused. "My understanding about one in particular had stirred up considerable interest in the hroltahg community."

"So we don't get our thoughts in a mix, can you please be more specific?"

"Something about a chosen one, or some sort of saviour, a catalyst in saving people – or is it uniting them – because this world is dying?"

"I see." Tipp looked to Leonie with an arched brow. "And have you heard any rumours recently."

"Word is the rollos are all congregating in Qelay," Krre'lo said.

"Did they perchance say why they were going away?"

"None. But it's curious, and concerning. Most of the hroltahg contingent here has already left. The dozen or so remaining will leave in stages."

"And I take it you deal regularly with sages?" Tipp stepped to the door and closed it, making sure no one was eaves-dropping.

"Too often, if you ask me," Krre'lo said. "Though I suspect they are more interested in my wine cellar. Where's this leading?"

"It's about the sage's convictions of all our unique origins."

"You're referring to the 'gateways to other worlds' theory? I've heard of it."

"What say you?"

"While it's hard to believe, it has merit. Even my limited understanding of the differences we all have makes me wonder; how did six completely different races develop?"

"And if there were portals, or gates to another place? How would you react to the fact?"

"After the laughing? Awe, I'd expect."

"Then I suggest you prepare for laughter and awe." Tipp turned to her. "Tell the magus what you saw."

"All of it?"

"Just the pertinent bits," Tipp suggested.

"There was this book I had to take to Qelay. I encountered the rollos over twenty years ago–"

"You mean the *Seer's Codex*? That was you?"

"Since that day," Leonie continued, "I have slowly learnt to do things."

"Didn't you die?"

"Several times, apparently. My last death was in Delta. I'm told the palace was destroyed by a crazy powershaper."

"Niaarin Grigorid. Go on." Krre'lo was leaning forward in his chair now.

Leonie went on to describe in condensed detail the first portal to Earth, that it took all this time to work out how to return, and on her way here to Reenat, she stumbled upon another portal in the Vale. "And that's why all the rollos are leaving. They're returning to Masevalon, their homeworld."

Krre'lo sat silent, looking from one to another. "And these other portals? Where are they?" he asked eventually.

"I can't be sure. Considering they haven't been found, they're either lost and buried, or perhaps on other skylands." She quickly explained her belief on the formation of the skylands.

"I will need to think on this." The First Magus paused, looking at Leonie for a full minute.

She started to feel uncomfortable with the scrutiny.

"Magus?" Tipp cleared his throat, politely prompting the magus.

"So, *you* are the chosen one?" Krre'lo asked finally.

"I was volunteered, if that's what you mean." Her tail lashed from side to side in annoyance.

"Why are you telling me all this?" the First Magus asked.

"Reenat is the largest, most cosmopolitan city in Shak'aran. It also has ambassadors of all countries and representatives of all species. It's possible that, with the backing of the Reenatian Royal House, continent-wide support and cooperation would be given in seeking out the remaining portals."

"This obviously needs to be taken to the highest level. It may take a few days, but I will get word to you both promptly."

There wasn't much to be said, after that so they made their farewells.

As Leonie and Tipp were about to leave, Krre'lo called out. "One final thing; I'll remove the guard escort. I doubt very much they'll be needed."

———

Leonie picked herself up off the sand, feeling dazed.

"You dropped your guard again," Krre'lo pointed out the obvious.

"Frag it. I don't reckon I'm going to get used to that. How can you mount an attack and defence at the same time?"

"Practice, practice, practice." Krre'lo readied himself for another bout.

"Maybe in a few years I'll get the hang of it." Leonie shook her head and massaged her shoulder where she'd landed heavily.

"How can you be so adept in the attack, yet so inept in defence?"

"Because I've never had anyone attack me magically before now."

"Your attacker won't care, and will use any means to defeat you."

Leonie decided in the next bout, she was going to be under-handed. She concentrated, gently scanning his mind. Krre'lo was about to use a very intense air-blast to knock her off her paws. The instant the magus released his spell, she disappeared. As the sand where she was standing swirled, she reached around behind him, claws against his thick neck.

"Like this?" she purred in his ear.

He froze. "Um, yes. How did you anticipate so accurately?"

"I followed your advice and used any means." She retracted her claws and stepped in front of him, now visible.

"You scanned me!" He laughed. "And I didn't feel a thing."

"You can blame the rollos for that."

In the distance a gong tolled.

The First Magus wiped the sweat from his brow. "Very well. At least you know what and how to do it. I have no doubt if you practice the techniques I showed you, it will come to you – assuming you survive long enough." He flashed her a grin. "Thank you for the entertainment."

"It's what I'm here for," she said as they strolled out the corridor. Behind the walls, at the back of the arena was a smaller, more secluded area used for practice sessions such as this. There were benefits to having the First Magus as your instructor; a quick word and suddenly the acolyte powershapers departed. She did note their backward glances and discussions, but a quick mind-scan revealed more curiosity than animosity.

Krre'lo was relentless during the training session, Leonie was so tired. Bidding him farewell, she decided to stroll back to the council chambers. If she was quick, she'd be in time for supper.

There was a decorative carriage with several soldiers out in front of the council chambers. They eyed her warily but let her pass. Thinking Tipp was entertaining someone of note, she wearily climbed the stairs and headed for her rooms. She caught sight of the bard the same time he saw her in the hallway.

"Ah, there you are. We have special guests; I make no jest." He escorted her to his official chambers. "Was the training draining?"

"Krre'lo is a tough one, but a good instructor. Well suited to his role," she said as they mounted the stairs. "I hate him today. Tomorrow, I'm sure will be different."

On the top floor, Tipp opened the door. Inside his office two ladies were sitting with Biell.

"Leonie, may I introduce the Princesses Siola and Phione," Tipp said.

The two women stood and faced her. They were slightly shorter than Leonie. Obviously sisters, as their looks were so similar. Both were tanned, indicating quite a bit of time outdoors, with black hair pulled back and plaited. Siola had green eyes, while Phione's were blue-grey. Close-fitting blouses and leggings displayed their athleticism. If she saw them in the street, she'd think they were thieves or dancers; the clothing allowed free-movement, and the grace with which they stood and walked over indicated agility. Apart from the black hair, Phione's blue eyes reminded her of Jade.

"Pleased to meet you both." Leonie smiled and nodded to Biell.

Biell returned the smile and quietly left.

"On the contrary." Princess Siola stepped over to shake hands. "It's our pleasure to meet you."

A quick look to the bard reassured Leonie there was no need for any undue etiquette. She put her paw out and shook the proffered hand. It was a surprisingly firm grip.

Princess Phione followed suit. She looked a bit younger, but as well-muscled as her older sister.

"I'm honoured you'd come to me. I was expecting a summons to the palace."

"Oh, it's a stuffy old place." Siola looked around the office. "Far more relaxing here and no need for pretence."

"Please be at ease," Tipp clucked, inviting them to sit. "Refreshments will arrive in moments." He pulled on an ornate rope hanging from the ceiling.

"I must smell like a di'anth. I have only just returned from Shaper Hall—"

"Oh yes. We heard about that. How did it go?" They all moved to the comfortable chairs by the balcony window overlooking the main street.

"Well enough, Princess. Lucky my fur covers the bruising."

"Please, Siola and Phione will be fine."

Leonie nodded, and shifted in her seat to adjust her tail. "So, what brings you here, if I may ask?"

"We can get to that shortly, but *please* tell us all about your recent adventures. I hear you are a very talented powershaper, self-trained and have fought those vile l'ith creatures. Surely that isn't true?"

"You can't believe everything you hear," Leonie said. "If today's efforts are any indication, I'm definitely not a talented powershaper."

"I told you, Phione." She turned to her sister. "Those guards tell these stories only to impress young girls."

"The fighting the l'ith part is correct, though." Leonie nodded with a smile. Again, with a deep breath, she regaled her edited version of the last twenty years, leaving out any direct mention of Earth, or wilders. The refreshments arrived; savoury pastries, fruit and wine.

"And you found a portal for the hroltahgs?" Siola continued at Leonie's nod. "Well, my father is very keen to help locate these other portals as well. You are aware Yarnik is getting warmer?"

"Not just a drought?" Leonie asked, making a selection of the foods.

"In our schooling, the tutors teach us many things – mostly boring stuff – but some very interesting lessons most people don't get to hear. We have two suns and while we circle Diphei each year, we are getting closer to Zastre, the other one." She said this matter-of-fact.

Leonie chuckled. "Siola, please assume I'm one of those most people. I didn't even know our sun had a name other than sun."

"Our astronomer sages tell us Diphei orbits Zastre much like Yarnik orbits Diphei, or like Luminor and Luxor orbit Yarnik. Diphei's orbit is however, very elongated. Meaning Yarnik has been a long way from Zastre for a long time. Longer than we have been on this world. They believe, from their studies, that Yarnik will get so close to Zastre, the hotter this world will become, and we won't survive. Only the l'ith will, as they are native to this world."

"And wyverns."

"Wyverns? Are they from here too?"

"Don't your scholars tell you about them?"

"It's touched on, but there is very little known about them. I assumed they were more myth than real, or an exaggeration of *something* else."

"No, they're quite real, I can assure you." Leonie helped herself to another wine after topping up the other two glasses.

"Where was I?" Siola wondered.

"Father wants to help," Phione said.

"Very much so." Siola nodded. "He feels it would be a great way to divert everyone's attention from the current troubles."

"This is the assassination attempts?"

"Yes."

"Are the Jart'lekk involved?"

"Some of it has been attributed to them, but there have been other attempts from other factions."

"Are there different groups after the throne, or is it one group using a variety of avenues to get the job done?"

"We are at peace with Lyhosa and Tesak. There is a rumour some internal rivalry is taking advantage of the unrest, but we are sure the main threat is from Delta."

"You mean Zander?"

"Word is you know Delta," Siola said quietly.

Leonie wondered who had told whom. "I've been there in my travels, yes. But it was many years ago."

"King Reindet would like you to go to Delta and remove Zander as a threat. When I say *remove*, my father means *kill*." Siola sat back, with a sigh. "Obviously, he can't get the Jart'lekk to do it. And frankly, he doesn't trust anyone else to succeed. Helping the king would put you in good favour."

Leonie also sat back to consider the conversation. She sipped her wine thoughtfully. "Have I a choice?"

"A choice? Of course." The slight hesitation and look on Siola's face showed more surprise that refusal was an option.

"But it's at the request of the *king*," Phione said, aghast.

"I hear request but I'm feeling it's something else entirely."

Siola gave Phione a worried look.

"Just kidding." Leonie chuckled. "While I have had my own troubles, Athglenn has been more or less good to me, but more importantly, good to my friends. If there was chaos in the capital, it would spread across the land, and that could cause trouble to my friends." There was palpable relief on the ladies' faces.

"It's a risky thing to ask though," Leonie continued. "Risky to me, at least. It's all well and good to be in favour to the king, but that's assuming I succeed. Is there anything to look forward to upfront?"

"I guess that depends on what it is you want."

"I'd like to meet the king. If I'm being asked to take some-one's life, I'd like to hear it from their mouth. Call it professional courtesy." Leonie drained her glass.

"Under the circumstances, that could be awkward." Siola considered.

"Surely he doesn't think I'm a threat? Hasn't he got a couple of rollo bodyguards? They'll read any ill intent long before the king was in harm's way. Also, since there's a mutual interest in finding these portals, I might have more information for him."

"We'll see what can be done. I assume you're staying here?"

"For as long as the bards can stand me."

11

———

THE KING

Maybe to Siola the palace was a stuffy old place, but for those not born into it, the palace was stunning. With spacious rooms and high ceilings, large paintings and tapestries adorned the white walls, and exotic plants filled the corners of the intricate mosaic-tiled floors.

As a matter of security protocol for powershaper visitors, Leonie had a thick collar clipped around her neck.

"This will light up if you begin to use the power. It also gets very hot. May I suggest for your comfort and safety, you do refrain from using it," a tall guard warned.

A blue and red liveried servant ushered her through the foyer into the reception hall, leaving two guards by the door. "King Reindet is currently indisposed," he said. "You are invited to partake of the refreshments until summoned. Good day."

Leonie clawed a piece of familiar-looking fruit and strolled around, examining the artwork. One tapestry caught her eye, looking vaguely familiar. She heard footfalls behind her. Turning, she saw the princesses and Count Trent enter.

While the ladies smiled, Trent baulked, his round face going red.

The princesses were wearing similar outfits to the other day, but their long hair was now loose. Trent wore shirt, vest, and trousers of good quality, and a thin circlet on his head.

"What is *that thing* doing here?" he spoke loudly, pointing at Leonie.

"Hush, now, Trent. She's a guest and will be treated as such," Siola berated him.

"Not by me." He nodded to the princesses and stomped out.

The ladies approached. "Leonie. I apologise for cousin Trent's outburst. He's not been the same since his mother died last month."

"On top of that, his evaluation was not what he hoped," Phione added.

"Sister," Siola chided. "That's a personal matter, not be aired. It also is no excuse for his rudeness."

"I don't mind hearing of his failure," Leonie grinned. "I won't tell anyone."

"I'm sure his retest – without distraction – will yield better results," Phione muttered defensively.

"Leonie, welcome to the palace," Siola stated. "I can only assume father has chosen to meet with you."

"You didn't know I was coming?"

"We passed on your request. What the king chooses after that isn't always disclosed to us *mere* girls."

"That's got to suck."

"Suck?"

"Not being told everything *because* you're female. As if having balls was an indication of superiority. Look at your cousin, for instance."

"Leonie, as a guest, it would be polite not to disparage family members."

"Fair enough. I forgot my manners."

"What do you think of this tapestry?" Siola changed the subject.

"I've seen it before."

"Only if you've been in that hovel called a palace in Delta."

"Ah ... yes." Leonie recalled that last night.

"So, you have been there?" Phione asked.

"Let's say in a previous life."

Phione was looking at Leonie curiously. "You don't look old enough."

"Thanks, I think. Why is that?"

"Perhaps I'm misjudging rrell age, but this tapestry arrived before I was born. You don't look old enough."

It was too tiresome to explain the nuances of her hybrid status. She decided to let it go unsaid. "I hide my age."

"You do it very well, it seems," Siola complimented. "But, all the better. If you've seen it, then you'll know the layout of the palace in Delta." She turned to Phione. "Sister, looks like we chose our assassin well."

"*You* chose me?" Leonie asked, surprised.

"We saw you at your evaluation." Siola nodded. "We were there for Trent, but then they switched agendas and there you were."

"A lot of people saw you," Phione added.

"And this is was why you came to make the request in person. Does your father actually know?"

"He does now. While you may not have come under his eye, once we approached him about it, he seemed very interested."

"How many have tried in the past?" Leonie watched them. "Surely this has been going on for a while." Leonie sauntered back to the table to choose another morsel.

"It has been going on for too long, which is why your talents will be ideal to end it once and for all. Are you considering backing down?"

"No. I have my own reasons why I'd consider doing this." She chewed her fruit.

"But you still need the king to ask it?" Siola asked.

"Call me an opportunist. One can never know when one needs a friend in high places." Leonie moved to the pastries.

"Were you looking for friends in high places the last time you were in the Delta palace, or were you being *opportunistic?"* Phione queried.

"I was after someone else, and they were no friend."

"To kill? Did it work?"

"In a manner of speaking. She did end up dead."

"If you could make Zander's death look like an accident, that would be good too." Siola pointed out. "Better for our international relations if they don't think we'd stoop to assassinating a rival."

They all turned at the sound of boots at the door. A stocky man, armoured and dressed in the royal colours entered.

"Ah, Castellan Willom, are we ready?" Siola smiled, asking politely.

"My ladies, the King will see you now," the castellan confirmed, bowing.

Swallowing the last of a pastry, Leonie followed the two princesses out. In the hallway were six soldiers, also in red and blue uniforms, but with metal breastplates, short swords and each holding a spear. The castellan took the lead, and four of the guards remained in the rear.

After a short walk deeper into the palace, they stopped at large double doors. Two men-at-arms opened them and stepped to the sides. The escort party continued inside. The doors closed behind them with barely a sound.

The audience hall was large and as elegant as the rest of the palace, except there were vaulted ceilings. Skylights allowed shafts of the afternoon light to play across the walls. As they entered, the guards peeled off to each side and stood at attention.

At the far end of the room, the king sat on his throne on the dais. The red and blue carpet stopped halfway, leaving the mosaic tiled floor exposed to the steps.

To one side was another table of juices and wines.

Four paces short of the first step, the castellan came to a halt.

"Your Highness, I have the honour to present the Princesses Siola and Phione, and the Lady Leonie."

Leonie nearly choked hearing *Lady.*

"Very good, Willom," the king said.

The castellan turned, bowed to the ladies, and joined his men by the doors.

As the princesses moved closer, Siola looked over her shoulder and motioned with her head Leonie should join them.

"Good afternoon, father," Siola said from the base of the stairs. "This is Leonie, the person we spoke about recently. Leonie, may I introduce King Reindet Moreward."

"Your Highness, it's an honour to meet you."

The king inclined his head. "You are welcome in this house, Leonie. I have heard interesting things about you. I'm in two minds; should I be concerned or glad at you being here?"

Glancing to the sisters, Leonie licked her lips. "I guess that depends on what you heard. Under the current circumstances, if you were concerned, then I wouldn't have gotten this close to you or be wearing the collar."

The king raised his eyebrows, before laughing. "Excellent points." He stood and removed his crown, placing it on the vacant throne. "Enough of that, I'm hungry. Please, ladies, would you join me in some refreshments?" He walked down the steps and, with the three women following, moved to the table.

At that time, a side door opened and a serving girl entered, looking flustered.

She curtsied. "My lord, apologies for the tardiness–"

"Nonsense girl. Bring the tray over." Once he sat down, the ladies chose a chair each and sat around the table; Siola at the opposite end to her father, and Phione opposite Leonie.

Nervously the serving girl walked over and placed the tray of food on the table. She then poured the wine, starting with the king then the princesses. When she served Leonie, the bottle slipped, knocking over the glass and spilling the contents over Leonie.

Leonie was up off the chair in an instant.

There was a shocked look on both Siola's and Phione's faces.

"Oh Gods, my lady, I'm terribly sorry." The serving girl

fussed; grabbing a towel from her pocket she started dabbing at Leonie's clothes.

As the king cursed at the clumsiness, two of the guards and the castellan rushed over.

"It's ok, really," Leonie said to the serving girl; fear clearly evident on her face. "I've spilt more wine on me than this."

Curtseying, she grabbed the tray and fled through the door to the kitchens.

"Clumsy girl," the king cursed. "Leonie, she will be reprimanded."

"Highness, please not on my account. We all get nervous from time to time."

"You're too forgiving, but in this instance, I will let it go. She is normally more dexterous." He returned to his seat. "Thank you, Willom," he said by way of dismissal of the castellan. The three men returned to their posts.

Leonie poured herself more wine, then decided to make a toast. "To the king, for his leniency and continued success."

They all raised their glasses and drank their wine.

Leonie seated herself, and waited quietly.

"My over-protective daughter tells me you have some special aptitude with powershaping, and also experience with Delta. How is this so?"

"I was born in Delta, your Highness. Sadly, I had no say in that. As for any abilities with the power, I can only say that I have the hroltahgs to thank – or blame – for opening my mind. Prior to that, I had barely any capacity for it."

"The hroltahgs gave you these powers?"

"My pardon, I believe they awakened or revealed latent abilities that would have otherwise remained dormant."

"Those hroltahgs are amazing creatures. Weird, but amazing."

"May I ask where they are? Have they all returned to Qelay now?"

"All that I know of. Yes." He must have noticed a change in Leonie's looks. "This disappoints you?"

"Highness, it was my hope to catch up with a friend. I thought he might be here."

"The elders said their farewells several days ago."

Leonie sipped her wine, thinking. "Doesn't that leave you exposed? I heard the rollos were your bodyguards."

"I have enough good and true men around." He pointed to the collar around her neck. "And as you can see, no visitors are permitted the use of power whilst in the palace." He stopped at a disturbance by the door.

Everyone at the table looked over to see Count Trent arguing with the guards. Behind him was the serving girl who recently spilled the wine.

"I am not too late. Thank the Gods, sire!" Trent called out. "I have some grave news."

With an irritated gesture of the king's hand the guards released the count, but they followed as he dragged the young girl behind him. "What is this news, young Trent. As you can see–"

"Sire, I believe this creature means you harm!" He pointed to Leonie.

"How so?" Reindet asked, looking at his guest in surprise.

"Poison, I believe, sire. When the lovely and vigilant Glynde here accidentally spilled the wine, she felt something in this *thing's* pocket. She thought it unusual, and with the recent threats on your life, came to me with her suspicions immediately."

"Truly." The king turned his steely gaze to Leonie. "Castellan, search our guest."

The castellan stepped over to Leonie. "Lady Leonie, please stand."

Leonie put her wine down and did as ordered, looking to the princesses then Trent. The dull colour of his fine circlet tickled her memory.

"This is foolishness," Siola said. "What's got into your head, Trent? Leonie is our guest."

"And that, in itself, is also a worry, your Highness," Trent addressed the king.

"Careful, Trent. Your circlet is slipping," Leonie said.

Reflexively, the young man's hand quickly came up to adjust the dark grey circlet.

Leonie sniggered. *Thanks for confirming my suspicions.*

Two palace guards stepped in and held her arms as the castellan checked Leonie's pockets. He withdrew an object from the pocket, still damp with wine.

"Sire." Willom held up what he found to the king; a vial with a dark purple liquid.

"This is crazy," Leonie said. "That serving girl must have put it there when she spilt the wine. No wonder she looked so nervous."

"Save your excuses and accusations," Trent crowed. "You've been found out by your superiors. Pure and simple."

"Father, I protest. This cannot be right," Siola objected, looking in shock between Trent and her father.

"I agree." Leonie looked at the smirking Trent. "This clown is a long way from being my *superior*."

The king ignored Leonie. "Nevertheless, daughter, let us find out what the vial contains. Unless your guest chooses to enlighten us. Leonie?" he asked.

Leonie looked at the vial, noting its colouring and viscosity. "The purple liquid is probably *dre'fiue*—"

"The very same poison that took our beloved queen! You come back to finish off our king?" Trent accused.

"How is it you know so much about it, Trent?" Leonie goaded. She turned back to the king. "My lord, I've not seen that vial before, but *dre'fiue* is quite common as a poison, and I do agree with what you said earlier. To plant that on me without me noticing, Glynde is still very dexterous."

Reindet sighed, deep in thought, glancing between Leonie and Trent. "We shall confirm with our apothecarist whether it is or is not the same poison. In the meantime, confine her to the guest quarters with guards."

"Surely this traitor must be taken to the dungeon—"

"*I* make the decisions here, Count Trent. If she's found guilty, then we will begin beheading anyone involved."

"But—"

"Enough!" the king shouted, glaring at him. "You've been a good lad bringing this warning to me, but do not overreach." He nodded to the guards, who frog-marched Leonie out of the room.

As she left, she heard Siola arguing and pleading with the king. In the hallway, the castellan remained stony-faced as he shackled her wrists and ankles. Two more guards appeared, taking her up a flight of stairs, along a corridor and finally into a room. The solid door was locked behind her.

"Those last two guards looked familiar," she muttered, wondering what the hell she got herself into this time. For Trent to so conveniently appear pointed towards him being involved with the frame-up. "Was this all because of shaming him at the testing?" she muttered. "Or simply because he despises rrells."

Leonie went to the narrow window and looked out. The palace was on top of the hill overlooking the city to the west, and the ocean to the east. Her view was out to the vast sea. Looking below, she saw a narrow path leading to a large stone quayside surrounded by rocks, roughly two hundred feet down. The walls were bare, with little to hold onto. *If only I could fly.*

Leonie turned back to the room and sat on the window sill. A large wardrobe was to one side of the room, next to the door. A fourposter bed filled most of the other wall, with two small tables either side. The opposite wall had a long, narrow desk with a bowl and mirror, with a stuffed chair and a small settee beside it.

She walked across the thick rug to the door and listened. All she heard was the breathing and mumblings of the two guards. *Where have I seen them before?* She wondered as she moved to the bed and lay down, luxuriating in its comfort.

An idea occurred to her; she tried to scan their minds, but nothing registered. *Maybe the collar prevents telepathy too!* "Think, girl!" she hissed to herself. She examined her shackles. "Fools should have locked them behind my back." Briefly attempting to use the power to unlock them, she immediately regretted it, feeling a burning sensation around her neck.

"Frack!" She cursed softly, trying to find a position with the least skin contact until it cooled. Leonie got up and paced the room, wondering how long it would be before anyone came for her.

She doubted Tipp had any influence in here; all the rollos had left, and with all their well-meaning protesting, how effective would a princess be against a king in fear of his life?

"It's up to you girl. How much of your old, neglected thief skills can you remember?" *You obviously forgot how to detect a pickpocket, idiot!*

Checking the desk and its drawers, under the bed, and inside the wardrobe took a couple of minutes. *Nothing!* She stood in the middle of the thick rug, clenching and unclenching her claws in the pile. Gazing around the room in an effort to devise a plan to escape. *Breaking the mirror would alert the guards, and the glass shards would be useless for picking locks.* Locks. Her eyes went to the wardrobe doors. There was a small key in the lock. Leonie leapt over and pulled the key out. *It has possibilities.*

Walking back to the window ledge, she started rubbing it against the rough stonework. The metal left scratches on the ledge, but the metal showed signs of wear. She quickly examined her shackle's keyhole again, then continued shaping the metal key, checking progress regularly.

She stopped when she heard voices in front of her room. It was the princess. Leonie held her breath. From the pleas, Siola wanted to come in, but the guards were adamantly refusing entry. "Orders from the King, princess," one said.

When the noise abated, Leonie continued, wondering who would visit next and how much time she still had.

Seemingly ages later, and satisfied the metal shaping was the best she could do, she sat on the bed and attempted to pick the shackles on her wrists. It was an awkward angle to work, but given the situation, any discomfort was pushed to the side. After a few minutes with little success, Leonie returned to the window and began scratching again, now believing it had to be made thinner. *But too thin will make it too soft.*

Again, she tried. It seemed to be working better this time, but as she feared, the metal pin was also bending. She took a deep breath and continued more slowly, more gently, coaxing the metal tumblers to turn.

Outside was dimming, indicating several hours had passed since her incarceration. Finally, there was a click and the shackles were loose. She rubbed her wrists, wanting to jump for joy in relief. Instead, she reshaped the pin to work on her ankles.

After a while she had to make a choice. The pin wasn't going to last much longer. She walked to the mirror and moved the collar around so she could see its lock mechanism and began to pick it.

With more noises growing louder in the corridor, she thought she felt something in the collar give with a last twist.

The keys rattled in the door.

Leonie dropped the bent key and put the shackles loosely back on her wrists, holding the cuffs against her body to keep them in place just as the door swung open.

The two guards stepped in, followed by Count Trent. A guard turned and kicked the door closed.

"I fear our King will be too soft to do what is needed. Take her," he ordered.

As the two guards reached for her she now recognised them as Trent's companions at the testing.

"Where are you taking me?" she asked.

"Not far," Trent laughed as they dragged her to the window. "You see, when you spend too much time with crazy old birds, you go crazy and end up thinking you can fly. Any last words before your *suicide*?"

"Are you man enough to tell a dying woman who you're really working for? You're too stupid to think of this yourself." *I really hope the collar is unlocked.*

The guards lifted her onto the window ledge. Trent drew his sword, pushing it against her. The point pricked her skin. "Take a moment to enjoy the view."

Leonie hissed at the jab in her back; it was where the crossbow bolt had struck, just below her ribs.

"Trent! What are you doing?" A woman's voice called from the door.

Leonie's heart skipped a beat. She risked a glance, recognising the princess's voice. The guards turned, but Trent held the sword firmly.

Siola stood in the doorway, a shocked look on her face. As usual, Phione was behind her, biting her lip and looking worried.

"Siola! I believe this traitor was trying to escape," Trent said.

"What? Out of a two-hundred-foot-high window?" Siola looked at Trent, with his sword at Leonie's back. "You're more of a fool than I took you for if you think anyone would believe that."

"People would go to any lengths in an attempt to escape a beheading," Trent replied.

"Throw her out!" Phione called from the door.

"Phione!" Siola whirled, facing her. "What are you saying?"

"I'm sick and tired of being in your shadow. I'm pushing in line, sister!"

Siola slapped her in shock. "Have you gone mad? You spend far too much time with your fool of a cousin."

Phione's cheek reddened quickly. "You know sister. You're right. I *have* gone mad. Mad at you always belittling me; belittling my Trent." Phione whipped her dagger out and thrust it hilt-deep into her sister's gut.

Everyone froze, stunned by the outburst.

Siola screamed, clutching her abdomen. Her fingers already slick with blood, she stared in shock at her younger sister, holding the bloodied dagger.

"Toss her out too," Phione cried.

"Guards, grab Siola!" Trent panicked. He forced Leonie out the window with a hard thrust.

Echoing Siola's scream of pain, Leonie twisted as the sword cut in. She lashed out with her foot. It was only a glancing blow, not enough to do more than a scratch and dislodge his circlet before she toppled backwards and out of sight.

12

ASSASSINS

With the castellan leading, half-a-dozen guards pounded up the corridor.

"I heard a scream. What's going on here?" Willom questioned as he stopped at the door, peering into the room. "Where's the rrell prisoner?"

"Oh, Willom," Phione cried, her voice shaking. "Siola entered alone in an effort to reach out to that traitorous rrell. I tried to stop her, but you know how Siola can be so stubborn. We heard the noise of a fight and then screams. We rushed in, but before we could do anything, they ... fell out through the window."

"What? Both of them? How?" The castellan pushed his way past to enter the room.

"Our furry assassin is as cunning as she is evil," Trent spoke up. "I can only assume, knowing beheading was the fate of assassins, she took what revenge she could – taking our dear Siola with her in her suicide."

Willom's face went pale. "That is indeed tragic. You all bore witness to this?"

The two guards nodded as vigorously as the princess and count.

"My dear sister, gone," Phione wept, turning to Trent and

burying her face in his chest. Trent looking as distraught, consoled her.

"Count, better take Princess Phione to her rooms. I will send the healer to ease her pain." He turned his gaze to the guards. "You two, my office to report. Now!" he barked at their hesitation.

As he stepped towards the window, his boot kicked something. Looking down, he saw the circlet. Willom picked it up, wondering why the Count hadn't noticed, and how it got there. He spotted the scratches on the stone ledge, then swore as he saw the dark shape carrying Siola fly up, disappearing over the roof.

"Come with me!" Willom called to his guards as he ran out of the room and down the corridor.

———

In sheer desperation and little time for anything else, Leonie pulled hard on her collar. She was certain she felt the lock undo earlier. The wind filled her head with noise as the rocks rush up to her.

Searing pain in her neck and paws burned deep as her fear and instincts took hold. "Pain is living!" she hissed. Her fall slowed and she changed direction, looking up just as Siola tumbled out the window.

Suddenly the collar flung open. The intense burning stopped, but her neck and paws, already blistering, throbbed in agony. Leonie raced up and as gracefully as she could, caught the unconscious princess. The front of Siola's blouse was soaked with blood.

Shifting her awkwardly to a more secure position, Leonie raced back around to the other side of the palace. She only had a minimal idea of the layout, but the areas she knew had guards everywhere. There was one area she could access easily without fear of bumping into Trent.

Leonie flew to the windows in the vaulted ceilings of the

main hall. *Yes!* As she approached, she blew a window out with a condensed burst of air, and shot through the opening, then descended rapidly to the floor, away from the glass shards.

"Help!" she yelled, laying the princess on the table used earlier to dine on.

Siola's face was pale, but she was still breathing.

"Willom!" Leonie called again. Taking a deep breath, Leonie attempted something she'd never consciously tried before, but it was something Krre'lo said in passing she now thought had merit. *Now or never.* Placing pressure around the wound, she deftly removed the dagger and attempted to heal. At first there was nothing but the beginning of a headache.

Headaches are good. It means something's working! Leonie persevered, feeling sweat mat her fur. She heard boots, seemingly far behind her. By the time they grabbed her, she was as weak as a kitten and couldn't resist even if she wanted.

"Hold!"

She was aware she'd been dragged back, but held firmly upright. There was a slick of blood along the floor where they dragged her. Blearily, she saw the castellan lean over the princess. "Is she dead?" Leonie mumbled.

One of the guards cursed at her to shut up, shaking her.

The castellan straightened and turned to her. "You saved her?"

"She's a friend," Leonie mumbled.

"Willom, what's going on?" She recognised King Reindet's voice over the sound of more boots running in.

"Why's everyone running?" Leonie wondered, watching through the pain as the castellan pointed to her, then the princess, then back to her. She couldn't make out the words. "Reckon I'm in for it this time."

The guard shook her again.

"Enough!" someone ordered. Her eyes closed as she passed out.

• • •

Leonie.

What?

I am pleased you live.

Me too. Is that you, Styx?

At your service?

So ... I'm not dead ... again ... yet, am I?

We've had this discussion before.

Where are you?

Here, beside you.

You didn't leave with the others?

I was away, but the only one left here.

Why?

I was waiting for you.

You didn't think to help earlier?

I was monitoring distantly. It was, as you say, touch and go, but you had it under control.

Fooled me.

Leonie's eyelids flickered briefly. The light was dim, but still too bright. Her pain returned; her head still ached, her side ached, her neck and her paws felt like they were still on fire. She groaned.

"She's coming around," she heard a real voice say. The next attempt at opening her eyes lasted longer. She looked around at her surroundings. The furniture and décor were as ostentatious as one of the rooms in the palace. The looming figures resolved into humanoid shapes.

Willom stood nearby, as did Tipp and Reindet. She searched the other direction for Styx.

I am still here.

You're such a short arse. "How is Princess Siola?" Leonie asked out loud.

"She is recovering, thanks to your heroic efforts."

"Pfft." Leonie waved a limp paw before remembering that there was a king present. "That's good to hear. Do you need me to tell you what happened?"

"It isn't necessary." Willom held the circlet. "The moment

you kicked this off, all was revealed. Trent's confession, and Phione's bloodied dagger condemned them both. Princess Siola also told us what she witnessed."

"Can I see her?"

"Soon enough."

After another rest, they filled her with food and drink. As a serving girl was taking the empty tray, Princess Siola came in.

"Hey, princess," Leonie coughed.

"Of all people, you don't need to call me that again. Ever."

"You're all better now?" Leonie asked.

"There is still some physical pain. But there's a deeper ache I fear will never go away."

"Ah. Yes. Phione. I'm sorry. That was a shocker!"

"You don't need to tell me!" Siola's face hardened. "She betrayed all of us."

"What happened to her and the Count?"

"Firstly, both were stripped from their titles and estates—"

"I bet the Count was crying over that."

"He did, up until the moment he lost his head. Everyone involved was dealt with accordingly." A tear ran down her cheek. "The law is clear; any assassin and those aiding him or her will suffer the same fate."

Leonie sat up. "Even ...?"

"Yes. Even ..." She wiped her face.

"I'm so very sorry," Leonie reached for Siola's hand. The firm grip was still there. She held it for a moment. "So, show me the scar. I hear men like them."

"Well, no thanks to you, they will be very disappointed." She lifted her shirt, revealing her flat stomach. All that remained as a reddened area. "It seems you didn't so much heal the wound, but transferred it into yourself."

"Ah." Leonie looked down at her abdomen and the wrapped linen bandage around her waist. "That would explain why my stomach hurts so much. I thought Trent stabbed me in the back."

"He did, but the healer says it wasn't too deep," Siola said.

"So, I better take healing off my list." Leonie laughed, hissing at the pain.

"Your neck and paws healed quickly enough. Our healer is good, but not *that* good. Even your fur is returning."

Leonie found the bristling of the stubby growth annoying at first, much like when she lost her fur with the first attempt at charging the portals. "How's your father?"

"He has secluded himself for a few days. The castellan and I are taking over the smaller matters."

"And this search for the other portals? Is that still going to happen?"

"Before his seclusion, he made an announcement that is to be spread far and wide; a reward of five thousand Reenatian gold ducats to any person or group that reveals the location of portals. Many adventurers have registered already and set off to cover the lands."

"Will that reward be made retrospectively?"

"What do you mean by that?" Siola asked.

"Since I brought the first portal to everyone's attention, will the reward still be made available?"

"I ... I'm sure something could be arranged." Siola looked unsure.

"It's okay," Leonie chuckled. "I'd have to share it with a dead wyvern."

The princess looked at Leonie for a moment, as if deciding she was joking or not. "You are a strange person, Leonie."

"So I've been told many times now," she agreed. "Did I mention there's a portal over in Fisbane and In'sha?"

"How can it be in both countries?"

"It's on a skyland," Leonie whispered, patting the bed. "Move closer and I'll tell you all about it."

The royal healer did excellent work, and Leonie was up and about a couple of days after the incident.

"I confess to not being the only one doing the work," the older woman said. "Your own healing made it much easier. How do you do that?" she asked as she was removing the last of the bandages, checking the area. "Fascinating. No scarring. The men will be disappointed."

Leonie chuckled. "My regeneration must be an inherited trait. I can't explain it, but it's been very beneficial."

The healer nodded. "What you did for Princess Siola was as fascinating as it was dangerous. If you're able to visit a few hours a day, perhaps after the morning meal, I can show you a few techniques that will not require you to take whole possession of wounds of others?"

"Thank you, I will try. That's most generous of you."

"For saving our Siola, it's the least I could do."

Leonie beamed. "Does that mean I can go?"

"It does, as long as you take it easy for a while."

"I'll do my best," she lied, glad to be out and about. "Thanks again." Leonie walked out the door. It was a part of the palace she hadn't seen before. As she was looking for an exit, someone called out her name. She turned, seeing Willom walking briskly towards her.

"Lady Leonie," the castellan greeted her. "I'm glad I caught you before you left. The king would like a quick word. If you would come this way."

She sighed, but followed, heading past the room she just vacated, and going further into the large building. Turning down a different corridor brought them into a courtyard with a fountain and topiarised gardens.

Across the courtyard, and up a flight of stairs they entered another wing. Not as ostentatious as the other halls it was much quieter. In a small refectory overlooking the garden, she met the King and Princess Siola.

"Ah, Leonie. So glad we caught you before you left us. I'm glad to see you are on your feet." He rose from his chair and walked to her, meeting her halfway across the floor, and took her paws in his hands.

"Your healer has done an amazing job." Leonie looked to Siola, then back to the king.

"No, it is you that has done that, and I've not had the opportunity to thank you personally. I should also ask your forgiveness at the premature arrest, and to have inadvertently put you in danger. I let my better judgement cloud my thoughts." He shook both her paws gently.

"Your Highness, there's nothing to forgive. These things happen. But, I'm sorry for your loss."

"You are gracious." He let go her paws. "Siola tells me you know the location of another portal."

"Oh, I was joking about the reward, but yes."

"Please be seated, and if I may ask you to indulge your company for a bit longer, what can you tell me about it? You have seen it? Can it be used?"

Leonie spent the best part of an hour telling them both as much as she could, including the Earth and Skyhome.

"Your world sounds as bad as this one in its way. So, if we can't stay here or Earth, where do we go?"

"Knowing that magic works there, Earth might still be a viable option, at least for the short term. However, perhaps there could also be an opportunity for some to go to other worlds. Obviously not Masevalon, but perhaps that of the glins'ool or rrell? We all breathe the same air and live under very similar climatic conditions. Maybe you can assist in negotiating those terms?"

"I dare say, whichever occurs, this reign will soon be over." The king's gaze drifted outside

"Father, what has happened cannot be undone. We can only remain positive and look to the future." Siola got Leonie's attention and indicated with her eyes to head for the door. "Wait outside," she mouthed.

Leonie crept outside and waited. Her eyes briefly met those of the castellan, realising he had been waiting patiently all this time. Siola joined them a few minutes later.

"Father feels guilty and depressed." Siola nodded and smiled at Willom before she moved off.

"Farewell, Leonie," Willom said as he went back inside to see to his king.

Leonie caught up with Siola while she continued speaking. "If Phione and Trent didn't force his hand, they would have seen the pointlessness of their actions. The monarchy will be over as soon as the people move away to whatever world will have us. Such a waste."

Leonie had little to say not already said. They continued across the courtyard in silence.

"There is now, of course, little point in assassinating Zander," Siola continued. "Once the news of the portals reaches Delta, there will be little point to any further attacks."

"You don't know Zander. That man is crazy."

"Well, we will keep on our guard until there is no longer any threat."

They chatted idly on minor matters until reaching the front entrance.

"I hope our paths cross again, Leonie." Siola reached for her and gave her a hug. "I hope we can remain friends."

"That is my wish too, Siola. And all the best with you and Willom."

"Oh ... you noticed?" Siola blushed.

"Didn't even need to be a telepath." Leonie winked. "Take care." She trotted down the stairs, deciding the walk outside would do her good.

13

REUNION

AS THE PALACE WAS THE HIGHEST POINT OF REENAT, THE PATH from here was all downhill. There were two options: using the roadway meant spiralling and zigzagging around the hill and passing all the establishments; the other option was the stairs. One very long and very straight flight of stairs cut down one side, intersecting with the road at each circuit.

The Reenatian Bardic Council wasn't too far away, so Leonie chose the road. With a similar layout to that of Delta, as one moved further away from the palace, the establishments generally grew less in stature.

A short time later, Leonie returned to the council chambers, deciding to fly up to her room and enter through the small balcony instead of through the main entrance.

Glad you have returned.

Hey Styx. I wondered where you had gone. Leonie had a drink of water then dropped onto her bed. She looked around the room, but he was nowhere to be seen.

You're assuming I went anywhere.

Why didn't you leave with the others? Leonie asked. As she waited for his reply, there was a knock at her door. Thinking it was unlikely to be Styx, she assumed it would be either Tipp or possibly Biell. "Come in," she called.

The door opened and Jade strolled in. "About time you showed up! I've been waiting several days now. Those upstarts wouldn't let me in the palace."

"Jade!" Leonie cried, leaping off the bed and racing over. She wrapped her arms around her old boss. Nothing was said for several minutes as the raw emotions of long-lost friends catching up after twenty years were released. Leonie looked up at a shadow in the doorway, Tipp was there with Biell. Even they had wet trails down their cheeks.

"There are refreshments at your disposal in the lounge, also ... other guests," Biell announced, sniffing.

Finally releasing her friend, Leonie nodded and wiped her face, as did Jade.

"I have so much to tell–" they both said at the same time, then laughed.

"Jade, it's good to see you again."

"Likewise. Tipp's told me a bit of it, and I'm sure you're sick of repeating it, but do you think you could indulge in one more telling?"

"For you, anything, but I doubt it will be my last time." She stepped back to get a good look. Jade was still fit and trim, despite the years, but she looked utterly exhausted and haggard.

"Let's go and get a drink and relax." Jade put her arm in Leonie's.

There was another surprise for Leonie when she entered the loungeroom.

"Hey Feiron! Phil!" she hurried forward and hugged both together. "And there you are, you rascal." She spied Styx to the side. His spikes were still evident but had greatly receded. He was still the swirling blend of red and orange. If anything, his colour was deeper and richer.

Thank you.

She could have sworn his colouring brightened for a moment. *Not blushing, are we?* Leonie turned back to her grinning friends. "You have to stop doing this to me." Leonie wiped her eyes again.

"It's a great relief to see you again. Jade caught up with us in Plenari," Phil told her.

"I was almost in Tesak when I received Tipp's unbelievable message of your return," Jade added. "I stabled Gretchen and hitched a ride back on Faldo."

"Who's Gretchen? Your gnasher?"

"Yes. How did you know about my bird?" Jade looked surprised.

"I ran into Rohan's family in Dalmellington. Has anyone seen Noldor?"

"He contacted Dorn about a week ago. He is ..." Philbert hesitated.

"Dead, yeah I know. It's a long story."

"Well, we're comfortable, we have food and drink ... may as well get started," Jade said before any despondency sunk in.

As they were sitting, Leonie's eyes kept welling with tears, so overjoyed just to see them all again. Her eyes kept going from one friend to another, still in disbelief. "How are the wyverns? I can't wait to see them again. Where are they?"

"Far away. I'm sure they're keeping themselves occupied, and not giving the Gryphon Riders any grief."

"Need I ask how you are, Styx?"

No need at all. You know how pleased I am you are here, and excited about the portal you delivered. You have done us all very proud.

Styx, since you are all so long-lived, do your people know anything about the portals? Leonie asked. *Like ... why they are where they are, and how?*

In the short period of our home reunion, this information has not been passed, but if we have it, I will definitely share it with you.

Tipp stood up. From a deep pocket in his robes, he withdrew a gold torc. "Leonie, Jade, if you would be so kind ..."

"What's this?" Leonie asked the bard, curious.

"A mere bardic formality, to return to long-awaited normality," he answered cryptically.

Jade had a strange, haunted look on her face upon seeing the torc. "You mean ...?" she let her question trail. She stood up and nervously reached for the torc with her long, slender fingers.

"It is time," Tipp nodded.

Leonie couldn't recall ever seeing Jade nervous. "What's going to happen?" She looked to Phil and Feiron for an answer, but they looked as bewildered as she was.

All will be revealed shortly.

She gave the rollo a scowl. Shaking her head, Leonie wrapped her fingers around the torc as well.

"Both paws." Tipp then let go. "Let the gods acknowledge the feat, the vow is now complete."

Vow? To Leonie, the torc became cold to the touch, feeling like her fingers were frozen in place. A tingling went up her arms. From the looks on Jade's face, she felt something too.

Everyone remained silent. Leonie was about to say something, but Tipp cut her off.

"Wait," he said simply. "But brace yourself."

It started as a soft breeze, billowing the drapes, growing in strength until they were almost horizontal. A peal of thunder rattled the glasses and plates on the table, followed by another, and yet another. Nine peals of thunder reverberated across the city, rattling the window panes and shattering glass in the distance.

The silence afterwards was deafening.

Tipp took hold of the torc as Jade let go. She collapsed onto the chair, unmoving.

"Jade!" Leonie leapt over, grabbing her hand. "What is it?" She turned to Tipp. "What the frack just happened?"

"When you left Delta by chaotic magic, Jade was grieving, distraught and tragic." Tipp put the frosty torc on the table. "With this torc she made a vow, to never rest ... until now."

"Rest? She's not ...?"

Leonie, your friend lives. She is in a very deep sleep, and will be for some time. I will monitor her. Philbert, Feiron – I prewarned the wyverns, they are calm.

"That's a relief. Thanks, Styx." Phil stood and after briefly resting his hand on Leonie's shoulder, walked to the balcony. Feiron joined him. Making sure Jade was comfortable, Leonie went out after them to witness the after-effects of what happened.

Outside was hot and dry, with a blue cloudless sky. The city was only now starting to move, babies and children wailing. In the streets, people were calming others, or trying to control their horses and other livestock.

"Looks like Styx couldn't calm everything."

I have limitations.

"What say we go out and help?" Phil suggested to them.

"Right you are. Coming Leonie?" Feiron asked.

"Later. For the moment I'm going to watch over Jade." She went back inside. Gathering Jade up in her arms, she carried her up to her room and lay her on her bed, removing Jade's boots and weapons belt.

"You idiot," Leonie said softly. Looking down at her mentor and friend, Leonie studied her. Jade had aged, but not two decades worth. The bags under her eyes, and lines on her face had already diminished, and even her white hair looked more vibrant. Her skin was deeply tanned, indicating she'd been on the road a lot, but she hadn't lost her shape; even at rest, she still looked like a tensioned spring. "You know, I've never seen you asleep." Leonie took a deep breath and sat in a chair near her. Eventually she too dozed, albeit fitfully.

She woke at some disturbance. There was a blanket over her. She was back in her own bed. "What the frack?" *How did I get here?*

"Leonie?"

She dragged herself out of bed and stuck her head out the door.

"Leonie, there is a delivery for you," Tipp called up the stairs.

"For me? Any idea who from?"

"Indeed," was all he said before heading into the lounge.

As Leonie walked out her door, pulling her shirt on, Jade came out from her room.

"Hey you." Leonie smiled, stopping at the lip of the stairs. "Good to see you up and about." She marvelled at how much better Jade looked already.

"I feel like a kid again."

"You almost look it. I hate to say, but you looked so haggard when I saw you yesterday."

"And you've hardly aged at all, despite everything that's happened, I find that incredible." Jade yawned and stretched. "What's this about a delivery?"

"Beats me," Leonie said. "Let's check it out together."

Jade nodded, as she walked behind Leonie.

Biell, Phil and Feiron were already present, and stood when the two women entered.

"Do you two sleep here or what?" Leonie laughed at them.

"No. We're lodging across the road, actually, but Tipp and Biell do have much to say."

"I hope you mean that in a nice way," Tipp warbled.

"And great company, of course. Indulging in his good wine is a bonus."

Leonie saw a small chest placed by the table.

"And there is also this communique. I'm sure we're keen to hear what it may say." Tipp handed her a scroll and also a small key.

"That's the royal seal?" Jade noted, looking at the rolled parchment.

"Which do you guys want first, the message or the contents?"

"The message." Feiron said.

"The chest." Jade gave Feiron a friendly nudge.

"Tell you what, Biell, why don't you read the letter while I'll open the box?" She handed the ranger the scroll.

"I'd be delighted. Thank you."

"Can't let the old bird have all the fun." Leonie pulled one of the chairs closer, sat and turned the key. "Here we go." She lifted the lid.

"'Dearest Leonie'," Biell started reading. "'I can barely comprehend all that you have told us – the stories of your travels, your adventures and your wondrous discoveries. For all that you have done, for me personally, and for all peoples, it is my hope these items can be of some use to you in your future efforts. Signed, King Reindet.' Then there is another note below that in different writing. 'It isn't as if our treasury needs the funds for much longer. Siola.'"

As Biell was reading, Leonie unwrapped the box's contents. In red and blue silk, there was a sheathed dagger. It had a jewel in the base of the hilt. When she withdrew the weapon, everyone gasped at the black crystal blade.

"That's incredible," Leonie said in awe, examining it. "Nice balance, and lightweight."

"That gem is a sapphire, looks to be about two, maybe three thousand ducats worth," Jade estimated.

"I better keep an eye on it then. Don't want some *thief* to get hold of it." Leonie chuckled, sheathing the blade, but passing it around for others to admire.

"Hey. I've retired from that!" Jade said. "Hurry up. What else is there?"

Leonie laughed, reaching into the chest for another item. It too was wrapped in the royal silk. She pulled it out slowly. "It's bigger and heavier than the dagger," Leonie teased. At Jade's impatient huff, she leisurely pulled at the silk edges. A note fell to the floor as a pair of arm greaves were revealed. "More black crystal," Leonie noted. "Greaves, I think?"

Jade grabbed the note. "I'll read this one," she declared before anyone else objected. "'You might need these, since your defence technique requires far too much work, signed Krre'lo.' Is that the First Magus?" Jade asked.

"Correct." Tipp nodded. "They did a bit of training together."

Studying one of the greaves closely Leonie noted the craftsmanship. "There's a hinge along this seam." Turning it over, she found a small pin at one end. When she pulled it, the device clicked open. She then slipped the greave over her wrist, clicking it closed, repeating the procedure for the other wrist.

"What's the significance of black crystal?" Feiron asked. "And how is crystal shaped like that?"

"It absorbs power," Jade informed him.

"If I'm attacked by a powershaper, these will absorb the bulk of the power," Leonie said. "As I rarely have anyone attack me magically, I have little knowledge in the ways of defence."

"Other than ripping throats out." Jade winked.

Tipp also explained to the illios how Earther monks were the only ones capable of shaping black crystal. He stopped talking as Leonie brought out yet another silk wrap. At first it looked to be a simple yet finely crafted silver medallion, but when Leonie handled it, an inscription on the back glowed.

'The bearer of this token is, by royal decree, to be given free passage and assistance in all matters.' The royal seal also glowed with it, but when Leonie passed it around, the glow faded.

"Looks like its attuned to you only," Phil noted.

"It might come in handy." Leonie popped it around her neck. "Just these sacks left." The moment she held one, by the weight alone she knew exactly what it was. She plonked it on the table with a thud.

"Aren't you going to tell us what's in it?" Feiron asked.

"Can't you tell?" Jade looked at them. "It's gold coins. The weight when she picked it up, the sound and shape as she put it down. Easy."

"Maybe easy for a retired thief," he chuckled. "How much?"

"One thousand Reenatian ducats in that sack," Leonie told them.

Everyone gasped, impressed.

"And there are five of them." Leonie laughed how their expressions changed when each one thudded on the table.

"You haven't counted them," Biell said. "Surely you can't tell that by weight alone."

"Please. Be my guest, go ahead and count." Leonie stood and buckled the dagger around her waist.

Biell's eye lit up as she opened the first bag and emptied the contents onto the table.

"I admit though, it does make for pleasant viewing." Leonie's eyes gleamed. "Jade, can you imagine this sort of haul in Delta?"

"I'd have retired earlier." Jade watched.

"Pfft. As if." Leonie laughed. She walked to the sideboard where the glasses and bottles of wines were. She brought back a tray of glasses and a bottle and started pouring drinks for everyone.

"One thousand ducats exactly," Biell declared. She looked inside the remaining bags. "And therefore, I assume five thousand in total."

"Isn't that the same amount the king declared for a portal finder's fee?"

"And Leonie found one." Jade slapped her friend on the back.

"While I'm in a good mood, let me make a toast to this success." She waited until everyone had a full glass. "Nothing I've done could have been accomplished without any of you," Leonie said. "Not only has Jade taught me everything I know, she saved me and raised me." She raised her glass. "To my mentor and friend."

Everyone had a drink, appreciating the fine wine.

"Feiron." Leonie turned to him. "I'm sure you thought I was as much of a pain in the arse as I thought you were, but we learned a lot in those early days; we looked after each other, saved each other. I never know what you're thinking, or even where you are looking, but I count you as a friend."

Again, everyone sipped their wine. Then Leonie topped up their glasses.

"Philbert, if it wasn't for you, Dorn, Faldo and Slana ... I don't know what would have happened, but you introduced us both to the ways of wyverns and taught us to fly. I wish they were here now, as I miss them, but that'll be remedied soon enough. You're all friends in my book."

She turned to the bard. "Tipp, I still think your doggerel is hilarious, but you came to me in the cell that day before I disappeared. You listened to my story even though you thought I was crazy, but you brought me hope. Would I have survived without you? I don't know, but then you got word to Jade and she was there – again – when I needed her." Leonie raised her glass and sipped.

"Biell, we only just met, but you helped Tipp in his searching for me, plus, you have all this knowledge of the skylands, which will come in very handy if we are to locate all these portals. If you have no objections to the company of thieves and rogues, I'd like to count you as a friend too." Leonie raised her glass to her, then drained it.

Wiping her face with the back of her paw, Leonie continued. "Now, before you lot get all sentimental at me, let me finish." She waved her paws at the wealth on the table. "None of this would be possible without any of you. Those bags of ducats are yours – one each, don't be greedy." She laughed. "I only wish it were more." She wiped her eyes. "I haven't cried so much in a long time. I reckon it must be the wine."

14

DELTA

The *Sundancer* partially phased-in two hundred metres above Delta, the harbour town of Leonie's origins. The ship hovered over the city. Not much had changed since David's last visit. The palace was still chained to the southern section of land, though it had moved slightly. There also seemed a lot of activity towards the central area.

Sussah, Bern and the agtechs crowded around the screen, staring in astonishment at the city below.

"And no one can see us?" Lerry asked.

"Just like back on Skyhome when I first arrived," David replied. "Not entirely phased-in yet. It's TAU's automatic setting for a partial phasing-in. They could probably see us if we were much closer, but at this height, we would look like a mirage, an indefinable ripple in the air – similar to the heat radiating from a hot surface. If we were fully-phased, then yes, they'd see a dull grey but very solid globe hanging in the air."

"But how can we see out?"

"The image you see isn't like looking through a window. These are live images from sophisticated sensors all around the hull precisely attuned to the frequency of our phasing. You've seen a strobing light somewhere in the tower at some point?" He continued at their nods. "And did you ever try blinking in rhythm with it?"

Sussah smiled in embarrassment. "Trying to make the light look like it wasn't blinking?"

"Exactly. When the frequency of the sensors matches the frequency of the tau-field surrounding the ship, then it's very much the same thing. We can *see* out."

"Oh," she said. "I think I understand."

"The same with these wristbands you all have. They emit a low-powered field that surrounds you. The frequency mirrors that of the ship so we can step through the exit without repercussions."

"What would happen if we didn't wear them?" Harrond asked.

"Massive disorientation at the least," he answered. "Don't worry. It's fully automatic; as you approach the force-field, the band will immediately detect it and resonate."

"Maybe it's better to not turn it off at all?" Lerry suggested.

"The power source would drain too quickly. To keep it compact it has a very small powerpac."

"That's where my parents had their tavern." Sussah pointed. "That's the Grand Plaza, with the seven temples." She fell silent as the memory of her last evening in Delta came to mind. It made her cold even after twenty years.

Harrond noticed her mood change. "Is that a festival?" he said to distract her.

"It must be the summer festival for Oes'het," Sussah said. "I remember them as a kid. So much happening, with travellers all over the land bringing unusual and exotic things. It was the only time my father's tavern was full," she said wistfully.

"Looking at the charts, it must be a winter festival."

"Winter? But it looks so hot and dry."

"With no other reference I can only go by what I see. The sun is to the south. All indications show it should be like Earth. Shak'aran is in the northern hemisphere. Something else we'll find out soon enough."

"What happened to the palace?" Sussah asked, shocked.

"Is that the same palace Leonie referred to?" David asked his mother. "Has it not always been there? Not another skyland, but captured?"

"There's only the one palace in Delta. And no, it was never like that. There was a headland, but it has gone. Some of the wharf area here is missing." Sussah studied the screen, pointing. "I'm sure it was bigger."

"Curious. Perhaps we'll find the answers to that later."

There was a tall gantry built adjacent to the palace front gate. As they watched, a cage inside was pulled up by large animals looking like the pictures of cows they'd seen.

"That's an elevator," David noted.

At the top of the gantry, a bridge extended to the surface of the small skyland. When the cage arrived, several people stepped off and crossed the bridge.

Slowly rotating the ship, David started looking for a landing area. The city itself held little promise, there being few spaces large or secluded enough. The outskirts were encroaching close to the dense jungle, and again were too populated.

A few kilometres north there was a clearing, between the road and a river. Moving closer he realised it was more or less a swamp, but it was only a short distance from the road leading north and back to the city. With no one in the area, he deactivated the tau-field.

"Looks like we have a bit of walking to do," David pointed out. As the *Sundancer* settled into the soft ground, the floor angled slightly. TAU compensated by adjusting the landing gear and redistributing the ballast.

"Won't we get stuck?" Sussah asked as the ramp lowered.

"No, mum," David laughed. "We will not get stuck."

"Are you laughing at your mother?" she huffed.

"Not at all – laughing *with* you." He gave her a quick hug to mollify her. "Welcome home."

As they descended the ramp, the hot humid air enveloped them.

"Frack, David! What is that horrid smell?" She dry-retched at the first whiff.

David screwed up his nose. "Stagnant vegetation, I believe. This *is* a swamp."

"You couldn't find anywhere else?" she complained.

"Sure, I could, but then we'd be walking tens of kilometres." He moved down the ramp.

"Well, it reeks." She waved her hand in front of her nose as if fanning it would help.

"No arguments from me, but there's little alternative. On the positive side, your olfactory nerve will adjust soon enough, then you won't notice it. Promise."

"I hope it's soon." Sussah gagged.

The agtechs chuckled along with Bern as they followed.

David wiped his eyes. "It is quite bad, isn't it?" he said to them as they grouped together at the base. He pulled a remote from a pocket and activated it. The ramp lifted and sealed shut. He reactivated the tau-field, but left the base clear.

"It's not completely covered," Lerry noted.

"If the field came into contact with the ground, it would disrupt it. It's on a minimal setting just for camouflage."

The group were now standing about ten paces from the road, but thick ferns and dense scrub surrounded them.

"My turn to do something I guess," Bern said, stepping forward. His clothing and thick hair protected him as he pushed his way through. He had to pull a few vines aside, but there was enough of a path to make it easier for the others who followed close behind.

On the road they brushed themselves down, but there was little to do about their muddy boots.

"In hindsight, lucky no one saw us." David looked up and down the road. "It would raise eyebrows as to why the five of us suddenly emerged from a swamp."

"Have you ever been this way?" Harrond asked Su.

"I've never left the city. Don't forget, I was seventeen the last time I was here, working in the tavern. There wasn't an opportunity, nor a need, to do so. I did want to stow away on a ship once."

"And now you've got one, and no need to hide on it." Harrond smiled.

"We better start walking," Lerry suggested.

"Should we mark the spot?" Bern asked. He looked towards the ship, but from here there was nothing to see and the dense scrub obscured any sight of the landing gear.

"Are you kidding?" Sussah answered. "My boy remembers everything."

"Okay, okay, Lerry's right, we should make a move." David started walking south. "It shouldn't take us too long to get there."

The humidity in the air soon had them all sweating. The buzzing insects had them swatting too.

"There are some things I *don't* miss about Delta." Sussah slapped at her arm.

"Much hotter here than on Skyhome, that's for sure," Lerry said, undoing his jumpsuit top.

Bern, now at the back, had already removed his shirt and had it draped over his shoulder. At a noise, he looked behind. "There's a vehicle coming."

They all moved to the side, but continued walking. As the horse-drawn cart passed them, the three people on it stared at them without saying a word.

"Not too talkative," Harrond said after the lack of response to his wave.

"Maybe it's not safe to talk to strangers around here?" Lerry suggested.

"We'll find out soon enough." David pointed ahead. The road straightened and the city wall rose in the distance. While there was jungle on either side, some areas on their right had been thinned to allow for some huts on stilts.

Another cart passed them before they finally reached the

gate. Even though Bern offered a greeting, no words were exchanged, but at least the driver doffed his hat and nodded.

Several men in thick leather shirts, cloth trousers and metal helmets lounged around the main gate. All had swords on their belts and three also held spears.

"I didn't think to bring the rifle," Harrond said softly to Lerry.

"I think it would create too much interest here. Better off without them." Then added, "I hope."

One of the guards came forward after sharing a joke with his colleagues.

"Let me guess, you're for the festival?" He looked at their clothing.

"Yes, we are," Sussah stepped forward. "Wouldn't miss it for the world."

"Hey there," the guard looked her up and down slowly. "If ya all come over here, we got to get details."

"Details?" Sussah repeated.

"Yeah. Where ya from, where ya stayin'. What company are ya? Those details."

"Oh." She looked hesitant. "I see. We're from Qelay."

He made a note. "And company?"

"Company?"

The guard took a deep breath. "Yeah. You're wearin' ya costumes. You all actors, jugglers? What?"

"Oh, yes. Jugglers, and theatrics."

"Right." He started writing. "Where's ya wagon n' ya gear?"

"Wagon?"

"Walked all the way from Qelay, did ya miss?"

"It broke a wheel a few kilometres back," Harrond offered.

"A few what?"

"Miles," David covered. "Our wagon broke a wheel a few miles back. Is there anyone here to help repair?"

"Sure, if ya got the money. Where ya stayin'"

"The Wharf Tavern, down the Bridgeway," Sussah said straightaway.

The man kept scribbling. "Names?"

He filled in their names as they called them. "All related, are we?" He looked up. "The Carter family, with no cart." He laughed at his own joke, some of his colleagues did also. Turning his gaze to Bern, the guard looked him up and down, noting all the hair with distaste. "Are ya part bear, or were you pullin' the cart?"

"No. Why?"

The guards chuckled more. "A comedy act," one sniggered.

The clip-clop of hooves made them look up. Three more wagons were trundling towards them. "Ok. More people comin'. Ya know the way?" He pointed anyway.

"Yes, thank you," Sussah said as Harrond hustled her through, keen to get away from them.

Once through the gate, the area opened up, with roads going east, west and south. There was a raised, circular section in the middle with a tall monument. They made their way around it and followed the busier road.

"The road to the west goes over the river to Portside and the palace, the one to the east breaks up into narrower streets and lanes. Not a good place to go, especially after dark."

"This is the Bridgeway?" Harrond asked.

"No, this is Upbridge, but it becomes the Bridgeway further down." Sussah looked excited, eyes taking it all in. "It goes all the way past the harbour to the tannery."

As they moved down the street, many people were gawking at them.

"I think our clothes are creating some attention," Sussah said.

"An oversight on my part." David shook his head.

"Can't think of everything." Lerry gave him a pat on the back. "We'll make do."

"And money?" Harrond queried. "How are we going to pay for anything?"

"By using our wits?" Bern didn't sound too convinced.

"How about we let mum see her parents first," David

suggested. "We can worry about that later. But I'll give it some thought."

Sussah nodded, and holding Harrond's hand, pulled him through the crowded street.

Eventually they came to the waterfront and moved closer to the stone harbour wall where it was marginally less crowded. The smell of the harbour was much stronger here, the salty water, the seaweed exposed as the tide changed.

Sussah continued being the tour guide. "The Urmaq River – that's the one we saw through the jungle – comes out back near the North Gate. From there, we have all these canals, and the islands. I don't know if I can remember them all."

"Not something we need to worry about. As long as you can remember the way to your father's tavern, that's the main thing." David was watching the crowd. "All these different races ... fascinating." He mentally named them according to Leonie's description. Seleth, a couple of voriens with their finned feet slapping the cobbles, glins'ool. He even saw an illios, the grey blob was unmistakeable as it oozed over the ground. He then wondered if there were more in the crowd, but in a different form. When a couple of rrell walked past he compared their appearance to Leonie. They were much leaner, and Leonie was definitely more womanly.

"You okay, David?" his mother asked. "I think you're getting too much sun; your face is red and flushed."

He looked around. "Sure. I'm fine. Just taking it all in. We are on another world."

"It is amazing," Lerry agreed, stepping back as two carts tried to pass each other. Wheels clashed together, and both vehicles came to an abrupt halt.

"Let's go," David advised.

They continued along the eastern harbour edge. As they passed by one island, others became visible beyond. Along this section, larger more elaborate bridges arched over the canal. "We're on the Bridgeway now, and that's Diamond Island, the largest one." She pointed. "It's where the Grand Plaza is; where we saw the festival."

"And your father's tavern?"

"Just past and opposite that bridge," Sussah pointed further south.

A few minutes later, they were at the front doors.

Even though the sign overhead clearly identified it, Sussah had to check the area first before she confirmed this was the right building. "It's been repainted. It almost looks new," she shouted over the noise.

The Wharf Tavern was very busy. They stepped aside as a couple of vorien staggered out. They somehow crossed the road without getting run down by a cart, and dived over the wall into the water.

"Shall we?" David suggested. He pushed through the door into the darker interior. Smoke from smoking pipes filled the air, obliterating the odour of the harbour. The noise of men arguing and people laughing grew louder, along with the sound of clinking glasses and clattering trays. Like poetry in motion, women wearing short skirts and low-cut blouses worked their way through the packed crowd, carrying drinks without spillage.

"Things are different in here, too," Sussah shouted, looking at the newer interior. "The bar should be towards the back."

She realised no one was paying attention to her, then realised their eyes were glued to the waitresses. Pulling Harrond close to her, she started pushing through the crowd. David, Lerry and Bern managed to follow without too much bother, though there were a few stares at Bern.

With a breath of relief, Sussah finally made it to the bar. "Oh, frack!" she cried in shock.

"Sussah?" the barman came rushing up. "By the gods. It *is* you!" He came around the bar, pushing his way between them and held her tight.

Harrond and the others were speechless at the response.

After an awkward time, Sussah pulled away looking

shocked, but also blushing in embarrassment. "Everyone, this is Rickard." She smiled nervously as he turned to greet the others, as if only seeing them now for the first time. "Rickard, this is David, Bern, Lerry and Harrond."

"Gents," he said in greetings. "This is a grand day. I thought I lost dear Su decades ago." He wiped his face. "My love, where have you been? We all thought you were dead when the palace was destroyed."

"I very nearly was, but it is a long, confusing story. What are you doing here, and where's ma and da?"

Rickard looked at her for a moment. "There was a fire here several years ago. Your ..." He looked at the others blankly. "Let's go into the back, shall we?" Holding Sussah's hand, he made his way past the bar and through the back door. "Gorle," he called to another man. "Could you watch the bar, thanks. I'll only be a minute."

Gorle nodded, looking curiously at the newcomers. Rickard wiped his hands on his apron and exited the kitchen adjacent to the back room. "Please, have a seat, Su. Sorry it's a mess." There were a couple of chairs next to an old, dilapidated table covered in trays, stacks of glasses and some old towels. Rickard quickly moved the trays further back and threw the towels into another room.

He sat down opposite, clenching her hands. "Three years ago, there was a fire here. I think it was a clogged chimney. Your ... your parents died in all the smoke."

"No." Sussah stared at him in horror. Her eyes started brimming with tears. As she stood up, Rickard did too, expecting her to come around to him. She stepped away from the table and reached out for Harrond, sobbing.

Rickard stood there looking at them both. He looked awkward, seeing the care they had for each other.

The others waited, despondent at the news.

"Umm, Rickard. We've only just arrived, but is there a place we can stay?" David had to ask twice before Rickard became aware of him.

"What? No. We're full, because of the festival."

"And there's nowhere else?"

"I doubt it. The preparation for this festival has been building for weeks now. Pretty sure everything is packed."

"Ah. Ok." David looked to the others, wondering about the next step.

"Look," Rickard said. "I've got to get back to the bar, but I've got an old fishing boat not in use. It will be cramped, but you can stay there if you want."

"We are strangers to these parts. At this point anything would be acceptable."

Rickard cocked his head, and looked at them as if noticing their attire for the first time. "You're not from around here, are you? Your clothing is ... different, and your accents."

"No. We are from a long way away–"

"As far as Lyhosa?"

"Fisbane," Lerry said. "From Doriel, the capital."

"That would explain it. A long way indeed." He sighed. "The boat's called the *Water Sprite*. It's green and white, same as the front of the tavern. And you'll find it under the next bridge down the Bridgeway."

Sussah and Harrond separated. Her eyes were swollen and cheeks red and puffy. "I'm sorry, Rickard. It was such a shock."

"It will be busy until late tonight. Can we talk first thing in the morning? We have a lot to catch up on." His eyes lingered on Harrond for a moment before meeting Sussah's gaze.

"Of course." She smiled. "That would be wonderful. We do have so much to talk about."

"I can arrange dinner to be brought to you if you'd like?"

"It's too much–"

"I insist. I can't give you a room, but I can do the food. I'll send one of the lasses down on dusk."

Sussah welled up again.

"We can't thank you enough, Rickard," David said. "We'll leave you to get back to work and see you in the morning."

"You can go out this side door." Rickard pointed. "No crowds."

Everyone nodded their thanks and farewell, leaving the Wharf Tavern through the side door. Back on the road they quietly moved to the harbour wall and turned south.

With the bulk of the festival-goers on Diamond Island, this part of the Bridgeway was much quieter and less crowded.

"There it is," Bern pointed. Like Rickard had said, the green and white vessel was moored underneath a high arched bridge. Beside the bridge was a stairway leading down to a rickety wooden dock that ran most of the length of the wall.

Watching their step as some of the planking was loose or missing, they boarded the vessel carefully.

The *Water Sprite* surprised them all, thinking they were going to find a small boat falling apart, but it looked like Rickard put as much pride and work into the boat as he did the tavern.

Other than the smell of fish and salty water, it was comfortable. Inside was a table and bench seats, and further towards the bow and down a few steps were six bunks, three on each side on top of one another.

Harrond found some glasses and water, sharing it around. They all sat, resting.

"I'm sorry about your parents," Lerry said to Sussah as he sipped.

Bern took his glass and drained it, while David held his glass, just looking at it.

While they sat there, the mooring lines creaked and strained as the wind shifted. The rocking of the boat was calming.

"I guess I should explain who Rickard is," Sussah said, breaking the growing silence.

"He's my father, isn't he?" David looked up.

"How could you know that?" Sussah's eyes went wide.

"Firstly, there was the way he reacted seeing you; not just a passing friendship. Then I saw the similarities; shape of his nose, his pinna – shape of the ears – and the eyes."

15

___

SOUTHBOUND AGAIN

After three weeks in Reenat, Leonie left the capital city on foot with the others. Styx left several days earlier, and it was just as sad to have to farewell Tipp and Biell, but life went on. Tipp still had his council duties to do, and Leonie still felt the urge to head to Delta. As promised, Biell supplied her with several scrolls in protective cases.

"These are not only the summaries of the skylands I've visited, but includes what other rangers have gleaned. I've marked the ones with glins'ool communities. They don't have portals on them, but could be used as supply points as the need arises."

In company with the others, she collected a few supplies from the early-morning traders as they traipsed down the circuitous path to the west gates. Overhead, the Gryphon Riders circled on their patrol.

Once the group covered several miles, the road branched; southwest to Qelay and north to Tesak. Being far enough away from any built-up area, it was a good place for Phil to call for the wyverns. The group moved to the grassy area to the side and waited, enjoying the morning air and peacefulness away from the hubbub of the capital.

Most of all, Leonie enjoyed the company. While deep down she knew this would all soon come to an end, it was still a disappointment when she heard Phil and Feiron were returning to Tesak.

"We are both now in the service of the Tesak'i," Philbert had explained. "No longer free agents to do as we wish. With the increased l'ith activity, even the few days away was grudgingly acceded, and only then because Noldor was doing such a great job."

"Don't they realise they wouldn't have the wyverns in the first place without your vision?" Leonie argued.

"At first, they were very appreciative, but after you've had something long enough, that wears off and it becomes commonplace. Now we keep Tesak safer by scouring the skies and lands to the west looking for l'ith incursion."

"And you, Jade?"

"Oh, I'm still a free spirit. I'll be in Qelay soon enough, but I'll need to collect Gretchen first. She's housed in the only place willing to take her. I fully expect they'll be wanting compensation for the extra stress."

"How long before you'll be heading south?"

"Once I leave Plenari, Qelay is a week's ride. Delta, about three days after that."

"Ok. I'll probably stay at White Cliffs for a day or so, then head to Delta and get a look at what's changed."

"Are you sure you want to do this though?" Phil asked her. "I understood Zander was no longer a threat to the monarchy?"

"This is for my reasons now. Twenty years ago, Dianah and Brendon attacked me to continue with their experiments. We fought, and I thought I killed them. Somehow, they survived. Now I'm going to do it properly."

"And Zander?"

"Before I left Earth, he tried to kill a close friend. If he gets the opportunity, I know he'll try it again. I'm pre-empting that."

"They say, 'when you are on the path of revenge, dig two graves'," Feiron said.

"I don't know who you've been talking to, but I'm planning on three."

"Here they come," Phil pointed.

Greetings, Leonie.

Greetings yourself. Leonie immediately recognised Dorn's mental speech. *Hi Slana, hi Faldo,* she replied

The three wyverns spiralled down, landing a few paces away.

"Wow, you two have grown so much." Leonie admired, walking up to them and scratching their chins.

Faldo's grown wider too. Slana barked a laugh.

"Still pinching other's breakfasts, I reckon." Leonie smiled. "Some things don't change." She helped Jade stow her gear on Slana.

Where is your ride? Slana asked Leonie.

I don't need one any more. Leonie did a quick circuit around them, much to their surprise and delight.

You too have changed, Dorn observed. *In more ways than one.*

You could say that, Leonie agreed. "I just remembered, Feiron, did you write that book yet?"

"It's a work-in-progress," he answered.

And has been for quite a while, Phil added with a chuckle.

"I heard that," the illios said, then laughed at Leonie's surprised look.

"How the frack did you hear that?" Leonie asked.

"Over the years, I've developed a modicum of telepathy. I think it might have been all those eggshells I absorbed back in Hell's Maw, but it only works when in contact with another telepath. When I'm on Faldo, I sense what he senses."

Without me, he is senseless, Faldo added, barking a laugh.

I so missed you guys! Leonie responded.

As we did you, Leonie, Dorn sent. *But it has not been boring.*

Phil and Feiron told me all about it. Did Noldor tell you about his adventures?

And yours too. Dorn added, *thank you for showing him the way home.*

"If there's anyone who never needs to thank me, it's you."

"Watch out," Jade called out. "If this keeps up, we'll all be crying again."

Leonie went around and hugged everyone farewell again. "I promise, this is the last time."

Phil and Jade climbed into their saddles whilst Feiron oozed into his.

She stepped back as they were about to launch. "I'm sure we'll meet again soon."

"No doubts about it," Feiron called down.

"And I'll see you in a couple of weeks at the latest," Jade said. "Oh, and Leonie? Try not to destroy the city again ... at least wait for me before the fun starts."

"I'll try, but won't promise anything." Leonie returned their waves as the wyverns leapt into the sky. She watched them circle and head north before taking to the sky herself for the southwest.

As she turned to follow the road, she saw a merchant with his wagon gaping at her and trying to keep his horses calm. With an apologetic wave, she moved off, gradually accelerating after finding her goggles in the bottom of her pack.

———

Later that afternoon she caught up with Styx in Qelay, with Riff and Dwer. They were the remaining hroltahgs in town until others from the surrounding lands arrived.

It will be our task to await all the others. Do not forget, we have covered most of this continent, and there are a few over in the Shattered Isles as well as Ghalena to the distant south.

"Are there other lands? All I hear about is Shak'aran and Ghalena."

They are, as far as we know, the only inhabited lands — at least by the seven known species. There are also vast ice regions to the far north and the far south.

"Sounds a bit like Earth." She let them scan her mind as she thought about it. "They call them the Arctic and Antarctic. How is it with you and other rollos?" she asked as Styx escorted her up to her room. "Are you accepted by them now?"

Only since the portal arrival, once they all saw what has become the norm at home.

"You mean you've been isolated all this time?" Leonie looked horrified.

Not isolated, as such, but it has been quiet. Plenty of time to contemplate.

Leonie had difficulty grasping the concept of being treated like that for two decades. They finally reached her door. "You know I can pay this time?"

You should be aware by now; we cannot accept payment from you after all you have done.

"Let's not get into that again."

Exactly.

"Is there anywhere on your world that's safe for me, or non-hroltahgs?"

There is not, unless something drastic has occurred in the last four-and-a-half centuries. Some areas, like the poles, might be the right temperature, but that would be it. The high gravity and toxic atmosphere would be fatal. You will recall your experiences in the caverns below.

"I just thought it would be nice to experience your world, as you can experience ours."

Only nice to us. You would be flat and asphyxiated in moments. Luckily, you wouldn't be alive to see the flesh dissolve off your bones.

"Not the best tour guide, are you?"

Not at all.

"Perhaps, like you did in the caverns, you will be able to create an environment suitable for non-hroltahgs?"

It is something worthy of consideration.

"What will happen to White Cliffs once you all go?" Leonie continued her questions.

Thinking of going into business with your new-found wealth?

"Hardly, not with the way the temperature's increasing over the next few years, if not sooner."

We are currently removing the heavy-gravity enchantment.

"How about all that gas?"

My people have imported some ... in your terms it would be vegetation, or algae, to absorb the bulk of the toxic gases. There were some fumes here originally. In the meantime, all those areas have been sealed until it is deemed safe. I will see you in the morning.

"Good night." Leonie strolled into her room and threw her pack onto a chair, along with her belt and new dagger. She then called down for water for a bath.

"Ma'am, I will get some hot water to you shortly," a maid said at the door.

"It's okay. Cold water is fine. I'll manage."

The maid looked at her blankly for a moment before heading off to fetch cold water. A short time later several staff emptied buckets of cold water into the tub. She thanked them and closed the door.

"Let's see how this goes." Leonie put her paw in and concentrated, gently summoning heat. After a few attempts, she managed the correct amount of control to bring the water to a comfortably hot temperature. She then stripped off and climbed in to relax and soak. When the water cooled, she simply increased the heat again. While lying there, Leonie decided to experiment further with water. "What can I really do?" she wondered.

By the time the headache was bad enough to prevent her concentration, she had worked out the basics of freezing and swirling the water, making water spouts, throwing water bombs, and willing the spilt water back into the bath, leaving the floor dry.

Afterwards, needing the fresh air, she strolled around Qelay and visited places not seen previously, then spent the remainder of the evening poring over the details of the skylands. She slept in and would have been longer if Styx didn't wake her.

Breakfast is ready in the dining hall.

"With your kind returning from the four corners of the land, what gossip do you have?" she asked when was at the table.

We do not spread– Ah. You jest.

"I've not changed that much."

But definitely changed where it counts. You have come a long way, Leonie. It maybe decades after the event, but I apologise for embedding those thoughts in your psyche.

"Water under the bridge. Stop changing the subject. Did Riff manage to get volunteers to remain as messengers?"

He did. All areas will be notified and encouraged to make plans to evacuate to the nearest major city. Once the portals have been located, word will get around quickly.

While she ate, Styx updated her on some of what had been reported from Lyhosa, Fisbane and In'sha. It was interesting, but not earth-shattering, and no surprise he had no further information on other portals, other than word was spreading about the reward for portal locations.

She was surprised to hear about the overnight abdication of King Reindet, and removing all possibility of Princess Siola taking over. In fact, he dissolved any chance of the monarchy reviving.

It was a sad turn of events. Reindet lost his wife and son several months ago, and now the loss of his youngest daughter ...

"I had no idea!" Leonie coughed, almost choking on her crust. "I did wonder about the absence of the queen, but not a word was mentioned about any prince. I thought Siola was next in line, assuming it follows either gender. What about the portal finder's fee?"

The royal lineage was not gender specific. But, with the news of the portals, Reindet deemed the continuation of the throne and the possibility of losing his last daughter over the short time remaining was not worthy of risk. He made one last decree before yielding complete authority; that order was for the Reenat Bardic Council and Shaper Hall to share responsibility between them. They have access and authority over the treasury. Rewards will still be paid.

Leonie slowly chewed, taking in this extraordinary news. "And Delta? What news from there?"

They are having a large winter festival. Many are travelling there from all over. Zander has managed to increase the influence of his little city-state, even though marginally.

"And pointless, now we know what's going to happen in the near future."

Perhaps. In fairness, he probably was ignorant of what we now know. Styx filled her head with the changes in Delta during her absence while she finished her breakfast. *It is now time for me to carry on with some duties.*

"I thought Riff and Dwer were running the place?"

They are. I am to visit Masevalon.

"That sounds exciting."

Does it?

"Pffft. You can stop the act. I can sense it in you."

As I said, you have come a long way.

"And will be going further. I'll be heading to Delta shortly."

No doubt I will see you again soon. Styx waddled out the dining hall.

Chuckling while pushing her chair back, Leonie too left the room. With little else to keep her occupied here, she packed her gear and maps and flew south. Even though she'd just been told all about it, she was impatient to see how Delta had changed in her twenty-year absence. Love it or loathe it, it had been her place of birth. There was a touch of nostalgia in it. She followed the Urmaq River, glimpsing Swangrove and Indras as she cruised overhead. When she saw the old ferry on the banks of the Deraz, the memory of Axorg came to mind and she wondered what the elemental wyvern was up to. Leonie even briefly contemplated if a transcended wyvern would be aware of Noldor. *It's not as if undead wyverns are common.*

High clouds painted the sky in the afternoon, but brought no rain.

Due to the late start, she arrived in Delta after dark. The

lights from the streets certainly indicated many people were partying and enjoying the warm *winter* evening.

While interested in looking over the city, she was keen to see the palace more.

Being told about what had happened to it wasn't the same as seeing it for herself. Leonie slowly flew around the palace several times, amazed at the result of the wayward spell. Niaarin had called for so much power, she had replicated – albeit on a much smaller scale – the devastation of Dromas.

She veered away when she saw a few glins'ool lazily flapping around the perimeter. Their lack of response was a sure sign she hadn't been spotted. "Too busy looking down, I reckon."

Leonie headed back to the Web, her old stamping ground. She wasn't interested in any possibly awkward reunions at the moment so went straight to her old room. Landing lightly on the shingle roof where she'd spent so much time sitting and contemplating her future, she was surprised when a flock of pigeons burst out of her window.

A quick whiff of inside was all she needed to start looking for another place. Needing drink to clear her throat, she sat on the roof like old times, took off her pack and began digging for her flask. She heard the clink of the ducats. In hindsight, she was glad Biell declined the bag of ducats, stating the one bag for Tipp would be sufficient for the both of them.

"Ha." Inspired by an idea, she finished her drink, donned the pack and raced across to Portside to find the most lavish room available. Whether lucky or unlucky, there was one suite left. The hefty price on it was the obvious reason why no one took it.

"A hundred and fifty gold ducats is absurd!" she hissed to the manager with the largest nose she had ever seen on a human face.

"Yes, ma'am." He looked her up and down through his spectacles, taking in her worn travelling attire. "I'm sure you can look elsewhere, perhaps somewhere more to *your* budget."

"Oh, the *budget* doesn't faze me, but these inflated prices, even for a suite, are over the top." She slammed the money on the counter, smiling at his shocked reaction. "Choke on it." Both elated at his surprise and annoyed at letting go so much coin, Leonie flew up the stairs, startling the other patrons. She loved seeing the look on the old fart's face, but even with the wealth she held, that price was against all her *thieving* principles.

In her rooms, she freshened up, changed her clothes and went down to have dinner. Most of the diners were guests who had witnessed her previous behaviour, and wisely kept to themselves. She generously tipped the waitress when the food and drink were brought out.

"Why, thank you, ma'am." The girl's eyes grew wide at the coins.

"You deserve it for putting up with that shithead."

The waitress fought back her smile, her white teeth contrasting against her dark skin. She curtsied and hurried away.

After dinner, which Leonie grudgingly considered one of the best meals she'd ever had, she went back to her rooms to think of her next move.

16

THE LAST RESORT

After a relaxing breakfast with a few sideways glances from other patrons, Leonie went searching for new clothes. Unless she wore the Earth jumpsuit, the clothes she'd purchased in Hellam looked worse for wear, and the alien clothing would bring too much attention.

Dressed in her new clothes Leonie explored Delta on foot while her old clothes were cleaned and repaired. First to check was the palace and headland. Even from ground level, she thought the damage was immense. Half of the old Portside she remembered was missing as well as the original headland. Where she stood now, the road ended abruptly with a stone wall. The other side was a forty-foot drop to the harbour.

Forming a very rough and jagged conical shape, the lowest portion of the palace bedrock now floated roughly twenty feet above the water with the bulk rising above the road and looming overhead.

Massive ropes, discoloured from years of exposure to the elements, snaked out from several strongpoints, anchoring it to the ground. She watched it for a while and saw the small skyland move, much like a ship moored at a dock. Further around the headland, and behind some warehouses, tall form-work stretched up, with a long narrow bridge at the top.

Leonie thought she knew what it was for, but she walked around the block curious to see it in action. Within the structure rested a bamboo cage held by ropes fed through a block and tackle at the top. The end of the rope was harnessed to several oxen. Counterweights were used to offset the load.

She shook her head. *Reckon I'll stick with flying.* Leonie turned and started threading her way across the many bridges, exploring the various islands along the way, including the festivities in the plaza. It was mid-afternoon by the time she reached Dockside.

It all came back to her, even after the long absence – the boardwalks and alleys – like she'd never left, the memories were so clear. Even the four thugs at the end of the alley were a nice touch to make her feel at home. She'd noticed a couple of them earlier following, thinking her new clothes and pack were worthy of attention.

"Hey guys. Is the Taker's Guild still in the warehouse around the corner?" she asked.

That surprised them.

"What do you want with the Takers, assumin' we know where it is?"

"I thought I'd join up." They laughed at that. "Come on. It can't be that hard if you lot are anything to go by. I spotted a couple of you several blocks away. So why the increased numbers? Did you need reinforcements?"

"I reckon I could take you by me'self."

"Want to bet? But, to be fair, I should warn you not to meddle with things you have not got a clue about."

"I reckon I've seen enough. You don't scare us."

She sighed. "Look, I'll tell you what ..." Leonie willed them all up as she flew above the roof-line. "I really couldn't be bothered." She dropped them on the nearest roof. "Yep, some things never change." Scanning their minds when she asked the question told her the location of the Takers. It had moved after all this time.

Leaving the thugs to work out how to get down, she headed over there. She was unsure exactly why, but put it down to closure; just to see who took over and how it was going. Jade had built it up to a pretty high standard. The calibre of those four thugs didn't overly impress her.

Having also been furnished with the password, she was escorted into the back room of a seedy tavern and up the stairs. At the door to the office, she was stopped.

"*We* don't know you," he said. The man had a cut to his forehead and his arm in a sling.

"I've been away for a while," she said.

"Must have. I've been here for years, and I still say we don't know you."

"Is the boss around?" she asked politely.

"Maybe he is, maybe he isn't. Who wants to know?"

She really began to think simply scanning everyone would so much more efficient, if impolite. "Me. Leonie. Tell him I'm an old friend of Jade's, the original guild-master."

As the doorman screwed up his face, thinking, the door behind him opened. "Who is it?"

"Sam? Is that you?" she said, surprised. Except for the black eye, the young man in front of her had a very good resemblance to one of the street kids she knew.

"Leonie?" Sam looked shocked to see her.

"You've grown so much."

"We thought—"

"Yeah, dead. I know. Can I come in, or are we going to chat here all day?"

"Fine, fine. Come in." He moved back and opened the door wider. "Thanks, Lark." He nodded to the doorman, as she passed, then closed the door behind her.

The office was surprisingly tidy, though cramped. Sam moved some scrolls off a chair for her to sit down. Looking around, she recognised some of the items from Jade's old office, but there were no tapestries.

He fetched another glass and poured a drink.

"Where have you been? What happened?"

Leonie spent the time telling him a version of what happened, but left out the travel to Earth. Instead, she had been stuck over on the west coast, making ends meet and slowly working her way back.

"Do you need work? We could sure use you here. Things have gone downhill, especially the last few months."

"No. You can probably see from my appearance, I came into a bit of money, so I'm fine. What's happened to make the Takers go downhill?"

"Our damn overlord, that's what. I reckon he's gone crazy this time. He goes on about taking the Reenatian throne, and he's recruiting as many powershapers and men-at-arms as he can, thinking that Reenat is going to attack. They're all taken out west to some training camp. I'm stuck with what's left in town."

"I can tell you there'll be no attack. The king's abdicated. There's bigger concerns brewing now than worrying about who's ruling the country."

"There is? What concerns are bigger than running the country?"

"You've not heard about the search for these portals to other worlds?"

Sam looked blankly at her. "We don't get much word from Reenat nowadays."

Leonie told him about the reward for finding these portals, and yes, they were real.

"Where's Helen?" she asked.

Sam's face grew dark. "She's a priestess at the Qevlir temple."

"Helen's an Earther now?"

"Four years, now." He nodded, draining his drink and poured himself another. "Maybe I should go and start looking for these portals. No point in *this* anymore."

"That's disappointing, but from what I've seen out there, probably better to cut and run." Leonie put her glass on the table for Sam to refill. She spied a partially covered parchment, but a section of a drawing caught her attention.

"May I look at this?" she pulled it out from the pile.

"Sure," Sam said. "Came in this morning."

Leonie studied the sketch. It looked like a device she was more familiar with. *What's tower tech doing here?*

"Just another indicator of him going crazy," Sam continued, "Reckons everyone should look high and low for it immediately. Huge reward too if you can believe them. They probably would've rounded up all the Takers if they could spare the manpower, but with the festival, all the guards are busy. Reckons it was picked from some traveller."

"Do you know who pick-pocketed it?"

"I've not heard. If they did and heard about the reward, they'd be there claiming it now."

"Anything else you can tell me?"

"About that? Nothing."

"No news of something or someone different? Did any spotters report in?"

"We've not had spotters for years. Why are you so interested? For the reward?"

"It's hard to explain, but I've seen something like this before." Leonie indicated the sketch.

"They also said it was a very dangerous powershaper device," Sam added.

Leonie had an idea. She took off her pack and unrolled her other clothes. "Have you seen someone wearing something like this?"

Sam looked at the clothes, then picked them up. "This is weird fabric. Not leather, not cloth ... and very light. Wow." He toyed with the zipper.

"But have you seen anything like it?" she repeated.

"I haven't, no. Lark!" he called out.

The door opened quickly as the doorman came in, looking

like he was ready to fight. "Easy, Lark. It's alright. Was this what you saw yesterday on those travellers?"

Lark looked from Leonie to Sam to what he was holding.

He nodded. "Yeah, boss."

"Where?" Leonie asked, scanning him. "The Wharf Tavern?" She saw his memory of the five of them mingling outside the green and white tavern. *Standing around and gawking like typical tourists.*

He nodded, blinking. "That's it."

"Great. Thanks, Lark." Leonie collected her clothes when Sam handed them to her. "Looks like that's where I'm going." She headed for the door. "Oh, and if anyone does find that device, I'll double the reward."

"But its twenty gold ducats," Sam exclaimed.

"Oh. Is that all? I'll triple it then to make it worth their while. Bye." Leonie left them staring and started briskly walking to the Bridgeway. "What the frack are they all doing here?"

It took her ten minutes to find the front of the green and white building. She pushed through the front doors, the sound and pipe smoke hitting her. Those nearest to the door stopped talking and stared. She ignored them, wending her way through the crowd to the bar.

"Hey, there," she said to a waitress. "Yesterday, did you see five travellers come through here wearing weird clothing?" Leonie scanned her mind, seeing the vision of the group heading into the back with Rickard. *Why did that name sound familiar?*

"I might have done," the waitress answered. "What's in it for me?"

"Thanks." Leonie turned and went back out the front door then turned into the side alley. There was a back door there and a lot less people. A quick scan suggested one person inside. Stealthily, she opened the door and stood there. "Hey there. Where's Rickard hiding?"

"Who are you?" the man asked, looking up from the oven.

Her scan showed an image of a green and white boat moored

under a bridge. Leonie turned and let the door close behind her. She loved how mind-scanning saved so much time.

On the Bridgeway she looked up and down for a bridge resembling the one she'd just seen. The bridge opposite was the wrong colour and the one north was the wrong shape. The style and shape of the southern bridge showed more promise. She dodged some carts and made her way to the harbour wall, and looked south.

There were dozens of boats moored against the wooden dock. With barely a thought, she hopped over the wall and quickly levitated down to the boardwalk and started trotting past the boats seeing her target boat about fifty paces ahead.

Leonie slowed when she was two more boats away. Most of the boats were empty and closed up for the festival. She could sense five bodies on the green and white boat. Four familiar minds were in a state of anxiety; Sussah, Bern and the agtechs. A fifth mind changed from what she sensed as adoration to rage to adoration again.

Rickard? she assumed. *Where is David?* She knew she couldn't read him. *But if one is Rickard, then there should be six people.*

She flew the short distance and landed on the roof and scanned again, concentrating. The information she got was they were tied up, except Rickard. Lerry, Harrond and Bern were in one section, and Sussah was trussed up towards the front.

Leonie concentrated on Rickard. His mind was in turmoil – and he had a knife! She had to get him away before he decided to do more with the weapon. With a deep breath, Leonie touched his mind, convincing him he had to go outside. When he stepped out of the back door, Leonie reached down and zapped him. He dropped to the deck, knife clattering beside him.

In an instant she hopped down, collected the knife and ran in. "Why am I always doing this?" They were gagged and tied up on the floor of the small cabin. If it wasn't so serious, she would have laughed at their surprised faces. In moments she had cut their bindings. "You can tell me everything in a minute," she said as she went to fetch Sussah.

"Where the frack is David?" she asked once they were all together. "And what are you guys doing here?" They all started talking. "Lerry first," she said.

The senior agtech told her about them visiting Delta. "We came to see Su's parents, but they died several years ago. We met Rickard instead."

"Why were you tied up?"

"I think Rickard, or someone, put something in the dinner last night. A bunch of guys came in and tied us when we were unconscious."

"If you were drugged, how would you know?"

"That idiot was gloating about friends in high places when we woke." Harrond looked at the body of Rickard. "Is he dead?"

"No. Unconscious. So, we need to go back a bit. Why all this?"

"Rickard is David's father," Lerry said.

"He was the—" Sussah started.

"Now I remember. You told me years ago. Does he know he's the father?"

"No. I've been wondering if I should tell him, but seeing how mad he is now, I don't think I should tell him at all. David worked it out though."

"Of course he did." Leonie nodded. "So, let me guess. Alexander's got David now?"

They shrugged. Rickard groaned.

"Should we go somewhere else to talk about this?" Harrond asked looking along the dock. No one had noticed or raised the alarm yet, but he appeared nervous.

"In a minute." Leonie walked over to Rickard. She willed his body up and over the side into the canal, dipping him in upside-down like a teabag.

"Wha?" He coughed up water and looked around in confusion, vainly wiping the saltwater streaming into his eyes.

"Where's David?" Leonie asked.

"Who are you?"

"Wrong answer." Leonie dropped him back into the water,

holding him there. She repeated the question when she pulled him out.

"I think Lord Zander has him," he spluttered.

"How did Zander find out about them?" She asked before he could get another word out.

"I don't know. A couple Watcher people came over—"

Leonie turned to the group. "I assume you guys came through the North Gate?" She looked at their clothing. "How did you get here? Wait—" She dropped Rickard back into the water so he couldn't overhear. "Now, Lerry."

"We landed the *Sundancer* near a swamp up the road." Lerry watched Rickard starting to thrash in the water; his feet kicking frantically. "We then walked down the road to the main gate."

"Wait—" Leonie let Rickard gasp a few breaths, then dropped him back in. "Continue."

"Um ... we had to give details of who we were, why we were here and where we were staying."

"Why the Wharf Tavern?"

"It was my da's tavern. It was the only place I knew. They died several years ago," Sussah added before Leonie asked. "But we only found that out when Rick told us."

Rickard surged out of the water and was dumped like a netted fish on the deck.

"What's in it for you, *Rick*?" Leonie questioned him, toying with the knife.

He coughed and spat water before he could answer. "I love Sussah. When they asked about them ... they only wanted David, and said they'd let me have her—"

"As if Su was anyone's to give away!" Leonie hissed. "No one is anyone's property."

"But I love her, and she loves me!" he cried. "Don't you Sussah?"

Sussah blushed, looking down. "I did have feelings, yes. But that was twenty years ago! Rick ... we were so young, and it was all so new ..."

"Can't we work something out?" Rickard pleaded, clearly in anguish.

Leonie sighed. "This is sad." She moved away to let them talk but kept an eye on him.

"Rick, what we had was so long ago. I was sent away and had to make a new life. No. We can't make it work out. I have Harrond now, and he has me. I'm sorry." Sussah ignored his pleas and awkwardly climbed off the boat onto the pier. Harrond followed her.

"What are you going to do with me?" Rickard asked Leonie.

"This." Leonie sent images into his head. He screamed and thrashed, but unable to escape his own mind. Leonie withdrew. "That's a small taste of what I'll do to you if you *ever* come near Sussah or these people, or if anything happens to them. Do you understand? Do not talk about us to anyone. Forget we were ever here!"

"Yes! Yes," he sobbed, nodding his head vigorously.

Leonie released him. He slumped down, crying.

"Let's go." She tossed the knife into the canal and jumped off the boat without looking back.

Lerry and Bern looked at each other then climbed out of the boat. Catching up with Su and Harrond, they made a circuitous path, avoiding the bulk of the crowds when they could.

"What did you do to him?" Bern asked her later as they neared Portside.

"To Rickard? I thought about some really nasty memories, and transferred them into his mind to let him know that's what would happen."

"They were your memories?"

"I had to be convincing," she growled as they crossed the last bridge and walked towards a large, imposing building. "Welcome to Portside."

"Looks expensive," Harrond noted the sign *Last Resort*.

"We haven't any—"

"I've already paid for this," she said.

As they walked in, the concierge looked up from his desk.

Before he said anything, Leonie hit his mind with an urgent bowel problem. Leaving two customers staring, he briskly disappeared through the back door.

"Follow me." Leonie led them upstairs and finally into her suite. "There aren't enough beds, but I reckon we can make do."

"Who's is all this?"

"Mine until 18th Polsert, or until I pay for more nights."

"What's Polsert?"

"It's this month. Today is Afel, one of the six days of the week here. I'll tell you everything later. For now, I need to find David, and you probably need to eat and rest."

"Can we help?"

"Not in this. This is my city and you may recall I'm not without some talents. I'll send a waitress up to deal with your needs." She went to the door, then turned. "If you're worried about this place, don't be. Everything is legit. Order whatever you want. I'll deal with the bill. Just don't go anywhere until I get back."

"How long will that be?"

"I have no idea." She closed the door behind her.

"Well, that was scary," Sussah said. "I've not seen her so angry before."

Lerry looked to Harrond. "We have."

Bern nodded in agreement.

A few minutes later as they were looking through the rooms and gasping at the refined furnishings and artwork, there was a polite knock at the door.

17

SAVING DAVID

THE PALACE WAS THE OBVIOUS PLACE TO START SEARCHING, BUT from what Leonie saw in her earlier visits, it was now fully-manned. Her last foray here was a different story, and she'd snuck in via the sewers.

There were also the glins'ool aerial patrols.

She walked around the headland, checking the skyland out from different locations. Every now and then she saw a faint glow. *So, he now has magical detection on his balconies and windows.*

While she walked, something niggled at the back of her mind, which only fed her frustration. She even scanned some of the guards at the gantry with no results. After a couple of hours of running scenarios through her head, she returned to the hotel.

As she entered, the concierge waved to get her attention. "You have too many guests in your room, *madam*," he said as soon as she walked over.

"You got any spare rooms?"

"Nothing has changed, we are full."

"Then they'll stay. How much extra to shut you up?" she asked. "No, forget that, she took off her pack and slammed a pawful of ducats onto the desk."

The man's eyes bulged with greed.

"Let me know when it runs out." Leonie left him speechless.

"Did you find David?" Sussah jumped off the settee the moment Leonie walked in. Bern and Harrond wandered in from the balcony and Lerry emerged from another room wiping sleep from his eyes.

"Not yet," she sighed, reaching for the wine. "You guys comfortable? All fed?"

"We're fine, Leonie," Lerry said. "Have to ask though ..." He looked around. "How is this possible?"

She removed her pack and sat down on one of the stuffed chairs and told them what she had been up to since she left Skyhome.

"One thousand gold ducats?" Harrond asked. "Is that a lot of money? It sounds like a lot."

"There was five thousand. I wasn't going to take any of it, but Biell insisted. Some people are too nice." She then showed them her arm greaves and dagger. "And you'll be happy, Su; I'm now a bona fide powershaper. Tested, registered and guilded."

"I knew you were all along," Sussah giggled. "And when will Jade turn up?"

"Maybe another ten days or so." Leonie sipped her wine. "Can you go through everything that happened to you again, once you were on the boat? There's something that rankles."

"Other than the smell of fish," Bern quipped.

Between them, they repeated the events in detail, correcting or corroborating each person's version.

"And then you saved us." Sussah smiled.

"That was pure luck." She reached forward and picked at the leftover food and sat back. "Nope." She considered what they told her. "Nothing rings a bell."

"Was it something you heard at the tavern, or what Rick said?" Lerry asked. "Who are these Watchers he spoke about?"

"We have eight deities, one for each of the temples based on a key elemental force. These forces are also the source of power – of magic." She told them about the pantheon most people on Shak'aran believed in. "It was because of some prophecies and the Watchers that Delta was eventually built. If we get a chance, maybe you'll get to see the temples at the plaza. Some people enjoy looking at them. Other than the palace, they're the oldest buildings in the city. But you won't see the temple for Time." Leonie thought for a few minutes.

"What is it?" Lerry asked at her pause.

"When I looked at the palace earlier, the ground where the temple had been built was gone. I wonder where the new temple is now? I'll be back in a minute." She walked swiftly out the door.

Downstairs she went to see the concierge, but he was with other guests. She spied the waitress from last night, and got her attention.

"Can you tell me where the new temple of Eternix is? Did it get destroyed when the palace went up?"

"Yes, ma'am. They built a new one around the plaza. It was the only area the council permitted."

"You're wonderful. Can you bring another bottle of red wine to my suite?"

"Of course." She was about to curtsy.

"None of that. Make it two bottles with four more glasses, and there's no rush." Leonie padded her way quickly back to her rooms.

"I think I've solved my little dilemma," she said as soon as she walked in.

"David?" Sussah looked up.

"Not that one, yet. Rickard said a couple of Watchers came to ask about you all."

"That's right. Is that significant?" Harrond asked.

"Maybe. Maybe not. I reckon I'd like to see this new temple though." She went out to the balcony that overlooked Portside and the harbour, but Emerald Island obscured the view of the plaza. Leonie heard a knock at the door. She came inside and grabbed a couple of coins from her pack as Lerry let the waitress in.

The waitress was surprised to see all the others here. She nodded hello and placed the tray on the sideboard.

"That was quick." Leonie handed her the coins. "Thank you, and keep the change, if there is any. No need to tell your boss."

"Any time, ma'am. Thank you very much." Her eyes sparkled at the coins.

"Can I ask a favour?"

"Certainly."

"If anyone comes snooping around asking questions about me or my friends here, would you let me know? If you can, I mean, without getting into trouble."

"Of course, ma'am."

"And no more of this 'ma'am'. Please call me Leonie."

"And I'm Anja." The waitress smiled and left.

"Drinks, anyone?" Leonie offered as she opened a bottle.

With full glasses in hand, they sat around the room. After several minutes, Lerry broke the silence. "What is Alexander up to? What's our next step?"

"For you." She looked at them. "A change of clothing. You can't go anywhere dressed like that without creating more attention. And attention is *not* what we want right now."

"And Alexander?"

"If he's anything like before, he's paranoid and crazy. I reckon he blames David for everything bad that's happened."

"How is it David's fault?" Sussah burst out.

"When I speak to the crazy man, I'll be sure to ask."

"Can you get to Alexander?" Lerry questioned.

"Probably, though it'll be tricky. But right now, he's not on my radar. My attention is on the Watchers. They're the ones asking questions. I would've thought Alex would send guards, not priests."

Sussah stifled a yawn.

Leonie realised they all looked tired. "There's three beds. After last night's crap, you guys need the rest more than me."

"Where will you sleep?" Sussah asked her.

"I'm fine with the settee. I don't need the blankets." Bern nodded.

"You sure, Bern? I'm not tired yet, besides, I'm going snooping. I could be out all night."

"If you're paying, the least we can do is let you be comfortable," the wilder replied.

"Fair enough. I'll see you in the morning for breakfast. Then we'll get you some clothes."

"Will you be okay?" Sussah asked, worried.

"I'm a big girl now." Leonie smiled at her concern, then walked to the balcony and flew off into the dark. To the east, the first of the moons was about to rise, leaking a pale luminescence to the horizon.

Wary of any glowing obelisks, she cruised over the city. Below, the festivals were still going in full swing. From her vantage point she could see jugglers with flaming hoops, acrobats and dancers thrilling the crowds.

The new temple for Eternix was built further back than the others, in what was a grassy reserve, if her memory was correct, squeezed in between a string of businesses and two other temples; Earth and Life.

She debated whether she like the crowd or not. Lots of people meant cover, and not being singled out, but it also created many witnesses if things didn't go to plan. "As if I had a plan," she muttered.

Four people emerged from the front of the temple. Even though they looked older, she recognised them immediately.

"Dianah and Brendon!" she hissed, also noting the two guards with them. There was far too much activity for her to do anything without creating more of a disturbance.

She tried scanning their minds, but their walls were sufficient to block her and the guards knew nothing. If she pushed too hard, they'd become aware of her presence. "But it does prove this *is* the place to be. Frack," she hissed as a crystal on the top of the temple started glowing.

She dropped down quickly, choosing her moment to land in

the shadows between the two temples. A couple of carousers jumped when she appeared, but then laughed and continued on their merry way.

Leonie waited in the shadows until there was a sufficient gap between the groups of revellers. She quickly padded across the pavers to the rear door. She didn't raise a sweat undoing the lock and was inside in moments.

Beyond the back door was a long, carpeted hallway, with other doors and passages alternating on each side. The interior was dimly lit by slow-burning torches roughly every ten paces, each opposite an exit.

Passing each door, she scanned the interior. Most were empty, but a few held sleepers. *Acolytes?* she guessed. She wondered which one took David, but to find out would mean waking them one at a time. *Maybe later, if need be.*

Opposite a branching corridor and beneath a torch, hung a mirror. Seeing her reflection, she considered, not for the first time, what an idiot she was. As she watched, her image slowly faded. *Better.* She moved on.

The stairs led up and down. Leonie chose down. In her experience, dungeons and cells were always below ground; cold, dank, and little natural light. *And no one can hear the screams.*

At the base of the first flight was an empty desk. A dozen heavy wooden doors ran down the stone-floored passage. More scanning as she crept along revealed nothing; all the cells were empty. *Which would explain the empty desk. No guards needed.*

The same result for the next floor down; the bottom floor. Retracing her footsteps, Leonie started going up stairs. The first-floor lighting was brighter, and the pattern on the carpet was rich in colours.

She checked her image in another mirror. *Still invisible.* Up ahead, hearing voices she slowly approached. Scanning the room, the room at the end had two occupants; one with a shielded mind. *David?* she wondered. Her perception as she neared grew in detail. He was shrouded by an aura. The other mind was ... blank? Like a fog, but the swirls were only vague thoughts. As if in a trance, or in the thralls of using the power.

Using it on David!

Trying the door handle, it was unlocked. Carefully she opened it and glanced in. A robed figure was sitting at a desk, eyes wide open, unblinking. Lips moving, a soft whispering now heard. In a trance, as she suspected.

Peering around the door, she saw David lying on a cot, shrouded by a luminescence.

He looked unharmed. She sighed in relief, risking a quick look behind her to make sure the hallway was still empty. She snuck in and closed the door.

The chanting stopped. Spinning around, her eyes met the Watcher.

"Welcome, Leonie. We have been waiting for you."

The shrouded figure on the bed disappeared.

"Ah, frack it!" She leapt at the acolyte, but he shifted and was suddenly on the other side of the room. The moment she flew across, he was gone again. "Keep still, damn it," she growled.

"Be calm, we were expecting you."

"How the hell were you expecting me?" she fumed, stomping over to the bed.

"We are Watchers," he said simply. "We were always expecting you."

"What, so you know exactly what will happen, and when it will happen?"

"Yes, and no. Please come with me?"

"Why should I?"

He beckoned as he walked out the door. "Because you will see David if you do, and won't see David if you don't," he called out from the hall.

He led her upstairs into a suite of rooms, not unlike hers at the Last Resort. The young man knocked on the door, then walked in. "I have brought Leonie to you, my lord."

She barely heard a response but the acolyte stepped back and waved her through. Once she was inside, he closed the door. The room was well-furnished and well-it. An antique table was to one side, in front of floor-to-ceiling windows. The curtains wafted slightly in the evening breeze.

A tall, robed figure with dark, short-cropped hair stood by the windows, looking out. Sounds of the festivities echoed from below.

The priest turned. "Greetings, Leonie. Please have a seat. Would you like some Tesakian Redleaf? I believe you like it."

"Where's David?" Leonie scanned his mind. Or tried to. She was blocked. *Or he's shielded.*

"David is safe for the moment." The priest brought over a tray from the sideboard with a steaming teapot and two cups.

"Is that a hint of a threat?" she growled.

"Not at all, just a fact." He sat and began to pour the tea.

"What's going on?"

"Time."

"What the frack does that mean?"

"Time is always going on. Allow me to introduce myself. I am Tieru Jerts, and the current High Priest to this Temple of Eternix. Welcome."

Leonie paced back and forth. "Am I a prisoner?"

"Do you see any guards?" He waved his arms around. "Is the door locked? Have we threatened you in anyway?"

"So, I can walk away?"

"Of course. Walk, fly, cartwheel if you like ... feel free, but you're here for David." Tieru placed her cup close to a chair and then helped himself to his tea. "As you know, Tesakian Redleaf is much better when it's hot."

Exasperated, Leonie hunched down in the chair. "If I drink, you'll tell me where David is?"

"I will gladly reveal what I can—"

"About where David is," Leonie insisted.

"It *is* one of the things I will reveal to you. Drink up."

She looked suspiciously at the steaming cup. "Why? Is it poisoned?" Leonie's mind went to her framing incident in Reenat.

"I'm sure you noticed; I *am* drinking from the very same pot."

"You could have an immunity to it." Leonie scowled.

"They said you were a suspicious one. What can I do to assure you that I mean you no harm? Quite the opposite, in fact."

"You can tell me where David is for a start."

Tieru sighed. "Very well. He is right behind you."

Leonie leapt out of the chair and whirled around. "Where?" There was no one else in the room.

"Concentrate. Look in the corner. What do you see?"

Staring intently at the corner, she thought she sensed more than saw anything. "What sort of a trick is this?"

"No *trick*, Leonie. More of a complicated use of power. David is right there, but ... we can alter time. Funny about that, being the time temple and all. He is ..." he paused looking for a phrase. "Out of phase."

"Like on another plane?" She stepped to the corner, putting her paw out and waving it slowly in the air.

"Another dimension would be more precise." The High Priest nodded. "Your tea?"

"And he is unharmed?" Leonie reluctantly walked back to her chair.

"He's completely unharmed, which is why we brought him here. To keep him safe."

"What interest is he to you?"

"David is a means to an end, as are you, as is Brendon and Dianah."

"I thought you worked for Zander."

"People might *think* that and we allow that perception to linger because it helps in achieving our aims. None of the temples really work *for* anyone other than carrying out the will of the Gods – or what is perceived as Their will."

"I just saw Dianah and Brendon leave. They walked out the front door! And you tell me you're not working for any of them?"

Tieru stood and walked around to her. "Leonie, make no mistake, we are all just pawns in this game of prophecy, tools to be used, discarded and forgotten at any stage. At the moment, David, Zander, even myself are a but a few of those pawns; those tools. We may be of use for ages, or discarded next week when another path is revealed."

"You didn't mention me."

"Well, no. Of course not. You are the *chosen one*, at least for this path and the many paths we do see. In fact, it is your encounter with Niaarin Grigorid that makes you so special."

That was a name she didn't expect to hear, but would never forget. "It does? Why?"

"Why?" He looked amazed. "You are the only one to have survived her teleportation spell. I don't abide her reasons or methods, but what she accomplished was truly amazing. Many of us here would be very interested in what those ramifications were for you; how you coped; what really happened ... anything you can tell us could further our studies—"

"I've been experimented on and quizzed much of my life. I don't share your enthusiasm." She watched the light leave his face. Leonie sighed. She should play nice since they had David captive.

"And what are *your* aims?" She decided to keep him talking until she knew how to get hold of David.

"All peoples on this world are doomed. We know this, and follow what we hope to be the correct path to achieve a satisfactory outcome. For everyone to survive."

"How long have you known about this doom?"

"We had an inkling for almost two centuries, but the climate over this last decade has confirmed it. It is why we sent a group of Watchers down here in the first place to await the arrival of Zander and his companions. The *High Ones*."

"What's to stop Dianah and Brendon telling Alexander that David is here? Will you stop him from bringing guards? He's already tried to kill him once."

The High Priest sipped his tea before replying. "If this occurs, a decision will be made at the time. We deal in and with time. Everything done – every path we take – is a necessary requirement to reach where we are today. We believe we've chosen the right path, though there have been a few pot-holes. Everything is possible, but we can only unravel a small part of the potential futures. Unfortunately, time has no set map." He placed his cup down and got up, pacing the room as he spoke.

"Think of it as an ocean, a vast empty expanse and we're beholden to the vagaries of the wind and currents. Every action from anyone at any time could change the outcome – with potentially unlimited and unfathomable results.

"While some individuals are obviously key, it's a gamble to choose who and where we should focus. You, for example, were an unknown. And that intrigued us. We had no idea what the outcomes of Dianah's experiments would lead to. We are only mortals, after all. You might very well be our *wind of change* we've been waiting for."

"So why hide David from me?"

"Because much of the minute-to-minute decisions you make are still unseen to us. We may see results *afterwards*, or trends of your actions, but in a temporal sense, you are invisible to us as much as one of your talents makes you invisible to mundane eyes."

"And now?"

"I'm still breathing, which is a bonus." He resumed his seat. "And I wanted to meet you. My reasoning is if I knew you better, had a handle on what you were about, then perhaps a better understanding would be made."

"How is that working out?"

"Time will tell." Tieru sat back and closed his eyes.

Leonie sat, watching, thinking he had gone to sleep. She felt a tingle; a rippling.

"Leonie!" David said behind her.

"Crap!" She leapt out of her chair, spilling her tea. "David!" She hastily put her cup down.

The young scientist stood up from a chair in the corner,

wiping his eyes and yawning. "I thought I was dreaming for a minute there. Where are we? It's great to see you."

"And you." Leonie went over and gave him a brief hug. "I seem to be doing that a lot lately." She laughed as she pulled away. "I blame your mum entirely."

"Where is mum and Harrond?" He looked around at the strange room, seeing Tieru.

"They're fine, resting in a hotel," she answered. "Seeing you safely back will definitely make them happier."

"When will that be?" he asked, still looking dazed.

"I don't know." Leonie turned to Tieru. "When will that be?"

The High Priest stood and walked over. "As we said, you were never a prisoner. We simply wanted to keep David safe."

"I still don't get why you allowed Dianah and Brendon in here. I assume they questioned David?"

Tieru smiled. "All will be revealed ... in time." He guided them through the tall doors beyond the curtains leading onto a balcony. "It has been a pleasure to meet you both *in the real*. I suspect you can make your way to the hotel from here."

"Wait." Leonie turned, looking at David, then Tieru.

"What is it?" David asked.

Tieru had a questioning look on his face.

"For a genius and a High Priest, you two aren't too bright," she exhaled in exasperation. "David, you are a genius scientist who has discovered time-travel; Tieru, you are the High Priest of the Time temple. Surely you should be brainstorming what you both know?"

Tieru shared a glance with David.

"I better make a fresh pot of tea," the High Priest said, walking back inside.

"Ready to fly, David?" Leonie yawned from the lounge when he shook her awake.

The two temporal specialists had been talking incessantly. She even learnt a trick or two and ended up talking in depth about her teleportation experience, but when the big words came out, she got some shut-eye.

He nodded. "I guess so. I hope mum and the others aren't too put out by my absence. I feel guilty about delaying my return."

"I'm sure they're fine. No doubt having a good sleep in luxury." She briefly told him about her accommodation arrangements as they strolled to the balcony escorted again by Tieru.

David looked below at the plaza. The flames, entertainers and the lively crowds had dwindled as it was almost dawn.

"I guess I should thank you." As she turned to bid the High Priest farewell, a woefully belated detail hit her in the face. "You're an illios," she gasped in surprise.

"All my life," Tieru replied.

"Now I have more questions than I'd like." She shook her head.

"Welcome to my world." Tieru smiled, watching as Leonie and David lifted off the floor. "Until we meet next time." He waved.

———

Zander paced back and forwards until finally Dianah and Brendon returned. "Well? What did you find out?" he asked the moment they entered the room.

"It is David—"

"I knew he'd come after me!" Alex paced even faster. "Call me paranoid now, do you?"

"He wasn't *after* you, Alex. He said he was here so his mother could visit her parents," Dianah said.

"His mother? From here?" Alex looked confused. "How the hell is that possible? No. He's too cunning. Mark my words, he tricked you and I'm his target. I always have been." He stopped at a window and glanced out furtively.

"Now you *are* being paranoid. You're safe in the palace, surrounded by guards and powershapers. There is no way he can get to you." Dianah turned to Brendon in exasperation.

"Brendon, I think we should go. No point talking to him when he's like this."

"Like what?" Alexander turned around before Dianah responded. "I can see clearly now. If what you say true, how did he get here?" Alex answered straight away. "Obviously in another time-machine! That device we're looking for is the key. I know it. Did we get it yet, or do I need to send the guards out and turn the city upside-down?"

"Right here." Brendon showed it to him, pulling it from a pocket. "It was brought straight to the front gates by a Taker earlier this afternoon."

"What are you doing with it?" Alexander asked, immediately suspicious.

"That's why we went to see David in the first place," Brendon replied. "I used it to ask David about it. It helped focus my questions."

"What is it exactly?" Alex put his hand out to hold it. "What did he say?"

"It's not what he said, it's what he thought about when I posed the questions to him." Brendon handed him the remote. "This remote allows access into the ship, which is currently invisible. With his stealth tech."

"What else?" Alex asked impatiently, looking at the device.

"I now know where the new time-machine is, and how to use it."

"Then we can go home!" Alex almost jumped for joy. "And leave that upstart marooned here. Let's see if he likes living in the dark ages for a century."

"Getting home is easy, it's staying alive that's the problem."

"Why? What problem?"

Dianah frowned at him. "You may recall we left under unfavourable circumstances."

"Nothing we can't handle now." Alexander waved his hand dismissively as his mind worked feverishly. "I have several dozen powershapers at my disposal, as well as an amassed army." He paced again, slower, more thoughtful. "We can forget about the Reenat royal household. Now we have the time-machine, we can finish off Nicholai and take over the tower as we originally planned. Once we have that under control, who's to stop us from expanding?"

"I don't think it will be that easy," Brendon stated.

"How can they stop magic? Our shapers pop in, blast away – or whatever they do – then pop out of harm's way." Alex was back at the window. "I've been watching them at the training grounds. Some of the things they can do are amazing; flying, disappearing, fire and lightning. The right combination could decimate any opposition armed with tower tech. With this ship, we can always come back for more troops."

"Why would you want to do this?"

"Why? Why? To have control but far better than what we could have had here. To be in charge. We can go home!" He repeated. "I no longer need to concern myself with Reenat, or any of Athglenn. And, Dianah, *you* will be able to carry out whatever genetic experiments you want. No one could stop you."

"What period would you like to go? I gather you no longer want 50 years in our future?"

"No. Can you do a month or two after we left? That'll be enough for them to drop their guard – thinking we were long gone." Alex went to his drinks cabinet and poured three glasses. After handing them theirs, he fetched his. "To the future, and our success." He sculled his drink. "How soon can we leave? Do you need to go over it for practice?"

"No. David's thoughts on it were quite detailed. Not too different from the first time." Brendon raised his glass. "To the *Sundancer*!"

"*Sundancer*?" Alex asked, pouring another celebratory drink.

"It's what David's calling it. He landed a few miles up the road. We should be able to leave whenever you want. I've seen it in his mind. We could take about ten, maybe fifteen, but they'll all have to stand in the corridors; there's only bunks for six. More I guess, if we really squeezed them in."

"I'm glad we're not sleeping in it," Dianah laughed.

"You recall I have a shaper that can shrink things," Alex said.

"Ah yes, Olekk, isn't it? Your First Mage?" Dianah asked.

Alex nodded.

"Well, we'll see what he can accomplish," Brendon said. His wristband clanked on the console. He pushed it further up his forearm, pulling his sleeve over it, briefly thinking of when Olekk gifted it to him.

The First Mage had approached him after overhearing one of the many loud and prolonged disagreements with Zander. Over the weeks of working with each other, he and the First Mage struck a rapport, both respecting each other's abilities. 'My Lord Brendon,' he had said. 'I'm sure you have good reasons for this continued relationship with Lord Zander. It is beyond my understanding, but I have dealt with rulers of a similar demeanour. Please take this.' Olekk handed him the blue, engraved wristband. 'If Lord Zander is on one of his rants, run your fingers over the runes and you will vanish – unseen – though you will still be heard.'

"Brendon! Wake up!" Alexander was glaring at him. "How long will it take?"

"Overall, the trip should take about half-an-hour," Brendon replied after clearing his throat.

"Thirty minutes? It's so quick! I can't believe it. Where's David now?"

"We left him at the temple. The Watchers have him under guard."

"I want to see him. I want him to know who bested him, and that it will be *me* leaving him here to rot until this world burns."

"We told him," Dianah lied. The time temple had creeped her out. "I think we should leave as soon as possible."

"There's more good news," Brendon added. "When we were returning, we came across guards who told us strangers were brought in. From their description, it looks like David brought some friends with him. They're now being made uncomfortable in the cells below. With them missing, he'll be too concerned looking for them to worry about us."

"That's even more fitting. He can rot here along with the unfortunates he calls friends." Alexander drained his glass. "Let's make ready to leave this swamp, finally."

18

PALACE REVISITED

LEONIE BROUGHT DAVID BACK TO THE *LAST RESORT*. WHEN THEY landed on the street, a couple of young surprised fisherman walked away quickly.

"I don't know about you, but I'm famished. We can let the others sleep in while we get some breakfast."

"Sounds good to me." David nodded.

Quickly padding up to the entrance, the clinking of plates and cutlery in the dining room reached her ears. Entering the large dining room, Leonie saw two waitresses setting out the tables. She heard other voices in the kitchen out the back and the smell of freshly-baked bread wafting past her nose made her mouth water.

Leonie and David walked over to a table by the window and sat down. As it was only dawn, they were the first ones here for breakfast.

"I hope we aren't too early," she spoke to the nearest waitress. "The smell of cooking is too tantalising."

"Not at all ma'am," one of the girls replied, weaving her way through the array of tables. "Good morning."

David smiled as she dug out a note pad and pencil.

After a quick study of the menu, they ordered breakfast then watched the activity outside while waiting. Being close to the waterfront, many workers were moving barrels and other crates around the wharf or onto the berthed ships, either by hand or davit, depending on size and weight.

Breakfast arrived in good time. David enthusiastically spoke about some of the ideas he now had, based on the information Tieru shared. The terminology and planned experiments made little sense to her, but Leonie had no doubts he'd accomplish his project. It also passed the time while she ate.

When finished, Leonie paid for breakfast and the pair headed back to the suite. She was ready to drag the lazy-bones out of their beds.

Defuol looked up from the front counter, surprised to see her and seeming quite annoyed, especially when he saw David accompanying her. He opened his mouth to say something, but paled at her intense, violet glare.

When Leonie reached her suite, she was surprised the door wasn't locked. She cautioned David to silence. Expecting to find Bern on the lounge, she stepped in quietly to give the wilder a scare. *Serve him right for leaving the door unlocked.*

When she found it empty, she chuckled, assuming he'd put the vacant bed to good use after all.

"Hey guys. David's here," she called out as she lit some lanterns.

"This looks quite upmarket," David commented at the décor.

Leonie went to knock on Sussah's door. There was no response, so she peeked in. The bed was empty and the sheets thrown haphazardly across the bed. A quick mind-scan indicated the other rooms were empty as well; there was no one here at all!

"This isn't right," she hissed.

"This is the *right* suite?" David asked.

She growled, physically checking all rooms. "Do you get a sense these rooms have been vacant for a while?"

"How do you mean?" he asked.

"A room has a sort of smell or feel about it when it's vacant.

I'm not getting that here, but I am getting a body odour smell that I don't recognise."

"How long were you away for?"

Leonie nodded. "Just long enough to find you. I wasn't expecting the long brainstorming session though. I should have left you there and come back—"

"You weren't to know, but something *does* feel awry."

"Look at the food." Leonie picked up the tray.

He pursed his lips at what he saw. "It's not very appetising."

"Exactly. There's slopped wine and a broken glass. I'm going back downstairs to get answers. Can you stay here?"

"Shouldn't I come too?"

"Look around, see if you can find any clues." In moments, she was sliding down the stair banister. She recognised Defuol's voice coming from the dining area. By the tone of his voice, he was not in a happy place. When Leonie padded in, she saw Defuol giving Anja an earful over some minor quibble with the cutlery.

Leonie sent him signals of another pending bladder emergency. He stopped mid-tirade, dropping the forks. He walked quickly out the back.

Anja picked up the forks and popped them into her apron pocket. She wiped her face before walking towards her to take her orders. Her eyes were red and swollen from crying.

"I've eaten already," Leonie informed the young girl. "Are you okay?"

"Just my boss doing the usual whinging." She dabbed at her eyes with the corner of her apron. "I apologise. My troubles aren't your concern, but thank you for asking."

Leonie waited until Anja had composed herself. "I was away last night. Have you seen my friends? They're not in the suite."

Anja wiped her hands and looked uneasy. She motioned with her head to follow her to a small passageway away from the kitchen and the other staff.

"They ... they were taken away last night."

"What?"

"Mr Defuol called in the constabulary and had your friends evicted. He claimed there were irregularities with the occupancy of the room."

"Did he now?" *Frag him!* Leonie's tail lashed from side to side in annoyance.

"Leonie. I'm sorry, but there was nothing I could do!"

"That's okay. I wouldn't expect you too, and he seems to have it in for you already. Thanks for letting me know." Leonie turned to head back to her room.

"I did see them being taken towards the palace, not the guardhouse," Anja called softly.

Leonie paused and nodded. When she was out of sight from anyone, she went invisible.

Defuol had just returned to the front counter looking unhappy and sweaty. As he was dealing with shuffling through some papers, she silently crept behind and floated into the back room where she'd seen the strongbox.

Originally Leonie was only going to take some of it, considering the outrageous prices charged, but after what he did to her friends and the way he treated his staff, she decided to take quite a bit more. She filled her pack.

Before Leonie left, she entered Defuol's mind again. She pictured Anja as clearly as possible; her poise, her smiling face and her courteous manner and overlaid his subconsciousness with those images. Then as she did with Rickard, she also implanted terrible visions, instilling a belief of what would happen to him if he mistreated her again.

Feeling a headache looming she withdrew from his mind, reinforced her invisibility and glided back to the suite where she told David the bad news.

"That's terrible," he said, standing up. "And you say this happened last night? I found a couple of drops of blood and there's an overturned chair in the rooms. The linen looks far more messed up than I'd expect."

"And since the lock wasn't broken, Defuol gave the guards

access," Leonie added. "Now Zander has your mum and with a head-start on whatever plans he wants to put into action."

"You're sure they're in the palace?"

"It's what I was told. I doubt he'd be taking them to the *Sundancer.*"

"How are we going to get them out?" David paced.

"We? *We* are going to do nothing. I, however, will go and find them."

"But—"

"David, believe me, if you could help, I would love it, but your genius won't help."

"Do you know where the *Skydancer* is?"

"Last I saw it was in a cavern under the palace."

"Take me there then, I'll see if I can fix it."

"With what? I don't see a toolbox or mech-droid in your pocket."

"When you first told me about the *Skydancer* – when you saw it originally – and we both realised Alex was going to steal it and end up here, you said it could be flown. It became clear to me it can't time-jump otherwise I'm sure they would've tried rather than be stuck here. With that foreknowledge, and I admit to bending one of my own rules, I secreted what spare parts I could throughout the ship in the off chance I'd find it again." He grinned. "Maybe not under *these* circumstances."

Leonie growled her unease. "I don't need to have to worry about you while I'm searching the palace."

"You think it's safe for me here? What's to stop the manager from getting *me* taken? He didn't look happy to see you at all."

"Okay," she grumbled. "I'll take you to the cavern. I only hope the ship's still there." She looked out the balcony window. The sun was now fully above the horizon. *Where is Alexander now?*

Together, they searched for anything left behind after the abduction. They found three shoes under the bed and put them in Leonie's backpack.

"I have an idea," she said. "Since I can make myself invisible,

I'm sure I can do it to you too, especially after Tieru's advice. It would make getting us both into the palace much easier. Come with me."

Standing in front of a large mirror in one of the rooms, she made herself invisible first.

"That is really ... weird," he admitted to the empty room.

"Now your turn. Put your hand out and look at the mirror," her incorporeal voice instructed.

As he did, she held it, and concentrated. It took Leonie a few tries, but after becoming a ghost form several times, he finally disappeared completely.

"That's fantastic. I can't see my reflection, but still see *me*, and I can see you now too."

"Yeah, weird as you say. Tieru tried to explain it, but who cares. It works." Leading him by the hand, she walked to the balcony and stood in front of him and crouched slightly. "You know the drill; arms over my shoulder," she instructed. She gripped them and held firm, then willed him up slowly. She rose as he did. "And away we go."

The cavern was where she remembered but with half the old cliff face missing. It was now open and exposed to the elements, more like a deep overhang than a cavern.

A light wall of bamboo had been put in place to hide the *Skydancer* from ships passing in the harbour, or prying glins'ool eyes. The interior had been cleared. All the remains of the fire that destroyed the sanctum were gone. The only evidence was the scorch marks on the walls and ceiling. *More than likely some from my fireball too.*

"I thought I destroyed this cave twenty years ago," Leonie said as she brought David quickly inside. With a little effort, she split the bamboo wall wide enough to slide through. "And looks like I hardly damaged the ship either."

"I did make sure it was resilient," David pointed out as he pushed through the bamboo staves. "Pointless having a spaceship that dents or breaks at the slightest bump."

"I reckon it was more than a slight bump, but here it is."

While Leonie went to check the stairs leading into the palace via the old library, David walked around the ship checking the exterior, especially the scratches and damage from the landing.

"How is it?" she asked upon her return.

"Hull integrity looks okay. I haven't been inside yet. If I have sufficient spares, we won't need to fly it, as long as it can jump." He walked inside and went straight to the command lounge. He took a deep breath and began activating the controls and studying the readouts.

Leonie watched on with interest, seeing the *shrine* through more knowledgeable eyes. Though now inured to modern technology, she reflected what could have happened all those years ago if only she had known its capabilities.

"Can I help?" she asked as David began removing panels underneath the console to study the internal parts. "Or I could leave you to it," Leonie said after a few minutes of silence. "There's a stairway to an old library. I'll make sure the door's secured so no one comes to disturb you while I'm off searching for everyone."

"Wait a minute." He climbed to his feet and nipped down the corridor. She followed.

At the rear of the craft, he manipulated a panel in the wall just off the floor. "Here you go." He handed her a comlink. "I'll let you know how I'm going; you do the same."

"If I can."

"One tap – bad; two taps –good."

"Why tap?" she asked. "If good, I can talk; if bad, I won't." As they walked to the entrance, she fitted the earpiece.

"Good luck; stay safe." David returned to the control centre, man on a mission.

"Right." Leonie chuckled and left him to his repairs.

Just like she remembered, the walls changed from bedrock and crystal to hewed stone as she ascended the stairs. At the top was the old library where Magda had lived. Leonie locked the door behind her and applied a small but intense stream of heat into the lock mechanism, lightly fusing its parts.

The library looked abandoned and had been for a long time going by the amount of dust. There was a trail of footprints on the floor, but they too were old. *No one's been to the ship for a while either.*

Leonie had to rack her memory for the location of the cells. When she was here to pay a visit to Niaarin she'd passed what she guessed were the corridor to the dungeons. She took a moment to reaffirm her invisibility. When she came to a corner or door, she scanned ahead for any signs of life, moving on if it was clear. In the back of her mind, because of who they were, she reckoned Sussah and everyone would be heavily guarded. *And therefore, more than likely part of a trap.*

She sensed eight minds ahead, though the thick stone walls made it unclear. Four were in the nearest room, and two each in other adjoining rooms down the corridor. None of the minds were familiar. Not all were overly alert but a couple of them felt formidable. "No doubt Alex will have some shapers on guard," she muttered.

Rounding the corner, she noticed an aura halfway along the dim passage. *A trap of some description?* She also saw six individuals around a table in a chamber at the end of the passage. Like the other areas she had passed, this chamber was illuminated by torches. The stone passage continued beyond.

Leonie rescanned, but strangely still detected only four minds in the first chamber. "Either there's a pair of guards wearing a device, or we have a couple of illios," she hissed softly.

But what to do about the trap? She stepped closely to it and concentrated, deciding it would alert them to her presence if it was breached. She concentrated on one mind at a time in the first room. They had the *feel* of men-at-arms, not shapers.

Going back to work on the first one, she thought about Dianah, Brendon and Zander. His response was unclear, but she got the impression they had all left with many others, power-shapers and armed men. Discouraged by this turn of events, she returned to the task at hand and encouraged him to visualise the others as his enemies.

He drew his sword. The others drew theirs, alert now, and queried him on what he heard. When he turned his attack on them, one went down with a large cut to his neck and shoulder, before the others turned to defend themselves.

They started yelling and grunting with the effort. Armed men fighting each other in a confined space become disorderly and bloody quickly. When her man went down, she withdrew her mind and waited. Everyone was wounded and breathing heavily with the exertion, except those with the minds she couldn't read. They all watched each other warily. The downed guards weren't dead, but they were no longer a threat to anyone.

She considered her observations from that experiment; the trap was still dormant and therefore only a physical presence would set it off – not ethereal or power-related; she also ascertained the fighting abilities of the remaining guards, and confirmed two were illios in human form.

Illios regenerated quickly. Hitting with swords or clubs did nothing to them as they'd reshape straight away. She also knew from Feiron's adventures, they were susceptible to heat and cold, but only intense levels after a lengthy period of time.

She didn't know how they reacted to electricity and considered that as a possible means of attack. Concentrating to draw in more power, she sent a bolt directly at one of the shapechangers.

It lost its shape immediately, and formed a grey oozing mass on the floor. The two upright guards jumped back from the spreading puddle, but one looked to where the bolt had come from.

Pausing long enough to draw more power, she cast a fireball as the guard started running at her, yelling. The fireball hit him squarely in the chest, throwing him back into the room. It killed him outright, but his bulk in the confined passageway blocked the full effect in the room behind.

Following in its wake, she burst in, her fists slamming the other guard back into the wall. The impact jolted her arms and shoulders, but she was in a far better condition than him. Sensing movement behind, she ducked and rolled as a sword swung past her head.

Right, so I lose invisibility when I attack, she realised.

The remaining illios formed more limbs as it now attacked with three swords. There was no style or finesse, but three whirling and jabbing blades would do sufficient damage regardless of technique.

With barely time to think, she zapped it with what she could muster in the few seconds. It was enough to stop the blades momentarily and she used the opportunity to zoom further into the dungeon.

Two doors opened simultaneously. One before her and one behind.

Frack! She stopped midway and strived for invisibility, claws out, trying to suck in air quietly and watched warily.

The illios guard dragged the swords with it as it slowly regained the multi-limbed form. From the room she had passed, two figures appeared. Both were female – one human, the other a rrell.

Leonie was concerned about the rrell, knowing feline eyesight and reflexes were as good as her own. *But can she see auras or invisibility? I'll find out soon enough.*

The rrell and human first looked down the corridor to the guard room, but seeing the illios guard heading their way, they turned in her direction.

And looked past her to the figures emerging from the other room. Here Leonie counted three figures. Since her mind-scan only indicated two entities, one was also an illios. All were robed, which didn't help. *How is an illios a powershaper? Does it have a device?*

Uncomfortable with being in the middle of these groups, she needed to come up with a way of getting past them. The width of the corridor would be a tight squeeze but, looking at the ceiling, there just might be enough room.

Leonie rose, flattening herself against the roof and moved

further along, deeper into the dungeon – dreading the moment someone spotted her.

As luck would have it, no one did. She moved cautiously over the heads of the last three and paused by the single torch at the top of the next set of stairs to look behind her to see if she was followed. The group of three moved to join the others, talking in low voices. No alarm was raised.

Gliding down to the next level, the foul air confirmed her suspicions of the cells being in this location. Scanning ahead for other minds, she continued a bit faster.

There were several cells along this dimly lit section, all quite small and empty. Another set of stairs down surprised her. *Why the need for so many cells?*

The cells below were larger, and she detected familiar minds by the time she was halfway down the stairs. Leonie sped up. Arriving at the barred door, she looked in before she said anything. All four were sharing the same cell.

"Hello everyone," she said softly.

Instantly they all looked up.

"Leonie?" Lerry said.

"Shh. Yes." She started working on the lock.

"Where are you?" he whispered coming up to the door.

"Oops. Here." She suddenly appeared in front of him.

He stepped back in surprise, knocking heads with Harrond who had also come to look.

As Leonie worked on the lock, she heard talking. "Keep it down."

"It's not us," Lerry said softly.

Leonie looked up momentarily. "Frack! Someone's coming." She concentrated on the lock, working as fast as possible before there was a snip of the mechanism. "Move back." She pushed open the door, hearing several boots coming down the stairs.

Before anyone in the cells could do or say anything, Leonie cut them off. "Listen," she whispered. "You'll have to trust me on this. Everyone move back against the wall and be utterly quiet, and put your hand on my shoulder or arms. We're all going invisible."

"Can you do that?" Bern asked in a soft rumble as he placed his hand on her shoulder.

"Pretty sure. Be still." Leonie concentrated like she did when she made David invisible, hoping she got the technique right and was able to do all of them. If not, then go to plan B. *Whatever that is.*

More torchlight illuminated the corridor, getting brighter. The voices and boots got louder. Suddenly the voices became shouts and the boots came running. A torch flared at the open door as two bodies filled the doorway. Some of the hands on her arm tightened, as did the smaller hand in her paw. There was a sharp intake of breath.

Leonie hoped it wasn't heard over the noise the guards were making.

"Is this the right cell?" asked one robed figure.

"First on the left. Definitely."

"It's empty!" The one carrying the torch stepped in waving it about to brighten every corner. "Where in the eight hells are they?"

If they both come in and move about, it could get cramped. Leonie waited nervously.

"Either someone stuffed up or they've escaped!"

"How could they escape? Where could they go? There's only one exit and no one passed us."

"I don't bloody know, do I?"

"Maybe that fight we heard before was them *escaping* – or being helped to escape – and *not* entering as we first suspected?"

"I think that damn illios has some explaining to do!" The torch bearer motioned for his companion to leave the cell. "You can never trust those damn blobs," he said as they ran back up the stairs.

Leonie waited for the footsteps to fade before relaxing. "Okay. We're safe for a few minutes."

"How did you do that?" Lerry asked.

"Lucky, I guess. No time to explain. David is fixing the *Skydancer–*"

"It's here?" Bern asked.

"You found David?" Sussah gasped.

She nodded, forgetting how dark it was for them. "Yes. For now, we'll give them a few minutes to panic and spread the search throughout the palace, then we will make good our escape."

Sussah hugged her. "We– I was so worried."

"All good now," Leonie reassured her. She briefly told them about her search for David. "The damn Watchers had him, but he's fine. I should ask if everyone here's alright?" She noticed everyone's bruised and blood-smeared faces. "What's happened? Did they question you?"

"They wanted to know where David and you were," Bern said. "Asked us about our weird clothes and where we were from, but we didn't tell them anything, really. I said we didn't know where you and David were – which was true – all we told them was we recently arrived from Qelay for the festival."

"They roughed us up, but we all kept to the same story, then they left us alone here," Harrond finished.

"They didn't know about David? Maybe there are different factions at work here?" she considered aloud.

Lerry filled her in on their version of events. "That old concierge came to speak with you. He was pretty pissed you weren't there. A couple of hours later, these soldiers came up and forced us out."

"There was this horrible, smelly wagon," Sussah added. "They pushed us all in. We had a bumpy ride. Then we were told to climb out and get inside some bamboo cage."

"Was that the elevator?" Leonie asked.

Sussah nodded. "And then they dragged us here."

"They didn't push us too hard for any answers, though," Bern said. "Do you think this is a trap to lure you here?"

"Maybe. It doesn't matter." She then told them her plan. "Now we know we can go invisible when we need to. I should be able to detect anyone ahead, and if so, we will keep silent and wait. Just like we did a few minutes ago."

"Should we go now?"

"Soon. I'm counting on them checking the nearest areas first and moving further away. I want the least number of guards to worry about." She activated her comlink. "Tap, tap." She winked at Sussah's surprised look.

"You can speak with him?" she asked.

Leonie nodded, waiting for a reply.

"Leonie?" She heard after a pause, putting the crackling down to interference from the bedrock surrounding them.

"I've found them. They're okay, but we're heading out of the cells in a minute. How about you?"

"It'll take too long to fix, but we can fly."

"I'll let you know how we go. Out." She turned to the others. "Stay close and be as quiet as you can. Su, you're going to see some nasty stuff up there," Leonie warned.

"I'm a big girl now."

"I never doubted it." She smiled at Harrond before she looked outside. The passage was clear. She waved them to follow and padded upstairs, then silently flew ahead to the next stairs, scanning the area while she waited for them to catch up.

Sensing no threat, she glided up the stairs, stopping at the first door to visually check. If there was an illios here, this is the only way she'd know for sure. The room was empty. She moved on and checked the second room. Empty. Leonie turned and waved for her retinue to come up to her.

"Okay," she whispered. "It's still clear, but this is where it got a bit lively earlier. Watch your footing, it could get slippery." The puddled illios was still there. *Taking a while to regenerate*, she thought.

"What's that?" Sussah whispered trying not to step into the muck.

"I don't know," Leonie lied. "They must have spilt something."

"It's a lot of something," Sussah replied, eyeing the substance dubiously.

Ascending the stairs, Leonie heard a noise ahead. Her group came to a junction; there were noises from both directions. She tried to scan, but the source was too far away, with too much rock in between.

"Which way do we go?" Lerry whispered.

"We're going left, but we'll wait; sounds like there's people down there."

"*Leonie?*" she heard on the comlink. The signal was clearer now.

"Yes, David? Everyone is safe with me."

"*They're trying to come through the library door.*"

"Are they now?" she answered.

"*Stay there. Probably too dangerous to risk anything while they're here.*"

"What are you going to do?" she asked him.

"*I'll think of someth–*" The link went dead after a lot of crackling. At the same time, they all heard a soft explosion.

"That can't be good," Leonie said. "Stay here." She raced off before they could reply. It wasn't long before she saw wisps of smoke coming through the doorway to the old library.

When she entered, she saw some of the bookcases had toppled and a few books were charred. Further back, the door to the cavern was hanging ajar on one hinge. There was no one else in here, and more yelling coming from below.

As she approached the door cautiously, she heard running footsteps behind her. Turning and preparing for an attack, Harrond was dragging Sussah, and Lerry was helping Bern.

"What happened?"

"We weren't the only ones to hear the noise. We couldn't stay where we were, so here we are."

"Bern?"

"Shot in the back. I think it's a crossbow bolt."

"Get behind me!" She moved behind an overturned desk. "How many?" she asked, quickly checking on Bern's injury as he slumped to the floor with a groan. Blood soaked his lower back and trickled down his thigh. Lerry made sure he rolled the wilder onto his side.

The bolt was deep. It looked bad. *Frack.*

"Can't be sure, eight or ten. They filled the corridor," Lerry panted. "This oaf is heavy!"

Leonie told them the news. "There's some downstairs, but not sure how many though. At least one's a powershaper." She thought fast. "I can jam that door, at least."

"And we're stuck in the middle," Harrond said as she moved away.

Closer to the door she heard running boots, Leonie willed the far door shut, then willed several bookcases across to block it. She laid them flat and stacked them on top of one another. She started to feel weary with the effort.

Almost immediately the banging start. Racing back to the others, she knelt by Bern.

"Harrond, watch that stairway; Lerry, watch the door." Thankfully, Bern was unconscious. She took a few deep breaths and drew what power she could, used it to help pull the bolt out, then immediately started trying to heal Bern before he lost too much more blood. *I wish I had more of those healing lessons in Reenat.* She felt dizzy.

"They're coming through." Lerry was barely heard over the sound of splintering wood.

"And someone's coming up the stairs," Harrond warned.

Frack! She stopped the bleeding, but Bern was still injured. "Everyone behind me and get down, take cover!" Her head was aching and the library was going out of focus as she drew in power but there was little to be found. *Fracking skyland,* she realised.

The door burst open. Bookcases were shoved to the side by powerful forces.

With little time to do much else, Leonie fire-balled the library entrance before she blacked out.

19

TOWER UPRISING

"When are we?" Alexander looked through the screen. Earth slowly rotated ten thousand kilometres below. From this distance, the whole continent of Australia was visible, along with New Zealand and Papua New Guinea.

There was a gasp from the crowd behind them. A dozen powershapers, the most powerful and influential of the army Alex could amass, all insisted on being in the control room. The many dozens of lesser shapers and armed militia – all in stasis to prevent them from touching anything – were crammed in the corridors and other compartments throughout the vessel.

"According to the readout, the year is 2351," Brendon said. "One month after our escape."

Alexander looked smug. "I can't wait to see the look on Nicholai's face when he sees us returned to the tower."

"Are you still planning on killing him?" Dianah asked. "It might be only a month here, but after all this time, you haven't reconsidered?"

"Oh, I am ... *after* I see his face. This time I'll make sure it isn't a damn clone either. Too bad David couldn't join him, but knowing he's stuck on a dying world is satisfying."

"This could actually work. We have the element of surprise, and several dozen powershapers to back us," Dianah said. "Unbelievable to think of the many decades marooned on Yarnik that so little time has passed here. I should still be able to recover a lot of my research. Thanks, Brendon."

"It's the least I could do." Brendon touched her face.

"Frack! Get a room you two. As soon as we get in, we'll deal with the Prime and take control first, then you can worry about your precious research. Brendon, get us down there."

Brendon manipulated the control panel. The ship swiftly descended through the atmosphere; first Papua New Guinea and then New Zealand disappeared from view as the Australian coastline rushed towards them.

"Aren't we coming in too fast?" Alexander watched nervously.

"We're fine. This is an amazing ship. A far cry from the *Skydancer*."

"This is your world?" one of the closer shapers asked, looking wide-eyed at the screen.

Alexander turned to his First Mage. "You're human, Olekk; this is the world of your ancestors too."

"I heard rumours ... but who believes sages?" Olekk shrugged, mesmerised by what he saw on the screen. His many companions, those that could see the vid screen, murmured their amazement.

"And we can go back home when we want to?" another shaper asked from the back.

"To Yarnik? Once the job you've all been paid for is completed, then we will take you back," Alexander paused. "Though why you would want to is beyond me. Your world will be unliveable in a matter of years. There's no future there. This is your future where you can bring your family."

More dark mutterings were heard, but no one protested the truth of his words.

"What are your orders, Lord Zander," the First Mage asked.

"With your aid, we will find and kill the man that exiled us with his false charges and accusations. We will land here." Alexander pointed towards the tower as it quickly came into view. "This area is like a port, but for flying vessels, not ships," he explained to the others. "If we're quick, we should find him in his offices two levels down.

"Once that's done and I have control, you and your men are free to do as you wish; take prisoners, do as you see fit to sate your needs. As long as it doesn't jeopardise my aims," he warned.

The other men cheered up at these words, nudging each other with their certain success.

With his stolen knowledge of the controls, it was easy enough for Brendon to reduce the ship's velocity. He adjusted the tau-field so it wouldn't affect the pad and manoeuvred between two waiting shuttles so the ramp was facing the terminal.

There was the faintest of jolts as the landing gear hit the pad.

Everyone started getting nervous when they saw people walking around the terminal.

"Relax, they cannot see us yet. We are still invisible," Brendon reassured them, though he licked his lips nervously.

"Olekk, we'll need shapers to take control of the area. While I'm sure our armed men are capable in what they do, they won't be able to compete with the weapons they'll soon face."

Alex cleared his throat. "This button will lower the ramp. Make sure whoever you send out there knows not to touch the white wall they will see. When they are ready, I'll deactivate it completely, and then your men can have at it. We'll make the terminal our bridgehead. Getting down to the Prime's office and residence on level eighteen is our priority, but we'll need to put men on each floor as we go to make sure we aren't attacked from behind. Once your men are dispersed, Brendon will return to Delta to collect the rest of the men."

"Just as we discussed before we left." Olekk nodded. "I will organise it now, but it will take a while. Those in stasis will need a few minutes to recover, and it will also take some time for them to revert to their normal size."

"How long? Why the delay?" Alexander looked away from the display, clearly annoyed.

"My Lord, this spell is still experimental. You wanted something done as soon as possible; this is it. The recipients were reduced in size. It will take time for them to readjust to normality."

"Just get it done."

"As you wish." The tall First Mage turned and wriggled his way through the crowd.

"Since they can't see us, what happens if another aircraft or shuttle tries to land in what they think is a vacant spot?" Dianah asked.

"I'm not certain, but I think it'll hit the energy field surrounding us and stop before the *Sundancer's* hull is touched. It distorts time in some way according to David's memories. We *shouldn't* feel a thing."

"Let's hope you're right. Couldn't we have landed on the roof instead? It's a large flat area." She pointed.

"We'd lose the element of surprise. Imagine how long it would take to get everyone down to the pad. This way we're right on their front door, and ready to hit them unawares," Alexander pointed out. "We'll deal with whatever happens when it happens. Let's not panic about nothing. Once we control the upper level, we can bring more in."

Dianah let it slide; no point arguing with him. A cam near the entrance ramp showed the First Mage proceeding with his orders.

The shimmering tau-field extended like a shawl beyond the hull surface to incorporate the landing gear. The condensed mass of men was moved outside so they could be enlarged to normal size. The camouflaged area under the curved hull was larger than the corridors or rooms. It was eerily silent.

Halfway through the procedure, the main console started beeping softly.

"What's that?" Alexander asked Brendon who was at the controls instantly.

"It looks like your nothing is about to arrive."

"What? A shuttle?"

"No, but a flyer is on approach." Brendon pointed to the blip on the screen.

"We can't move; our men are on the pad outside," Alexander stepped closer to the console, made harder by the other shapers also trying to see.

They started muttering among themselves.

"I hope you're right about this energy field," Dianah said as she watched the screen in trepidation.

The approaching flyer, oblivious to the large bulk of the *Sundancer* blocking their path, slowed on its optimum approach trajectory. The instant the underside of the flyer made contact, it started disintegrating; shrapnel flew in all directions. The pilot reacted incredibly swiftly. The momentum slowed sufficiently to save the flyer from immediate destruction, but it was now out of control. The engines smoked as the flyer careened towards the rooftop. It crashed, sliding along the expanse of plascrete, sparks and flames erupting as it took out communications towers along with several air exhaust ducts.

"Frack it!" Alex cursed.

The various cams showed the debris strewn over the pad and roof. Some of the shrapnel hit the shuttles on the pad, damaging fuselage and a wing. TowerPol and other personnel ran out; some hit the invisible tau-field and bounced back, collapsing in a writhing heap.

"Time to panic now?" Dianah said snidely.

Outside, the on-oncoming rush of people stopped in confusion. The TowerPol officers now hesitantly approached, using their weapons as a prod. When they encountered the invisible barrier, the tip of their rifles flared and disintegrated.

"It reacts to metal differently than flesh," a shaper behind Dianah observed.

In time, the cautious officers established a perimeter a few metres back from where their comrades had fallen. Some were already being treated. On the roof, personnel were emerging from stairways to render aid to the downed craft.

"What are your plans now?" Olekk called from along the corridor. "The men are ready to go."

"Tell him to—" Alexander started to yell. With a sigh, he pushed his way through the crowd and along the corridor. "Olekk," he called from the ramp. "There are armed troops along this side of the barrier." His eyes scanned the shimmering white haze with uncertainty. "We'll drop the barrier. Tell your men to deal with them the best way they can. We need to do this quickly."

Olekk nodded and began issuing orders. "Ready, my lord."

"Drop the wall!" Alexander called back down the corridor to Brendon.

Outside, the shimmering faded then disappeared completely.

The tower shuttle terminal was directly in front of them, as were the dozens of stupefied troops and personnel.

The shapers and armed men went to work immediately. Depending on the particular expertise of the powershaper, some men dropped unconscious, some burst into flame or were frozen. Others were lifted and thrown over the side, or simply blown over by strong gusts of wind. Olekk strode back inside the ship to begin the process of bringing out more of his miniaturised army. Time was of the essence if there was any hope of success.

As the surprised people dropped, the armed men rushed in, striking with their swords or clubs. Several men ran inside the building, chasing survivors. Within a couple of minutes, the invaders were the only living people on the pad.

At a command from Alexander, the rest of the attackers – shapers and armed militia – rushed inside the terminal to deal with whatever they found. He followed at a safe distance.

The engines of the two awaiting shuttles increased in volume as they were preparing to depart.

"Can anyone stop them?" he yelled. Either busy with their

own survival or no one heard him over all the noise, the shuttles took off a few minutes apart.

"Frag you all!" Alexander waved his fists at the dwindling craft; one turning to the north and one flying south. He turned to the *Sundancer*. "Maybe Brendon—"

The *Sundancer* vanished.

20

SKYHOME

"Where are we?" Leonie asked weakly from the lounge. As she asked, her eyes focused on the control panel of the *Skydancer*.

David swivelled around in the chair. "Keep still, Leonie, and rest. I've taken us out of the city. We're on a swampy clearing to the north of Delta. It's where I landed the *Sundancer*."

"I gather it's gone then?" Leonie asked.

David nodded. "We couldn't land here if it was."

"Any idea when they left?"

"Not long, but I can't say for certain. There were many footprints, which the swamp hadn't reclaimed, given the short timeframe."

"How convenient! Do you think he's gone back to the tower?"

"It's the most logical option for the same reason why we visited Delta in the first place. After twenty years of being away, the first thing mum wanted to do was to catch up with those she left behind. So yes, if I was them, I'd be wanting to go back to what I knew; what I was most comfortable with – or to finish the job – especially if I had help."

"Don't they realise they're wanted people back there?" She rolled to a more comfortable position.

"I have no doubt they remembered, hence the hired help."

"How's Bern?" she asked as her last memories came back. "How did I get here? How did *we* get here?"

"Looks like someone gets to save you for a change. It's a good feeling."

"You had one of those hidden too?" she asked, seeing the rifle on the console behind him.

"It's quite surprising how many nooks and crannies one can find if there's a need."

"In another life, I'd be proud of your smuggling abilities."

Sussah came into the room and knelt beside her, resting a hand on Leonie's shoulder. "I was so worried," she wept in elation. The others surrounded her too, relief showing on their faces.

"I'm okay, Su." Leonie patted her hand. "Tell me what happened?"

"As usual, you over did it, again," Lerry admonished, but there was no heat in his words.

"Where's Bern? How is he?" she asked again.

"He's recovering nicely on the medicomp, and that's where you're going soon as he's finished."

"You probably saved his life with your healing," Harrond told her.

"That's generally the plan." Leonie lay back.

"How did you get shot in the back?" Susah asked. "There was no one near you to shoot."

"I transferred his wound to me," Leonie explained. "I can heal faster."

"That's just stupid." Sussah wiped her face.

"It worked. We're both alive." She looked around. "And we're all safe. What happened ... after?" she repeated the question.

"David had to save us this time." Lerry recounted the details. "You incinerated half the room before you collapsed. Then David came up the stairs brandishing the rifle. He covered our escape as I took Bern, and Harrond carried you to the *Skydancer*."

"Looks like your heroics are rubbing off," David joked.

"David told us what happened at the Time temple," Harrond added. "I don't know if I'll ever get used to this place; aliens everywhere, people casting fireballs, people mucking around with time—"

"Yet people making time-machines, people using pulse rifles or spaceships doesn't faze you?" Leonie asked.

"That's different. That's technology."

"And magic is *their* version of technology." Leonie slowly stood up. "I'm feeling a bit peckish. I don't suppose there's any food on board? Or water?"

"Afraid not," David said. "But you need to relax."

"I am relaxed. What I need is to walk around a bit and see Bern. Is my pack in the medbay?"

"It is," David affirmed, following Leonie.

Harrond helped Sussah stand and Lerry led the way to the medbay. "It took all four of us to get him up there," Lerry pointed out.

Bern looked comfortable, even though the medicomp couldn't hold all of him. To fit his left arm into the unit, he was hanging over one side so his right arm had to be folded over his stomach to stop it from hanging down.

David stepped passed and checked the monitors. "He should be up and about in an hour or so," he said.

"I'll probably have healed myself by then. Look, we need to get back to the tower," she said. "If Alexander has gone back there with powershapers and armed men, I think he's going to try to cause trouble, or take over the tower. He's got at least a day's head-start."

"How did you find this out?" Sussah asked.

"I sort of read it in one of the guards' minds. Are we able to get out of here now?"

"Sure can. We can't jump, but I'll get us airborne and headed west to Skyhome." David left them, heading straight to the control room.

Leonie grabbed her backpack and slowly followed David.

"Did they tell you what happened to them after the fishing boat incident?" she asked. Back in the control room, she settled back on the lounge with a sigh.

"We told him what we knew. It's all quite confusing and convoluted," Lerry said behind her.

He and Harrond sat in the arm chairs and Sussah joined her on the lounge.

"We should be arriving at Skyhome in two and a half hours," David informed them.

"Don't run into any skylands. There's a lot more than I realised, but some are very small and are much higher up." Leonie reached into her backpack. She pulled out the flask and had a quick drink before offering it around to the others. Then she grabbed a nutri-bar and told them her version of what happened.

"As you know, I suspected the Watchers of being involved. I went to their new temple on the plaza. I didn't know for sure if David was there, but seeing Brendon and Dianah leaving confirmed it."

Sussah looked horrified. "Why did those two want to see him?"

"And how did they know where *we* were?" Harrond asked.

"Why, is because Brendon can only mind-read David with skin contact – and only then because ..." Leonie continued quickly away from the recent news David and Brendon were brothers. "As to how they knew; there are many ways to spy in Delta." Leonie explained about the Watcher spy network around the city. "And the Watchers have been helping Zander and company for centuries for their own ends."

"Brendon had my remote with him," David said. "How did he know about that? It was in my pocket and not in plain view."

"I reckon you were pick-pocketed." Leonie recounted her visit to the Takers earlier. "They had a sketch of something definitely tower tech and a big reward was posted for whoever brought it in. I didn't even know you were in town at that point."

David continued, "As said, Brendon's telepathy on me is only activated with physical contact. I tried to keep my mind occupied to deflect the bulk of his questions. My presence here obviously means another ship. He now knows everything about the *Sundancer* and how to use it. Brendon also took my wristband."

"Wristband?" Leonie asked.

"To get into the *Sundancer* through the tau-field." David explained the significance of the wristbands. "But once deactivated anyone can get on board."

Lerry showed her his wristband. "We've all still got ours."

"They didn't search you very well when those guards grabbed you," Leonie scoffed.

"They didn't search at all. Just dragged us to those horrible cells and left us there," Sussah said.

"And asked their questions," Harrond added.

"One would think it was a trap," Leonie considered. "Did Brendon know about us?"

David shrugged. "I can't be certain. Neither he nor Dianah asked about any of you specifically, so you weren't in my thoughts."

"Well, we know the Watchers knew, but as Tieru explained, they have their own agenda. Maybe Brendon only found out when Defuol evicted you?"

By the time they arrived at Skyhome, Bern was up and about and Leonie had finished her course of treatment on the medicomp, though the hug of appreciation from Bern for saving his life threatened to put her back on it.

David landed the *Skydancer* on the grassy field between the community accommodation and the portal. Rhiannon stood alone. A look of relief crossed her face when Leonie walked through the exit followed by the others.

The seer turned and waved to the other wilders who emerged from hiding.

"We were unsure who was flying." She stepped forward to

greet Leonie. "Last we saw the rest of you was in the *Sundancer*." She was soon joined by the many wilders in greeting them.

"I caught up with this lot in Delta," Leonie explained. "It's a long story, and I'm sure they can tell you all about it. Right now, I need to get to the tower urgently." As she moved off, the agtechs started to follow. "Best if you stay here. Explain what's happened so far. I just want to see if it's safe or not, and I can look after myself if I don't have others to worry about."

"We can bring pulse rifles," Lerry argued.

"I know and if the time comes, we might need them, but let me check first before we commit ourselves. Please."

"I'll need to come too if I'm going to design a portal sensor," David stated.

Leonie turned to David. "Give me a few minutes. If SciCorps is safe, I'll let you all know." She flew off and through the portal before they could object.

A quick flit around the labs showed no sign of intrusion and the corridor cams were clear. The news vids though were a different story. Reports of bloody violence, fires and explosions coming from the Prime's office were prominent. Security forces were called in, as well as reinforcements from the lower levels. All of White Zone was in lockdown. It was only a matter of time before the mayhem spread to the tower's lower levels.

The vid showed drone footage, both internal and external, of smoke-filled corridors and billowing out of broken windows. There was also footage of the rooftop where a wrecked flyer was smouldering, and a large spherical spaceship took up half the shuttle pad. It had the same dull external appearance of the *Skydancer*.

"Interesting," she muttered. Leonie scribbled a note on a pad and tossed it through the portal.

'Safe to come through, but stay in the labs for now. Don't look for me.'

As the drone zoomed in, text played across the screen. 'Alien craft lands at shuttle terminal causing a crash. Dozens of personnel massacred.' Many bodies lay between the ship and the terminal. There was some wreckage of a flyer strewn on the pad, but the bulk of the fuselage was smoking on the roof.

Leonie quickly made her way to the dock area, partially opened the door leading outside and did a quick circuit of the tower. There were quite a few damaged areas – large broken windows with smoke swirling away with the late afternoon breeze; the sun was touching the western horizon.

Descending to the most damaged section, she hovered outside a window with a large hole taking out most of the thick, triple glazing. She waited and listened to the unmistakable sounds of energy weapons discharging, followed by explosions. Leonie also felt power being drawn in, which confirmed what she'd scanned about shapers being recruited to Alexander's cause.

Once inside and keeping low to the floor to avoid most of the smoke, she flew towards the noise. Down a long corridor, she saw several shapers throwing fireballs over a balcony, with energy pulses and bullets returning seconds later.

Going invisible, she drifted closer. Four shapers in all. Regardless of how she felt about the security forces, these shapers were here at Alex's behest and they were no friends of hers. Drawing in power, she gave the shapers the equivalent of an EMP to stun them, then willed the four over the railing. She doubted the security could hold them even if they managed to capture them.

Having confirmed Alex must have returned here with a group of shapers, Leonie turned to leave. A barrage of energy pulses and bullets sprayed the wall above her as she came under fire from below.

"Fracking security dimwits!" Leonie ducked, went invisible and quickly returned to SciCorps. She found David and the agtechs now gathered around the vid-screen. As she approached, a snippet of vid replay showed four robed individuals fall over a railing. Two plummeted the eighteen floors to the bottom, but two recovered in time and slowed their fall before flying away.

"Your doing?" Lerry asked.

"I confess," Leonie replied.

"They'll know you're here now too once they see that." Harrond pointed to the screen as the scene changed to an outside shot. On the screen was a view of the drone recording the fires from outside. Leonie was clearly seen flying around the building.

"I better stay invisible as much as I can then." Her tail lashed side to side in annoyance. She turned to the scientist. "David, is the *Sundancer* a large, round spaceship?"

"A sphere, yes."

"It's up at the shuttle dock. Want me to get you up there so you can bring it here? Let's get it away from them so they can't escape. You can make it disappear, yeah?"

"I can. Good idea, but my pad isn't large enough. We'll have to land it on the ground."

"You sure?"

"Anywhere else could risk someone flying into it. A couple of kilometres from the tower base should be suitable."

"Fair enough. I'll have to fly you back. We can go whenever you're ready."

"Then we better have a bracelet each." He turned to Lerry and Harrond, who slipped theirs off.

"Let's go," Leonie said, examining the bracelet.

"What about us?" Harrond asked.

"Too dangerous to take all of you, and we're several thousand metres up. Maybe stay here and keep note of what's happening. I don't know how many shapers Alex has, or how many soldiers."

"Who are they after?"

"I suspect Alex is trying to get rid of the Prime again so he can take control." She indicated the turmoil on the screen. "The Prime's office is on that level."

"You mean his father?" Harrond asked.

"You saw the vid earlier of the assassination attempt. He's already tried once. We shouldn't be long." Leonie turned, following David to the loading dock.

Before they went outside, she rendered them invisible and carried David up to the tower's main landing pad near the roof. There were two men-at-arms patrolling near the ramp. The pad's lights were on as night was fast approaching; the light from the terminal splashed across the base of the ship.

Toward the outer edge of the landing pad was a small amount of wreckage from the downed flyer. As they moved closer, the discoloured smears on the deck nearest the terminal turned out to be blood; lots of it. Leonie paused get a better understanding. Many people were killed as evident by the number of bloodstains – now mostly dry. The trail leading to the edge of the pad explaining what they did with the bodies.

"The moment I deal with them we'll become visible," Leonie whispered fiercely.

David tapped her. "The ramp is down," he replied softly in her ear. "How about we try to sneak on board first?"

"We can do that," she agreed reluctantly.

As they approached, three more armed men were visible within the terminal.

Taking her time and allowing for the extra bulk of David, Leonie negotiated the area between the guards and the ramp. She came in from above and followed the curved hull of the ship. She had to pause as one of the guards turned and sat on the ramp itself.

A drone buzzed around the hull and flew into her shoulder. The drone, bouncing off, took a second to reorient itself before continuing its path.

Realising their invisibility was compromised, Leonie reacted. *Was I quick enough?* Holding her breath, she waited for the alert, surprised they couldn't hear her racing heartbeat.

"Better not get caught loungin' around," one of the other guards said, pointing to one of the many drones; their tell-tale lights blinking in the darkening sky.

Cursing, the guard stood up and spat.

No one noticed. She exhaled slowly and continued. Leonie silently floated over their heads and angled inside. Not having been inside this ship before she paused at the end of the corridor.

"Where to now?" she whispered.

"Put me down." David kept in contact with her so he wouldn't become visible. He then keyed a pad on the wall. The elevator doors slid open.

Leonie kept watch out the entrance in case anyone heard anything.

"Let's go," David whispered as he entered.

She stepped backwards into the lift. The doors closed silently.

"Everything looks brand new and pristine," she said as they became visible.

"Except for their muddy boots." David quickly led her to the control centre when the elevator arrived on the next floor. After touching a few buttons, she felt a vibration through the floor. "We're now phased out – invisible – and warming up to leave."

The screen showed the panicked guards outside, looking perplexed at the now empty pad.

'Welcome back, David.' A voice came over the speakers.

"Thanks TAU. I hope they didn't damage you."

'Everything is functioning per design parameters.'

"Good to know. This is Leonie."

'Welcome, Leonie,' TAU said.

"Err. Hi." She turned to David. "Who am I talking to?"

"The ship, or more precisely the AI running the ship." He addressed the AI. "TAU, were you able to determine the number of passengers?"

'Only by estimation from the extra 4.8 tonnes of biologic mass.'

"Tonnes?"

'There were some anomalies – four masses of approximately 1.6 tonnes each, as well as twelve specific entities.'

"Any data on the biologic mass?"

'Negative.'

"What about atmospherics?"

'The percentages are now on screen. You'll note the subsequent trips differed.'

"What does all that mean?" Leonie asked, looking over his shoulder at a swag of numbers on a chart.

"Biological mass is something living. From this data, with the amount of oxygen, nitrogen and carbon-dioxide exchange, they have somehow brought approximately fifty-five people with them given an average of 85kgs each. And they did four return-trips. They must have unloaded and returned immediately each trip. It looks like there's possibly over two hundred people here."

"Is there enough room for that many people in four trips?" she asked.

"Hardly, but what gets me is these large individual masses. Did you see anything unusual other than the shaper army?"

"Nothing weighing that much." She looked around. "You've got no cams to check?"

"Something to be remedied. When we land we'll remain invisible. The bracelet will allow us to walk through the tau-field without a concern." He briefly reminded her how it worked. "It's easier than going through the portal. Ready?"

"Sure." Leonie nodded.

It took several minutes to land the ship at a suitable location amongst the tough scrub on the ground.

"TAU, remain in stealth mode until I get back." Then he added as an afterthought, "And only obey my voice commands from now on."

'Very good, David.'

Following David to the exit, Leonie went down the ramp and with only a momentary pause walked through the white wall, David close behind.

"I'm going to assume that storm will have no effect?" she pointed at the approaching wall of dust.

"If anyone was nearby and observing, they'd definitely see something unusual."

"Unlikely scenario. Hop on," she instructed.

In plenty of time to avoid the dust storm, they flew up to the SciCorps dock and joined the agtechs by the vid for an update.

"Not too much happening," Lerry reported. "Only a little bit of progress. There's a report the Prime used a personal flyer and escaped. Mind you, there are also numerous reports saying he's dead."

"Did they breach Nicholai's quarters yet?" David asked. "Maybe it's another clone? He had one made, chances are he has several."

"It's not clear. No vid about it." Lerry shook his head.

"What about numbers? Has there been any mention of how many people Alexander's got with him?" Leonie asked.

"I'll memorise the vid feeds and tally what I can," David suggested. "Then we can confirm if its anywhere near two hundred."

"Two hundred?" Harrond questioned. "The ship isn't big enough."

"It is a conundrum," David admitted. He began scrolling through the previous footage from drones in different areas. Much of it was smoke-filled corridors and halls littered with the bodies of security guards and other tower people. Citizens.

The vid replayed the four shapers Leonie threw over the railings, followed by the two recovering shapers slow their fall, fly back up and blast the surprised security guards on their return.

"I count a minimum of fifty shapers and one hundred and twenty armed men," David said after ten minutes.

"Plus those at the terminal. I didn't see Alexander and company in any of that footage," Leonie said. "He'll be keeping a low profile with a few shapers with him for personal protection as well. To be honest, I thought he'd make an attempt to get in here."

"SciCorps is no doubt a target, but it looks like getting the Prime is his priority," David observed. "Once he's out of the way, it will be easier to take control. What about Dianah and Brendon? Surely they have protection?"

"If they've split up, I bet they're down at HelixR."

"Leonie, I know you want to go after them, but they aren't going anywhere now and they're not the threat we need to concern ourselves with this minute," David said. "We've got Alexander and a large number of shapers and armed men with him. They are who we need to concentrate on now."

"Since he has so many men, we've little chance of success, but we need to do something and quickly. I have advanced droid prototypes. They may be of use, maybe not. They haven't been field-tested yet."

"How soon can they be sent out?" Lerry asked.

"About an hour to reprogram them all. I just need to decide what their protocols will be. Can't just say *kill bad guys*. Maybe radiation levels ... this army won't have any."

"Handy to have three degrees. In the meantime, I'll go back out and see what mischief I can come up with." Before she left, Leonie turned back. "I promise not to visit HelixR." *Revenge can wait a bit longer.*

"Don't forget the comlink?" he advised.

21

______

GET THE PRIME

GOING INVISIBLE, LEONIE ONCE AGAIN FLEW AROUND TO A LARGE broken window near Nicholai's suite and entered cautiously. She glided towards the centre of the tower where she knew from memory the Prime's office overlooked the central atrium. There were noises coming from several directions; forward, below and above. The air was thick with smoke – too much for the ventilation fans to cater for.

Further down, the corridor opened to a view of the atrium. She watched several TowerPol officers facing a wall of intense heat as it spread closer. They were on one of the many walkways that crisscrossed the open space at various levels. Their retreat was cut off by a large gap in the walkway floor. She couldn't believe what she was about to do, but she needed allies and information. Ducking behind a column, she willed all four of them up and quickly moved them across the gap, nearer to her.

They looked around, bewildered at their fortune, coughing with the smoke.

Preparing for the worst, she called out to them. "Not everyone here is your enemy."

They all turned with raised weapons towards the hidden voice. "Who said that?" one asked.

"Lower your weapons and I'll show myself," Leonie replied.

"We'll be giving the orders around here," another called arrogantly.

"Seriously?" she hissed. Willing them to point their weapons down, Leonie stepped out from behind the column.

As expected, their eyes bulged at the sight of her and they strained to lift their rifles in fear. One bright-spark let go of his rifle and went for his blaster. Leonie ripped the blaster from his hands and lifted him to dangle over the atrium, immobile.

"I could have let you get incinerated." She pointed as the wall of fire reached the gap. "Or you could have risked not breaking your legs with the jump to the next floor."

"Who are you?" the first guard asked.

"What are you?" another asked.

"Who and what I am is irrelevant. What's relevant is I'm here to help stop this takeover any way I can. Where's the Prime? Is he still safe?"

As the first guard was about to speak, one of his friends stopped him. "She could be tricking us to get information," he muttered.

"Want to join your friend? You guys are clearly outmatched. It's only a matter of time before they reach the Prime's suite, unless he's already escaped."

They remained silent, unsure.

"I can rip the information from your minds, but I'd rather it was volunteered. You'll need me more than I'll need you." She pointed to the chaos. "These clowns arrived ... what, a few hours ago, and look what they've done already? Ask me anything about the tower, but make it quick, the longer we waste time here, the more chance the Prime will be killed." Then added, "And that fire is getting closer."

"What do you know about the Prime?" the second guard asked.

"His name is Nicholai Zodaich and is the grandson of the last Founder. He had one son, Alexander – who is currently leading this rabble. The Prime's partner, Ivana, was murdered by

Redmond Collins about twelve years ago. Nicholai later partnered with Veronica Felton – she used to be the partner to Stefan Felton before he was arrested for unsanctioned genetic research and cloning. Veronica was recently murdered by Alexander, Brendon and Dianah Felton—"

"Wrong. Veronica was murdered by David Osbourne—"

"Wrong yourself. That was a clone of David Osbourne controlled by Brendon, built by Dianah and HelixR at the behest of Alexander in their conspiracy to kill the Prime and take his place as sole heir. Nicholai's clone also fell, as did that of Osbourne. The coup was discovered and the three escaped." While she spoke, she kept the guards immobile. She watched the firewall getting closer. "It must be getting hot over there."

"Okay, okay. I'm convinced." The first guard yelled in panic. "The Prime is alive, but he's trapped in his office."

"When I release you, better not shoot me, not with your friend dangling," she warned.

They nodded. Suddenly set free, the three of them moved away from the oncoming heat, but still remained cautious of her, staring at this strange feline figure in front of them.

"How did you know all that about the Prime?" one of the officers asked.

"I've lived here for over twenty years." These officers were all much the same height, and dressed exactly the same; black uniforms with helmets and armoured segments covering chest torso and limbs.

"But how—"

"She must be the Shadow!" His companion pointed.

"The what?" Leonie asked. They were staring at her more, if that was possible.

"The Shadow. Even before I joined TowerPol, I heard about this dark shape rumoured to be flitting around the tower. No one could see you clearly; it was either too dark, you were too quick, or the cameras were mysteriously faulty, but they say they heard you a lot, bouncing around the air ducts."

"Now that's a lie. I wasn't that noisy ... was I?" She willed their dangling colleague back to the balcony.

"It's what I heard them say." One shrugged.

"Alright, this is fun, but how can I get to the Prime and help him out?"

"All access has been cut off. We were trying to get through ourselves. Half of TowerPol is between them and the Prime's suite."

"As well as what we could get from corporate security," the other added.

"Any idea of the numbers of shapers?" she asked.

"Of what?"

"The enemy. The attackers. How many?"

"I've heard about forty," an officer told her.

"There's a small army as well," another guard added. "They're running around creating havoc everywhere else."

"Possibly just to stretch TowerPol resources?" Leonie suggested, thinking.

"That's a thought." They agreed, nodding.

"Much of the power is shut down too. No electricity, just for emergency lighting and equipment."

Leonie looked over the railing. Down below she could see people running in panic. Several areas were on fire. "Is this the 18th floor of the White Zone?" she asked.

They nodded.

She considered. "And no one has broken in from the outside? Through the windows?"

"From outside? We're over two thousand metres up!"

And yet, I'm here. Leonie nodded absently. *No flyers in this group?* "How large is his suite? Does he take up half the floor? Is his office located in a corner of the tower?"

"His main office is closer to the centre, overlooking the atrium, but his residence is towards the outer windows. He's not in the corner, more towards the middle. Why?"

"Because I reckon I can get him out that way. Get him to safety."

"Where to?"

She looked at them, making a decision. "SciCorps."

"Doesn't Osbourne own that?"

"He does, and he is also an enemy of Alexander. Believe me, SciCorps is like a fortress." *She hoped it was.*

"How can we help?"

"You can't. Not directly." She saw the disappointment on their faces. "Let me explain something. What you are dealing with here is an army of magic—"

"Magic?" they mocked.

"Umm. Did you not just float over a gaping hole? Isn't there a mysterious wall of fire coming closer?" The wall was dissipating, but she moved back along the corridor and continued as they followed. "Did I not just force you to lower your weapons against your will? Hard to believe, but a fact, nevertheless." She created a small fireball and let them examine it before she tossed it at the approaching wall where it flared and dissipated.

"Magic can work here," she continued. "They know this. Your pulse rifles are okay, but if someone can go invisible or create fire from nothing, you have to admit, it's going to be hard to beat. How do you think I managed to keep alive here for two decades?" She looked at them, not expecting an answer, but she could see the reality of the current situation in their eyes.

"Look, I've got to go. Maybe you can get below and deal with those harassing the citizens? Don't say anything over the comlink about me, but if you see your buddies, tell them not to — Tell them 'Don't shoot the cat'." Before they responded, she vanished.

Leonie flew to where she estimated the windows to Nicholai's suite were located. As it turned out, there was a small landing pad, empty but for a bit of debris. Looking towards the ground she spotted more wreckage. "Either the Prime's personal flyer, or someone tried this way and the security got it." She scrutinised the area near the pad. There were bulges at regular intervals, indicating small but powerful laser turrets.

"Just like SciCorps." Taking all precautions, Leonie came in from above and hugged the outside of the tower; what she hoped would be outside the scope of the security sensors.

Now hovering on the pad, she studied the entrance in the darkness. Unlike SciCorps, this was a normal door, not for the transfer of goods. It was locked and reinforced. Without knowing what was on the other side, she placed her paw on the entry pad beside the door frame and gave it a little charge while trying the handle. Still locked. *So much for the subtle approach.* Increasing the charge made the pad smoke, but the door remained locked.

Stepping back, she applied her force of will. If she could lift several tonnes, even a security door shouldn't be too much trouble. Leonie increased the pressure, slowly feeling the door buckle. With a bit more of a nudge, the door sprung open.

A quick thought to reduce her will stopped the door from bursting away and clattering to the floor; instead, it floated to the side to rest against the wall. Immediately, lasers burst from the interior, hitting the pad and doorframe. Light, although dim, now spilled out across the pad.

When the shooting stopped, Leonie checked inside after reaffirming her invisibility. TowerPol and corporate security guards were strategically arranged around the foyer, energy weapons aimed at the doorway.

She tentatively put her paw out. No one took a shot at her, so her presence didn't register on their weapons. *That's a relief.* Feeling confident, Leonie zoomed in silently and started searching for Nicholai.

Leonie had to float almost ceiling height to avoid the milling bodies. There were TowerPol officers – both men and women – everywhere, more so towards the centre of the tower and the Prime's main offices. If her reasoning was sound, the Prime would be where the officers were the thickest, he wasn't far away now.

Finally, she spotted him. He was at his desk talking heatedly on the vid-com to several people. In the background, she heard many sounds including pulse weapon discharges and various explosions. Amongst it all were the sounds of men either yelling or screaming in pain.

Leonie waited for him to finish. She was going to mind-speak and didn't want his shocked response on display to all and sundry. When he finally clicked off the com, he sat back and drained his glass of water.

Nicholai. I am a friend who can help you.

As expected, he froze wide-eyed, dropping his glass to clunk on the carpeted floor, looking everywhere for the voice.

Leonie tried not to laugh at his antics as it would give her location away.

I can't show myself because your men would blast me instantly, but SciCorps will be your safest place.

"With David Osbourne? How? Why?" he asked.

Leave the how up to me. As to why: to save you from your son—

"Alexander?" The Prime looked confused. "He's here?"

Yes, and leading this attack, along with Dianah and Brendon. It's a long story, and you won't believe me. What I need from you though is complete trust.

"What assurances do I have?" Nicholai stood, warily walking around the room, searching.

Other than my word, which would mean nothing to you? You're still alive, and your men have no idea where I am.

"Sir? Are you okay?" His commander spoke to him.

"How would I get out?" Nicholai ignored his commander. "There's some impossible army at the front door and my flyer is ruined. How did they get into the building? Where are they from?"

"Sir?" His commander looked alarmed as the Prime was talking to himself.

I can answer all those questions, though it will take time to convince you once you hear it. Call SciCorps.

After a moment of hesitation, Nicholai went back to his desk and put the call through.

Ask him if you can trust Leonie, she prompted peering past his shoulder.

In a matter of moments, she saw David appear on the screen.

"Osbourne. I ... I have this ... *voice* in my head that said I should trust it."

"If it's Leonie, then you can. I'd trust her with my life," David said. "How is it up there?"

"Quite dire." As if on cue, a blast shook the air. The line crackled. "I believe they're almost through."

"You haven't much time then," David said. "Believe me, if Leonie says she can get you out, she can."

Zodaich ended the call. "What do you want me to do?" He asked softly to the air.

I can take you and your commander to safety.

"Why the commander?" he asked looking at the confused man beside him.

Because when the shit hits the fan the military will more than likely trust him over you.

"You mean this isn't bad enough?" He looked distraught at the many wounded men and women sitting or lying in the corridors.

This is nothing to what is about to be unleashed.

Nicholai considered this as the fighting – and the screaming – got louder. "What do you want me to do?"

Have you got another room where we can talk in private?

"Very well." He stood and summoned his commander. "Follow me, Jay."

The Prime strode to his ornate display cabinet. Waving a hand near a hidden sensor, it clicked open, revealing a smaller room. With his commander close behind, he entered.

Leave the door ajar.

"Sir, we need to formulate a strategy—" Jay protested, no surprise registering on his face about the secret room.

"That's what I'm doing right now," Nicholai assured him.

Leonie had to be quick. Now they were close together and out of sight from the rest of the officers, Leonie took a deep breath and gently zapped them both. She became visible briefly. There were no cries of alarms; no one noticed anything before she reaffirmed her invisibility.

Grasping an arm of both men, she made them disappear and rise. Slowly and cautiously, she retraced her path back to the flight-pad door after closing the cabinet behind her.

A few of the guards guarding the external door had moved closer; two were outside waving their torches as they examined the wreckage of the personal flyer.

And no doubt puzzling over what blew the door out. Leonie smiled.

"David, heading your way," she spoke into the comlink when she was clear.

The SciCorps loading dock was three levels below on the other side of the tower. They arrived a few minutes later. When they landed and became visible, David came out to greet them.

"Glad to see you made it safely. What happened to them?" he asked, concerned at the slumped figures.

"Just unconscious." She willed them inside. "This was the quickest way to get them here."

"No other injuries? Perhaps a quick turn on the medicomp?" David suggested.

"Fine." Leonie moved them into the medlab. Putting the Prime on the bed first, he was checked and treated for ten minutes before he came around, confused but healthy.

"Osbourne?" Nicholai looked around, unsure. "How—" he stared when he saw the creature standing beside the scientist. The Prime cried in shock and fainted.

Leonie sighed.

David opened a small tube and waved it under the Prime's nose. Even from a distance Leonie got a whiff of the strong and pungent odour. Nicholai's head jolted; his eyes snapped open. Once again, he became aware of his surroundings.

"This is Leonie and she's helping us all," David said as he helped the Prime off the medicomp.

Leonie then willed the commander onto the bed and set it up the same as they did for the Prime.

"Resorting to kidnapping now? Why am I here, Osbourne?" the Prime asked, clearly uneasy with this turn of events. "What's your plan?"

"My plan? Was I supposed to have one? When Leonie tells me, I'll know."

"I would've thought a genius with three degrees would have one by now," Leonie teased.

"You listen to *that* ...?"

"She has saved my life several times, and many others as well, including yours. I think you should give her the respect she deserves."

"Is she a mutant?" Nicholai eyed her dubiously, taking in her black fur, pointed ears and tail. "Or is she one of these invaders betraying her own kind?"

"Can I zap him again?" Leonie hissed, Clenching and unclenching her claws in annoyance. She started pacing the room. "Just a little prick?"

Nicholai's face paled as he witnessed her vexation.

"Okay," David started. "We're up against over two hundred shapers and armed men—"

"Shapers?"

David sighed, turning the vid around so Nicholai could see. "Call them magicians if you want—" He paused at the scoff from Nicholai. "Did you forget a few minutes ago an invisible cat flew you from your office without your men knowing? I suggest you take this seriously. Now, from what we see on the vid feeds, energy weapons are next to useless against them. The shapers either create some field for protection, deflect the shots or simply vanish. On the other hand, they send officers over the railings or slam them into walls, casting fireballs, or bolts of electricity."

"Surely there's a rational explanation to all that, but *magic*?"

"Call it what you will. It makes little difference to me, but it just saved your arse." Leonie turned to him. "Are you shallow enough to let your inability to comprehend what's happening stop you from saving other lives?"

Nicholai sighed, coming to a decision. "I will accept whatever assistance is offered, regardless of *who* offers it or how it's accomplished."

Unlike the Prime, the commander didn't faint at the sight of Leonie when he revived, but he was definitely nervous and unsure. He did keep his distance though as he got off the bed and joined the Prime in the loungeroom.

To emphasise the use of magic, Leonie willed a tray of refreshments to the small table in front of the lounge, and they got down to discussing a strategy. After being informed of the threat they were facing, Nicholai and Jay shared their information and answered questions.

"The tower has around 5,000 TowerPol, and the same in SecForce," Jay told them, appalled at what he saw on the vid.

"Is there a difference?" Leonie took a sip from her mug. "Why so few to guard over a million citizens?"

"With most citizens controlled by a subliminal process they don't need too many officers," David replied.

"The TowerPol cater for simple crimes and misdemeanours – of which there are few—"

"Because of the subliminal control," David interjected.

"And SecForce," Jay continued, "deals with more military concerns – mainly external; mutant attacks, that sort of thing." He paused. "I recall several reports of a large flying black cat, but that was years ago, and it was reported as being killed." He looked her up and down warily. "There's also an exclusive clause, specifically to White Zone citizens."

"What clause is that?" Leonie asked.

"SecForce is forbidden to enter White Zone."

"Forbidden? That's crazy—"

"Perhaps. The founders instituted a clause long before Nicholai was in charge. The upper levels have always been for the hierarchy, and therefore required no military oversight," Jay explained.

"Why hasn't it changed since then?" She directed the question at Nicholai.

"We like the status quo." The Prime shrugged. "Up until now, there was no need."

Leonie's tail twitched with the stupidity of it. "How quickly can your men be sent out?" she asked, getting back on topic.

"If the corridors are clear of the public, squads can be deployed quite rapidly. Other than our two main garrisons, we also have a small bureau with ten officers on every other floor," Jay said. "As Osbourne stated, everyone from birth has had subliminal messaging; this is needed to keep the masses from uprising or rioting. This sort of thing was never anticipated when the towers were designed, but the guards can block the stairwells to prevent anyone trying to move between levels."

"How does the messaging work?"

"Quite effectively."

Leonie growled.

"Oh. Other than conditioning from birth, there is a sub-aural tone constantly generated."

"I've heard it, but thought it was just the background noise of the building. That's why everyone is more or less docile?" Leonie mused. "What about the lifts?"

"They can be overridden by us, and we can control what floors they go to if need be," Jay continued. "Some lifts are on the blink because of damage and fires. There is an automatic cut-out if smoke or undue heat hits the sensors. That we cannot override. We need maintenance staff to get to work."

"These shapers can fly down the lift shafts. If they are invisible – like I was – they can easily bypass your blocks, and they may be able to bring fighters with them. Your men also have the disadvantage of keeping the citizens safe, reducing the effectiveness of their capabilities; the shapers haven't got those qualms."

"So, even with our high-tech and overwhelming numbers, we're outmatched?" Nicholai sounded resentful.

"If you were willing to lay waste to everything, then the tech would win – but at the cost of thousands of citizens' lives."

"We can't have that," the Prime said, though he didn't sound adamant.

"I agree." Leonie nodded. "But while that's a concern for us, I don't think they're going to worry about the body count. What we need is our own powershaper army." She put her empty cup down. "And I know exactly where to find them."

22

PRIME TIME

"We've searched his residence and office. This Nicholai Zodaich is nowhere to be found." Olekk reported dabbed at his forearm where a laser had scored his flesh. There was no bleeding from the cauterised wound.

"Are you sure? You must have missed him in the darkness. Did you check the panic room? My informant was adamant of the Prime's location and there's no other way out." Alexander clenched his fist in frustration at his First Mage's shaking head.

"If by panic room you mean a small room behind his office desk, then yes, it too was empty," Olekk confirmed. "Only a few lights were out in his offices, so it wasn't too dark to miss him."

They were back in Alexander's apartment. A few things were missing, but the bulk of his furnishings remained. Dianah and Brendon sat on the lounge, listening to the report.

"We can assume he had help. The door to his landing pad was opened from the outside with great force," Olekk continued. "Perhaps someone secreted him away, perhaps to another tower? One of my men scanned some of the minds of his guards; the Prime was talking a lot on his comlink, then to himself. His commander is also missing."

"Talking to himself? Maybe he's finally gone mad," Alex wondered aloud.

Seems to run in the family, Dianah sent to Brendon, who snorted.

Olekk looked at Brendon, annoyed by his brief laugh. "Is there anywhere else he could have gone?"

Alex thought about the question. "No reports of any craft leaving the tower, not since our arrival at least." He wondered about the two shuttles that escaped when they first arrived.

"No other hidden or secret way out?" Dianah asked.

"None that we can find. It is a mystery," Olekk replied. "Is he capable of going invisible?"

"Not unless one of your people has betrayed you."

"That could not happen." The First Mage shook his head vigorously. "We've only been here for a short time. Who could he turn to and how would he be able to in such a short time without anyone else knowing?"

"Frack it!" Alex screamed his frustration.

"I've sent copies of his image out. We will do what we must, my lord."

"But we also need to get control of the tower as soon as we can." He scrolled through images on the screen. "You recall the floor plans I showed you earlier? These areas are where the TowerPol are stationed. The SecForce are only stationed in the lower zones and won't be an issue. Get your shapers out there and do what you need to do; they currently control the elevators – and therefore access to all levels."

"I have some ideas on that—"

"I should hope so. Get to it before this takeover goes to shit."

Olekk nodded and strode purposefully out of the room, grumbling under his breath.

"I'll head back to the terminal with a shaper or two and use the *Sundancer* to get more troops," Brendon suggested. "We still have plenty of men left at the boot-camp. Thanks to that flyer crash, our element of surprise didn't go as well as we liked. Time for plan B."

———

"Are you sure this is a good idea?" Jay protested. "I should remain here with you."

"No doubt Alexander realises by now the Prime is not dead or captured," Leonie said before Nicholai could answer. "He'll be sending his people out to search. You'll be better placed with your troops to prevent that."

"It's the logical thing to do," David added. "If he doesn't know where you are, his next step should be to get to the troops – they are his biggest threat."

"Then the Prime should come with me. Surely a few thousand troops can protect him?"

"If they are the next target, then he'll be in the line of fire – the troops will be as ineffectual as they were when you were *safe* in your office. An empty and heavily fortified research facility would be one of the least likely places for him to be."

"How fortified can it be?" the commander queried. He looked around the lab area.

"Let's just say I have several efficient and quite lethal projects in place—"

"Don't say any more in case he's scanned," Leonie warned. "Just him knowing the Prime's here is enough of a risk."

"Scanned? You mean mind-reading?" Jay scoffed.

"This is the only reason I saved you," Leonie said tensely. "If you can't do this, then you aren't any use to anyone."

"I will take my orders from my Prime—"

"Jay," Nicholai cut him off. "Do it. You know I appreciate your loyalty, but I'm fully aware of Osbourne's capabilities even if you aren't."

"TowerPol is on the first and tenth level," Jay informed them. "I can call them and arrange a lift. We're on level fifteen?" He was about to activate his link.

"Stop!" Leonie ordered. "They're more than likely listening in. Alexander is crazy, but he's not stupid. SciCorps is supposed to be derelict. Even if they were working, an elevator coming to this level from TowerPol would only arouse suspicion and interest."

"But without the lifts, how will I get down there?" the commander asked.

"Same way as I got you here. We'll fly down to the TowerPol pad."

"We're nearly two thousand metres up. Isn't there another way?" Jay looked anxious. "Maybe the stairs?"

"There's quite a bit of distance to any emergency stairs, and too much going on between here and there to risk it. This is much quicker and safer."

"I get vertigo easily," he confessed. "I can't go outside. I get a cold sweat even by you telling me you flew me here from ... out there."

"There's the lift shaft. That's only a 150-metre drop," Leonie teased. The commander's face drained of colour. "I could stun you, but then your troops wouldn't see me as an ally. How about you close your eyes. It will only take a minute or so once we're in the shaft."

After a bit more coaxing and encouragement, it was decided. David deactivated the lasers. With Lerry and Harrond as security, Leonie and the commander exited SciCorps and quickly made their way to the nearby elevator doors.

"Stand back," Leonie cautioned as she willed the doors apart revealing the empty elevator shaft. The odour of smoke lingered in the still air. She popped her head in to look. From here she could see both stationary lifts; one two levels up and the other five levels down. "How convenient; the lift is on your floor."

"All security forces have priority. The default setting is the lifts will always return to the nearest TowerPol or SecForce level until called by a citizen – when not stopped by the sensors or overridden."

"Ready?" She looked to the commander.

"And you say it'll only take a minute?" Jay asked.

"Much quicker if I let you freefall."

"You're one cruel individual." Jay stepped closer to the door.

"Okay. I'll stop. But just to let you know, I've never received anything other than abuse and derision from your kind."

"Humans?"

"Militia, guards, troops ... you're all the same. Only brave when holding a sword or a blaster." She floated into the shaft. "Thanks, guys," she said to the agtechs. "I'll see you shortly." Leonie addressed Jay. "Ready?"

Jay shook his head. Regardless, she willed the commander up and into the shaft. She heard his sharp intake of breath when he saw the depths of the shaft. "Don't look down. This is level fifteen. How about concentrating on counting the levels so we can be sure we don't get out on the wrong floor?" She closed the doors and began the descent after Jay's nod.

Leonie descended relatively quickly, but not so fast to make the commander's stomach churn. "I count five floors, and it only took thirty seconds."

"This is the tenth level," Jay confirmed as he settled on the lift roof, letting out a sigh of relief.

Leonie scanned the elevator below and the hallway beyond its doors, picking up several minds with military type thoughts.

"Get your hands dirty," she said.

"Why?" he asked as he rubbed his hands over the greasy rails. a look of distaste on his face.

Not used to getting his hands dirty. "I'll make you a hero," she answered, then gently pried open the elevator hatch. "Want me to lower you in?"

"I can manage."

"Good." Leonie stuck her head through the hatch once he was through. "Just so we're all working off the same page," Leonie started a list in a soft voice. "These invaders are working for Alexander Zodaich; they can do magic and a whole lot more, as I'm sure you've found by now. Whether you believe that or not is up to you. So far, they're only on the top four levels. Like me, some of them can fly, so they might even try using these shafts; consider keeping them under guard too.

"Dianah Felton is part of this group; she might try to head

for HelixR. I suggest you get some men to watch that area and don't let her through; there's also a landing pad there. She'll have help with her. Do not make the mistake of thinking she is incapable of being a very nasty bitch. Got that?"

"Any other day what you say would be so inconceivable, but yes, I got it."

"I'll let your men know you're here." Leonie sent a thought to the waiting troops along with an image. *Your commander is about to come through the elevator door.* They were instantly alert and wary of the unseen voice. *Remain calm and don't shoot him.*

"Last thing – try to keep anything about SciCorps out of it. You and the Prime were separated in the attack and you only just managed to escape. Tell them you managed to overcome your vertigo and climbed down the shaft, hence your dirty hands. Is that heroic or what?"

Ready to take control if need be, she willed the door ajar. She scanned again and picked up a name of one of them. "Your men are nervous. Better give them some reassurance it's really you," she suggested to the commander. "Do you know a Sergeant Bretton?"

The commander nodded. "What about you?"

"I'm not here." She went invisible.

"Hey Bretton," the commander called. "Are you still shagging that corporal from Blue 100?"

There was a pause. "Commander? Is that you?" Sergeant Bretton replied.

"Who else, you dimwit. Help me open these damn doors!"

Leonie registered their surprise and relief when the guards saw him. Jay related the story as per her suggestion and she picked up thoughts of admiration for their commander, knowing his fear of heights and risking the climb.

"What a hero," Leonie grinned as she raced back up to the fifteenth floor. The agtechs were still there, guarding the gloomy passage.

"All good?

"Yep. Let's get back to SciCorps. We've got to recruit a shaper army of our own."

————

"Where could he have gone?" Alexander paced back and forth on the plush carpet in his old suite, fretting on how Nicholai escaped and his whereabouts. "Someone must be hiding him. One of *his* allies!" His plan of taking over the tower seemed to be crumbling as quickly as it started. "I've met some of my contacts; nothing seen or heard. Not even a rumour."

"Pull yourself together." Dianah was sitting on the lounge, apprehensive about his mood swings over the last few hours. "Perhaps you can connect with more of your allies? See who would be in a position to hide him?"

They both turned at the sound of the door opening. In the corridor beyond, two henchmen ushered Brendon in. Since the failed coup with the Prime, Alexander insisted he have a dozen militia and shapers protecting him. They were now arrayed in the passageway to his suite.

"You could go somewhere else, where they'd least expect you," Dianah suggested.

"That's what a coward would do. I—"

"The *Sundancer* is not where I left it at the shuttle port," Brendon said quietly.

Alexander stopped his pacing. "What the frag do you mean gone? Gone where? Are you certain it isn't invisible?"

"I searched the entire pad. It's gone." Brendon shook his head. "I—"

"Who could have taken it?" Alexander's pacing became more frantic as did the wild look in his eyes. "It's David isn't it? He's come after me again!"

"How could he?" Dianah spoke up from the lounge. "We left him stranded in Delta. I think your paranoia is returning. It would be impossible for him to get back here, and so soon."

"Because he's a genius! He's always bringing me down. You

think I'm paranoid? For decades I *knew* he'd find me, and what happens? He turns up in Delta, then lets me grab his new toy, and now it's fragging gone! He's toying with me. That's what he's doing!"

"Is it coincidental that Nicholai is missing, and now the ship?" Dianah considered, reluctant to side with Alexander's paranoia.

"How could the Prime have gotten to it? Or even known about it?" Brendon asked.

"Yes, Brendon. A good question. How *could* he have known? You're the only one here who knows."

"You're crazy if you think I had anything to do with it. Either way, we're here, now and permanently. We can't get any reinforcements."

"I bet all the answers are in SciCorps. That's where we should concentrate our attacks. Maybe Nicholai is hiding there? We haven't been able to access it."

"We lost quite a few people so far—"

"Who cares? They can be replaced, but without access to SciCorps, we've nothing."

"Alex, you've got a lot of people blackmailed. Why not use that leverage to your advantage?" Dianah tried to coax his ego. "Surely their fear of you and what you can still do to them should give you the edge. They're the ones who should stick their necks out first – these powershapers are a unique element and not to be squandered. Do what you're good at; use your guile, not a full-on attack. When you put your mind to it, you can be just as smart."

Alex's pacing slowed, as did his breathing. "I can," he mumbled. "I can do this. Osbourne is just an upstart. I was dux until he came along."

"Exactly," Dianah encouraged. "Call your people; tell them what to do or else."

"I will tell them what will happen if they fail me." He sent a message to his allies to meet in his boardroom and that an *escort* for each was on the way.

23

RECRUITING SHAPERS

DESCENDING SWIFTLY THROUGH THE HIGH CLOUDS, THE *SUNDANCER* made a spectacular sight for the city's denizens. From the sheer numbers, Leonie estimated every able-bodied Gryphon Rider was in the air in a fruitless effort to defend the city.

"How good is your hull to crossbow bolts?"

"I'm confident, though admittedly it isn't a parameter I considered when designing her."

Nicholai Zodaich stared at the screen in stunned silence.

"Wh-where are we again?" he stammered.

"Reenat," Leonie said.

David flicked to another screen, briefly showing the star charts. "That blue dot is Sol and the green dot is us."

"How far?"

"We are 3,211.47 light-years from Earth. A time-machine is good for traversing vast distances in space as well as through time." David's attention was drawn back to the landing when faint popping sounds echoed through the hull. "These are the crossbow bolts you mentioned?"

"Reckon so. There's the arena." She pointed at the screen. "The ideal place for this ship."

"This is truly unbelievable," the Prime said, staring at the fantastic city.

"You haven't seen anything yet, Nick," Leonie stated. *If he thinks this is weird, wait until he sees an illios!* She chuckled quietly.

It was a snug fit between the four black crystal statues in the arena, but the *Sundancer* landed in the centre of the arena.

David opened the ramp once the dust settled. Already a throng of people were gathering along the viewing area. Dozens of guards came running.

"Don't go anywhere near the entrance yet," Leonie reminded them. "Otherwise, you'll be peppered with bolts before you get a word out."

"You know these ... people?" Nick asked, unsure what to call some of the beings visible on the screen.

"Yep. I'm a bona fide powershaper, registered and all," she answered before continuing. "I'll go invisible and contact Krre'lo. He's the large black man there." She pointed to the figure in the growing crowd. "He's the First Mage of the city – or was when I left – one of the people now in charge. Once I get him on side, everyone else will fall in line."

They made their way to the lounge area.

"I'll make coffee," David said.

"For me, yes please. For them, tea would be better if you've got it," Leonie suggested as she left.

David nodded. "Nicholai, here's another screen." He activated it so the Prime could keep staring at the unbelievable sight outside while he fixed the beverages.

Leonie summoned the elevator and went invisible after she entered. The first thing she noticed when she flew outside was the heat. It was less humid but just as hot here as in Delta.

Below, the wall of troops now surrounded the ramp, but at a safe distance, their polearms all levelled and directed towards the entrance. Overhead, the Gryphon Riders circled. Enhanced by the arena acoustics, the guttural noises the gryphons were making could be plainly heard by everyone.

The First Mage, as expected of his rank, moved to the front of the lesser mages and directly beside the garrison commander. In a few minutes she was hovering over him, positioning herself to sidle up behind him without bumping into anyone. Everyone's attention was glued to the open ramp of the alien sphere now filling their arena.

Leonie descended and tapped the First Mage on the shoulder as soon as a gap appeared next to him. "Hello Krre'lo," she said.

The big man turned absently. He looked pleasantly surprised at the sight of her. "Leonie! I wasn't sure what had become of you." He put his hand out to shake her paw. "Isn't this fascinating?" He turned back to the ship.

"I believe it is. How would you like to look inside? There is someone I'd like you to meet. You too, commander, if you'd like."

"You? Me? In there? What have you got to do with it?" Krre'lo asked, bewildered.

"Everything. I'm the chosen one, remember? We have a situation and need your help. You're the first person I thought of for this problem. In fact, I reckon we can help each other. I'll explain everything to you, but we better to do it in there away from prying minds and ears."

The First Mage turned to her, then back to the ship then back to her while he made up his mind.

"My lord, you know this person?" The commander asked, looking dubiously at the newcomer.

"I do." The First Mage started moving forwards. "I'll do it."

"Make way," the commander called out in his booming voice, quickly striding in front of the First Mage.

The troops immediately moved left and right, clearing a path. As trained as they were, their mutterings audible as the trio walked up the ramp.

"This is ..." Krre'lo was lost for words. He walked slowly along the corridor, touching the wall and the floor, trying to look everywhere.

"You have vessels that travel across the sea. This one travels vast distances across the sky. Remember how we spoke about other worlds, including Earth – the homeworld of humans?" Leonie summoned the elevator. The doors slid opened instantly. She invited them inside and continued. "This vessel comes from there. The people you'll meet are also human. One is the designer of this ship – think of him as a brilliant sage – the other one is your equal, a leader among the humans there. He wishes to talk to you. Both of you."

The elevator opened and she stepped out. The look of them seeing the new area almost made her laugh.

"Where is the other room?" the commander asked, baffled.

"This is another floor." She guided the two men to the lounge. "Krre'lo, First Mage of Reenat, please meet Nicholai Zodaich, First Prime of Blue Mountains Tower."

The First Mage shook Nicholai's hand firmly, as did the commander.

"And this is David Osbourne, commander and designer of the *Sundancer*." She shrugged at David's questioning look at the rank.

"Welcome, gentlemen. Please be seated." David directed them to the lounges.

"Thank you," Krre'lo acknowledged. "Also, this is my trusted garrison commander, Ergnat Wolfden-Farlor."

The commander nodded as he sat down, briefly startled as the chair moved to form around him.

Leonie fetched the tea and coffee. She poured the dark liquid into the cups.

"This could be an acquired taste, it's not like your Tesakian Redleaf. Careful, it's hot," Leonie warned as she brought the cups over on a tray. "Our apologies, we have nothing alcoholic."

No one laughed at the faces the guests made at first taste. To their credit, the guests didn't spit it out straight away.

"It is quite warm." Krre'lo put his cup down after a few tentative sips.

"There are only the three of you controlling a vessel this size?" Ergnat asked.

"Yes. Most of the functions are automatic," David replied.

The garrison commander looked confused at the answer.

"It's *our* magic," Leonie intervened. "We have much to share. Prime, would you like me to begin the preliminaries?"

"That would be gracious of you." The Prime nodded sitting back and sipping his coffee.

Leonie went into the details of how the upstart ruler of Delta had made his way back to Earth with a cohort of shapers and militia and attacked the Prime's city. "You see, while we have our own type of magic like this vessel, Earth is as unaccustomed to your magic as you are to ours." She then went on to describe the towers, and the vastly different way of life.

"In short, Lord Zander is creating havoc and unless we can combine our forces – that of the shapers in Reenat and of Earth's troops – there will be a tragic loss of life," Leonie finished.

"Firstly, I would be glad to discuss how we can be of assistance," the First Mage stated. "However, many of my colleagues will be wanting to know how would we benefit?"

"I'll leave the finer details to the Prime," Leonie started, "but Yarnik will soon be unliveable. Where will you all go? Have any other portals been discovered yet?"

"They have not," Krre'lo admitted, looking sullen. "But it has only been a week or so."

"Other than the possibility of providing aid and shelter to as many humans as we can, David here is busy working on how to locate the portals."

"A project I'm eager to get started with," David agreed.

"You know I've already located the portal to Earth? Without portal access, everyone on Yarnik will die. My apologies, Nicholai." She looked to the Prime. "Time for your negotiations, methinks."

The Prime frowned. "I'm not sure there is all that much left to discuss." He turned to the two guests. "But I can assure you both, with your aid we can overcome this upstart. Once that danger is nullified, any and every resource I have will be put towards the saving of your people."

Krre'lo pursed his lips in consideration. "I would like to

invite you all to Shaper Hall for a banquet this evening. What you have here is truly remarkable, and I am most favourable to our mutual assistance. However, I'm not the only one to be persuaded. May I suggest dinner after sunset? That should give the kitchen ample time to whip up something."

"You're too kind. We would be delighted." Nicholai stood to shake their hands. "Thank you."

Leonie escorted them off the ship, much to the relief of the troops and many shapers still waiting outside. "I'll probably visit Tipp shortly. Will he be dining as well? I can get word to him for you."

"Most assuredly he will be there. I wouldn't hear the end of it if he missed out," Krre'lo chuckled. He slapped the commander on the back. "Let's go, Ergnat. Much to do and little time to do it."

Feeling somewhat satisfied with the outcome, Leonie wandered back inside.

"If you gents feel up to it, how about we go for a stroll in the city? I have a couple of friends I'd like you to meet." Leonie turned to Nicholai. "You've taken to my appearance relatively smoothly. When we leave here, you'll soon realise I am not the most bizarre form."

The Prime nodded, draining his coffee. "I will do my best not to stare. What are these portals you mentioned?"

When they left the ship, David closed the ramp with his remote.

On the way to the Bardic Council chambers, Leonie and David educated him to the significance of the portals, and the dire consequences facing this world. It was a good distraction for him as they passed many glins'ool, seleth and rrells.

"So, we have them over a barrel?" he decided.

"We do, but with their magic ability and their numbers, if you thought Alex and his small cohort was giving you trouble, imagine what a thousand of them could do if you crossed them," Leonie advised.

"Nicholai, this isn't really something to be bargaining or

undercutting for best profits," David added his thoughts. "We're talking about the survival of tens of thousands of sentient beings."

"Imagine the benefits Blue Mountains Tower would have with a few hundred loyal shapers doing things technology can't hope to replicate," Leonie finished.

"Okay, okay." The Prime raised his hands. "I will do what I can to assist them, assuming I'm in a position to do so once this is over." Try as he might, he couldn't help but gawk at all the aliens calmly walking along the road, shopping and chatting.

"Here we are." Leonie steered him towards the Bardic chambers. "If we're lucky, Tipp won't be speaking his usual doggerel. It can get ... tedious."

She led them inside. *Hey, Tipp. It's Leonie,* she sent a greeting.

There was a squawk. With a flurry of feathers, Tipp fluttered down from the top floor.

"Leonie! A pleasant surprise for my eyes. I heard gossip about a sky-ship. If it wasn't for council duty, I would come for the scrutiny."

"Tipp nul Chor Tukk, this is Nicholai Zodaich and David Osbourne. They are visiting from Earth."

"A pleasure, gentlemen," the bard replied after a brief pause to take in his guests. "What brings you to my den?" He shook their hands in turn and escorted them up the wide, winding stairs. "I assume you've been back to your homeworld?" the bard noted.

"Our trip to Reenat is complicated, but our visit here is to invite you and Biell to the banquet Krre'lo is holding tonight." Leonie looked around. "Where is she?"

"Biell's assisting with an investigation at Siola's invitation."

They settled in the comfortable chairs in the bard's lounge on the first floor.

"Investigation?" Leonie queried.

"To sort through their extensive library. Between you and me, I suspect Siola wanted female company. Did you know Reindet's ancestry goes way back to Dromas city?"

"I didn't." Leonie shook her head. "We only met briefly."

Tipp clucked. "How remiss. Food and wine, I insist!" He fetched a bottle of wine and glasses. "Leonie, would you care to pour? I'll fetch snacks for four."

As he strutted out the door, Leonie looked for David and Nick's reactions. David had already encountered several races in Delta, but from the Prime's glances, he still needed a lot more acclimatising.

While they got a taste of the local wine, Tipp returned with a tray of sweetmeats, cheeses and dips. He brought her up to speed on the local news since her departure.

"News of Siola and Willom's engagement has been shared. Reindet is well, and Styx is loitering somewhere."

"That's lovely news. I have no doubts they'll be attending this evening too." She took a sip from her glass. "Why is Styx here?"

Tipp shrugged. "Who would know about the rollo."

"Have you heard any word on the portals? Maybe something on your bard network Krre'lo hasn't heard yet?"

"No news since your last goodbye, but Jade's arrival in Qelay is nigh."

"I haven't forgotten. She said it would be about a week before she got to Qelay. I was thinking of visiting tomorrow, or leaving a message with the rollos if I miss her arrival."

"Be advised to keep her by your side. She'll never confess how your absence caused her stress. Searching for you all these years has brought about many tears."

"I understand, really. We still have a lot to catch up, but—"

"Leonie," David suggested. "Go meet your friends. I'm sure I can recruit Lerry and Harrond like I did when we evacuated the wilders."

"Are you sure?"

"Certainly. You have good people here who have done so much for you, and you can do with respite."

"How long will you be away?"

"If we leave first thing in the morning, we should be back by late afternoon."

"Ha. Almost a *whole* day off." She rolled her eyes. "How will I cope—"

"Good. That's settled." David gave little indication of noting the sarcasm.

"Is this why you've come by?" Tipp inquired.

"Partly, but we're here to request the First Mage's assistance." Leonie filled Tipp in on the recent activities in Delta, and the outcome. "We require the services of a hundred powershapers."

"And his answer was what?"

"Yes, of course. I'm the chosen one, remember?" Leonie rolled her eyes.

———

After catching up with Reindet, Siola and Willom at the banquet, the trio were introduced to a dozen of the top powershapers in Reenat, discussing their abilities and how they could assist the cause.

It was clear some of them thought it beneath them to vend their abilities like it was a mere commodity. Leonie's hackles rose in frustration.

"I'm sure you'll be rethinking that when you're stuck here, smelling your flesh burn off your bones," Leonie hissed at one particular upstart. "We'll let you know if we deem *you* worthy."

He was most taken aback by her tone. Leonie moved on, ignoring his complaining.

"Don't forget, we need these people," Nicholai urged as she stalked away.

"We do, and once he realises he needs us just as much, he'll change his demeanour, as will I, but I'll not be spoken to like that. It's this sort of superior-than-though attitude I grew to loathe when growing up helpless and alone on the streets in Delta." She took a drink from a passing waiter and drained the glass. "I'm not so helpless now," she finished.

By the end of the evening and after much discussion from Krre'lo, with the aid of Reindet's backing, convincing arguments from Tipp, and hard and fast facts from Styx, the council agreed; all registered shapers would be summoned to assist in defending the tower. For their unwavering support, their families would be given priority when the inevitable evacuation came.

"How exactly will we be getting all these people to the tower?" Nicholai asked after the banquet had finished. They were in a lounge opposite the dining hall, and just down the corridor from the rooms Krre'lo had arranged for them.

"You remember the portals we spoke about?" Leonie continued at his nod. "There's one for Earth, but it's on the other side of the continent. David will come up with a solution to bring it across here." She looked to the scientist as he rested his eyes, lying on the other couch.

"I can manage that," David said, not opening his eyes. "When the room stops spinning."

"I told you the wine here had a kick." Leonie smiled. "Do you need to medicomp?"

"See how I feel tomorrow."

"And this portal you speak of? I assume it's connected to another on Earth?"

Leonie looked to Nicholai. "Yes. We know where the sister portal is."

Nicholai waited for more information. "Where, exactly?"

"David?"

"SciCorps," he groaned.

"Yes. SciCorps ... what about it?"

"The portal. It's *in* SciCorps."

"Inside SciCorps?" Nicholai looked shocked. "You have a doorway to an alien world *inside* the tower?"

"Well ... when you put it like that ..."

"How else should I put it?" The Prime stood and paced the room. "I can't believe this!"

"Pfft," Leonie scoffed. "After everything you've seen so far, and *that* is what you don't believe?"

"I'm the Prime! I should have known. Of course, it's something that needed discussing."

"Hey, I know what, let's discuss it now," Leonie offered.

"It's too damn late for that."

"Then it's settled," she growled. "It had to be done with very little time to convince your Elite Council and then put it to the vote."

"Why?"

"Because people were dying! Tower people – or more accurately Dianah's minions – were attacking and killing any wilder in the region. Ever seen what a ship's blaster can do to a child?" Leonie glared. "The few that weren't killed were being used for experiments!"

Nicholai shook his head. "Dianah did this?"

"People in her employ. HelixR people." Leonie nodded. "They recently murdered at least a couple of dozen wilders of all ages that we know of, and it's been happening for years."

"It was my idea to bring the portal into the tower," David admitted as he sat up. "We needed a safe and secure place for it, and that's SciCorps. It couldn't be anywhere outside in case Dianah's people found it. There's very little chance of anything bad coming through. The one here is well-protected."

Nicholai abruptly stopped pacing the room. "I'm going to bed." He turned to the doorway, clearly still vexed.

"I think I might do the same." David got unsteadily to his feet. "G'night."

"I'll head to Qelay in the morning. Say hi for me at Skyhome."

24

WHITE CLIFF TRIO

I BELIEVE YOUR FRIENDS ARE ARRIVING. LEONIE RECOGNISED RIFF'S thoughts. *I have directed them to the field north of us.*

Thanks. Leonie went invisible as she flew out the window and headed north, scanning the skies while she waited. The two green wyverns spiralled down towards the township. She flew above, ghosting them as they landed behind the hills. Feiron was on Faldo, and Jade was mounted on Slana.

Where's Dorn and Philbert? Leonie asked trying not to laugh as both wyvern heads snaked around to look for the unseen source.

Furry one? Slana replied. *Mother and Singer are still fending off the l'ith around the west Plenari forests.*

Leonie landed between them and reappeared. She'd not seen a wyvern jump before, let alone two. "Ha. Surprised you both!" she laughed. "It's okay though, I won't tell anyone."

"I will though," Jade chuckled.

We weren't surprised, Faldo objected.

We just moved away before we stepped on you, Slana finished. *Mother would be upset at your squishing.*

"Oh, I'm sure was what it was." She smiled. "How are you, Feiron?" she turned to the shapechanger.

"I'm well enough. I see you are too." The illios oozed off Faldo's back beside her.

"No saddles," Leonie noted.

"You forget, I have two decades experience in riding now."

She turned to Jade. "Where's Gretchen? Didn't you have a gnasher?"

"We went directly to Dalmellington, arriving last night." Jade dismounted.

"I know only a week has passed, but it's very good to see you again."

"Likewise." Jade hesitated. "To be honest, I wasn't sure you'd be here."

"You know my previous absence was out of my control." Leonie put her paws on her shoulders and gazed into her blue eyes. "Jade, while I'm sure we will both regret it in a few weeks, we'll not part again. You have my word."

"Okay, this is getting embarrassing," Jade laughed, looking away.

Even Slana and Faldo snorted, but Leonie noted a hint of a tear as she pulled away to grab her pack.

"Have you spent all those Reenatian ducats yet?" Jade asked.

Leonie smiled and told her the exorbitant costs for lodging at the *Last Resort*.

"I hope you didn't pay!" Jade protested.

"Oh, I did, just to shut him up. The look on his face when I dropped a pawful of gold ducats in front of him was worth it."

"I'm deeply disappointed—"

"I didn't let him keep it!" Leonie laughed. "I even made a small profit when I left."

"That's what I like to hear." Jade slapped her on the back. "Shall we?"

"How are things in Tesak?" she asked.

"Not so desperate that they can't spare the pair of us for this search for the portals."

"The Investigator's Guild allowed that?" Leonie questioned Feiron.

"It was permitted as a token of merit for my dedication within Tesak."

"Ah yes, the spying. Got you." She winked.

"Under the circumstances, this search is now the priority."

Leonie gave both wyverns a scratch on the snouts when they moved their heads closer. "And you two are well enough, I see."

We are, though Faldo is still fatter.

"Still stealing Phil's breakfast, no doubt," Leonie replied.

Taste-testing is not stealing. Faldo defended himself. *Singer is an important personage. I am simply ensuring his good health.*

"If you keep telling yourself that, Faldo, you'll believe it."

We will return at dawn. Slana and her brother unfurled their wings.

"It's so good to see you both again," Leonie called out as they took off.

And you too, furry one.

She watched them fly off, no doubt in search of food. "I hope they don't eat any cows." Leonie turned to Jade and Feiron. "How would you like to meet some of my friends tomorrow?"

"We are at your disposal and would be delighted," Feiron spoke for the both of them. "It will be nice to see White Cliffs again. I've not had the opportunity to visit for many years."

"Why are you here?" Jade asked. "I was expecting to see you in Delta."

"Been there, done that." Leonie explained her recent travails as they strolled to the cavern resort.

"You've travelled across Shak'aran, been romping around Delta, travelled to your Earth, and then back to Reenat? All in less than a week?" Jade sounded stunned.

"All true. And now we'll be heading back to Earth tomorrow. Zander is trying to start a war in the tower."

"Why are we waiting?" Feiron asked. "I'd think that's your priority."

"And get blamed for disappearing again?" Leonie told them about retrieving the portal. "Apart from an idea I had, they insisted I come here while they fetched it. In the meantime, Krre'lo is putting an army of powershaper volunteers to help."

"Are we invited?"

"Sure, but can you?"

"I'm on leave from the guild."

"And I'm a free spirit, remember? Can't get rid of us that easily."

The trio arrived at the rollo resort.

Greetings Jade and Feiron.

"Hi Riff," Feiron replied.

Dwer, at your service.

"Apologies."

"You said you could only communicate when touching?" Leonie pointed out.

"That is with the wyverns. The rollos seem much stronger, or I'm more sensitive to them at close range."

It is complex, but that will suffice, Dwer confirmed.

After a quick wash, Jade joined Leonie and Feiron in the dining room. "What's this other idea you mentioned before?" she asked looking at the array of dishes to choose from.

Leonie poured the wine. "The rollos are the only ones I know that can get messages across the country quickly. I need to ask if they are in a position to spread the word about the portals, and inevitable evacuation."

"We don't know if we'll find more yet," Jade pointed out.

"That's irrelevant. Earth can take them all if need be, but food and shelter will be a concern – better than roasting though. Everyone needs to gather to their nearest major city. The best hope of getting as many people as possible away is to have them centralised. There's no agenda yet, but to get the maximum number through the portal. Perhaps for a week each, we can have the portal at each city."

"Can you cover those cities that fast?" Jade asked, between mouthfuls.

"With the *Sundancer*, we can get there in a blink."

"What about the temples?" Feiron absorbed his food, and simply created a mouth to speak clearly.

"Temples? What about them?"

"They too have their inter-temple communications."

"Do they," Leonie pondered. "Maybe they're useful after all."

"And they're everywhere; even the most remote village will have a temple of one order or another. We might entice the glins'ool to visit skylands in their regions, to narrow down the field," Feiron also suggested.

"And the wyverns," Jade added. "Dorn and Noldor can contact their brethren and see what they know."

"I thought wyverns cared little about our history."

"It can't hurt."

"True enough." She brought out the timetables. "Here's what we know so far."

25

ELABORATE PLANS

Leonie returned to Reenat around midday, Jade and Feiron walking by her side, having left the wyverns back at the cross-roads. Her trip to Qelay was uneventful, but even though they had been reunited a week earlier, seeing Jade and Feiron again brought more emotions to the surface.

Nearing Shaper Hall, many citizens were lining up to get inside. One of the guards recognised Leonie and waved her through. Several citizens waiting in line objected, to no avail.

As the trio walked down the stairs towards the barricade wall and the arena, Leonie explained what they were seeing. Jade was familiar with the arena and the black crystal, but Feiron had not set foot here previously.

"There was no need. I'm not nor ever will be a powershaper," the illios in the guise of a young man admitted.

In the centre of the arena's sandy floor stood a crowd of robed individuals. Most of them were human, but there were a couple of rrell, glins'ool and seleth among them. Towards the northern side of the arena was the portal, with a powerpac beside it. Two gryphons and their riders were on opposite sides, wary as their mounts circled it.

Giving the gryphons ample space, Lerry removed the cable

and sling used to transport the portal. Towards the southern wall was the *Skydancer*. If she wasn't mistaken, it looked in better condition than the last time she saw it.

"Here we go." Willing the pair up and over the wall, they glided towards the spaceship.

"How was it?" Leonie asked when she caught up with David. She nodded to Nicholai who emerged from the ship.

"The *Sundancer* wasn't suitable for this task, and the hold wasn't large enough. Looks like I need to design a bigger one."

"Already obsolete in a matter of weeks." Leonie smiled. "When did you get the chance to repair it?" She pointed to the fixed tail section.

"Last week after we returned to Skyhome, when you decided to race off to check on the tower, I reprogrammed a couple of the mech-droids to carry out repairs. It still can't time-jump though. Also, the skyland has dropped seventeen hundred metres."

"Is that because of the absorption of power?"

"I believe so. I could confirm with longer tests."

"Or I could compare the strength of a fireball. How will the drop in height affect the flight path?" She waved to Lerry who joined them. He dropped the coil of cabling by the steps of the ship then wiped sweat from his brow.

"On the plus side, it isn't low enough to strike anything yet," David advised.

"No Sussah and Harrond?" She turned to Lerry.

"It was agreed they stay at SciCorps," Lerry said. "They can keep us updated on any major developments."

"Of course, and she can have her bath." Leonie smiled. "And where's Bern?"

"He felt he was more use in Skyhome." Lerry watched with interest as more exotic visitors gathered around the arena to see the portal and sky-ship. "They've been coming and going all morning."

"We saw a long line of them outside. This is Jade and Feiron by the way," she introduced her friends. "How is it back in the tower?" Leonie asked, watching the milling crowd. Some took seats while others made a circuit of the arena to see everything at different angles. "Any idea how the people have been affected?"

"Things aren't great. Other than the SciCorps corridor, Alex's group have the top ten floors in lockdown. Most of the fires have stopped, but we don't get much news out of there, and no real idea of how the citizens are being dealt with. The occasional drone sends vids before it gets zapped; there look to be many casualties.

"David has a few drones of his own that Su or Harrond can send out and tap into. The garrison on level 10 has managed to stop the bulk of the rebels, but at a high cost. There are sporadic skirmishes on lower floors. The only thing keeping them viable is the reinforcements making their way up from the other zones."

"It sounds like Jay has managed to organise them," Lerry added.

"Have there been any attacks in the other zones?" she asked.

Lerry shook his head. "No, everything is confined to the White Zone, as far as we can tell. A few groups had tried to fly outside and come in through private docks, but the security lasers took them out when they got too close."

"What about SciCorps?" she asked.

"Same thing with the dock. The corridor is littered with corpses of militia and a few shapers when they tried to get in." The agtech turned to David. "Looks like your upgraded security system is quite formidable."

As they talked, a large dark man in robes broke from the cluster of shapers and sauntered over. Leonie introduced Krre'lo to the others.

"Jade I know already," the First Mage said. Nodding to the others. "We have news from your world?"

Lerry repeated the news so far.

"One of the aspects in your favour, and Leonie we touched on this during your training, is that many of those shapers are only adept in one, maybe two elements. Since you are capable of five, you have the advantage."

"But I'm one against dozens—"

"Not all of those shapers are registered at Shaper Hall. While a couple are no doubt formidable, most are untrained, raw talents. What you've got here is over four dozen highly trained shapers."

"We've seen how the others fight; one will do fire, one might do lightning, but they need another to get them around," Lerry added.

"How did you witness this and survive?" Krre'lo asked in interest.

Leonie explained what a drone and vid was. "It's like a vision, or looking through a crystal display. There's no immediate danger to the viewer." She looked towards the shapers. "This is great, but I thought there'd be more?"

"It's only been a couple of days; give it time. Not all have arrived. So, when would you like to start?"

"I'll need to go through first and move the portal somewhere more practical." She explained where the sister portal was within the tower. She turned to David. "What do you say?"

"Once the portal is out of SciCorps, it will become vulnerable and a target. As will you."

"I'll do my best to protect it." She hoped her work with Jay and the troops would be an asset.

"The advantage of a mobile portal means a large number of shapers can be moved quickly anywhere," David continued.

"Forgive my intrusion, but you're forgetting our other assets," Krre'lo suggested.

"What other assets?"

"Our Gryphon Riders." He pointed to the circling patrol.

And me, at your service.

Leonie spun around as the crowd gasped, parting quickly as the reddish spiked rollo trundled into the arena.

"What the hell's that?" Nicholai squawked, going pale seeing the hroltahg for the first time.

I heard you were in town. Leonie watched the rollo entering. *You want to be part of this?*

I have been part of this for a long time.

After a quick lunch the group wandered back to the arena. It was just as warm outside than inside, but the breeze and fresh air made it marginally more comfortable.

With the information gleaned from David's mind they formulated a more detailed plan. Styx would then relay the floor plan of the tower to the shapers, a distinct advantage over the rebel shapers.

Part of the strategy was for Leonie to mobilise the portal, and maintain invisibility during the process. She moved closer to it and willed it up a few feet. While it hovered, she turned it invisible. This part of the experiment was new, as she didn't have to make contact with it.

Your skills have improved remarkably, Styx complimented.

I had more training here, and also a bit of advice on technique from the Eternix High Priest. Another aspect of her modified talent was to be able to see it whilst it was invisible. For practice, Leonie moved the portal up and down a bit more before replacing it.

In the first phase, Gryphon Riders would escort a group of shapers and take control of the spaceport. Once she manoeuvred the portal into the atrium, she'd coordinate with tower troops. At her signal, shapers would come through and begin their assault. She just had to work out how to get the portal from the outside of the tower to the inside.

"That's all well and good for the White Zone, but what about the other zones if the fight spreads there?"

"They can get in like I did twenty years ago, via the railway tube. Once they get into the terminal, it's a short trip along the corridors to access the Red Zone atrium. From there it's easier to reach the Green and Blue Zones."

"Is it that easy to breach the tower?" the Prime asked, appalled.

"Only if one can do magic. Don't stress; for anyone else it would be very difficult."

"What do you need me to do?" David asked.

"Apart from causing as much trouble to Alexander as we can, I'm hoping to distract him from an all-out assault on SciCorps. We need you to do what you do best; invent stuff. A portal sensor or something similar."

I can assist there. Styx thought to all concerned.

"How can you assist, Styx?" Leonie asked.

I have studied our portal, and other than destination, there are consistencies with yours. There is a faint web of energy.

"And this energy you sense, you can use that to trace a portal?"

I can.

"Fascinating," David said softly.

David has stated he can devise a sensor. I'll provide the details of what he is to look for.

"Sounds good to me."

It is beyond your human audio range.

Leonie laughed, looking at David. "See what I had to put up with?"

"I need to be doing something," Nicholai stated.

"You've not been forgotten." Leonie turned to him. "How's your negotiating skills?"

"I'd like to think they are quite reasonable. Why?"

"There's going to be a huge influx of people heading to Earth in the next month or so if not sooner. Where will they live? If the terrain outside isn't viable, they'll need your help and that of the other towers."

"I have a reasonable affiliation with several southern towers, but these people have no skills—"

"Why the frack does that matter? They live and breathe and need refuge."

"I understand perfectly; what I was getting at is *how* I sell the idea to the Primes of the other towers. How do they benefit assuming goodwill isn't sufficient? They all have their problems too."

"Is outside bad everywhere like it is around Blue Mountains Tower?"

Nicholai licked his lips. "No. Not at all. There are tracts of land quite clean. How many people are we talking about?"

Leonie turned to Krre'lo. "Any idea?"

"It's a few years out of date, but the last estimate was around four-and-a-half million people—"

"Humans?" Nick coughed.

"Oh no, no. That's in total. Humans, glins'ool, seleth, rrell, vorien and illios."

"Vorien? Illios? Have I seen any of them?"

"Voriens are aquarians, or mermen ... they live predominantly in the sea."

"We have a lot of that. Earth's surface is about 80% water. And this other ..."

"The illios," Leonie supplied. "Do you really want to see one?" She winked at Feiron.

"I should have an idea of—" He looked faint as the young man beside him suddenly melted into a puddle. It then reformed into several other shapes before reverting back to the original young man.

Nicholai's mouth hung open for a while.

"I reckon they can come in handy," Leonie broke the silence. "Let's not get ahead of ourselves. That's the worst-case scenario if the other portals aren't located in time. How many humans are there?"

Krre'lo considered. "Possibly one-and-a-half million."

It took a nudge from Leonie to get the Prime to focus.

"Very well then." He paused, looking around at the group. "We could possibly take about twenty percent of that."

"And the rest?"

Nicholai pursed his lips. "Negotiations will be needed with La Trobe and Warburton Towers. They are further south; the terrain is also more viable than these parts."

"Then that's your job. Once it's safe and we can get a flyer—"

"In person? I'll need a pilot. It's been far too long since I flew anything."

"If we sought one out, will you arrange to talk to them? I think the personal approach is better."

"Even so, they will never believe me."

If it will save lives, I will volunteer. I do have some ambassadorial skills, and I am curious to see your homeworld too.

Nick looked nervous. "It— *he* looks quite ..."

"Protective, I think is the word you're looking for. Other than wyverns, no one will get close enough to you to cause harm."

There was a call. One of the Gryphon Riders quickly strode towards them.

"My lord, this just came through the portal." The rider handed Krre'lo a piece of paper tied to a paperweight. The First Mage handed it straight to Leonie. She read it quickly and swore, then handed it to David.

"From Harrond. Looks like the shapers are making a concerted effort to get into your labs." She turned to the mage. "I've no idea what's going on, but can I get maybe six of your shapers to come with me?"

"At once." The dark man turned and barked some orders. Half a dozen shapers separated from the milling group.

"Gentlemen – and ladies," she started, noting two female shapers. "Going through the portal is initially uncomfortable. You'll feel an intense cold and maybe dizziness. It will seem like it's lasting a long time, but is in fact about thirty seconds."

They looked quizzically at her.

"I mean it's only for a short time. Don't stress. Also, what you see on the other side will be completely alien to you. Just relax and don't touch anything. When I go through, count to ten then come through in pairs with the same interval between each transition. Got that?" She looked around at the confirmed nods. "Good."

She turned to her companions. "You guys coming?" Leonie called out. Without glancing back, she flew through the portal.

26

SCICORPS

She picked up the odour of smoke immediately after her arrival. Su and Harrond, waiting anxiously nearby, sighed when Leonie appeared.

"Thank goodness you're here." Sussah came to her straight away to hold her paw with a smile of relief.

"We would have come through to you, but we didn't know where the portal was," Harrond said.

"Safe now if you want to leave, but let's see what's going on out there." Leonie pulled Sussah away from the portal as she moved to the vid on the desk. Jade and Feiron arrived a second later. Jade stumbled a few steps, but retained her balance.

"Does that happen every time?" Jade asked, shivering. Feiron looked discomforted by her side.

"More or less, but you get used to it," Leonie answered over her shoulder.

"I hope so," Feiron stated. "Ever since the White Cliff caverns, I have been more susceptible to the cold."

"I'd rather not do it enough to get used to it." Jade nodded a greeting.

Leonie introduced them all as she watched the monitor. A vid showed the corridor outside full of smoke.

"Lasers are less effective in smoke," Harrond explained. "With ventilation cut off, it's getting quite thick out there. I think they started a fire on purpose to disrupt the lasers."

"And I guess the lasers are still working because SciCorps is on an isolated circuit?" Leonie suggested, noting the clearer air inside.

Harrond agreed. "Power fluctuations outside only. So far, we've been fine in here."

"Just so you're prepared, there are more people coming through any second." Leonie turned to the portal. "They'll be helping us."

A few seconds later, two more people in strange garb appeared. Quick to react, Jade and Feiron reached out to prevent them from falling over.

"It can be disorienting," Leonie said to them. "Welcome to Earth." She let the new arrivals regain their senses as they were guided to the side. It wasn't long before the six shapers were walking around; astonished by what they saw, and studying the alien walls and furniture. David, Nicholai and Styx made the final appearance.

Sussah had seen seleth before, but covered her mouth to prevent a scream at the sight of the reddish spikey ball.

"If SciCorps is under attack, I should be here," the scientist said.

"No argument from me," Leonie agreed. "There's a build-up of smoke in the corridor outside—"

"Which reduces the laser's capabilities." David joined her by the monitor, seeing the external corridor.

"Not much to look at," Leonie stated. "If I can get a breeze going in there the lasers firing up should slow them down."

In the distance came the sound of muffled explosions. "Sounds like they're attacking the dock as well." David flicked to the external view of the dock. They could see a group of rebel shapers hovering beyond the security sensor's range. Anything closer was blasted.

"What's that on the pad?" Sussah asked.

"Looks like wreckage of a flyer," David noted. "Did anything happen earlier?"

"There was a noise," Harrond replied. "Nothing like now though, just a few soft thumping sounds."

"Laser cannon." David nodded. "Someone tried to access the pad without the correct protocols."

"This will be our priority," Leonie spoke up as she addressed the shapers. "We'll need to get rid of them, one way or the other."

"It's safe to take them through. I've deactivated the internal security," David added. "It'll take too long to put everyone in the system."

Leonie nodded and started to lead the shapers from the back of the laboratory complex to the main entrance and docking area. The smoke odour was stronger, and the larger door leading to the landing pad was darkened and bulged slightly at its centre. "Any ideas?"

She heard the expected responses. "Blast them with fireballs; I can zap them." Others called out similar suggestions.

"What about you?" Leonie noticed a shaper in brown robes who hadn't yet responded. "Anything?"

"Agnetta hass nothing to attack with," a black-robed seleth stated.

"I doubt the First Mage would pick someone without skills or merit," Leonie spoke over him. "Agnetta, is it? What can you bring to the party?"

"With assistance, I can suck the power from all of them."

"Prepossterouss!" the seleth claimed, his thick tail thumping the floor.

"How? What assistance?" Leonie asked.

"Kizgra is right. I'm an Earther, we do not *attack*. Our training is in defence and protection only."

More rumbling sounded against the door.

"Fine, but how? And be quick!" The group reached the docking area. The large door shook as another blast hit it.

Agnetta looked around at the alien flooring with distaste. "I am not connected to the ground, but if we all link by touch, my ability is to drain power from the targets."

"So, they stand behind you and hold your shoulder?" Leonie guessed.

"Just one has to make contact with me, but everyone else needs to grab another like a chain."

"Okay then. Sounds like a plan to me." Leonie reached for the normal-sized side door. "Everyone line up behind Agnetta."

"Then we can kill them," one said as they reached out to grab the other's shoulder.

"Actually, I want a prisoner to question," Leonie informed them. "To find out what Lord Zander has planned." She used Zander as it was the name they'd be familiar with. "Only Agnetta will be in front. The rest of you stay inside and out of sight. You sure this can work?"

Agnetta, concentrating, nodded.

"I'm going invisible. Don't worry about me, just take them out. Here we go."

She pulled the door open and disappeared.

With all shapers linked, Agnetta stepped to the threshold and began chanting, both arms forward and palms facing out.

A fireball in mid-flight shrivelled and dissipated before contacting the door. Some in the rebel group pointed at the new target, but as they conjured up bolts of electricity or fireballs, the energy drained from them. The rebel shapers panicked and tried to escape, but suddenly dropped out of sight.

With relief, those behind the Earther mage relaxed their hold on each other, breaking the power chain. Agnetta slumped against the door frame, sweat beading on her brow.

One of her powershaper companions patted her on the back. "So, even protective incantations can be lethal," he commented as he ventured outside. Acknowledging her successful tactic as they passed, her colleagues ventured outside as well. Buffeted by strong wind gusts, they kept away from the edge, gazing wide-eyed at their surrounds and the vista the dock's height provided.

Suddenly two rebel shapers flew over the edge of the platform. Before the group could do anything, they crashed hard against the large door and fell immobile to the dock.

Leonie appeared and landed beside them. "Well done. I'll question these two later, but now we have to deal with those in the corridor." Before she re-entered the docking area, she flicked the wreckage of the flyer off the pad.

As they entered, loud banging came from the other side of the front doors.

"All done out there I take it?" David asked as he and Jade waited by the entrance doors. He had a pulse rifle and she held two daggers. Styx looked like a statue in the centre of the room.

"All done," Leonie replied. "I was going to clear the smoke and let the lasers do their work, but if they're at the door already—"

I can immobilise all eight of them, Styx suggested to her.

Do it. Leonie then spoke quickly of her plans to her shapers. "Can any of you manipulate air?" They shook their heads. "Okay. Pick your target; eight of them left to right, and do what you do best."

The shapers prepared themselves and lined up facing the entry.

"David, when I say so, unlock the doors, open them and move back."

He moved close to the doorway, shouldering the rifle.

They are immobile.

"Now," Leonie ordered.

Using the keypad, the scientist unlocked the doors and pulled both of them open before prudently stepping out of the line of fire. Swirls of smoke began to infiltrate the room. The blaring of the smoke alarms, muted by the security doors, now filled their ears.

Directly in front were four militia, swords in hand; behind were four rebel shapers. Smoke curled around them, but remained clear of their faces. All were frozen in place, but their new predicament plainly showing in their eyes.

As Leonie created a strong breeze to blow the smoke clear of the room and back down the corridor, her allies let loose with controlled fireballs or bolts of electricity. The intruders all slumped to the floor when Styx released them.

The smoke quickly dissipated and the lasers started firing at targets further down the corridor. It was over in seconds.

Leonie stepped forward and snatched a glance around the corridor. "That should keep them away for a while."

"You guys have all the fun," Jade grumbled, sheathing her knives.

"Next time. Promise." Leonie chuckled as she willed the doors closed. There were sighs of relief with the alarms muted again. "What now?" She looked at David.

"I still believe my best role is to design a sensor." He came over to activate the door locking mechanism.

"Do you have enough information to go by?" Leonie asked.

"Styx here has what I need."

I do. I will take the liberty of portalling back to Reenat first. Once I have embedded the floor plans for the levels into the minds of the other shapers, I will return. Nicholai and I can then begin our travels and negotiations with the other tower Primes. The rollo made his way across the room to the far exit.

On the other side of the room Nicholai quickly sidestepped the departing hroltahg and approached David's personal flyer parked by the wall near the dock door. "Will we be using this?"

"It's ideal as it has the stealth technology," David agreed. "And dock security won't blow it out of the sky."

"Reassuring to know." Nicholai nodded.

"And I still have two rebels to interrogate outside." Leonie made her way towards the landing pad.

"Not any more you haven't," Agnetta said meekly from her position by the large dock door.

"What happened?" Leonie questioned.

"One revived. He grabbed his colleague and was flying away. You were busy ..." Agnetta studied her shoes.

"You drained him?" another shaper asked.

"It was that or let them escape," Agnetta said in her defence.

"It's okay," Leonie reassured the Earther. "I'm not sure what we would have done with them afterwards anyway."

"What do we do about those in the corridor?" Lerry asked.

"Recyc as usual." Nicholai shrugged.

"Recyc? Is that a burial ceremony?" Feiron asked.

"We utilise everything we—"

"You reuse bodies?" a shaper asked in disgust. Others echoed their displeasure.

"For horticultural and medical needs. It's the standard procedure. Nothing goes to waste," the Prime finished.

"Okay then," Leonie interrupted, changing the subject. "David, is your flyer ready for flight?"

"I'll need to run over the diagnostics quickly."

"Then perhaps, Nicholai, you'd like to freshen up for your trip? Looks like you and David are similar sizes?"

"Now? I guess so."

"I'll show you to the bathroom and then fetch a change of clothes," David offered, leading the flustered Prime away.

Leonie turned to the other shapers. "This world is not ideal and far different from what you're used to. It has had centuries of problems, but is slowly on the improve. Unfortunately, Yarnik will soon be uninhabitable. If we succeed here, you could be the start of change here. That's where Nicholai is going, to arrange for safe havens for all of you, either here or elsewhere."

"Is there anything in particular planned for us now?" Agnetta asked.

"Not at this moment. I'm about to fetch the portal and move it to other areas around the tower. Once your colleagues arrive and everyone's in place, we can coordinate a strategy. I'm hoping you can wait here until then?"

The shapers considered this, discussing amongst themselves. Agnetta finally spoke for her group. "I assume this place is safe for the moment?"

"It is. I doubt Zander will try another attack like that, and very shortly he'll have much more to worry about." She spoke to Sussah and Harrond briefly then turned back to the group. "I reckon after all that, you're hungry? There's food and drinks in this area." She pointed to the kitchen. "My friends here can help you out."

They nodded. "That would be good, yes."

"I won't be long." Leaving Jade and Feiron with the others to get a meal, she made her way back through the labs. After making certain it was charged to full capacity with David's ad hoc powerpac still attached to the base, Leonie left the portal by the docking bay door.

The smell of food made her realise a lot had happened since her lunch in Shaper Hall. Not knowing when the next meal would be, she decided to join the others. As she dished out her food, the shapers were staring in amazement at the tablet as Harrond brought up information and vids.

"Sussah, Harrond and Lerry, can you stay here?" Leonie asked. "David will be busy but might need some assistance. At the least we'll need someone to maintain communications." She went to a drawer and searched for comlinks. She found a couple and gave one to Lerry and kept one for herself.

Sussah looked up from Harrond's demonstration. "I'm a pilot now," she said proudly.

"You're a what?" Leonie nearly spat out her food.

"A qualified pilot." While you were away and galivanting around Yarnik, Harrond helped me hook up to the database. We downloaded all the data, went through the course, and then I qualified. I've been training on and off since the portal was on Skyhome."

"I even have her certification right here." Harrond proudly showed Leonie the e-certificate he called up on the tablet.

"I can also fly those air bikes, and even manage a few technical repairs on electronics." Sussah laughed. "You probably thought I've been sitting around having baths all the time."

"Who? Me?" Leonie backpedalled. "The thought never crossed my mind. That's great news." She rested her paws on her friend's shoulder. "It's a good thing to learn. You want to fly the Prime to La Trobe?"

"Can I?" she asked, wide-eyed.

"Why not? Unless there's another pilot available? With Styx along, it will probably be the next safest place for you, unless you want to go to Reenat?"

"Oh no. Here is fine. I'm happy to finally be of use."

"Everyone does what they can. You've been no exception," Leonie encouraged. "Are you happy with that arrangement, Harrond?"

"Regardless of what I've been telling her, Su's been looking for a way to pull her weight. This will be good for her." Harrond hugged her when she walked to him.

She looked at Lerry and Harrond. "That leaves you two to help the powershapers while David keeps busy in his lab."

"I think Feiron and I will see what we can do this end," Jade confirmed.

"What are you two up to?" Leonie asked suspiciously.

"You've enough to worry about without us getting in the way," Jade said. "While you're busy with the portal, we might see what Alexander is up to. Take some of the action to him instead, maybe divide his forces and make your job easier."

"You two better be careful." Leonie regarded Jade then Feiron. "Things here are very different."

"The two of us have worked together on and off for two decades. We'll be okay."

"I've no doubt, but there are things here which neither of you has any understanding."

"We're quick learners." Jade patted Leonie's shoulder. "And I bet they haven't seen what a shapeshifter can do."

"So, who's coming through first?" the illios asked, stalling further concerns.

Leonie sighed at them for their stubbornness. "If they're ready, the Gryphon Riders should be. I better get the portal up to the roof."

At that moment, Styx returned through the shimmer and rolled across the floor towards them.

"That could have been awkward, Styx," Leonie chided. "I

was about to take it outside. I don't reckon even you could survive a fall from this height."

Considering who trained you, I am confident in your skills. He stopped by her side. *All the powershapers have been given the floor plans of this zone. They are ready for deployment, as are the Gryphon Riders.* He unfolded himself and handed her a fist-sized black crystal cube. *This is the signal for commencement. Toss this back when you are in position. They will then come through.*

"I didn't know you had a pouch," she said, surprised.

We call them pockets. Styx trundled to the flyer. *Here is Nicholai now.*

Sussah finished her drink and stood, watching as the spikey ball rolled under the craft. The belly of the fuselage was less than a metre above the floor.

David returned. Nicholai followed in a change of fresh clothes. "Is this ... Styx ... able to climb into the flyer?" he asked, seeing the red alien under the ship.

"Now there's something I hadn't considered," Leonie admitted. "Jumping is out of the question." *Are you able to levitate?* she asked him.

I am fully capable of climbing. I believe there is a ladder.

Sussah walked over and tapped a panel. A small ladder extended from the hull and several niches revealed in the side just forward of the short wings. "There you go."

Excellent. Thank you. Styx unfolded into his stubby wedge-shape and climbed the ladder with his short arms and legs with care so as not to puncture the hull with his claws. Once inside, he settled into the area behind the seats. *So my spikes don't puncture your seats,* he explained.

With only the briefest hesitation, Nicholai climbed in and got comfortable.

Sussah made sure he was secure then climbed in and familiarised herself with the controls while David operated the main door to the outside landing pad. Because of the damage by the rebel shapers, it only opened halfway, but enough for the flyer to pass through.

Leonie walked outside onto the pad, keeping an eye out for any potential threats. "You don't seem surprised about your mum being a pilot now," she said loudly over the wind.

"I knew of her keenness to help out. It seemed the better option," David winked. "And I saw the logs. She had considered getting arms training to be a more affirmative female like yourself."

"Pfft."

"That's what I said."

"To what? Her getting arms training, or me being an affirmative female?"

Any response was lost in the excited talking from the shapers who came out to watch with interest as Sussah manoeuvred the flyer out onto the pad as soon as the door was open.

David stepped closer and leant in, pointing to the additional controls. "This won't be in your training. These activate the stealth mode." He flicked a switch and adjusted a dial. The fuselage became a mirage, barely visible, only the interior being discernible through the open cockpit. "I suggest you keep it activated until you're well out of Blue Mountains Tower airspace."

"And just do what you did in reverse to cancel it?" his mother asked.

"Precisely. Enjoy the flight, mum. Good luck, Nicholai. Take care of them, Styx."

Of course.

David stepped away as the canopy lowered and sealed, rendering the entire craft virtually invisible. If one looked carefully, they'd see rippling air. The hum of the craft faded quickly in the distance.

"I'm surprised Nick went so easily with Styx," Leonie said to David.

"Oh. We had a discussion about it," David informed her. "He finally came around to the inevitability of it. I expressed my doubts of anyone believing a word he said without irrefutable evidence. Styx is that evidence. Then there's his telepathy, ambassadorial experience and of being a bodyguard."

"Let me guess, the bodyguard aspect was what convinced him?"

"Nicholai isn't perfect, but he is quite astute when he needs to be, and the flyer does have stealth tech. I'm sure someone would be interested in it. I hope the talks works out." David said as they stepped back inside with the others.

"If Styx can't convince them, it'll be a worry." Leonie drained her now cold coffee and finished the last of her meal. "I better get this portal to the roof. They'll be restless at the delay." She checked her comlink with Lerry before moving the portal outside. "Hey," Leonie turned and called to the shapers. Once the flyer departed, they were now back inside, making themselves comfortable on the lounge chairs. "It's going to get hectic and we might not get a chance to talk for a while. Thank you all for your help here."

Surprised, the shapers nodded and murmured their acknowledgments.

"I'll be on coms in the back lab," David said as the large door closed. "You know where to find me." He waved over his shoulder.

———

Leonie settled the portal on the rooftop far enough away from the tower's edges and crashed flyer wreckage to allow plenty of space for the gryphons' arrival. She tossed the crystal cube through and waited.

She gazed around the vast flat windswept expanse surrounding her. In all her time at the tower, she hadn't spent much time up here. *For good reason.* Leonie strolled over to the multi-windowed glass pyramid structure in the centre of the tower. "Must be the atrium skylight to let the natural light into the centre of White Zone," Leonie considered. "And about the only natural light many of these people get."

The wind filled her ears and ruffled her fur while she wandered over to the burnt-out carcass of the crashed flyer.

Scooping up a pawful of the red sand, detritus of the recent tempest, she let it sift through her fingers then watched the dust storm on the horizon continuing its path to the southwest.

A grey gryphon emerged at a trot with a roar. The following gryphons also shook and roared at the discomfort, fluttering their large wings. Their riders, no doubt affected by the transition themselves, managed to retain enough control to keep their mounts moving so as not to hinder those behind. They all moved to one side, far more than needed, considering the last gryphon had already emerged.

The leader of the riders dismounted and walked around, searching.

"Over here." Leonie called out, then realised she was still invisible. With a laugh, she dismissed the spell to greet the rider, recognising her to be the one that confronted her on her first arrival to Reenat, where she was greeted with a crossbow bolt in the ribs.

"Well met," the rider said, realising now who it was she spoke to. "I'm Flight Leader Adera Belaarus, and the Grey Wing is at your service as instructed by the First Mage."

"Welcome to Earth. Do you have an idea of the layout?"

"From the hroltahg, we do," she confirmed.

"When you're ready, I'll take you over and point out a few things."

"Very good, ma'am, but there are still others to come through."

"Others? I counted twenty ..."

"Not gryphons, ma'am," she stated without elaboration.

The whiskered snout of a green wyvern appeared, followed by the head, long neck and the rest of its length. Being smaller than Noldor, it had no trouble fitting through.

"Faldo?"

Greetings, furry one!

"What the frack are you doing here?" Leonie growled.

I'm keeping Slana company. As Faldo moved away, his sister emerged behind him.

That was much worse than the puddleman described, Slana complained.

She turned as the gryphons roared their discomfort at the huge creatures' presence, the riders working hard to keep them at bay. "I better deal with this first." She motioned for Adera follow as she flew towards the space port.

The Flight Leader mounted her gryphon. "Rise," she ordered as she followed after Leonie. Turning in her direction, the Grey Wing gryphons unfurled their wings, took three running strides and launched in pairs.

"As you would have been told," Leonie called out to Adera. "This was used as the main entry point for Zander's forces. It may hold strategic significance. Have you any powershapers among your troops?"

"Only those with minimal skills. Anyone with more talent is encouraged to join Shaper Hall."

"Better than nothing. I have no doubts your Grey Wing is capable of controlling the area. Do that and you strike a blow to the rebel's confidence. They will see it as their escape route has been taken from them."

"A blow to their morale, but if this area is so important, there will be repercussions to our presence." Adera looked down curiously at the port they were now circling. "Before I forget, I was told you'd need this again." She scooped the black crystal out of her saddlebag.

Leonie put the cube in her pouch. "If all goes to plan, they'll be too busy elsewhere to give you too much grief. Good luck." She waved a farewell and turned back towards the centre of the roof where the two green wyverns looked so out of place on the massive structure.

"It's great to see you two, but you're too big to go inside," she said when she landed next to them. "Did Feiron have anything to do with this?"

Puddleman? No. We wanted to see this world for ourselves after Noldor's stories, Slana replied.

We can explore nearby, acclimatise and get our bearings, Faldo added.

"And there's a big, wide ocean over there to the east," Leonie pointed.

There might be a meal or two to be had, Faldo craned his neck to see.

Typical, Slana barked her amusement.

———

There were two TowerPol garrisons in White Zone; on the tenth and first levels, each with its own landing pad. The external docking area made it convenient to use as a staging area for the portal.

With her encrypted comlink, she managed to contact the commander regarding access for her companions. Feiron was in disguise as there was no way his natural form would be stomached without time for adjustment; time they didn't have.

Jay met them on the dock. He looked curiously at the portal as she explained what was going to happen. "And this leads to this other world you mention?" he sounded sceptical.

"I haven't time to explain, but you'll see soon enough. We've arranged for groups of allied shapers to come through and help. They will be wearing a blue arm-band—"

"Blue for the tower?"

"Correct. Let your men know not to attack them. They're here to help."

"And the Prime? Is he safe?"

"He's on his way to La Trobe Tower to negotiate assistance for these shapers and their families."

"La Trobe? Alone?"

"He has one of our best bodyguards with him. I reckon he's safer than you are with your garrison of troops. Anyway, our allies are waiting for me so they can come through."

At an order, the roller door opened fully, revealing several flyers within taking up half the docking bay. To one side, there was a side door with white-gowned people looking out.

"Are they medics?" she asked.

"Yes. There is a hospital attached to each garrison, and a smaller medbay adjacent to each of our bureaus."

At the back of the bay a handful of black-uniformed troops were milling in the doorway. Talking ceased as she entered, and all eyes were watching; some out of curiosity, some with fear and uncertainty. A couple of the officers she met on the walkway gave a brief wave, triggering an inundation of whispered questions from their colleagues. She heard *shadow* mentioned a couple of times.

"Is this sufficient space for your needs?" Jay was asking.

"Hmm? This will do fine." She nodded, moving the portal into position. She moved back, advising Jay to do the same. "Feiron, you can toss it through now."

Several minutes after the cube disappeared, pairs of shapers appeared. Although forewarned, the tower commander jolted upright in shock, especially seeing glins'ool, seleth and more rrells. In all, fifteen pairs arrived.

Leonie spoke to them softly as they came to grips with their alien surrounds.

One rrell shaper looked around, noticing for the first time the audience of the troops bunching up in the corridor. "I'm Truskot," he said. "Where would you like us deployed?" He studied her with curiosity as he handed her the crystal cube. "I've heard about you."

"What are the capabilities of the squad?" Leonie asked him, ignoring his last comment and pocketed the cube.

After a brief pause, Truskot detailed the group's various talents, Leonie realised Krre'lo had banded as many of the elements as possible. "Can any of you fly or levitate?"

"Yes, the First Mage surmised the ability to fly and carry would be useful."

"That's good to know. The rebels have only a few with that ability, so they're limited in what and where they can attack."

She guided the shaper by the arm. "This is the garrison commander. Jay? Where can you use them best?"

"I ..."

"Where is the most likely place for the rebels to attack? What's your weak point?"

"The atrium," he said immediately. "It is such a large space to cover with many access points."

"Not the elevator shafts?"

"We managed to station a few of those SciCorps security droids in there, so the shafts are fine. And we are manning the stairways."

"Great. Last thing; can we coordinate communications?"

"I'll have an equal number of my men deployed with them for support," the commander decided. "They can relay any messages. I recommend splitting into four groups; one for each side of the atrium."

"That sounds acceptable, commander." Truskot nodded, tail swaying back and forth. He turned and started organising four groups, each with a cross-section of abilities.

"I'm on coms, so call me if you need anything," Leonie said to both of them.

"Where will you go next?" Jay asked.

"Your other TowerPol station on level one," she answered. "And anywhere within White Zone with a docking bay."

"I'll send men around and wait for you. How many *shapers* are you expecting?"

"I think about sixty for the moment." She nodded, rising with the portal in tow. Before she moved to the next pad, she checked the portal's powerpac levels; almost depleted. *Time for a recharge.* She detoured to SciCorps to change the pac, briefed the others on progress then continued as planned. Within the hour, fifty-six powershapers had come through and been taken in an orderly fashion to where they were needed the most.

She dropped the last group on the Prime's personal pad and walked inside with the shapers as they made their way to the atrium. There were gasps from some of them; other than the damage from fire and other magical forces, the area was strewn with bodies.

"This is where the leader runs the tower – a bit like Reindet runs Reenat from the palace – I managed to get him out ... but not everyone."

"It looks like a war zone," one shaper noted to a colleague. Walking on in subdued silence, they reached the centre of the building. In equal amounts of amazement and bewilderment, they peered in all directions at the huge interior space.

"I know this is all very strange to you," she said, giving them the same pep talk as she gave the previous shapers on their arrival. "Your targets are rebel shapers, or anyone with a sword, axe or anything *you* recognise as a weapon. Everyone in a dark uniform is friendly," she advised. "Make sure you keep those blue armbands visible at all times, otherwise they'll shoot first and ask questions later."

They nodded their understanding and began looking for the rebels.

Feeling exhausted, she traipsed back through Nicholai's office to collect the portal and return to SciCorps. Desperately weary after all the power she'd expended, she reluctantly decided to rest for a couple of hours.

"You know, you do too much. I reckon the rest of us can look after ourselves for a while," Lerry said. "Then you can come back, all refreshed and save us."

"Or maybe I won't." She trudged to her bedroom in the residential section of SciCorps. It seemed like ages since she'd slept in her own bed. She stripped and washed before sinking into the soft mattress with a sigh.

27

A TROUBLESOME TRIO

Alex stared at the vid screen again. "These powershapers aren't ours! Where are they coming from? And those Gryphon Riders! How the frag did he get them?" Alexander raged, dragging himself away from the viewer and began pacing up and down his loungeroom. "Did Osbourne go back and recruit his own army? It was far too quick to be anything but planned. I *told* you he was after me."

"That's absurd," Dianah rebuked, worried his paranoia would make him do something stupid. "How did he get here to retrieve the *Sundancer*? How could he possibly have arranged to have a shaper army ready and waiting?"

"Time-travel, woman!" The wine in his glass slopped onto the floor as he waved his arms. "He could've started working on them years ago!" He looked around, wide-eyed. "Where's Brendon? What's he up to now?"

"He's probably dealing with our people, getting reports and directing them as he sees best."

"What *he* sees? Who made him boss? I'm in charge!"

"Then act like it! There's a wing of those Reenatian Gryphon Riders patrolling outside. The elevator shafts have high-tech droids, the stairs have TowerPol guards; most of our people are stuck on different levels with the atrium being heavily patrolled, and we can't get our people outside to get anywhere. The moment your father evaded us and things didn't go your way, you've holed up in here."

Alex threw his empty wine glass at the wall behind her.

"You need to get a grip on yourself." Startled at the anger, Dianah stood and stormed out. "So much for your guile and leverage," were her parting words.

Alexander swore, pacing back and forth frantically, muttering to himself. He stopped in front of the mirror, staring vacantly at his reflection. "I'm in control ..." he mumbled over and over.

Eventually, he picked up the comlink and jabbed a number. "It's me. I need something to take out a bunch of enemy *flyers* outside the tower. If you can't, I'll find someone else who can. Then I will destroy you, your business and your entire family. You will be so humiliated; they'll be laughing at your name for decades as far as Mars!" He nodded at the frantic voice.

"It better work. You say this old fighter doesn't have the AI capability and can't be overridden? Use it. Obliterate them. I don't care what it costs. Do it and you're in the clear. And before you try to double-cross me, if my death is from anything other than natural causes a long time from now, that data will be released." He slammed the link down. "I *am* in control."

Appalled at the carnage he encountered, Brendon stealthily made his way higher. Even the small rag-tag army he led years ago wouldn't molest or injure women or children, and if they didn't have a weapon, they became prisoners only. *And well-treated ones at that.*

Hearing crying, he tried a door, but it was locked. The crying stopped, but he heard it start again as he walked away. "How did we come to this?" he asked himself. *Once we win, I'll make changes.*

Fuming at being blamed for the loss of the ship, Brendon left the arguing to Alex and Dianah, deciding to put his efforts into finding out how the *Sundancer* was taken.

Only David and I can fly it, he mused as he trudged up the stairs to the shuttle port. *Was it on some sort of auto-recall? David never mentioned it. Because you asked the wrong questions, idiot!*

The guards he questioned earlier saw nothing and knew even less, and since the arrival of the Gryphon Riders, they were beyond another interrogation. *Despite their lack of any sense of humour, it was handy having an Opsyss priest or two to help get information from the dead. Maybe we can again, if we get on top of this mess.*

Careful to not alert the Gryphon Riders resting on the pad, Brendon snuck into the rear security room to scrutinise the local vid-feed on the hard drives. Like much of the White Zone, it was dimly lit, but as he hoped, the battery backup still functioned.

He locked the door and sat at the desk. The screen was still on, so he replayed the relevant timeline over and over. Sure enough, other than one guard sitting on the ramp minutes before it vanished, the guards were doing their job. Leaning back in the chair and rubbing his eyes, Brendon took a brief rest before continuing.

He selected a recording from the drones, hoping a different angle might shed some light. The footage of the flyer crash on their arrival was the most interesting thing so far. *Why so many drones?* he complained watching the ninth one.

Much like the others, this view was simply an angle above the pad, doing a circuit with the ship as its focus. As it cruised around, the sitting guard came into view. Having seen the same image several times, he reached to change vids. The drone's image jarred as it hit something. There was a blur of an image, then the normal scene. The drone moved on its course.

He paused and replayed the scene several times, trying to make sense of what he observed. An image filled the screen for a second. He slowed the vid down, then paused at the moment of impact.

Enlarging and enhancing the image, he sat back and swore.

He ported the image onto his wrist-com to show Dianah and Alex. In his haste to share the news, Brendon almost forgot about the riders. He paused at the doorway and glanced out, waiting for the right moment. Once sure their attention was elsewhere, he bolted across the passageway and ducked into the stairwell.

He had no idea how Leonie or David got here, or even how they somehow teamed up ... there was definitely something happening no one had any idea about. Brendon paused on the stairway and looked again at the image. *Are my eyes deceiving me?* Leaning against the railing, he breathed in and out slowly several times before studying it again.

The lower left corner was definitely the face of David, or part of it. The right side of the image was a black furry neck and a pointed ear. A feline ear.

Maybe it's only a rrell shaper after all? Brendon reconsidered. *Maybe not Leonie.* "But that's definitely David Osbourne," he whispered. "Working with these Reenatian powershapers."

Full of enthusiasm, like a kid he bounded down the stairs with the intentions of telling them the truth. 'It wasn't my fault!' he'd say. He stopped now and then to check his wrist-com, making sure he hadn't been dreaming. Looking around, he recognised the corridor of Dianah's apartment and decided to freshen up first.

I must be a mess, with all the running around. There was blood on his clothing, and he had to admit, he smelled a bit ripe.

Dianah needed time to consider the immediate future. Things weren't going to plan, and Alex was losing it. *Again.*

With her pair of militia protectors – apparently no shapers were available for her – she made her way to one of the balconies to view the atrium, where she could hear fighting. From this vantage point, as long as she remained out of sight, she could get an idea of the progress of their takeover.

The civilian part of her mind registered the bodies seen

inside some apartments or piled to the sides of the passageways; the scientist part acknowledged casualties were to be expected.

Their powershapers and militia were battling the newcomers below. It didn't take long to see it wasn't going as well as expected. While power was thrown back and forth, she saw TowerPol moving in from the flanks.

"Someone is coordinating this lot ... and better than us." *Where has Brendon gone?*

"What is your bidding, lady?" one of her guards asked, seeing his comrades being hemmed in.

"See what you can do to help them. We've not seen any danger on this level. I will head back to my apartment. I'll be safe there."

They left after a brief bow.

She knew Alexander still had powerful contacts, but whether they were in a position to help in time ... she had doubts. Her priority was always HelixR and her research, but it was awkward to get to now with well over a hundred floors to traverse, especially with TowerPol – and now Osbourne's shapers – on the scene. It was a conundrum to get there; stairs were unlikely, the lifts weren't an option, and any request for a shaper to assist would need to get past Olekk. *Fat chance, considering they had none to spare to protect me.*

Now that the shrewd mage saw first-hand how divine Lord Zander really was, it wouldn't surprise her one bit if Olekk and his closest shapers didn't have their own ambitions. *Best to keep away from him now.*

She considered it time to make alternative arrangements for herself. Secretive communiques with anonymous peers revealed other towers would pay for research like hers; even the colonies were an option.

Though the moon or Mars will remain at the bottom of my list. Running through her possible remaining allies, her mind set on Drake and his crew. Though wild and unscrupulous, her number one mercenary leader had always been there for her in the past and she had little doubt he had coped okay in her absence. *His type always come out on top.*

Resolved in her decision, Dianah returned to her apartment. Only when she had a hot espresso in her hand did she activate her personal sat-com link in her desk and put through an encrypted call. waiting apprehensively until it was finally answered. His vid was dark as usual. "Drake?" There was static on the line. "It's Dianah."

There was a pause. "Dianah Felton?" he sounded surprised. "You— Where the frag have you been? Where are you now?" His voice changed back to the rough, no-nonsense tone she was used to. "It's been a while. I'm actually surprised you called."

"I'm back in my apartment in White Zone. I need to get to HelixR, then leave the tower for good."

"Of course you do. I'm hearing mixed reports White Zone is having issues."

"I'll explain more later, but the lifts are all out. Can you come and collect me?"

"Sure. You haven't got a landing pad. Can you get to the shuttle port?"

"Shuttle port? Yes, I can try. You might find some resistance though."

"We can handle ourselves."

She heard the confident and cocky Drake as always. "How long?" she asked, checking her chrono.

"Give me an hour."

"An hour?"

"I'm not exactly cooling my jets in a Blue Zone bar. I'm busy right now. Anyone else with you?"

"Fair enough. No. I'm alone. See you in an hour."

"Oh, you will. Most definitely." He cut the call.

"Well, that went smoothly enough," Dianah muttered as she considered how to get to the shuttle pad. Like Alex's apartment, her suite was on the thirteenth level and on the opposite side to the port. The corridors weren't her issue as they'd be empty with most of the good citizens thinking they'd be safe locked in their homes. Taking the stairs was her only option for going up. The guards were only blocking the lower levels, if the information from her informants was accurate. Still, there were the enemy shapers to deal with. Maybe if they didn't suspect who she was, she'd manage. *Would a shaper from* Reenat *recognise me?*

Dianah relaxed once walking through her rooms. When she discovered they were still accessible and untouched, she was surprised but then had to consider – to those in the tower – she'd only been gone for a month or so, the evidence of her absence being the small amount of dust. With glee, she raided her wardrobe for a change of clean – modern – clothes and headed for a long shower, albeit with low water pressure.

She stopped in the bathroom, noting the damp, recently-used towel and the wet shower booth.

"Brendon?" she called out. "Are you here?" Only silence responded. *No doubt doing his own thing, just like what I am doing.* She shrugged.

After her shower, Dianah searched her meagre pantry.

Refreshed and fed – even though it was nutri-bars – her spirits lifted. She relished the basic modern amenities missed for so long. Seeing her reflection in the mirror on the wall in her sleeping quarters, she regarded the change in her appearance. No longer the youthful and attractive, forty-year-old female scientist; what stared back was a much older-looking woman. *Like the poor in the lower levels unable to afford ReJuv.*

Her skin, once milky and smooth was now tanned and far more weather-beaten than she would have contemplated, but with the blemishes of her desperate experimentation. The withdrawal from the rejuvenating drug was clearly evident. The medicomp on the *Skydancer* was unable to completely restore her youthful appearance, nor remove the effects of hroltahg genetic integration. And there was no time to do it on the *Sundancer*.

"Stupid woman," she chided. "Scarred and looking like an old hag! Was the small increase in psionics worth it?" She angrily brushed the tears that spilled from her eyes. *Yes, the risk is always worth it.*

Flipping the mirror to the side, she opened the safe and extracted the compact blaster tucked away. She'd never used it; never needed to other than at practice droids. The charge was full. "Of course it is. You only put it there a couple of months ago." *When Brendon first came into my life.*

She laughed now at her foolish, almost childlike concerns, fearing his aggressive feral-roots would come back.

———

Brendon stepped out of the shower and was towelling himself dry when he heard her voice.

Who was Dianah talking to? Her tone made it clear it wasn't Alex, and under the circumstances it was highly unlikely she'd invite anyone here.

'I'm back in my apartment in White Zone. I need to get to HelixR, then leave the tower for good.'

She's talking on the link? Someone who knows her and HelixR. He listened in, curious, donning his clothes.

'Shuttle port? Yes, I can try. How long?'

In a silent daze he put on fresh clothes. *I should speak to her? She's leaving, without even a goodbye ...*

'No. I'm alone. See you in an hour.'

Alone! Quietly, he stepped out of the bathroom into the hallway. He heard her walking across the loungeroom; her unmistakeable tread across the tiled floor. *How many times have I heard that sound?* He quickly ran his fingers over the runes on his wristband and blinked out.

Feeling numb and lost, he left her suite; the image on his wrist-com forgotten. Unsure where to go he rubbed his face to think. *Back to the shuttle port to wait.*

28

WHERE'S ALEXANDER?

JADE STUDIED THE WEIRD CONTRAPTION ON THE DESK. "IS THIS working?" she asked, smacking it again.

"It's amazing," Harrond said as he strolled over, smiling. "You've been here for a few hours and have already mastered the fine art of computer maintenance."

"What?" Jade looked up from the screen, flustered.

"Hitting hi-tech, delicate appliances works eighty-five percent of the time."

"Should I hit it again?" she asked in all seriousness.

"Here," Lerry stepped in and tapped the screen. "What are you looking for?" The screen came to life in his hands.

Jade, realising Harrond was clowning around, scowled at him. "I should remind you I have some very powerful and very hungry friends."

Harrond looked unsure of what she was talking about.

"There are two of them, about eighty-feet long, and green." Feiron slid up beside him. "Survivors call them wyverns."

"What survivors?" Jade laughed.

"Of course, silly me." He grinned as Harrond's face paled. "They don't leave any."

"Does this tell me where Alexander lives?" Jade addressed the senior agtech.

Lerry wiped the smile off his face when his son looked at him. "It should list his living quarters as well as his business address." Lerry typed in the information. "You realise he'd be stupid to be there?"

"This is Zander we're talking about. He's been known to be an arrogant, cocky bastard," she replied.

Lerry glanced down at the screen. "There it is – W13S/2B."

"What does that mean?" Jade asked.

"White zone, level 13, south side, apartment 2B – probably a suite; anything above level 12 is generally Elite living quarters or white-collar industries, much like SciCorps. It's two levels down on the other side of the building. But how will you get there? The lasers cover the corridor again and David's indisposed, so you can't go that way."

"How did Leonie get around for so long?" Feiron asked.

"She said something about the airducts?" Jade said, unsure.

"And lived in them for the better part of two decades." Lerry explained the function of airducts. "They go everywhere and can vary greatly in size, depending on the volume of air needed to be moved. Nearer the shopping malls, there are also maintenance corridors – keeping the workers out of sight from citizens."

"You are strange people." Feiron oozed over to the wall, eyeing the rectangular covering. "Is that a duct?"

"Yep." Lerry brought over a chair and levered the vent out.

"I don't know where it leads though. Leonie could probably tell you if she were here."

"We'll manage." Feiron oozed up into it. "I'll check it out and be back soon."

While waiting, Jade spent a few more minutes on the comp before checking her equipment, ensuring she had her knives; balanced for throwing if the need ever presented itself. She then had some water, grabbed a snack and was doing stretches by the time the illios emerged.

"There is a junction further along. One of them goes to the elevator shaft," he told her.

"The computer registered your movement in there," Lerry informed them.

"An alarm, but no lasers. That's reassuring," Feiron sighed.

"Great." Jade strode over and stepped up onto the chair. "Let's go." With agility defying her age, Jade easily wriggled through the gap.

Finally reaching a lift shaft, Feiron hung over the edge, and stretched to the next ledge.

"Is that as far as you can go?" Jade stuck her head out of the ducting. She twisted to look up and down. Both directions disappeared into darkness.

"If I stretch myself any further, I can't guarantee to be able to hold you."

"There better not be a fat joke in that." Jade swivelled to her back and sat up.

"Pardon me." Feiron bunched up beneath her, supporting her backside.

With just enough grip on the metal sheets to steady herself, she dragged her legs out one at a time.

Feiron slowly lowered her until she was hanging onto the vent edge. "Give me a moment to establish a secure hold," he advised. "Ready," he said a moment later.

Jade wrapped her hand around him, feeling the texture of his illios body harden as he took her weight. It was like gripping a thick, smooth rope, but not rough like those on ships, with a slight spring.

"I reckon you'll be taller after this," she joked as she lowered herself slowly and steadily.

Feiron remained silent.

When she reached the next vent, she wedged her feet inside and briefly eased cramps out of each hand and arms. While she did this, Feiron gathered himself and oozed inside the vent to reform and rest. "One more level to go." He rolled down the wall and repeated the process as before.

As Jade lowered herself hand over hand, she heard an almighty boom echo down the shaft, followed by an ear-piercing scraping of metal grinding on a hard surface. As she looked up, the roof of the elevator shaft disappeared in a bright ball of flame.

She loosened her grip slightly to slide down Feiron, then clung tightly to the next duct as metal and rubble rained down, clattering and spinning off the walls and disappearing into the darkness below.

"Feiron, get inside," she gasped.

Once the illios was safely within the ducting, he helped drag her inside too.

"What the blazes was that?"

"I wasn't in a position to notice much, so have no idea. But I definitely felt the rumbling through the walls," Feiron replied.

As they speculated, they heard several explosions and felt a series of vibrations. It stopped after what felt like a particularly large but remote explosion. The noises after were distant and indistinct, but she assumed there were many terrified or injured people.

"This should be level thirteen. Let's find Zander." She crawled on. "Which way's south?"

Alex paced back and forth behind his desk. He had been trying to use his coms, but they cut out after the crash. His apartment was dimly lit with emergency lighting.

"Why are you here and not out there?" he raved at the group of people standing in his office.

"We lost several shapers and quite a few militia when that flying craft crashed, not to mention what the Gryphon Riders have cost us, or trying to get into that laboratory you're so keen on. These TowerPol officers are also quite efficient when not having to face power.

"Many are now wounded and laying low wherever they can. They ask where our leader is ... and here you are cowering where you think it's safe and not leading us out there!" Olekk retorted.

"You forget, I am Lord Zander—"

"Maybe your Watchers think so, but it is plain to see you are no lord. You are a snivelling man-child in an ageing body who hides behind his desk. When things aren't going your way, you blame others for your failings."

"Just like you are now, blaming me!"

"This was *your* plan; from the moment we arrived, *your* plan fell apart. We're finished with you, while there's some of us left alive—"

"Where can you go? There's no way home with the ship gone. Reckon you can survive the 24th century without me?"

"Considering what I've seen so far, yes. Brendon has shown more leadership qualities. I've worked with him before. He's quite amenable—"

"I knew it! You can never trust those feral mutants. Where is he hiding? Dianah deserves him."

"Seems you can't trust her either – or she doesn't trust you; Dianah was seen heading upstairs. She looked dressed for a long trip. We will also take our leave."

As Olekk turned away, Alex grabbed a blaster from a drawer. "You'll be leaving in a body bag." Alexander's body tingled as he tried to aim and fire his blaster, but couldn't move his fingers; even breathing was a chore. "Wha—" His mouth and tongue refused to function.

Olekk turned back, seeing how close he'd come to being killed. "My thanks, Sme'na. I knew your quick reflexes would be handy," he said stepping closer to Zander, frozen in place.

"I could kill you here and now – I should – but I see your little world crumbling around you, and how much failure hurts your feeble ego. The ongoing misery this brings to you will be my reward."

The First Mage pivoted and left the room, his retinue following.

29

RAPTORS IN THE NIGHT

THE *VULTURE* APPROACHED FROM THE SOUTH, COMING IN SO LOW the crop stalks flattened in its wake. Drake was savouring meeting Dianah for the trouble she had caused him. Even with his mercenary skills, the last weeks had been difficult; moving from outpost to outpost to raid for supplies, even skulking in caves to avoid detection and capture from SecForce. Having left the tower in a rush, he was now out of anti-rad pills and medical supplies, so remained on his ship as much as possible to stay safe. Only his navigator, Blanchard – who stank like a month-old howler carcass – remained from his original crew.

"Boss, there's a craft coming in from the west," Blanchard called from his nav-console. "It's a big'un. Transponder says it's the ... *Eidolon!*"

"Is that rust-bucket still flying?" Drake searched to the west from his pilot seat, but night was approaching and it was too dim to see objects at a distance.

"You know of it?"

"I served on her in my early days. She was a dilapidated wreck then. Should have been decommissioned and scrapped several decades ago."

"Well, the scope ain't lying. It's her, alright. If she's close enough, thermal imaging might pick her up." He activated a secondary screen and manipulated the dial.

"There it is." Drake spied the bright blot on the display.

"She's burning hot," Blanchard noted at the intensity of the image.

"That'll be the older fusion drive; the last of its kind."

"Coming from the pit mines according to its flight path. Nothing else that way except damn ferals—"

"And not even them anymore since they all disappeared." He had wondered where they had all gone so quickly. One minute they were there for target practice, the next day, nada. For a few weeks he'd scoured the barren hills, revisiting the hovels they called home. Sure, there were signs they left in a hurry, but no tracks to follow; they all simply vanished abruptly. He had considered someone flying them out, but who, where and why? Something on a scale that large from the tower, he would have heard. He had a suspicion of a competitor, but nothing was heard through his usual contacts.

Blanchard kept whining. "Good riddance, I say. Filthy animals."

"Idiot. Animals or not, that was half our income. Gone."

"What were they so useful for, other than target practice?" he chuckled.

"ReJuv, I hear. HelixR was able to extract some enzyme from some of them, which was what they used to make their longevity drug."

"No more ReJuv? So, no more hundred-year-olds waltzing around like thirty-somethings?"

"They've got a synthetic formula going, but it's not the same. Lucky no one knows the truth yet, but I reckon it'll soon show."

"Funny how this Dianah chick calls you out of the blue after a month of nothing," Blanchard noted.

"Yeah." Drake nodded. "A big surprise, considering the bitch left us hanging. I lost half the crew because of her and that damn investigation she left in her wake."

Blanchard mucked around with his console. "Yeah, good men gone," he said absently. They were getting closer to the tower so he adjusted the scope to the shorter range, increasing the resolution. "What happened to her?"

"She buggered off after the attempt to murder the Prime, along with that dick, Alexander and some other nimrod. What was she thinking, getting involved with assassinations?"

"Where's she been hiding?" Switching to the higher res created some glitches above the tower. He banged it with his fist a few times. No change.

"If I knew that, I would have kicked her sorry arse to hell and back. She has some explaining to do – as well as a shitload of compensating. If that Alexander nimrod is with her, we should be right soon enough."

"Isn't he the Prime's son?"

"Yep, and loaded."

"They all are, those damned Elites!"

"Don't worry. Pretty soon we'll get our share, and more."

Blanchard scrutinised his screen. "There's something weird on the scope, boss."

"Weird in what way?" Outside through his window, all he saw was the darkening landscape and the silhouette of the tower in the distance.

"I thought it was a glitch – we've been overdue with maintenance for months—"

"Yeah, yeah. Once we got the credits, we'll get the old bird overhauled. Now, what glitches you on about?" Drake turned in his seat and leant back to view the scope.

"Bogies above the tower. A few of them. Very small, too small and too slow to be flyers; no transponder." On the nav-console screen a large blotch was easily discernible as the tower, but blinking above it were faint dots, moving erratically.

"Not hovering vid-drones? Those morons do love their newsfeed."

"Nah, even drones have a signal. This is ... weird. If I guessed, I'd say it was a flock of birds."

"Huge birds to register on the scope," Drake laughed, but still watched, curious. "Are they making a formation?" Several other glitches appeared from the tower and were forming into two groups. The individual glitches became two larger dots. "Increase the res."

"Can't. Maxed already." Blanchard turned the dial anyway to prove the point.

Drake looked back outside. The tower was a darkness against the twilight sky, but whatever was flying around the tower was still too small to make out even on the thermo-scan. He turned back to the scope.

The two dots separated, one descended and moved to the south while the other dot ascended and moved to the north, making their way around the tower. Drake continued watching in case those dipping to the south were interested in the *Vulture*, but they were heading towards the *Eidolon*. "This could be interesting. Whatever those glitches are, their moves are coordinated. I reckon they're going to attack the *Eidolon*.

"Someone's in for a surprise. She might be old, but she's armoured and armed to the hilt. It'll obliterate them, who or whatever they are." As he spoke, the scope buzzed as another bogie popped on the screen. "What the frag is that?" Drake pointed to a larger dot on the extreme edge of the scope.

Blanchard studied the nav-console. "Frack it! We'll have to get closer to see anything clearly."

"I'm keen." Drake altered course, but not altitude. Hugging the terrain had its drawbacks, but by doing this they posed no threat. As they got nearer, the shadows took shape.

Blanchard stood to look out the viewport, leaning over Drake's shoulder. It took him a while to find his words. "Looks like a flying lizard ..."

"You're a great help." Drake pushed him back into his seat. "Ever seen a thirty-metre flying lizard, idiot?"

"Have now."

It does look lizard-like. Swearing under his breath, Drake turned to give the tower a wider berth as he waited and watched. He never liked rushing into unknown situations, and there were too many unknowns here. "There's two of them!" he exclaimed. Whatever they were looking at had been flying close together. From the angle they were now observing, the one resolved into two, large flying creatures.

———

Omodamos screeched as the large craft approached from the west, a dark profile against the rich crimson horizon.

"I see it, Omo," Adera responded to her gryphon. She pulled a tube from within her vest and blew on it, but it was such a high pitch only those with extreme aural abilities would detect it. Those gryphons patrolling other areas around the tower immediately banked to join their leader to face the oncoming vessel. The gryphons resting on the pad acknowledged the call with deep crowing; their riders mounted swiftly and launched.

"This is a much larger craft than the previous ones we've encountered," Tholart, second in command, noted from his position above and behind Omo's right wing.

"I agree." Adera searched the horizon. "Omo, recall the wyverns if you can, we may need them." She felt the buzzing in her head as her gryphon sent out the telepathic summons.

"We have another craft; low and to the south," one of the riders pointed. "Not as large, and a different configuration to anything before. They seem to have as many different types of flying craft as we have ships in—"

"Silence," Adera ordered, waiting for Omo's response.

Omo turned her head to the east, letting out staccato squawks.

Following her gaze, Adera finally saw the two distant shapes fly up from the ocean. Quietly, she was relieved; this alien world with its alien craft were a threat the likes of which her wing had never encountered. She turned her attention back to the west. What Tholart said was true, the size of this one dwarfed any previous flyers.

To the south, the second, smaller craft, slowed and moved in a wide arc – not approaching directly. "Are they manoeuvring for another attack vector, or simply avoiding any confrontation?" she muttered. "Tholart," she ordered, "take your squad up and come in after us; we will go low."

With his three piercing whistles rising in pitch, Tholart led his team high. At the same time, Adera descended, using the bulk of the tower to cover their movement. Once out of sight, she banked to the left to go around the huge building and make her attack run from below on their flank.

With crossbows loaded, Adera led her squad from the south, timing her run to meet the cumbersome craft as it crossed the threshold of the tower wall. Coming up from below was considered a strategic move. Unseen, they let loose their bolts. A few peppered the side of the vessel as they raced past; depending on the angle, some bolts shattered and penetrated the windows while other bolts glanced off the armoured walls barely leaving a mark. They circled away to the rear, reloading as the second wave began their attack run from above.

Seeing the outcome of the first attack, Tholart led his squad in a dive towards the front, concentrating their fire on the large windows. He could easily see the pilots pointing frantically at them. The larger windows here were tougher, harder to penetrate, and they only managed to crack one of the curved panes before they had to wheel around to reload.

Adera's squad moved in to continue her attack, but now from the other side. This time the prepared crew returned fire. A loud rat-a-tat-a-tat burst from a dome underneath the craft.

Confusion reigned and the riders peeled off in all directions, eventually regrouping behind the craft at a distance so the jet blast didn't send them spinning like fledglings caught in the summer thermals. Adera checked her squad. All were accounted for but no bolts had been released.

"What was that?" one rider asked.

"I have no knowledge of that kind of weapon," their leader

replied stoically, but deep down fighting the shock. *Damn this alien world with its alien craft,* she cursed again.

Another rider struggled to keep her screeching gryphon steady. "Mandilo has been injured!" the rider cried out, pointing.

Moving closer to observe, Adera saw the blood seeping from a thigh wound. "Florin, get grounded and apply aid. We will deal with this."

As she spoke, Tholart started his next attack. The same rattling sound but from a different direction reached their ears. This time, to their horror, three riders were taken out; two riders fell – blown off from their mounts by an unseen force, and one gryphon spiralled into the side of the tower. Both the rider and mount dropped, glancing off the wall as they fell.

Tholart whistled three rapid low-pitched bursts and the squad split, banking away and diving below the roof using the tower's bulk as cover. The craft, heavy and unwieldly turned to follow. Again, the loud staccato noise erupted from the craft.

A departing gryphon was struck, going limp almost immediately. They saw the rider leap off as her wing-mate dived in close. The rider landed on the gryphon's hind, where she quickly held onto the rear of the saddle, screaming in shared pain and sorrow as her ride spiralled to the distant ground.

Undeterred, the gunner picked another target and began firing. Screeches of agony were barely heard over the sound of the weapons and roar of the jets as another gryphon and rider was taken out.

Beware! Faldo gave a warning as he and his sister dropped from above, legs outstretched as they crashed into the top of the craft. Even a vessel this size felt the effects of the mass of two wyverns. The ship yawed, and dipped perilously close to the roof.

Again the rapid-fire sound burst from the craft. Both Faldo and Slana roared their pain and anger.

The vessel plunged towards the tower roof. The thrust of the jets sent it ploughing across the expanse of plascrete, taking out a myriad of structures along its path. Combined with the friction

from the roof, the large pyramid structure in the centre was sufficient to slow its momentum. The *Eidolon* crashed into it, twisting
the metal and shattering the thousands of tempered glass panes.
The nose of the craft dipped into the atrium. With no support
below, the jets drove it over the edge before they cut out.

———

Dianah considered being shrouded in darkness was as much a
saving grace as a hindrance as she made her way up the stairwell. Stubbing her toe again, she swore under her breath, not
that anyone would hear her over the hubbub of the tower's
background noises.

Perhaps the acoustics of the stairway picked up the sounds of
ventilation fans, water pipes, and a myriad other noises of this
massive entity that housed so much humanity, and amplified it
along the vertical plascrete tube.

And it was uncomfortably cool. Not so surprising considering she was nearing the roof at over two thousand metres. She
wished she'd considered that before leaving her apartment and
donned an extra layer of clothing. Checking her watch, she still
had time to return for warmer clothes, but she'd be in HelixR
shortly. She could endure a few minutes of discomfort. Dianah
plodded on, the knowledge her research would soon be in her
hands enough to keep her warm.

The sound of the wind encroached as she neared the shuttle
port. There were only a few flights before the exit. As she got
closer, a sliver of brighter light shone down.

A loud, unearthly screech made her go rigid with terror. She
collapsed in a daze. Her head throbbed and she felt warmth
trickle down her cheeks. She moved to a sitting position on the
dusty steps until the throbbing stopped. It was too dim to see,
but her finger tips came away damp and sticky. *Blood from my
ears?*

"What the frag was that?" Dianah whimpered into the
darkness.

Gripping the railing, she pulled herself to a standing position not daring to move until she was steadier on her feet. Another sound smothered that of the wind, getting louder and higher in pitch. The stairs quivered. There was a resounding crash. The structure housing the top of the stairs was obliterated as something huge swept past in a mass of flames. Rubble and burning debris rained down, most of it falling through the centre of the stairwell to the levels below, bouncing and clanging off the railings.

If she were another floor up, she'd be incinerated. She coughed at the smoke and dust. The heat left as quickly as it came, whisked away by the incessant wind, but there was still an ear-piercing scraping sound.

Dianah realised she was at the shuttle port level. The exit door was by her left hand. Giving the handle a twist and a pull, the door was halfway open when she heard the screeching of the gryphons as they landed. She risked a glance. It was getting too crowded with over a dozen riders milling about in a frenzy.

Ducking back and looking up, she decided to go for the roof. *Drake's switched on. He'll see the riders as I have, and come to the same conclusion. His thermal imaging will find me.*

More noise followed – metal striking metal, and then glass shattering. A brief moment of silence preceded a distant crash, followed by another muted crash. Vibrations followed each impact, but growing fainter.

Thinking the incident over, the next explosion surprised her. She sensed it was far below her, but larger than the previous ones. "What the frag is going on?" Dianah steadied herself, waiting, but there were no more explosions; no more floor vibrations. "And you're starting to swear like Alexander." As she shook her head, she noticed the shadows on the underside of the stairs above her.

Glancing down the stairwell, a bright ball of flame was rapidly moving up, engulfing each level. With both legs moving in panic, she raced the last flight to the roof.

Reaching the roof, the gusting wind blew her off her feet.

Falling to her knees she scuttled away, cursing at the bruising of her knees and stinging palms. Her hair caught on the jagged edge of twisted metal, she persevered, leaving multiple strands behind as the flames reached the open air, licking at her heels.

In seconds it was over. She lay there breathing heavily along the scorched and buckled ventilation unit. Resting with her eyes closed, she sensed a presence. *What now?* she wondered, opening her eyes.

She saw two huge lizard creatures, wings folded along their sides and one's spiked tail thumping the roof as if in irritation. They were both looking into the ruins of the skylight.

Her mouth worked, but she was too terrified to utter a sound. Injuries and pain forgotten, she jumped up and ran in the opposite direction, looking to put distance and cover between herself and the monster. *'Dragon!'* came to her overwrought mind. Even as the thought registered, the scientist mind scoffed at her primal fear.

Dragons have four legs! she heard in her head.

"You're getting delirious!" Dianah forced her legs to move, simply wanting to put as much distance between herself and those creatures. Moving away from the trail of carnage she headed towards the northern side of the roof.

Once settled out of the wind, she put through another call. This time it was answered immediately with little static interference. "Drake? Change of plans. I'm on the rooftop —"

"There's some weird shit happening up there, lady."

"All I know is something crashed onto the roof. I think it fell into the atrium."

"Where are you now? Not the shuttle port, I take it."

"No. Roof. North-west corner." She looked around for something obvious. "It looks like a group of vent cowlings."

"I'm two minutes away." The call cut off.

Dianah crawled around the vent to see where the creatures were. *Maybe I should have warned Drake about them?* They stood in the distance partially lit by the dim emergency lighting from the atrium.

She blinked hard as another creature flew out of the darkness to join them.

"No way is that possible!" she stared. *Not dead?* The shape had an uncanny resemblance to Leonie.

Silly. Of course the furry one is very much alive.

"It should be down here," Jade whispered, edging around the corner. The lights flickered again. When they went off completely, emergency lighting came on, only to shut down when the main lights flicked on again. This had been happening for the past twenty minutes.

Several minutes after the explosion they emerged into a corridor where they encountered many people. Some were panic-stricken, some were running to the nearest stairway, others were huddling with their crying children in doorways. Everyone ignored them, busy with their own concerns.

Seeing no guards stationed outside Zander's apartment, Jade approached the door and listened for sound. When she tried the door, she rolled her eyes at Feiron, discovering it was unlocked. "Where's the challenge in that?" They entered.

The place was a mess. Not the mess of someone who didn't care, but the kind of mess of someone who lost his temper. Shattered glass covered the floor and some of the chairs – those that weren't overturned; wine and other beverages had stained and dripped down the walls.

"I think he left in a hurry, and not too long ago." Feiron indicated the wine still dripping from the fronds of the fake foliage.

"Maybe that rumbling had something to do with it?" Out of habit, Jade rummaged through the drawers and cupboards, pocketing anything of interest. "I honestly didn't think he was that stupid to come here, but I had to check."

"It would appear he was that stupid ... or that arrogant. Where to now?" the illios asked. "Dianah's?"

"She lives on this floor, but on another side." Jade said moving to the entrance.

"One thing's for certain, he didn't go past us. Lead on."

Back in the corridor, she could smell the smoke. "First though, I'm going to that big empty space in the middle to see what the hell's going on."

"You mean the atrium?"

30

WHITE ZONE

A MASSIVE EXPLOSION ROCKED THE FLOOR AND WOKE HER UP. THE lighting in the corridor flickered on and off briefly, then resumed.

"Slistorf's balls!" As she spoke, another more distant explosion reached her ears. Throwing her clothes on quickly, Leonie bolted back to the loungeroom where she found Harrond and the shapers gathered around the vid. It was flickering on and off.

"What the frack was that?"

"We can't say for sure," Harrond answered. "Only a few of the remaining drones are in the air, and only one anywhere near the roof. And all it showed was a flash of light, but it was out of the drone's angle of view."

"Where's Lerry?" she asked.

"Gone to check on David."

"I'll take a look outside." Leonie raced through the dock doorway. Outside, she turned and flew backwards, scanning the tower to see what was happening.

Smoke wasn't so unusual these days, but when it came out of so many of places at once, it meant something huge had happened. She sped around the tower; most vents on the lower level of White Zone's east side had smoke issuing from them.

That's level one TowerPol station. As she watched, the plumes got thicker and blacker. The only place where so much smoke could originate at the same time must be the atrium.

But why is there smoke down there when there was an explosion on the roof? Leonie wondered as she shot to the roof.

She recognised Adera as the gryphon leader broke formation near the shuttle port and came over to her. Leonie nodded to her as she hovered close by. "What happened here?"

"A large flying craft attacked us. We ... several riders were killed."

"Frag! I'm ... I'm deeply sorry." Leonie hesitated, sensing the distress in the flight leader.

"The craft crashed onto the roof and then through that structure." Adera pointed to the large skylight, where Slana and Faldo were on the edge peering in.

Leonie noted the scoring of the roof, signs of a very heavy craft sliding before hitting the glass pyramid and then toppling over. "Did your riders manage to destroy it?"

"No." Adera looked down. "It was destroying us."

I believe I was responsible, Faldo declared.

With Adera following, Leonie landed between them. She sensed the pain and distress in his thoughts, then saw the damage to his wing; several holes ran along one side, dripping blood onto the roof.

The craft was attacking the other riders. When we intervened, it fired its weapons at us! I mind-blasted it to stop it, Faldo added.

"I see." Leonie sighed, having done the very same thing herself years ago. *Are you okay? What about you, Slana?*

I am alright. Is Faldo in trouble again?

"No, not this time. He probably saved many riders." Leonie walked closer to the edge of the skylight. Looking down all she could see was flaming chaos. The majority of the walkways crisscrossing the atrium had been struck, some completely smashed.

"I'm going in to see what I can do to help." She reached up and gave their snouts a quick scratch. "Rest yourselves. We'll talk later."

There is a woman over there. Slana sent a mental image of the area. Leonie recognised the group of ventilation housing. *She is not only crazy, but insulting.*

In what way?

She called us dragons. Everyone knows dragons are lazy and have four legs!

Leonie laughed. *Was that the insult or the crazy part?*

The insult, of course. Her craziness was thinking you *were dead.*

Me, dead? Leonie stopped laughing. *How—* "Dianah is up here?" She turned in the direction of the vents. A small ship was hovering over the area, then landed. It looked familiar ... like the one she saw at Jenolan after the wilders were decimated! As she was about to launch herself after it, there was another explosion far below.

"Frag!" she hissed, caught between a terrible want and an urgent need.

Slana picked up on her quandary. *We can stop them if you wish?*

Don't attack them. I want them alive. Just follow for now.

We will do this, Slana promised.

Thank you. Leonie looked down again as a cloud of smoke rose from the wreck. "I better get down there." She dived in.

Those flashing lights can't be a good sign. Down below, many levels had orange lights blinking on and off. "I've never seen that before."

Seated in the darkened security room, Brendon waited for Dianah to appear. To conserve power, he turned the other screens off, and used the one – flicking through the various views regularly as he felt his world collapse around him. It was all he could do to not scream at his pain and anguish after hearing her words. *'No. I'm alone. See you in an hour.'*

The Gryphon Riders outside came and went in pairs; resting their mounts, stretching their legs and drinking water. He tensed when there was a rattle at the door, but it was just the once. The footsteps receded.

Oh, Dianah ... Dianah. Not for the first time, he pulled himself together. It wasn't like him to get so emotional, but those words cut him so deeply.

'I'm alone. See you in an hour.' He looked at his chrono. *Anytime now.*

"Drake. Wasn't he the one who captured me?" Brendon berated himself for his gullibility. "Wasn't Drake the one she sent out to capture Rhiannon too?" *Who was I to think she could feel anything for me – a wilder ... just a* mutant! *After all we've been through, all those memories ... and she seeks help from Drake over me.*

Almost mesmerised, he watched the screen flick from viewpoint to another viewpoint. As the last view changed, something happened. He scrolled back and panned back. The riders were grouping together, the leader pointing.

"What's happening to get them riled up?" he wondered.

They suddenly split into two groups and raced out of view. No cameras could be found with a view to show him anything other than the empty pad and foyer. The shuttle port was now clear.

"Good time to stretch my legs and find the toilet." He listened at the door before unlocking it. The corridor and terminal beyond were empty.

After relieving himself he wandered around the port. Nearing the pad, he heard a loud but distant staccato sound over the wind. "What the frag was that?" Above, in the night sky, he saw several riders come into view, wheeling and diving.

Who are they fighting? He didn't know of any of his power-shapers capable of taking the riders on in their own element.

More of the rattling sound reached his ears. There was the roaring of a jet-engine as well. "Sounds like one of those flying craft in an old vid I saw."

A gryphon and rider smashed to the pad in a bloody heap. There were cries and screeching filling the sky. He saw the dark shape of another gryphon spiralling out of sight, its rider falling beside it.

More jets roaring, and more staccato noise, fading. An almighty roar! He felt dizzy. *Mind-blast?* He rubbed his head as it throbbed. *Who here was powerful enough to do that to* me? Then the floor rumbled. *Not good at two thousand metres!*

There were loud noises and explosions coming from above. Then the gryphons began returning in pairs, the riders leaping off to help their fallen comrade or see to other wounded.

Brendon activated his wristband and retreated in the darkness to the security room. By the glow of the monitor, he witnessed more gryphons landing on the pad, some awkwardly, indicating injuries. He hadn't realised how many there were. *And some had already been killed.* It dawned on him this area was going to get busy soon. Before that happened, he decided he wouldn't be here and headed for the stairwell.

The floor vibration stopped. "Is that it?" he wondered. A heartbeat later there was a bang and muffled explosion. Followed by another. "Weird it's fading?"

Curiosity getting the better of him, he went upstairs instead of down to see what was attacking the gryphons. To the far side, he saw the tangled remains of the atrium skylight. *And two wyverns!* A rrell flew in from out of the darkness and landed between them! He looked at the image on his comlink, then back to the rrell.

"Damn. It *is* Leonie!"

Another more familiar sound emanated from around the corner. He carefully stepped out from the stairwell exit and peered around the wall.

"Looks like ... the *Vulture.*" He recognised the craft when it landed as the same one that had captured him. A door slid open on the side and a man stepped out, disappearing behind the vent cowling. *Drake!*

Brendon turned to watch the wyverns. Leonie reached up to their chins, then she dived into the atrium. The two wyverns' heads bent down to watch. When they came back up, one of them turned his way. Forgetting being invisible, he reflexively ducked behind the wall, fighting the urge to run. "I need to get to the *Vulture*! I've got to see her before I lose her."

After a few heartbeats, he risked a glance. The wyverns had taken off. He barely caught sight of them flapping higher and higher. With a deep breath he started running towards the flyer. He was halfway across the vast expanse when the *Vulture's* door closed and the craft took off.

"Nooo!" he cried, collapsing to his knees.

———

The two wyverns followed the *Vulture* at a distance to where it landed in a patch of dense scrub to the west where the tower was barely visible. As the moon rose, they spiralled high, waiting to see what it would do next.

Spying furtive movement below, Faldo banked and dove, tracking the dark shape. He pounced. Once he regained altitude, he tossed it into the air. The creature let out another ear-splitting howl before it was consumed whole.

That creature tasted horrible! Faldo almost gagged as he joined his sister. *And far too scrawny.*

You do not taste! Slana barked in amusement. *You swallow everything all at once.*

The fish here are much nicer, he ignored her barb. Still, he kept an eye out for more.

The moon had moved halfway up the night sky before the craft moved again. As it rose on its droning engines, a volley of shots came their way before it turned to the south.

They are aware of us, brother.

It is a shame we cannot mind-blast. His head swivelled around to examine the bullet holes in his wing.

True. Maybe later, but we can follow their minds from much further.

You mean to let them think we are no longer a threat?
Exactly.

The wyverns turned away, making it clear they were not in pursuit; instead, they spiralled higher and higher, eventually losing sight of the craft far to the south.

———

Leonie witnessed fires, large and small, all the way down to level one of White Zone. Quite a few citizens on the upper levels came out to stare at the wreckage from the higher atrium balconies. When they saw her flying down, they gasped or screamed, pointing feverishly.

Swearing under her breath, Leonie waved and continued her descent, realising there were no flashing orange lights above the fourth level. On the lowest level there were no lights at all, except from the flames licking around parts of the large craft. She saw a group of officers on one of the levels. As she approached one was about to raise his pulse rifle, but one of his companions berated him, pointing.

Leonie grinned, remembering the blue armband she was wearing.

"Did you do this?" one officer asked, eyeing her suspiciously as he approached.

"Not I." She dropped the smile. "I'm as shocked as you. Have you got the commander on your link?"

"Our links cut off when this thing crashed and exploded," another man answered, wary of her.

"Guess I better go and see him in person then." Leonie turned.

"Tell him we have to clear everyone. That old ship's full of ammunition and explosives. When it blows, it'll do a lot of damage."

With a bad feeling, Leonie raced up to the 10th level TowerPol section. As it turned out, the commander had made his way to the atrium balcony to see the carnage for himself.

"Did you do this?" Jay glanced over the railing paling at the sight.

What is it with these people? "Of course I didn't. One of your men tells me that craft is full of explosive ammunition."

"No doubt. It's an older model. We'll need to get everyone away from the area; most of the lifts are offline, but they'd be too dangerous anyway. Best to take them upstairs."

"I gather your coms are out now too?"

"Mostly." He nodded. "I—" The words caught in his throat as he was lifted up and over the railing.

"Sorry, Jay." She flew at break-neck speed to the level she'd just vacated. "I'm taking you down to give the orders. I doubt anyone will listen to me."

"Y– you could have a-asked." His voice shook at the rate of descent.

"Any idea how many men you have down here?" Just as she asked, she spied a uniform through the haze." She zoomed over, feeling the heat of the blaze waft over her as she landed near the officer. It was the one she just spoke to earlier. His companions were absent, and he was dragging a woman further away from the edge. Cries and screams came from the passages leading away.

"Sergeant, who else is down here?" Jay called out.

Leonie ran to the injured lady. She was dazed with a cut to her head. Leonie knelt beside her and placed a paw over the wound. Careful not to overdo it as before, she only healed the woman enough to be able to walk.

White-faced, the woman screamed at seeing her dark, furry benefactor. She crawled away then stumbled upright as she fled.

"You're welcome," Leonie grunted under her breath.

"Captain Wester is back there, sir," the sergeant said to his superior. He looked sideways at Leonie. "There are only five of us around here."

"Good. We need you to get everybody up the stairs. Tell them to go as high as they can." With a white-knuckle grip on the railing, the commander glanced down fleetingly. "I think we've lost the garrison down there."

"I can go outside and see what remains from—" She turned

with the others at the sound of voices. The sergeant was about to draw his blaster at the two approaching powershapers.

Leonie didn't know their names, but recognised them and their armbands. "Blue ribbons." Leonie reminded him. "They're friendly." She addressed the shapers. "Can you get any others here to help? Our communications are down and we need to get everyone to the higher levels."

"Possibly, I can amplify my voice. Did you say you wanted everyone to the higher levels?"

"Yes." She thought for a moment. "Jay? You reckon the shuttle port?"

"If they can, the roof is the largest area. Anywhere upstairs is better than here. Maybe we can get people away on flyers?" He sounded dubious.

Leonie nodded to the shaper. "There's your message. All citizens are to get to the shuttle port or roof." *I hope the wyverns are gone by that time, or these people will probably prefer to risk the explosions.*

"I've seen you before," the powershaper responded. "You can fly, can't you?" He continued at Leonie's nod. "The two of us will be quicker."

"You're okay here, Jay?"

"I'll be doing what I can, and find out if anyone is left at the level 1 station," he responded. "Also, add 'Code Omega' to your message."

"Code Omega? Okay." She turned to the shaper who was talking to his companion. "What's your name, and what do you need?"

"Kade. All I need is mobility, but you'll need these." He handed her earmuffs from his satchel. "They're designed for humans, but will be better than nothing."

Leonie donned the muffs. They were an awkward fit. "We better concentrate on the lowest levels first before moving higher," she yelled.

He gave her the thumbs-up, and she willed him up and over the edge.

They spent a hot and chaotic time, getting down to the second level and began weaving in and out of the various smoky malls and passageways, Kade constantly blaring out the message. "Code Omega. All citizens are to make their way via the stairs to the shuttle port and roof."

They saw citizens emerging from their apartments or from the malls where they had been cowering, making their way along corridors to the exit; looks of fright and horror on their faces when encountering bodies. It didn't take long for the stairs to fill with fleeing people.

As they flew around a corner of a darkened mall, they encountered a large crowd filling the corridor. No one was making any progress.

"What's the problem here?" Leonie called. Those nearer to her position turned and screamed at the flying feline. Some fainted, some caught by whoever was closest.

"Bugger!" *Every damn time! Too late to go invisible.* "Relax, we're here to help."

"Be calm, citizens. We mean no harm," Kade called out. "You need to ascend to the roof."

Recognising him as the voice that was alerting them, several citizens stood their ground, though apprehensive. "There are armed men in the stairwell threatening us," one man spoke up.

Armed men? Leonie landed slowly, not wanting to cause any more panic, she released Kade. Even so, the crowd jammed themselves up against the walls to keep as far away as possible. As Kade spoke softly to them in reassuring tones, she went to check out the stairwell; she felt a subtle power in his words.

There was one citizen lying bloodied at the base of the steps; his abdomen sliced open. Scanning inside, there was definitely a number of mercenaries just beyond the entrance. Looking back, the milling crowd were traumatised enough, any more violence or bloodshed would send them over the edge into a mad panic. Taking a deep breath and concentrating, she went invisible. The crowd gasped.

Ignoring them, she stepped inside and silently mounted the

stairs getting as close as possible to the sword-wielding mercenaries, noting they were all human. Once she was beside them, she reverted to the old trick used with the flyers years ago. She sent a mental blast to stun them. *Just like Faldo had done.* Leonie then bundled them all and willed them up the next level and dumped them with little regard in the nearest corridor, out of sight of the citizens. While doing so, she came across several dead people, killed by swords from the looks of their injuries.

Her hackles rose in anger at this killing, and while she had done her share, never innocent and defenceless civilians. Slaying this lot now wouldn't serve any purpose – assuming they were the ones responsible – but she took a moment to scar each right cheek with a claw slash for identification. If she found them later, she'd get her answers.

As she descended the stairs, she removed the bloodied body, gently moving it out of sight lower down, regretting she could do little more.

Kade had calmed the crowd by the time she returned. There were also now two TowerPol officers present. Leonie quickly filled them in on the details.

A series of loud bangs and rumbles from the crashed flyer got the citizens fidgeting and moaning with concern. Children, sobbing before, began wailing in earnest.

"Best get them moving." She stepped away as the crowd surged forward.

Leonie and Kade resumed their task, spiralling the atrium, calling for calm while evacuating. As the shaper's voice boomed out, Leonie looked down again. The mottled blue and green paint job of the hull had turned to a blistered and scorched black in many areas. The impact of the crash destroyed anything within a fifty-metre radius. Bodies, some charred, lay on the lowest level; whether they had been at ground zero, or from the damaged walkways was academic. There were too many. No telling how many underneath the burning wreck; rubble from the skylight and walkways littered the level.

From what she could remember, the first four levels had been

RecZones and shopping malls, with the university on level 3. The TowerPol station on the west side of the tower was where she had dropped off a dozen shapers, Kade had been one of them.

"Where are all your companions?" she asked in a quiet moment while Kade was resting his throat. She hovered, slipping the earmuffs around her neck.

"Scattered about. We left in pairs, each with one of those guards. When this crashed, our man ran off." He motioned for the muffs, then bellowed out the message a few times as they circled the open areas.

The shockwave of a larger explosion pitched them sideways. Dazed, Leonie dropped Kade, but recovered quickly enough to prevent him falling far. Once they were together again, she headed for the nearest floor. Blood trickled from both their noses.

"You okay?" she asked when they landed.

"Maybe a rest and a drink." He nodded, wiping his face, grimacing at the blood.

Leonie left him for a few minutes. They were on the seventh level. The areas around the balconies were dotted with self-serve machines. She forced the doors open and grabbed some nutri-bars and drinks.

"Try this." She handed him a bottle and some nutri-bars. "It might take getting used to the flavour, but they aren't too bad. And it's all we've got for the moment."

He looked quizzically at it for a moment.

Leonie ripped the cover off it. "Try now."

More rumbles came from below; the floor vibrated every time.

"This definitely doesn't sound good," she said, stating the obvious. Leonie stood up and walked to the edge. She had no idea what combustibles were on board the ship, but the fire had now spread further across the floor, engulfing the previously seen bodies and wreckage. As she watched, another minor explosion blew out more of the side sending shrapnel and globs of molten metal further out creating more spot fires.

Leonie turned to the sound of approaching footsteps; three powershapers with blue armbands came trotting along the concourse, skirting rubble.

"Are you alright?" one asked coughing at the dust and smoke.

"We're fine. Anything to report?" she asked.

"Anyone capable of moving has left the area but are now stuck around level twelve. Many stairwells are clogged. Those guards are redirecting them to other stairs as best they can."

"It's good news that they're clear, but the clogging of the stairway is to be expected, considering the number of citizens," Leonie mused. "They'll need to stay away until this thing blows or is put out. That could mean all night."

She paced along the railing, thinking. "Kade, can I leave you here? I reckon your amplified voice has done the trick. You can join your colleagues while I figure out what more can be done for the survivors up top."

"Sure. We'll help where we can in the stairways, even if it's just keeping them calm."

"Works for me. Take care." Leonie leapt off the balcony and soared back up to the shattered skylight. Every now and then she glimpsed people still wandering around the upper floors and looking over the railing to the destruction below.

At the shuttle port a large group was milling within the foyer. Most of those she saw looked uninjured, but there were a few with cuts and bruises or bandages. Considering the available space, it was going to get very crowded soon.

She dropped to the pad and looked for someone with authority. A woman screamed at seeing her, drawing attention. Suddenly there was mass panic as the already traumatised people came to grips with an alien in their midst. Cries of *mutant,* were plentiful.

Damn, should have gone invisible! "You!" she called out to a uniformed officer. "Who's in charge here?"

The young man stared at her for a second. "Captain G-Gill," he stammered, pointing.

Leonie tried to make her way in the indicated direction, but the crowd was too thick. Even though everyone tried to back away in fear, there was simply no room. Cursing to herself, she went invisible and rose to the ceiling. The crowd was still wary, but relieved all the same when they couldn't see her.

Captain Gill. We need to direct more people to the roof. There are too many here now.

As expected, the man was dumbfounded, looking everywhere for the source of the voice.

Forget about me. Use your brain! Look around you. Pretty soon they'll be pushing each other off the pad. I doubt Commander Jay will think highly of you when it comes time for promotion. Move these people TO THE ROOF!

He jolted at her blast, holding his head. "Jenkins. Direct that lot up the stairs to the roof." He pointed to the two emergency exits each side of the interior. "Do it now!"

Bewildered, Jenkins and his colleagues started herding the newcomers further up. There was confusion at first, but after a bit of rough handling they started moving up. Children were crying, but order was quickly restored and, like sheep, those still coming up the stairwell just kept plodding on. It was going slow though, and the shuttle area was still overcrowded, but it wasn't getting any worse.

Something would have to be done, and soon. She raced back to SciCorps to finally report to David.

His lab set-up was still functioning, but there were no vid feeds. "From your description, I believe that older style fighter craft had some antiquated ordinance. I'm surprised anyone still uses it."

"I've no idea about that, but things are getting desperate up in the shuttle port."

"That craft has radioactive components. Safe when enclosed, but with the explosions and fires those lower levels could be toxic." He thought for a moment. "And you were there? For how long?"

"Flying around, clearing the area as best we could. Maybe forty minutes."

As she spoke, David went to a cupboard under a workbench and brought out a device she hadn't seen before. He turned it on and waved a wand at her. The device started clicking.

"Strange. You should've copped quite lot more rad. Did you see any flashing lights?" He reset the device and started testing again.

"Orange ones?" She nodded. "I've had rad before. Isn't the lower dose a good thing?"

"Oh, low is definitely better than high." He considered. "What were you doing exactly?"

"The usual." She went on to explain how they communicated to the population.

"So, you both used power quite a bit? It would help if I could check this other shaper."

She nodded. "Could be tricky to find him at the moment. Why?"

"Just a theory ... but in the meantime I suggest you get on the medicomp for a check-up and I'll also administer anti-rad."

"I feel fine and it'll have to wait. We've got almost thirty-thousand scared people and kids crawling to the roof. They need to be evacuated."

David put the device down, turning to her. "I think I know where you're going with this, and being suddenly exposed to outside will only create more panic for many."

"We're lucky it's night and the full impact of the wide-open space of outside won't affect them as much. There aren't enough flyers; we can't possibly ferry everyone to the ground before they start stumbling over the edge. We'll need to use the portal like we did with the wilders."

"And send people to Reenat," David surmised.

"It'll have to be a temporary measure, but you'll need to recharge it and have extra powerpacs available."

"Most of my powerpacs are on Skyhome. I've only three fully-charged pacs remaining here; the same with less than half-charge before the power grid shut down – insufficient to transport everyone."

"It'll have to do for now. Mind you, I recall years ago, the agtech vehicles have similar powerpacs," she said.

"Good to know. Let's see how long the power is out for. If our shapers and TowerPol can quell these rebel shapers, then maintenance can start doing repairs quickly and safely."

———

We are far above you. Slana sent to her their location when she reemerged from the tower. *We have news?*

Stay there. You'll scare everyone. She ascended to join them, soon feeling the chill. *How is your wing?* She asked Faldo on arrival.

It is a minimal pain, the wyvern replied. *But the holes leak air. I have to rebalance constantly.*

Sorry. You said you had news, Slana?

We do. Slana told her about their prey. *It shot at us again, so we decided to track their minds from afar.*

And you know their location?

It is far to the south. She shared to Leonie the image in one of the minds. The craft flew to an outpost. The southern rail tube curved a few kilometres to the west of it.

"That's great! I'll confirm with Lerry which outpost it is."

The mind of the female registered much pain, Slana added.

Not as much as mine, Faldo griped.

I don't know how long I'll be away. If the craft is a long way away, why not land and rest? But do it away from the tower. I'll see you when I get back. Thank you for the news.

31

FALLING BETWEEN WORLDS

THE ARENA AT SHAPER HALL WAS WELL-LIT BY LARGE GLOWING balls hovering over the area. Beyond, the sky was dark and Luminor and Luxor were nowhere to be seen. The night was uncomfortably warm. When Leonie stepped out of the portal, a shout echoed around the arena. Several men-at-arms stepped forward. When they realised who it was, they relaxed.

To her surprise, Willom came forward. "It's good to see you again, Lady Leonie. And a surprise. I trust things are going well in your world?"

She moved away from the portal. A few heartbeats later, the Gryphon Riders began their return. The reduced numbers were noted. The worst of their injured had received first aid. With a salute from Adera, the Grey Wing returned to their garrison for rest and respite and more treatment.

"Yes and no. Your shapers are succeeding in quelling the rebellion, but another dire situation has arisen." She briefly explained the situation. "We need to evacuate some of our citizens quickly. I need to speak to Krre'lo ... and Reindet if he's available." She remembered to forgo the king honorific since his relinquishment of the throne. "I don't know what hour it is here, but it is urgent."

If Willom had any doubts or confusion about the request, he didn't show it. "I'm certain you wouldn't be here on a mere whim. Please, come with me." After sending one of his men to inform Reindet that Lady Leonie was requesting an urgent audience, he escorted her towards the First Mage's chambers.

"How is Siola?" she asked, making small talk. She actually liked this couple.

"Siola is well. She's been kept busy enough with the many groups either registering to seek the portals, as well as sending investigators to confirm the bona fides of supposed found portals."

"And have any been found?"

"Not the ones we require, no," he laughed. "People will go to extraordinary lengths for five thousand gold ducats."

"I imagine she has her hands full."

"It's a good distraction for her." He went silent after that as they entered the buildings.

Leonie bit her tongue as she was about to ask from what, before she recalled. *A good distraction from no longer being a princess, and for the execution of her traitorous sister.*

They continued in silence until they reached the First Mage's door. There was music coming from within. Willom knocked politely.

"Enter," came a familiar voice from beyond the door.

"I bid you goodnight, Lady Leonie," Willom said.

"Thank you, Will, but cut this *lady* crap. Please say hello to Siola for me. We need to catch up sometime soon."

"She will be pleased." He bowed and stepped back.

Leonie smiled and pushed the door open.

Reindet arrived a few minutes after the First Mage had poured the first glasses of wine, wearing slippers and a night robe.

After the thanks for attending the impromptu visit and giving them a brief progress report on the shaper conflict, she got down to explaining in detail the dire circumstances. The two leaders sat back, considering the news Leonie gave them. It had only been a few days since she last saw them, but there was a big change in Reindet. As king, while he had a commanding presence the weight of responsibility of leading a country showed. But now, the man in front of her looked ten years younger, and still with the air of confidence of a ruler.

"I know it's short notice, but with the crisis now upon us, the portal is really the best solution," Leonie emphasised.

Reindet stood and refilled his glass, bringing the bottle over for Leonie and the mage.

"With that many people, the arena would not fit them," Krre'lo advised.

"Perhaps not." Reindet looked thoughtful. "How many people visit us during the summer festival?" he asked Krre'lo.

"Over the festival period, we've counted at least fifty thousand, but not all in one day."

"Nevertheless, I believe this isn't long term – nothing is these days?" He looked to Leonie for confirmation.

"Just an emergency measure, I assure you," she said. "Several days at the least, no more than a week." She had little knowledge of how long their festival lasted.

"Exactly, and since they are going to take over a million of us, how can we say nay to a few thousand of theirs?"

"So, you're saying we set this up like the summer festival?" Krre'lo asked.

"I am, but without the vendors, jesters and minstrels. All the marquees can be set up for protection from the elements, and the food can be brought in by the wagon-load. This hot weather has brought rain and bumper crops. The only other difference is the season – though it is warm enough to be a summer festival."

The First Mage turned to Leonie. "How will your people cope? I recall you saying they are quite … insular?"

"Oh, they won't cope at all." Leonie shrugged a shoulder. "But panic attacks, vertigo and agoraphobia are far better than being dead by falling two thousand metres off the roof. And, if we can, only humans to cater for them."

"Um, no doubt. When do you propose sending people through?" Krre'lo asked.

"To be honest, as soon as you can manage here."

"I'll start mobilising the garrison; get the usual fields sorted out, and arrange for food and water cartage."

"In the meantime, I'll get back to Earth and get things going. When we're ready, I'll return to move this portal."

"The field is to the west of the road, at the base of the hill. I'll send a runner down with a few torches to mark the location for you."

————

"Did you get the other powerpacs?" Leonie asked David on her return. She sat with a sigh at the table, reaching for a drink then after a long swig, hooked a claw around a piece of dried fruit.

"All on the roof. Lerry, Harrond and a couple of our shapers went down to the maintenance bay and retrieved a dozen heavy-duty pacs from the agtech harvesters. More are also being moved to the roof as we speak. I told you we were capable of doing things. You take too much on your shoulders as it is. How did it go in Reenat? Were they amenable?"

"Chosen one, remember." She pointed to herself. "It'll take them a few hours to get organised." Leonie clawed another titbit of food.

"In that case, I insist you rest." David insisted.

"We've got too much to do—" she began.

"Incorrect. *We* have tasks to do; *you* have time for at least an hour on the medicomp." He cut her off before she could respond. "You said yourself it would take them a few hours to prepare. How much sleep did you get earlier? I can tell it wasn't enough. You do too much, but you aren't the only one involved. I insist you rest before you fall in a heap. *That* will be your own doing. I'll ensure everyone knows it too."

Leonie glanced up to see the wyverns now landing outside. *I thought you were resting?*

We were bored and saw you return.

She sensed a mental shrug, as if that was enough of an answer.

For a human, David is quite smart. He helped Faldo a great deal.

Did he? "Slana tells me you helped Faldo," she said, turning back to the scientist.

"Just a big dose of nanites to give him a boost." David shrugged.

"Do those things work on wyverns?" There were several vials in a stand on the table. She picked one up and studied the viscous liquid content, turning it in the light. While not seeing the individual nanites, she did see faint flecks of reflected light.

"Leave the shiny things alone." David gently took it out of her paws and replaced it. "Once their bioscan analysis came through, it was easy enough to reprogram the nanites."

"How did you get him on the medicomp?" She fought from yawning. "Has there been any word about Alexander or Brendon?"

"Nothing yet. Coms are back online, but sporadic. Jade and Feiron have gone off exploring for Alexander." David explained what Lerry and Harrond told him.

"I was wondering where they were. They aren't without their own resources and after working together over the years, should be okay."

At that moment, the agtechs returned via the main door. They came over to join them.

"I gather the lasers are deactivated?" Leonie noted.

"The rebel shapers have dispersed," Lerry said. "Some are surrendering, some are dead. None are near here to cause a threat."

"Another reason why this is the ideal time for you to rest," David reiterated. "And I'm sure Lerry and Harrond agree."

"Definitely. Or we'll get Sussah to start harassing you."

We have noted your weariness, even if you do not acknowledge it, Slana added.

"Fine," she hissed in frustration at them. "No more than an hour."

"You'll be monitored the entire time." He gave her a few minutes to finish her drink and snack then ushered her to the medbay.

"Aren't you supposed to be designing a portal sensor or something?" she whined.

"I have done what I can for now. TAU is working on it now."

"The *Sundancer* AI?" she asked, laying down and sliding her arm into the medidoc.

David nodded. "I'll get notification once the numbers are crunched."

"The shapers that helped with the powerpacs flew you down?"

"Exactly." In a matter of minutes, she was hooked up and resting. Satisfied she was asleep, he set the timer for two hours and commenced the diagnostic program.

"One hour for resting, and one for that analysis I always promised," he muttered.

The furry one will be cross when she awakens, Faldo sent.

"I've dealt with a cross furry one before," David reassured him.

Shall we move the portal now? Slana asked.

"Please. Grip around the outer edges."

Noldor told us about it already. Slana gripped the outer edge as instructed and gently rose, the portal lifting easily, swaying as she turned.

"We said an hour," Leonie cursed, jumping up.

"*You* said an hour; I said 'at least'. You got your one hour of rest," David assured her.

"I checked the time beforehand. I was under for two hours!"

"I amended our agreement." He finalised the medicomp and deactivated it.

"It doesn't work that way," she argued, but not too stridently. She did feel much better.

"I also took the opportunity to program your analysis. Bonus!" He poured her a glass of water.

"What analysis?" she asked, accepting the drink.

"The one promised much earlier," he reminded her. "To ascertain everything we can about your genetic makeup."

"And you had to do it now?" She took a sip. "I thought you did that already?"

"It was inconclusive, and we had time to spare."

"What did it tell you?" Leonie stalked out of the room to the docking bay. "Did it mention anything about what an irate creature with really, really sharp claws can do to a man?"

"It will take a long time to digest the data. Once we have dealt with the situation at hand, we will have a sit down and discuss it in greater detail."

"We better." She saw the empty pad. "Someone steal the portal?"

"Slana has taken it to the roof, much like Noldor did when we evacuated the wilders."

"And how are things going below with the crashed flyer?"

"It's slow, but there is progress. The SecForce and TowerPol officers are attempting to put the fires out and keep it cool."

"Cool?"

"To reduce the chance of more explosions." He gave her a brief rundown on other news.

She nodded. "And Lerry and Harrond?"

"Back on the roof with the six shapers from here."

"I better get up there so we can get the roof cleared." Leonie tossed him the empty glass. A few minutes later, she landed beside the two agtechs. The portal was charged and ready on the roof, the shimmering as bright as it had been for many weeks.

"Enjoy your catnap?" Harrond asked.

"Not half as much as a couple of green friends of mine would enjoy you as a snack." She gazed at him with her violet eyes before she turned to Lerry. "Do you think Sussah would miss him all that much?"

"I think she'd be pouting constantly," Lerry replied after consideration.

"We don't want *that* now." With a sigh, Leonie agreed. "If everything is fine on the other side, I'll move the portal. No idea where I'll be, so don't let anyone through until I return." At their nods, she jumped through the bright shimmer.

"Why is everyone threatening to feed me to the wyverns?" Harrond muttered.

―――――

By the time Brendon recovered from his fit of despair and self-remorse, the stairway was full of frightened citizens, all clambering to get to the roof. Facing a wall of people, he had to either go with the flow or risk being trodden underfoot. There was little fear of anyone recognising him; once they reached the roof, most of them kept their heads down.

Because many have never seen outside, let alone been here, he realised. *Much like Alex and Dianah were when they first crashed on Yarnik.*

Moving around the nervous group of citizens, he realised his wristband power had depleted; he was now visible. Hidden among the nervous crowd, Brendon curiously watched as TowerPol officers and some powershapers warned people to move back from the edges. Mingling with the thousands of people, he overheard many conversations, learning quickly what had occurred.

Based on the sounds he'd heard and these stories, it all came together; an antiquated flyer that hit the roof, fell through the atrium and crashed onto level one. Now there was a potential radiation threat, enough to clear everyone from below level fifteen. This portal was to take them to a safe place until the danger had passed.

A safe place? He chuckled to himself. *If only you knew.*

His previous research had made him aware of the impending doom on Yarnik for anything that wasn't indigenous. If he escaped, he could get help from his contacts in Reenat. There might still be a place for him here by the time he returned. He took the opportunity to edge even closer to the portal.

Like everyone else, he hadn't seen it before, only now recalling a brief report of a 'search for other portals' back in Delta before they left in the second time-machine. *And there's one here too? Does that mean there's a pair of portals for every other race?*

"If they have a portal, then why did they need the *Sundancer*?" He brooded, thinking back. "So, this portal isn't in Delta. Of course. Reenat, hence the Gryphon Riders and the other powershapers." *Is the other portal in Shaper Hall?* he wondered. *I know people there too.*

When Leonie jumped through the pearly shimmer and disappeared, anyone near enough to see it gasped. Lerry and Harrond walked towards a TowerPol officer who had waved them over.

Seeing his chance, Brendon bolted for the portal. *Almost there.*

There was a yell from one of the TowerPol officers. Several moved to intervene, but they were too far away. He put on a burst of speed.

Lerry turned, seeing the movement too late. "Brendon? Don't!" he yelled out, recognising who it was, but too far to reach.

Ha. Brendon leapt through, feeling the uncomfortable coldness immediately. As the seconds passed, he felt the cold seep into his bones. To keep warm, he imagined the surprise on Leonie's whiskered face when he showed up.

———

Leonie waved to Krre'lo and once clear of the arena headed for the high west wall and to the designated position on the field outside the city walls. She turned to glide onto her back to watch as the suns inched over the horizon.

It would be a shame to lose it, she thought. The capital was a beautiful city, seeing the stucco walls of the buildings as they spiralled around the main road to the castle on the dominant hill. A far cry from the palace at Delta. *Though Delta did have its many bridges and blue harbour,* she reminisced.

Krre'lo told her sunrise and sunset were the best time to see the two suns, Diphei and Zastre together. Diphei was soon wiped out by the brilliance of Zastre as the larger sun made its appearance. Almost immediately as the light shone on her, she felt the temperature rising.

The fading scream shocked her out of her reverie, making her jump. She looked around. "Where—" *Someone had come through the portal!*

As quickly as possible she tried to slow the fall, but she couldn't risk losing control of the portal. Her futile efforts were too little; too late. Swiftly descending, once the portal was safely on the ground she raced to the body.

There were other calls as farmhands and guards ran towards them.

"Slistorf's balls! Brendon?" Leonie recognised him when closer, sensing the catastrophic damage he suffered internally and externally. She reeled at the excruciating pain he was broadcasting. With an effort, she blocked most of it. He was on his side near the edge of the designated field. Even the damp ground had little effect to soften his fall or lessen his injuries.

"What the frack were you thinking?" she knelt beside him.

His breathing was shallow, barely perceptible if not for the blood bubbling on his lips.

... My biggest ... regret is sending them ... to Rhiannon. Please ... apologise to ... wilders of Jenol—

"I will tell her, and she will no doubt forgive you. But half of them are dead because of what you did. Do you think they will forgive you for that?" is what she wanted to say, but only, "I will," passed her lips.

There was no response. The red bubbling stopped and he remained utterly still.

32

SOME GOOD NEWS

The craft returns, Slana messaged her brother who was scanning the ocean again for a meal.

Shall we summon furry one?

Let us see what happens. She is very busy.

Furry one is always *busy!* He pivoted and plummeted into the blue water. A moment later, he appeared with a large fish in his claws. Great sheets of water poured off his back as he rose to join his sister who had turned towards the tower. *Wait for me.*

The *Vulture* landed on another pad much lower down from the roof. As the pair of wyverns watched, they saw three people exit the craft and walk inside. The two men had to help the woman; the wyverns sensed her injuries, that she was unable to walk by herself.

What do you think, brother? Slana asked.

I think if they enter the craft again, they might escape this time. We were lucky they returned. These craft can go a long way quickly.

My thoughts too, so if they have no craft to enter ...

They cannot get away again. I think together we can do this.

We can do anything together.

The siblings landed lightly on the pad after scanning the area.

While they could sense hundreds of minds within the tower, none were in the vicinity and the craft was empty.

Shall we? They moved above the flyer and gripped each end with their talons. There was the sound of metal bending and glass shattering, but no one was around to hear it. With mighty flaps of their wings, they rose laboriously and manoeuvred to the side, off the pad.

It is not as bulky as that other one that crashed.

That would have been very difficult to move, Slana agreed.

At the same time, they released their hold. The *Vulture* quickly dropped away, slowly tumbling as it fell the 1300 metres. When it hit, there was a bright explosion, then flames.

Technically, we didn't attack them, Faldo stated

As long as the people are still alive, furry one will be pleased.

The wyverns once again spiralled nearby to keep an eye on the landing dock. One of the other pads with several dark flyers along one side in a row showed activity as a group of people were quickly making their way to one of them.

I think we are going to have company. Again, Slana observed.

They are persistent. Is this not the third time since we arrived? Shall we?

They flew closer and mind-blasted the small people before they could board the craft.

I have noticed they don't survive if we do that once they are in the air, Slana said.

More lives saved. Something else furry one will be pleased with. Maybe we should do something to discourage more from coming out, Faldo suggested.

The sibling wyverns landed on each black craft, damaging them with their weight, and smashing the front windows with their barbed tails.

Now we wait for furry one, Slana said as they launched into the sky.

I hope she isn't too much longer. I am hungry. Faldo looked wistfully at the ocean, gleaming with the light of the single small moon. *They need another moon.*

David was waiting on the dock as his returning flyer came into view. When Sussah called to inform him of their return, he told her that stealth mode was now unnecessary. Once they landed, Sussah activated the ladder and climbed out. She gave her waiting son a hug. "Miss me?"

"Of course." He returned the hug. "Did you like the flying?"

"I can see why Leonie loves it so much." She smiled. "Where is she? Out saving the world still?"

"I believe she's with the wyverns. They are chasing Dianah."

"I'm sure she'll be fine. I've been flying for hours. I need a wash." His mother gave him another quick embrace before disappearing to the living quarters.

"What the frag happened on the roof?" the Prime queried as he climbed painfully out of the cockpit. He winced when on the pad and stopped to stretch his legs.

Your mother flew very well. Styx climbed down and rolled inside.

David filled them in on the details of the attack on the gryphons and the crashed warcraft as they followed the rollo in. Jade and Feiron were having a discussion in the lounge room, along with Lerry. Styx was in the corner.

"You say it came from the pit-mine? Did Alexander have anything to do with it?"

David nodded. "According to our information, though I don't think he expected this to happen." He invited them to the lounge where he had snacks and beverages prepared.

"Can we get a tech onto his comp? I want anyone Alexander communicated with to be rounded up for investigation. Coerced or not, others in the tower helped," Nicholai stated, settling into a chair with a sigh. "And where's Jay?"

"The commander is coordinating the search and rescue. We have Blue Zone SecForce units here as well. The two remaining TowerGov people are looking after them and organising the repairs as well as." David cut Nicholai's protest about the *clause*.

"When the warcraft crashed, it damaged the adjoining zone floor sufficiently to cause concern with Blue Zone. We also have their engineers, maintenance staff and droids to help rectify all the White Zone damage." David then recited various reports, supplying the Prime with a comprehensive idea of the damage.

Nicholai listened attentively as he massaged his calves. "And everyone from White Zone is now in that city we visited?"

"As many as we could get." David nodded. "We're keeping essential personnel. Only a few from TowerGov volunteered to help. We haven't been able to tally all the dead, but it's definitely in the hundreds, possibly thousands."

Nicholai looked stunned at the numbers. "I should inspect the area."

"That would be a good idea." David passed him a glass of water, which he drained before speaking again.

"And Alexander?" the Prime asked. "Anyone know if he's alive or ... not?"

"We checked his apartment, and Dianah's," Jade said. "Both were empty, though there were indications of recent use. They've buggered off somewhere."

"Could they have portalled back to Reenat?" Nicholai asked.

"I very much doubt it," David informed him. "They are too well-known. Word is, Alex and Dianah had a falling out and went their separate ways. Leonie is on her trail as we speak." David added, "There was an outbound shuttle about an hour ago. A TowerGov registered craft."

"We'll arrange to notify the orbitals," Nicholai said.

"Don't they have diplomatic immunity?" Lerry asked.

"Yes, but at least we'll know where it docked. Maybe who was on it. Didn't Dianah have a partner?"

"Brendon is dead. In his attempt to escape, prior to the evacuation getting into full swing, he followed Leonie through the portal. She was moving it over Reenat at the time ... he didn't survive the fall," Lerry finished.

They quietly picked at the food for a few minutes. Lerry went off to make some more coffee.

"On the plus side," David continued, "your quarters are repaired, and most of the rebel shapers and militia have surrendered. They were abandoning Alex anyway. We found a few others, but I don't believe we found them all. Some may have also managed to hide among the evacuees. No doubt many were killed."

"I'll go and have a quick wash in my apartment, then visit the affected area." Nicholai stood up. "See you tomorrow."

———

When the trio emerged from HelixR, Dianah was no longer limping. Drake held a small case, and Blanchard's rifle was held loosely in one hand.

"Frack! Where's the *Vulture*?" Blanchard ran forward, staring at the empty pad.

"Did you do this?" Drake turned on Dianah. "Back-stabbing us again?"

"I have no idea! We have a deal." She spoke forcefully, but shied away from his raised hand. "It's not in my interest to get stuck here, fool."

"I found your ship." Leonie hovered nearby, dimly lit by the pad's landing lights. "Though I can't take the credit."

All three jumped at her voice.

"Frack!" Blanchard swore, stumbling as his rifle was ripped from his shoulder. It disappeared over the edge.

"Leonie—" Dianah started.

Both men attempted to draw blasters, but struggled to move, muscles bulging with the effort.

Leonie willed the weapons out of their holsters and they went with the rifle into the darkness.

"Where's my flyer, mutant?" Drake snarled. "What have you done with it?"

"Want to see?" she asked. Before he could reply, both mercenaries rose off the ground and floated into the open air. "Look down." She inverted them anyway.

Dianah turned to run, but was held in place. *You aren't going anywhere,* Leonie sent to her.

"What're you doing?" Blanchard yelled. "You can't do this. I– I surrender. Let me go."

"Now there's a poor choice of words." Leonie hovered nearby.

As the two dangling mercenaries made out the small fire far below around a shape similar to the *Vulture,* Leonie sensed their mixed anger, confusion and terror. A deep scan of their memories told her all she needed to know, confirming her suspicions.

"Did you allow the wilders at Jenolan to surrender?" She directed the question at Blanchard. "Did you give *them* that chance?"

"Wilders?" he asked in confusion.

She picked up on his thoughts. *Ferals.* "Ah yes, *target practice* you call them. Your wish is granted." She let him go. His scream cut off as a dark shape intercepted him.

"What about you, Drake? Going to plead for mercy too?"

"Not from these lips, you feral low-life."

"Do you remember blasting a little girl?" Leonie flew up to him, staring at him. "Her name was Jojo. She lived with many others at Jenolan, the wilder community west of here you and your cowards destroyed."

"A feral pup?" The mercenary snarled, though she sensed his fear. "I don't give names to animals."

"Even for murdering innocents I would have allowed a clean death," Leonie hissed through gritted teeth. "But you should never have pissed on her grave." Leonie showed him the memory of what she witnessed that night. "Consider yourself lucky. You won't have a grave for anyone to desecrate." She grabbed the case he held and let him go. *Faldo, still hungry?*

Need you ask? Greedy Slana took the first one.

I'm just faster than you, fatty.

Dianah screamed as she saw the massive dark shape swoop down, following Drake as he fell.

"What to do with you, I wonder?" Leonie landed near the scientist.

"You wouldn't exist—"

"Not that bullshit again." Leonie feigned a yawn. "You tried that back in Delta. I gave you and Brendon a chance then, and still you tried to kill me."

Dianah cried as Leonie lifted her up. "I– I have valuable information!"

"Maybe now *I* have the valuable information?" Leonie studied the case.

"It's encrypted, and useless without me," Dianah argued desperately.

Are we getting dessert?

Dianah's face drained of colour, sensing Slana's query.

"What can you possibly do to redeem yourself?" Leonie growled, flying slowly around her as she moved the scientist further from the tower.

The geneticist whimpered and shook uncontrollably when her body floated over the edge, eyes wide at the sight of the dark ground far below. "I ... I can save your wilders."

"I don't know why I asked. You'd say anything to save your skin. You've lived too long as it is." Leonie let her fall.

"My research ..." she shrieked, her long hair streaming behind. "Wilder ... genetic ... structure!" Dianah's struggled to scream over the wind.

Leonie raced after her as she continued to fall. *How?*

"Medicomp ... program ... reverses ... mutation," Dianah squealed, seeing the ground race up to her. She wasn't making much sense with her terror, but Leonie read her thoughts.

Both stopped a few hundred metres off the ground.

"If you lie or fail, we will be revisiting this experience ... unless Faldo intervenes before I can stop him."

Dianah whimpered her assent.

Looks like no dessert, brother.

At a speed taking her breath away, Dianah found herself soaring up the side of the tower. Leonie returned to SciCorps where she spied the flyer parked to the side. "They're back?" she asked David when she landed on the pad.

"About twenty minutes ago. Mum's having a wash, Nicholai is doing a quick tour of the damaged area and Styx is with him." He noted the immobile but frightened woman with her. "I see you were successful." David turned to Dianah. "Hello again. As you can see, the family's all here."

Leonie floated inside and with little ceremony, Dianah was secured onto the medicomp. "I don't trust anywhere else to hold you. She might still have friends out there. Can you set up an induced coma?"

The scientist tapped at the keyboard.

"At least I get to sleep," Dianah simpered, relieved to be in familiar territory and not hanging thousands of metres in the air.

Leonie pulled the straps roughly to get her attention. "Brendon's dead." *Dream on that.*

The medicomp cut in, freezing the dismayed look on the geneticist's face.

———

The Prime returned to his personal living quarters after his White Zone tour, looking pale at seeing the resulting damage. When he called in to SciCorps the following morning, they thought he looked marginally refreshed.

David was chatting at the table with Leonie and his mother having breakfast. Styx was out on the pad in the sun. "How did the trip to La Trobe go?" David asked to take Nicholai's mind off the chaos.

"I do believe our negotiations went well. La Trobe and Carlton Towers are amenable to taking a third each of the refugees." He nodded to Sussah as she poured herself coffee.

"That seems generous – not disparaging your negotiation skills – but what do they expect out of it?" the scientist asked.

"We've arranged a sharing of SciCorps tech—"

"Not with time-travel?"

"Of course not, but it seems your reputation is widespread. They'll benefit somewhat with your efficient and cost-saving production technology. Their increased efficiency will help us in the long run, especially if we are going to be connecting more with them."

"And what did they think of Styx?" Leonie smiled.

Nick laughed. "His powers of persuasion are greater than mine."

I merely showed them the benefits of mutual cooperation.

"This is true, but inserting images directly into their minds ... not the most diplomatic of methods."

It worked, and they are now on the same page, *I believe is the term.*

"Basically, he scared them to death," Nicholai stated.

Pffft. They live. Sometimes the truth can be daunting. The weak heart was unforeseen though. It was good he recovered. Styx changed the conversation. *Nicholai was saying your mother is an excellent pilot.*

"That's very kind of you, Nicholai," Sussah beamed.

"What did you get up to while you were there?" David asked his mother. "I'm assuming diplomatic discussions weren't on your résumé as well as the piloting?"

"Our apartments were quite well-appointed," she started.

"You didn't spend all those days in a bath?" Leonie asked, jokingly.

"Not *all* day," she laughed. "I did find time to roam the malls, meet people – did you know their agtechs are allowed to mingle with the rest of the citizenry?"

"Their subliminal messaging is faulty?" David asked.

"It's non-existent," Nicholai said in shock.

"They have much less rad down their way. Keeping people inside constantly wasn't a necessity for them as much as for us. They actually have community gardens," Sussah said, and she became animated with describing their fresh produce. "Not as good as your hydroponics, though."

"Thanks, mum," David turned to Nicholai. "In other news,

Leonie captured Dianah. She is now in an induced coma on the medicomp."

"She's still alive?" Nicholai nodded to Leonie. "I'm surprised you kept your temper."

"Dianah claims her research will help wilders – to remove their mutations." Leonie held up the case. "All her research is in here. That's the only reason why she's still breathing."

"What do we care about these ferals?" Nicholai shrugged.

"I care," Leonie growled, glaring at him. "Most are better humans than I've experienced in the tower!" She took a deep, calming breath and turned to the rollo. "Styx, can you deep scan Dianah and find out if she's telling the truth? I have plans for her otherwise."

At your service.

Thank you.

"When all this has been dealt with, we will need to arrange a court hearing and make sure everyone sees justice is done. There was a lot of news about the assassination attempt, then their sudden disappearance. Many people need to see this is being resolved once and for all." He sipped his coffee. "What's next?" the Prime asked.

"Now that you're back, we'll return to Shak'aran. You, Jay and who you can find of TowerGov can take care of the tower. I have designed and manufactured two portal sensors—"

"Do they work?" Nick asked.

Leonie chuckled.

David looked hurt but continued. "It registers our portal from over three hundred kilometres. With an area of 6,353,243 square kilometres, the Shak'aran continent is smaller than Australia. With the *Skydancer* assistance, we should be able to criss-cross the land in a few days and triangulate the location of any portal we find."

"Isn't there another continent to the south?"

"There is," Leonie confirmed. "The population is sparse. However, from some personal experience and the knowledge gained from close friends in Reenat, skylands do not go beyond the coasts. That is the only way portals could get to Ghalena."

"And the portals are only on the one continent? There aren't two ... bases?"

Leonie looked to David before answering. "None to our knowledge. No one has ever mentioned it."

"If there are, we can check," David assured him. "Either way, once we find a portal, we'll make sure it's charged and get it to the cities as soon as we can. Wherever they're needed."

Leonie added, "I've already arranged for notification be sent to most of the population to get to their nearest capital city or major townships."

"You've been busy," Nicholai noted.

"I got this started when we three visited Reenat – on my day off I might add." She explained how the remaining hroltahgs along with the temples, were going to blanket their areas with the message regarding the portals and the evacuation."

"Don't some of those temples hate each other?" David asked.

"True, but they all have one love – living. Ironically, even the Deathers."

———

The return of the evacuees to White Zone commenced the following morning. Half of the walkways had been replaced, and the same for the damaged lower level once the hulking wreckage was cut up and recycled.

"Have you managed to deal with the radiation?" Leonie asked.

"We have made great progress. Remember when we spoke after you and that shaper cleared the lower levels of White Zone?"

"I was supposed to get a high dose of rad."

"And you did, but then it disappeared."

"No doubt you have a theory."

"With the assistance of several powershapers I recently

conducted a series of experiments. I had a few items with rad; when they carried out some powershaping, the rad was reduced. We did this several times – different levels, different items, different magic – all resulting the same: powershaping diminishes radiation."

"Did you get any Earther to try their 'draining' method?"

"Good point. She did, but it simply redistributed the rad. We need to *expend* the power to reduce the radiation threat."

"And there's no danger to the shaper?"

"None so far ..." he paused. "But you don't get injured when you produce fireballs or lightning. This must be similar. Also consider, with all the magic you've been using here over the last twenty years, your rad levels are non-existent."

"That's outstanding news, but won't the returning citizens be suspicious?"

"The radiation warning will be called a false alarm; that the rad sensors going off was a short-circuit caused by the crash. Citizens are used to bureaucratic bungling."

Leonie thought about the ramifications of this news. "That means, given time, the radiation outside can be eradicated?"

"Precisely. Powershaping – magic – can save us and the planet."

33

THE SWARMING

It was a hot, late afternoon over the western edge of the Tesakian great forest. With the sun on the horizon, it would soon be turning into a hot evening. Philbert on Dorn and Jade on Slana cruised north to Garangoa, the next township on their map.

They kept an eye on the ranges to their left; unlike the massive trees of the forest below, those on the slopes were stunted with poorer soil and the cooler climate.

"I'm sure glad it's winter!" Phil called to Jade.

"We better not be around by the time next summer begins."

There is a wyvern approaching, Dorn sent.

I see. Phil squinted to the west into the setting sun. "Rider coming in." He pointed for Jade. She shaded her eyes to look. And sneezed.

It is ... Limma. She is gravely injured. She is weakening, but saying the ... l'ith are beginning to swarm.

That is a bad thing indeed, Phil answered. *Indala is her rider?*

Yes. She is unconscious.

They raced up to intercept as Limma descended, Indala slumped in the saddle, held on by the safety harness.

Dorn, tell Limma to turn north. Garangoa is not far now.

Dorn relayed the message. Sensing her great pain and fatigue she added, *Stay strong, brave one.*

I ... will not ... make it.

It is not far to go! Dorn encouraged.

Take Indala ... my rider, Limma urged. *I may still make it, but the landing will not be good, my legs ... I am too badly damaged.*

As you wish. We will do this.

I hear you both, Philbert acknowledged.

Dorn flared her wings to slow briefly and dropped in altitude to glide under Limma. As she did this, Phil looked up and saw the damage to her legs, belly and neck. Limma had pulled a l'ith off her, but its head was still attached with its mandibles still imbedded – like a wild dog not letting go a bone.

"It's a wonder she made it this far," he said to himself in awe.

Are you ready, Singer?

I am. Phil stood in the stirrups and braced, arms out in preparation. As he did, he sensed something in the air ... but ... *Dorn? What is that?*

Limma is sharing her remaining essence!

Sharing with whom?

Phil felt a subtle buzz. He recognised this as a private conversation, between Limma and Indala.

Indala leant forward and hugged her wyvern. Sitting up and wiping her eyes, she unbuckled her harness and turned, making her way back behind the wings to the base of the long tail. She crouched for balance and braced against the turbulent wind. Waiting for the best time, judging the wind, the distance and the wing beats, she gave a quick hand signal, then dropped.

Phil reached to grab her but her tunic ripped. His heart leapt to his throat as she fell with a scream out of sight below Dorn.

Jade has her, Slana sent, having dropped below Dorn as backup.

Well done, daughter. Dorn banked slightly once Phil had seated himself.

Excellent work, Slana. Give Jade my thanks, Phil said. He gave his companion the thumbs-up.

The injured wyvern, no longer burdened by the safety of her rider, surrendered to the welcoming darkness.

Limma, no! Dorn's mind screamed. Even Phil winced at the impact to his senses.

Limma's wings lost their rigidity, causing her to spiral; her head sagged.

I ... only waited for Indala's ...

Cradled in Jade's arms, Indala lost consciousness, the shared essence of her dying wyvern spent.

———

Garangoa was a rural mining and logging town with about three hundred inhabitants in the town itself and as many in the surrounding region. There were three predominant races living here, seleth, humans and glins'ool; illios and rrell were a minority.

When the wyverns landed on the road at the southern edge of the town, many folk stopped their daily tasks and gathered in numbers. Wyverns were not unknown here, but rarely did they land.

Out of the group, a rrell came forward wearing the medallion of the mayor. He spied the injured rider with his keen eyesight and turned to summon the healers, but they were already approaching, along with Rmero, the last hroltahg in the area.

"We are honoured to have you visit, but I see you have injured." He met them as Phil and Jade carried Indala up the main road. "Please come with me to my chambers. There are healers waiting."

"There are thousands of them. I've never seen so many!" Indala declared earnestly, clearly terrified. "I would say there were more there at this one time than we have managed to kill in all these years."

"Why did your wyvern not send a message ahead?"

With regret, Limma's strength to communicate is much weaker than others. She hung her head down. *Her strengths lie elsewhere ...*

No need to feel shame, no one else has done what you two have done. "By going further into the Vale than anyone, both of you may have saved many lives."

We did convey our message to those on the ground as we passed.

"Again, lives saved. I hope they took heed. We have a resident hroltahg, Rmero, who will convey the message ahead. Rest now."

"They are coming ... this way!" Indala slumped. "You must all ... leave."

Dorn, can't you get the message out? Phil asked.

I can, but the hroltahg is more powerful.

Why not both? Rmero asked.

———

"This snow stuff is bloody cold!" Leonie stated, trudging over the slushy incline. She decided to fly back to the ship.

David chuckled. And was still chuckling when he slogged up to the ramp. "Now we wait for Styx to return." He stomped his boots to clear the snow. "Thanks for carrying the powerpac. The portal should be fully charged in an hour or so." He sat down, enjoying the sunshine. "At least it isn't boiling here yet."

"I suppose the higher temperature was a benefit in this case to have melted the – what did you call it – *permafrost*?"

"Correct. I'm confident the sensor would still have picked up the signal; ice wouldn't affect it."

"I'm getting a coffee. Interested?"

"Why not." David lay back, hands behind his head.

"Does *Sir* want a pillow?" Leonie inquired as she glided over his prone form.

"If you can manage without spilling the coffee."

Leonie disappeared with a growl.

• • •

A few minutes later, she returned with two steaming mugs.

"Thanks." David took the mug before he wore it. "No pillow?"

He shuffled over so there was room for them both side-by-side. The pair sipped their coffee, looking at the portal while they waited. In the distance she saw two specks in the sky. Noldor and Faldo, off to find something to eat.

What was first thought a hill turned out to be a lopsided skyland. The *Sundancer* landed at the base where the skyland had gouged into the ground when it crashed. So acute was the angle, the portal had toppled face down like the one she retrieved from inside the cleft at the Vale, preventing travel in either direction.

It was still embedded in the packed ice. Leonie warmed up the area to loosen it, then willed it down to level ground closer to the ship.

I return.

What they saw at the base of the portal was absurd. Instead of the usual reddish spiked sphere, they saw a large mass of *jelly*.

I suspect these are illios wardens. They have wrapped themselves around me I believe in the expectation of detaining or smothering me.

Frack! Styx, are you okay? Leonie quickly handed David her mug and raced to him.

A minor inconvenience. Styx rolled slightly. *As we learnt from friend Feiron, I understand they do not like the cold.* As he rolled, a portion of jelly – of illios – now a shade of grey, remained in the snow. Motionless. Over the course of several minutes, more of his reddish exterior became visible as he rolled in the snow.

Leonie willed the illios remains back through the portal. *Perhaps they'll regenerate.*

I concur. I have no animosity to them. They were doing what they thought right. And maybe they'll see this as an act of mercy – that our intentions are not to be violent.

The hroltahg sped up the hill, the spikes giving him good traction. Leonie flew up with him.

"I see we've found Torone," David said as they arrived.

"Better summon Feiron and give him the good news." Leonie brushed the slush off her legs.

I can get word to Faldo and Noldor, if you'd like.

I'm sure he'd appreciate it. Leonie nodded and said, "Under the circumstances, that would be a good idea. We'll need to send an illios through to let them know what's happening."

"No telling what they are thinking on the homeworld after that little mishap," David said.

They have been informed, and will be here shortly. Faldo says Feiron is excited.

"What was Torone like?" David asked the hroltahg.

The climate is similar to here before the heat; moderate, I believe. It was daytime, but I have insufficient knowledge to determine the portal's position globally.

"Before they attacked you, was there any attempt at communication from anyone?"

You will recall, the illios are not capable of mind communication as we are.

"But what about Feiron?" David inquired. "He has an ability to communicate with Faldo, albeit only when making physical contact."

He is an exceptional case, I believe, because of the absorption of many wyvern eggshells two decades ago.

"Sounds like a research project."

"What are you two conspiring now?" Leonie coughed her drink.

Perhaps a diagnostic of Feiron.

"A what?"

"We're going to pull him apart and find out where his mind is," David explained.

"Good luck with that." She laughed and finished her drink. "We could go in to this village and say g'day?"

"It can't hurt."

No need. There are villagers approaching, Styx informed them.

Leonie tossed her mug in the snow and rose in one motion. David put his coffee down, gripped her outstretched paw and she hauled him to his feet. Together they trudged around the hull to greet the villagers.

There were seven of them, wearing furs and carrying spears and axes. They stopped when they saw a rrell and a man come into view with a hroltahg.

"Hey there," Leonie called out with a wave.

They resumed their approach cautiously, looking at the strange craft, never having seen its like before.

"Who might you be?" a bulky man asked? "What business brings you southrons here?"

"We came here to collect that portal. You've heard about them?" Leonie watched them warily

The group glanced at the portal and the ship. "It's ours," the leader said.

"Is it now?" Leonie shared a glance with David before she continued. "How do you come to that conclusion?"

"The land here is ours. We claim this thing as ours. We get the reward. Not you southrons."

Leonie nodded. "And who might you be?"

"I'm Graja," the spokesman said. "Leader of Kalingirga."

"Do you know what it does?" she asked.

The men looked at each other, mumbling softly. "A gate to take us away from here."

"To where exactly?" David asked.

Graja hesitated and the others shuffled their feet.

"It doesn't matter," David said. "We're not disputing *whose* it is."

"And the reward?" The men grew silent, fidgeting, waiting.

"Sure. As soon as we let them know in Reenat, they'll have the ducats ready for you all."

A shadow flashed on the ground. Looking up, the two wyverns were circling. Faldo was coming to land.

The men watched the wyverns nervously.

"Are there any illios in your village?" David asked, getting their attention.

"No. Just people." Graja shook his head. "But there was one

of them. Came last week, he told the message." He pointed to Styx. "But not red, and no spikes. Is it a girl one?"

I believe the term is protogynous hermaphrodites.

I hope you get better. Leonie chuckled. She turned to Graja. "When you say people ... I assume you mean humans?"

"Sure. As I said, people."

The men jumped when Faldo's talons crunched into the snow.

Feiron oozed off and slid over to them quickly. The wyvern launched again. *That is very cold.*

"Are you sure it's my homeworld? Torone?" Feiron asked as he came over. As Noldor stated, he was very excited.

"Unless there's a world covered in aggressive jelly." Leonie briefly recounted the incident with Styx. As she did so, she lifted him out of the snow. "It seems your kind can't handle much of this coldness."

"We cannot. Though I have had experience with freezing previously." Feiron shuddered, recalling the near-death experience in White Cliffs. "I will go there and inform them of what is happening."

"Want me to go with you?" Leonie offered.

"Better not. With what has just occurred, the appearance of another alien might upset them. One of their own should mollify them."

"If you say so, but hear this, we'll wait a reasonable time, but if you don't return soon after we send through a signal, we're coming in after you. And they can get as upset as they want."

"I hear you. Let's hope it doesn't come to that." He sounded excited.

"Good luck," Leonie gave him a slap of encouragement. "Ready?" She willed him through the portal at his nod.

Dumbfounded at this exchange and seeing the illios, first come off the back of a wyvern, then fly into the portal, the men from the village remained silent, staring at the place he'd disappeared.

"We now know it goes to the illios homeworld," Leonie explained to them. They looked indifferent.

David cleared his throat. "We'll bring the Earth portal up when the southern regions are done."

Being brought back to their current situation, the men grumbled. "Why do we have to wait?"

"We're always last," another complained.

"Because the l'ith like the heat and won't be up here for a while yet. Ertuk is not under threat."

"Never seen a l'ith ... Are they not fairy tales?" The men chuckled, nudging one another at the silliness of southrons.

They are not children's stories. Styx's affirmation seemed to mollify them. *I have encountered them myself many times.*

"And we'll get the reward?" Graja continued.

"Tell them, Styx. Perhaps they'll believe you more."

I can confirm the ducats will be awarded and equally distributed to all the members of the Kalingirgan environs.

Leonie, being more sensitive to telepathy sensed an irritating buzzing. She turned to look at Styx.

I have just received a message! Styx and Noldor both informed them at the same time. The large wyvern hovered nearby, causing the villagers to move back a few steps.

"Both of you? From the same source?" Leonie asked.

Mine is from Dorn, Noldor stated.

Mine is from Rmero, a hroltahg in Tesak.

"What message?" David asked. He ignored the villagers asking questions.

The l'ith are swarming! They number in the thousands and are heading in all directions. Rmero is a hroltahg in Garangoa, a mining town north of the Tesak forest. She sends they are in danger.

Mine is from Dorn. It is similar. A wyvern died in getting the information to them.

"What's the village population?" David asked.

Noldor paused. *There are normally six hundred in the area, but because of the portal messages, this has blossomed to nearly two thousand.*

"How quickly can you and Faldo get there?" David asked.

It will be half a day at best. Dorn informs me all the wyverns have been summoned.

"That's good news, but if there's a swarming they'll be needed everywhere," Leonie reasoned.

True.

"Noldor, we'll see you when you get there," David said.

We will do our best.

"Is the powerpac attached firmly?" Leonie asked David.

"As firmly as any other portal. It should be okay. And the portal will be fully charged on arrival." He turned and hurried up the ramp.

Noldor, you know what to do. Also, just in case, watch out in case Feiron makes a hasty arrival.

"What's happening?" Graja asked loudly, frustrated at being ignored.

"We have to go. You'll see someone in a few weeks with the Earth portal. Tell your people to be ready," Leonie advised them.

"And they will bring the gold?"

"That's not for me to say. You can always remain behind since you don't believe in the l'ith. But, when the ground is dry as a bone and your skin is peeling off you, you might think a few ducats wasn't that important." Leonie turned and entered the ship, Styx at her heels.

Again, the group of men watched nervously as Noldor moved to the portal, gripping the outer rim with his great claws, then slowly rose with mighty sweeps of his wings.

Once inside the ship, Leonie hit the button to raise the ramp and made her way to join David in the command centre. "All set?"

"I've punched in the coordinates for Garangoa."

"You're so violent." She joked softly, nodding as she took in the view.

The wyverns were higher now, winging their way south, while the villagers stood there; some staring at the wyverns, some watching the ship. The view became a pearly luminescence as the tau-field activated.

"Haven't we got blasters somewhere?" Leonie asked moving back to the console. "You know, like in those hiding places you found in the *Skydancer*?"

"I do have a couple, not enough to fight off thousands though."

"Maybe, if those bugs are going everywhere, we won't need to face big numbers. Either way, it'll be better than nothing until we can get those people to safety. How long will it take us?"

"Not long."

The pearly luminescence faded revealing a scene not much different to Qelay, other than the absence of a lake.

"Not long at all." Leonie stared, punching him in the shoulder.

"I wasn't following a portal signal this time." David shrugged, landing near the town.

Outside, the planted fields – burnt dry with the arid air – stretched to the north and east. Between the ship and the Central Ranges to the west, Garangoa sat with its quaint wooden and stone buildings. The only difference was the lack of people. The town looked completely abandoned; doors were left ajar and carts in the street.

"Where is everyone?" Leonie asked, moving closer to the viewport. "Noldor said there'd be a couple of thousand."

"At least there's no bodies, and no hordes of l'ith." David scanned the area. "But no indication of life-signs in the town. Wait ..."

We are here.

Dorn?

And Philbert, Slana and Jade. The populace has retreated into the mines.

That's good news.

"A better place to defend until help or a portal arrives," Leonie expressed her relief.

You didn't bring it with you? How long will it be? Philbert asked.

"Noldor and Faldo are bringing one from the north. They'll be several hours at best." Leonie spoke aloud so David could keep abreast of both sides of the conversation. "How is everyone?"

The townsfolk are safe for now. A couple of minor injuries in the rush, and a wyvern rider, Indala, was severely injured when she and her wyvern were attacked.

"I'll come to you and bring her back to the ship. We have a healing device that will help her greatly."

I will pass the word on. In the meantime, there are a dozen wyvern-riders heading this way from Plenari. There are other townships along the ranges to protect.

"We have some weapons here to help."

More potent than a wyvern?

"Of course not." She smiled.

Hmm. You are not convincing. We shall see.

"Any idea where the l'ith are at the moment?" She looked to David. "We could fly further west and see for ourselves. Maybe reduce their numbers before they get too close."

David nodded. "As soon as we get Indala aboard, we can go."

"I'll be back in a minute." Leonie moved to the elevator as she spoke.

I will go to the mine and remain with them until you return. Styx joined her before the elevator closed.

Once Indala was on board and hooked up to the ship's medicomp, David cruised over the mountains searching for the swarming l'ith.

"There they are." He pointed to the display, steering the ship towards them. "An estimated hundred or so. They're too close together to get exact numbers."

"That's more than double what Noldor and I faced at Arilaso."

"They still have ninety kilometres of mountainous terrain to traverse before becoming a threat to the town." As they approached, more appeared. "That's strange ..."

"Those ones are flying." She pointed to the south. "Hunters."

David counted the blips. "There is roughly a dozen of them."

Leonie hefted one of the laser rifles she had retrieved from the storage unit, along with a belt containing five spare power-pacs. "Will the ramp open in flight?"

David activated another display and tapped at the keyboard. "It will now."

"Great.' She headed for the elevator. "Try to get above them and keep the ramp aimed towards them."

"Will do." David turned to her. "Don't forget your comlink." He fished one from a drawer and tossed it to her.

With the ramp frozen half-open, Leonie lay down and took aim at the unsuspecting l'ith, the spare pacs within easy reach by her side. She counted twenty-one l'ith hunters and had taken seven out before they turned their attention to her and the ship.

Her aim wasn't the best, sometimes clipping them, but the damage was enough for them to plummet to the ground. Some managed to land, some smashed into a cliff face. Either way, they were no longer a threat.

She continued her barrage of fire until they were all gone. "Done. Let's get to those on the ground," she called into her comlink.

"Will do," she heard the reply.

The terrain below changed as the *Sundancer* rotated back to the north-west.

Checking the remaining charges, she readied herself for the next lot. As they came into view, she had to lean further forward to aim down, but she was hanging out too far to be practicable.

"Any more hunters out there?"

"None on the scope," she heard.

"I'm going out. Let me know the moment any do."

"Be careful," he cautioned.

She rolled off the ramp and flew towards the many scuttling oversized bugs. "Aren't I always?"

"Rarely," he retorted. "And don't roll your eyes."

Pfft.

"I heard that," he chuckled.

She laughed, spun slowly and gave him a hand gesture. "No, you didn't."

———

Noldor and Faldo covered most of the distance when they got word the emergency was over. Being so close, they continued, but at a slower pace, arriving in the early evening.

Noldor placed the Torone portal on the roadway leading north then flew up to join Dorn. Faldo landed in the field next to the *Sundancer*. The younger wyvern promptly lay down, exhausted.

Hey brother, there is a lake full of fish. Shall we get dinner. Slana circled overhead.

I am too weary to eat.

I will bring something back for you, fatty. She flew off.

Leonie glided over to him.

Why is Noldor not tired, he asked peevishly.

That's because he's dead ... sort of. It is an anomaly. She gave him a hard scratching on the snout. *Well done,* she said before she joined the group gathering before the portal.

David was talking to Philbert and Jade.

"How long has he been in there?" Jade asked.

"Four-and-a-half hours," David said as he hooked up a fresh powerpac.

"We've got a dozen illios keen to head home."

"I'm going too," Leonie told them.

"You are?" Jade turned, surprised.

"I can go invisible, see how things are. If they're friendly, all good, if they're not ..." She dug into her pouch, extracting a black cube. "I'll toss this through."

"If you're going, so am I," Jade said.

———

"There you are. Enjoying the view?" Leonie spied Sussah sitting on the edge of the pad. Accompanied by Jade and Feiron, the trio walked out with their coffee mugs to join her.

"Surprisingly, yes. Once I started piloting, I've grown accustomed to heights," Sussah replied.

"And with either your profession or simply residing almost two thousand metres up, that can't be a bad thing."

They beheld the expansive view as the sun was setting.

"How are you Feiron?" Sussah asked. "Adjusted to our world yet?"

"More than I expected to. More to the point, many here have adjusted to me."

"I still don't understand why your own kind held you prisoner. You'd think after all these centuries, they'd be ecstatic to connect with one of their own."

He laughed, but not as loudly as Leonie. "I wasn't a prisoner."

Sussah blushed. "You weren't?"

"When Feiron returned, they worshipped him as a god," Jade laughed.

"Feiron? A god?"

"I know. Crazy, right?" Leonie gave him a friendly punch.

"I don't think *god* was the right term—" Feiron started.

"We were there, we saw everything," Jade poked him. "Pedestal, candles ... and were they flowers they were throwing over you?"

"Well ... maybe someone of importance ..." He changed hue in embarrassment.

"Anyway," Leonie continued, "like all civilisation has done over the ages, when there's something they don't understand, they try to reason it out until it made sense to them. Once they decided what occurred, it stuck and the concept grew over time, changing depending on who was saying it."

"And what was the story?"

"Many illios went through the portal and never returned. Some thought it a gateway to hell. By not returning, they suffered their penance. Every now and then, if an illios was guilty of a serious crime, he was forced through."

"What happened to them?"

"Who knows? A better life? Killed? Depending on when the skyland crashed in the snow, who's to say they didn't simply freeze?"

"To the illios, the cold is our worst nightmare," Feiron acknowledged. "Hell would be apt."

"So, when Styx arrived in Torone, they thought he was a demon—"

"And again, a hroltahg is everything we are not; hard, solid, multi-hued and spiky."

"That's funny, Styx a demon." Leonie laughed.

Not really.

Eavesdropper. Where are you? she asked the rollo.

With the judiciary in their chambers.

Any news?

Find out in two more days.

Pfft. Demon.

Jade continued the conversation. "The appearance of a hideous demon confirmed the portal was a gateway to hell, and when Feiron returned after centuries, he was regarded as a deity, for surely only one who is pure and righteous could return unharmed from hell?"

"However, when all the others appeared a few hours later, it was realised perhaps I wasn't so special after all."

"You're special to us," Leonie whispered with a wink.

"Hence my return. I couldn't disappoint my true followers."

"Anyway," Jade stood. "We're off. There are some people here from Plenari we said we'd look in on. Nice seeing you again, Su." Jade and Feiron bid them farewell.

"I'll see you out. I'm going to get some wine anyway." Leonie got up with them. She was back a few minutes later.

"We've come a long way," Sussah mused, taking her glass.

"You certainly have. No longer the goofy young girl I escaped with." Leonie sat down, dangling her legs over the ledge.

"Goofy?" She looked across at her companion.

"Definitely." Leonie's whiskers twitched. "I think the word was *bimbo* – but, now you're far more responsible and mature."

Sussah sighed. "I suppose ..."

"Still. Here we are; me a thief from the slums and you a tavern wench—"

"I was never a—" Sussah cut her protest at Leonie's laughing. She poked her tongue out instead.

"Ah well ... nice to know some things never change."

"We've *both* come a long way." Su looked back out. "How are things progressing elsewhere?"

"For starters, they're changing the subliminal messaging in the tower," Leonie said.

"I thought it was going completely?"

"They'll be reversing it to adapt to the new paradigm. Soon it will be non-existent, as will the morbid fear of aliens, agtechs and the outside." Leonie sipped her wine then continued, "White Zone is mostly repaired and resettled. We've got the powershapers removing pockets of rad around La Trobe and Carlton Towers to the south, which has more arable land than us. Overall, we're doing well with relocating everyone."

"That's good." Sussah studied her wine. "How's the trial going?" she asked.

"They're getting through it all and should be finished within a couple of days."

"We were all up there, earlier today. It must have been hard, having to say all those things about your life and what Dianah has done."

"Not so hard." Leonie shrugged. "I've had my life to come to terms with it. It's just words now. I've moved on."

"And the wilders? I've not visited them yet."

"Most of them are outside where they are happiest."

"I meant the treatment. Did Dianah's research help?"

"Her research, I have to say, is amazing – and I don't know much about it even though David has tried to explain it – the main thing is, *he* is amazed."

"Which must count for something."

Leonie nodded. "Progress with the wilders is promising. Quite a few are showing improvement with their regular sessions on the medicomps. She wants her efforts with her research to be considered in her favour."

"Will they consider it?"

"Probably – *humanitarian* reasons and all that – but at the most, all it'll do is remove the death penalty. She'll more than likely get a life-sentence like her father."

"Is it the Elites looking after one of their own?"

"No. It isn't only Elites with a vested interest in this case, that's why we have independent members selected. The main councillors are from other towers, so they are neutral, and with ambassadors from each of the five races, she will get a fair hearing. Don't forget, Dianah was on Shak'aran for well over a century, interfering with their lives as well. What she did not only impacted humans, but all the known races."

"I haven't seen David since lunchtime. Have you?" Sussah asked.

"He left a note. He has come across some very important information, and he wouldn't be long. I don't know where he's gone, but he's taken the *Sundancer*."

34

THE TRIAL OF DIANAH FELTON

THE ATRIUM CONFERENCE CHAMBER HADN'T BEEN USED FOR OFFICIAL business since the assassination attempt on Nicholai Zodaich, the Prime of Blue Mountains Tower. Now after days of hearing evidence, the place was full with members of TowerGov, Elites and anyone who had enough privileges to get a seat.

It all started quietly enough, but as more reports of what was happening got out, the interest exploded. The air was abuzz with drones; so many of the tower population were keen to hear the outcome, mostly to see a high-rolling Elite fall. Some just came to see the aliens. Part of the hype was allowing aliens to be part of a special judicial council for the trial of Dianah Felton. To ensure complete fairness, no one from the Blue Mountains Tower held a position in this special judiciary. The speaker was Councillor Peratta, a tall, thin woman from La Trobe Tower; and the judiciary included Councillor Nan'chu from Carlton Towers and an ambassador from each of the races; Tipp, for the glins'ool; Rmero, for the hroltahg; Slarrnok, for the rrell; Lieroh, for the illios; and Zakari, for the seleth.

Because of the increased interest, and because several rebels were still at large, SecForce guards lined the walls, stairs and entrance. Security was high, and an elaborate screening process was now required before entry was permitted. There was also the possible threat to safety as not all Alexander or Dianah's potential associates were behind bars.

With the powershaper attack, much of the White Zone population had been on edge. On top of that, with the recent crash, radiation scare and the traumatic evacuation to an alien world, the population needed something to take it out of their minds; to put it all behind them. Nothing said 'all systems normal' than a scandal at the top of society.

Some of the citizens recognised Dianah's name from when her father, Stefan Felton, was convicted of illegal genetic engineering and cloning involving the tragic murder of Ivana Zodaich – the Prime's beautiful wife. However, the majority knew her as the drive behind HelixR, the bio-pharmaceutical company providing the possibility of an extended life with ReJuv, their number one product.

There was a time when Dianah was the 'golden-girl', much like her mother, with the constant socialite lifestyle. Then it waned. Rumours abounded it was because of her new lover partner, a large, mysterious man known only as Brendon – from unknown origins – making the gossip all the more spicy.

That this golden-girl had followed in her father's footsteps and was involved in similar acts of genetic engineering and cloning raised eyebrows in some circles, but since the alleged involvement of the terrible murder of Veronica Felton Zodaich – her own mother – the chatter and rumours really started.

What did Alexander have to do with it? Was this mysterious lover part of it? People speculated Brendon had escaped during the evacuation. Wasn't he seen chasing Leonie, that cat-woman, through the portal? Some said they were both involved; others just as adamant Leonie had killed him. He had not been seen since.

At the sounding of the gong everyone stood. The hubbub died as the judiciary members returned. There was no applause, just quiet observance, even when that strange reddish ball appeared. Some thought it was cute, even with those spikes;

some considered it a pet and wondered where they could purchase one for themselves.

As for the other aliens, the crowd had not been disappointed. These *aliens* were intriguing, and not as monstrous as expected, other than the large lizard. The witnesses brought forward were mainly human; staff at HelixR and the zoo, but the most damning witness was the cat-creature named Leonie.

"Members of TowerGov, Elites, ladies and gentlemen, be seated as we commence the finalisation of this hearing," Council Peratta of the judicial council declared as she banged her gavel.

The elevator platform normally used in the inductee ceremony of new Elites activated. Moments later, Dianah Felton appeared, seated and dressed in a simple, unadorned grey robe. Those in the audience missing the previous hearings babbled among themselves as this was the first time they had seen the accused.

The speaker took a drink from her flask to allow a few moments for the audience to settle before she began. Many drones hovered silently, focused on her and the judiciary members. A few drones slowly swept over the heads of the crowd, and as many focused on the accused.

"In this session we will summarise what we have heard, the evidence, and the judiciary's final decision to the fate of Dianah Felton.

"The most heinous crime of the accused is the alleged conspiracy to assassinate the Prime, Nicholai Zodaich and Veronica Felton Zodaich and the murder of David Osbourne. We have independently confirmed two of the three bodies recovered were clones, those being of Nicholai Zodaich and David Osbourne. As they were simulacrums, there is no charge of murder. Clones are not covered in Blue Mountains Tower charter. The Prime Lady, Veronica Felton Zodaich, was the only human killed and therefore the assassination charge stands. In this charge we also took into account matricide.

"We have seen the evidence regarding the illegal cloning done by the accused, utilising the HelixR premises and equipment. The bulk of this evidence has been contained in files kept by Alexander Zodaich, including voice recordings of the accused, all of which has independently verified.

"We have seen evidence and heard the testimony from those affected by the actions of the accused into genetic engineering experimentation. To point out the most gross of these actions – that of the creation of Leonie. A full analysis of her genetic makeup includes the DNA of human, rrell, and in smaller amounts illios, hroltahg, seleth and glins'ool." She turned and acknowledged the ambassadors behind her before returning to address the chamber.

"You will be aware these are representatives of the new alien races recently discovered and welcomed to our alliance. The accused has grossly violated and manipulated the genetic code of five of the known sapient races. The evidence of this has been independently verified.

"The allegation of the accused in the destruction of the Shrine in Delta, causing the alleged deaths of dozens of women and children, cannot be determined completely, therefore those charges will be dropped."

Peratta took another drink from her flask before continuing.

"Now, I will declare the verdict of the council in each of these charges.

"For the charge of conspiracy to assassinate Veronica Felton Zodaich, the judiciary finds her guilty. The penalty for this crime is death by Recyc.

"For the charge of illegal cloning, the judiciary finds her guilty. The penalty for this crime is death by Recyc.

"For the charge of genetic engineering and the gross manipulation of alien genetic code, the judiciary finds the accused guilty. The penalty for this crime is death by Recyc."

She raised her voice over the rising noise, banging the gavel loudly several times as the gathered audience erupted, some in cheers, some in consternation.

"Order. Order!" she shouted.

Leonie flew up and over the railings. She landed and stood

there, silent. Eyes glowing. The shock at seeing her silenced everyone far more effectively than the speaker banging her gavel.

Two SecForce guards turned to intercept her. She ignored them as she stepped forward.

"Your honour, if I may address the judiciary and the chamber?"

"This is highly irregular—" the speaker stood, looking to Nicholai Zodaich, overseeing the hearings every day. He gave a subtle nod, muttering to Krre'lo and Reindet siting each side of him.

"What here these last months hasn't been highly irregular? It's trending. Go with it."

"The judiciary recognises Leonie," Peratta uttered as she sat down.

"Thank you." She increased the volume of her voice slightly. "You heard the verdicts, however, as unusual as it would appear, I would like to propose an eleventh-hour reprieve."

The crowd muttered.

Leonie spoke over them "Who here has used the HelixR product, ReJuv?"

Half the hands raised, some fast, some slow.

"A product Dianah Felton designed," she called out. "Who here has used the medicomp to heal injuries and disease?"

More hands were raised.

"Dianah Felton's research was used to make that device possible." Leonie strode up and down the front of the crowd, seeing the agtechs and Sussah to the side. "The bulk of you, and dare I say the bulk of Blue Mountains Tower population, would not be enjoying the health conditions you currently have if not for the research this woman has carried out. I know this for the truth that it is. I have seen her research – every bit of it. For better or worse I would not be here if not for her, but who here did have that choice? Can you opt out in utero? Of course you can't.

"Has Dianah done wrong? Yes, she has. Did she do it out of greed for power like Alexander Zodaich? No. Did she do if for wealth or personal gain? No. She did it for the one and only thing she cared about, knowledge. To do the best she could. You could say it's in her DNA."

Some of the chamber chuckled nervously at what they perceived as a joke.

Leonie strode closer to where Dianah was watching her. Nervous. Scared. *What are you up to?* Dianah messaged.

Leonie continued, "Many will say she chose to do these things, but did she? She, like us, is a product of our environment. Over the last couple of weeks, I have spent time with her as she worked to save many of my friends. I have delved into her mind. There is no animosity there, no yearning for greed, no yearning for power, just a yearning for anything to increase her knowledge in the field she loves.

"Most of you will know of SciCorps, and its brilliant founder, David Osbourne. Again, much of what you use in everyday life in the tower has been improved by his genius and drive for efficiency. So, you will understand that when I say he has uncovered some pivotal information, you will know I speak the truth."

"What is this new information?" Councillor Peratta asked loudly, standing up at the podium. "Why was it not brought before us to consider?"

"David has been absent and only recently returned with this information. Your honour, if I may present David Osbourne to address the judiciary and chamber?"

The speaker rolled her eyes. "Very well, if he can be quick."

Leonie willed David over the rails from the level below where he had been waiting. With him was a very thin, pale man who could barely stand up. She assisted by keeping him elevated, and enhancing his frail voice.

"Father?" Dianah cried out in utter shock. She openly wept.

"State your name."

"Doctor Stefan Felton," he answered.

Several Elites stood up in distress at the name, cursing. They sat down quickly when SecForce guards tensed.

"Doctor Felton, tell the judiciary and the audience what you revealed to myself and David."

He cleared his throat. "I am and have always been an ambitious scientist; a geneticist. Without bragging, I believe I am gifted. You may scoff, but the evidence has been in front of you for quite a long time." He chuckled.

"Continue," Leonie encouraged.

"It is virtually impossible to determine a well-made clone without the utmost careful analysis. I understand a clone of young David was used to murder Nicholai and dear Veronica ..." he paused, catching his breath. "The simulacrum was sufficient to pass casual scrutiny, but was easily determined to be what it was. The clone of Nicholai was not made by Dianah Felton, but under the direction of the Prime himself."

Accusing eyes turned to the Prime. By the dark look on his face, he was clearly not expecting this turn of events.

"And who could forget dear Ivana Zodaich," Stefan continued, "such a wonder to behold, the most exquisite woman anyone has ever laid eyes on; perfect symmetry, perfect voice, perfect in every way. One might say too perfect. Unless she was a clone. AI designed her, and I created her for my good friend Nicholai."

Again the crowd argued and disputed the claims of this convicted madman, standing up and shaking fists and heads; some at the convicted scientists, some at the Prime.

Silence all of you! Styx entered their minds long enough to shock them into submission.

"And my dear daughter, Dianah," Stefan continued. "To remove any suspicion I specifically designed her to have the flaws usually found in humans, but I did make sure she had an inquiring mind."

"You're saying Dianah Felton, your daughter, is a clone?" the speaker asked, shocked.

"I am saying exactly that, councillor."

Dianah screamed, then fainted, slumping in her chair.

The crowd gasped, but wary enough not to get too loud less

the alien enter their minds again.

He is speaking the truth, Styx confirmed.

Eyes looked to him nervously.

"And so, your honour," Leonie spoke up, "as you pointed out, under the Blue Mountains charter, a clone is a non-entity which has no legal rights, therefore it cannot be tried or punished for the very same reasons. It is designed to look the way it looks, and programmed for what it does and the way it acts. Do you blame the blaster, or the person behind the trigger?

"As much as an elevator goes up and down; or a spaceship flies ... Dianah Felton did do these things, but by design only. To that end, I call to the judiciary to renounce your verdict. Dianah Felton cannot be found guilty of any crimes; a clone cannot be judged under our laws."

Again, the audience erupted, creating a great disturbance. The drones whizzed by overhead to take it all in for the ravenous citizens of the tower. It became evident more force was required.

The guards formed a barrier around the judicial members and raised their weapons in preparation.

STOP!

All movement in the chamber froze except for Leonie and David. Only the drones continued whirring overhead.

"Thank you, Styx."

At your service. Ambassador Rmero is assisting.

The SecForce guards were released first, and they quickly escorted the judiciary to their chambers; only when they were clear was the crowd released and ushered away.

"What was the meaning of that fiasco?" Nicholai strode into SciCorps. He made a beeline for Leonie.

Involved in an animated discussion with Leonie about what happened in the trial, Sussah, Harrond and Lerry looked up from their chairs in surprise.

Nicholai continued his tirade. "I've been on coms all day

having to explain myself to every damn TowerGov nobody, and influential socialites."

"Which part was the fiasco?" Leonie's ears flattened in vexation. "The part where we learned you had a sex-doll? Or the part where you used illegal tech for yourself? Do you not see it as hypocritical to punish somebody for doing exactly what you did?"

"I did no such thing—"

"When Stefan was arrested, you shunted him off-world, out of the way. Your friend! Then you used his research for your own ends."

"He broke the law—"

"As did you," she growled.

"I'm Prime," he said, as if that was answer enough. "It was a security measure only, in case of assassination attempts. Clearly, that was a prudent measure."

"And Ivana? Was she a security measure too?" Leonie argued.

Nicholai stared, lost for words, unable to argue this blatant truth. He would never admit his loneliness.

"Nick, I'm not judging," Leonie softened her voice. "I've also done terrible things. Things I could justify at the time; others may not feel the same way. All I am saying is if he is guilty, you are also; if you punish him you need to punish yourself."

"And what of you," he countered. "Were you not engineered? Are you not a clone – a simulacrum."

Lerry and Harrond stood up at these words. Leonie stopped them.

"If I am, I'm not covered by your laws." She stalked closer, circling him. "I reckon I can do what I wanted to you, with no repercussions. We just proved that."

He swallowed loudly.

"She isn't, actually." David entered the room.

"Isn't what?" Nicholai asked, stepping away from Leonie.

"Leonie is not a clone. True, genetically modified, but a real living and breathing entity."

35

TRANSITION STATION

With the portal dome now permanently established on the roof of the Blue Mountains Tower, a decision to relocate those portals on Shak'aran needed to be made.

Within a month of the last portal being found, there was concern the l'ith could find them and use them to infiltrate the homeworlds. Some races, like the hroltahg, might be formidable enough to compete with them, but the other races had severe physical limitations.

David waited for the Prime and Reindet to hear his presentation. He had the droids clean the entire lounge, kitchen and docking area. To while away the time, he harvested some of the produce from his hydroponic garden, finding peace with growing things.

I find it strange for a person of your capabilities in science to find such solace in gardening.

"I can't explain it, Styx. One of the mysteries of the universe." He laughed, putting the last of the fruit in his basket. "Thank you for being here tonight, and for your assistance over the last few weeks."

Whatever I have aided in recently is nothing compared to what you and Leonie have done for us. For all of us. Not everything was foreseen, though some tomes on prophecy are still lost to us. Still, some of the outcomes were a surprise. As you say, one of the mysteries of the universe.

"Don't underrate yourself. Without your presence, mapping the stars for all the other homeworlds would have been much slower, and much more difficult."

After the centuries on Yarnik with all races interacting in relative harmony, it was a revelation to see how those on the homeworlds reacted when seeing aliens for the first time. If it wasn't for my previous ambassadorial duties in Reenat, I doubt even I would have been welcome.

"Glad to have such a reputable individual at my disposal."

At your service.

"Better be careful what you wish for." David smiled.

One of your guests has arrived.

"Welcome to SciCorps," David greeted the former monarch.

"Nicholai sends his apologies, but he will be attending short-ly," Reindet said. "Personally, from his banter, he doesn't need to go through another tour. I, on the other hand, can't wait." He turned and looked down. "How are you, Styx?"

I am always fine.

"Then please allow me." David took him on a tour of the SciCorps labs. Styx trundled behind.

On completion they moved to the lounge where their discussions could take place in comfort. A selection of David's fresh hydroponic fruits was laid out, along with glasses and wine.

"This is all very impressive," Reindet complimented. "Not that I have the slightest idea of what I'm looking at."

The Prime is here.

Nicholai was still frosty over the trial incident. David actually thought he'd go into cardiac arrest when he signed the release of Stefan Felton. The Prime had avoided going out in public if he could get away with it.

He gave a non-committal grunt as he took his seat.

"Pleasant tour?" he asked Reindet.

"Fascinating."

"Good. Shall we get to it?" he said abruptly.

The three men got down to the first item on their agenda; the portals. The discussion had been going on for several weeks now. While the populace had been safely evacuated, what to do with the portals was still a major concern.

"It's not as if we can expect the wyverns to defend the portals for ... How long was it?" Reindet smacked his lips, savouring the wine.

"The high summer will last for 738 years. If we waited for 740 years—"

"How do we cover that length of time. Is there something you can do with your time-machine?" Nicholai interrupted David.

Reindet looked up from his reading of the tablets he and Nicholai had before them. "With thousands of those l'ith scuttling about further and further, it's only a matter of time before they stumble upon them. If they get through, that would be catastrophic to most homeworlds."

Except Masevalon, but we hroltahg couldn't offer assistance to every homeworld. Out of our natural environment, the l'ith would be quite a challenge.

"If what we know of the l'ithnamagri is accurate, there'll be nowhere to guarantee the portal integrity," David said.

"Not on a remote island? We know they hate water," Nicholai suggested.

"The extrapolated data indicates the only substantial free-standing water would be at the poles. It would be insufficient to deter the l'ith, especially considering they can fly or easily burrow to it if they chose to."

"Do we destroy them?" Reindet sounded dubious. "Or somehow make them unworkable? What about draining them?"

"They are far too valuable for interstellar trade and diplomacy to destroy," Nicholai argued. "We should secure them at all costs."

"And we will, Nicholai; we need to work out the details of how to do it." David turned back to Reindet. "Draining them, and keeping them drained would be problematic. There's no guarantee they won't recharge, and we will be in no position to prevent it. Besides, while we managed to get everyone we could find off-world, we still have many people on other worlds who want and need to get back to their own worlds."

The two men looked hopeless. They flicked through their own prepared notes in the off chance an idea would come to mind.

"Why keep them on Yarnik at all?" David suggested quietly.

"Why ...?" Nicholai looked unsure. "Where then?"

"There are two large moons – they are uninhabited – we could consider either a dome or a subterranean enclosure."

Reindet looked unsure "Underground? On the moon? Which one? Luminor or Luxor?"

"It does have merit," Nicholai considered the option. "Regardless of which one. But is it possible?"

"Our very own portal here, and those on the skylands, have proven they aren't beholden to a specific area, but hardwire to each other only. I believe moving them to a moon would make little difference to their functionality."

"Okay. A moon base, then what?"

"The portals could be set up and a transfer station established."

"Transfer station?"

"Now that we have knowledge of several other sapient life forms, I assume trade would ensue," David suggested. "We have much tech that could benefit them, and I'm sure they have much we desire – food and produce for starters."

Nicholai tapped his stylus on his knee, thinking. "That would require some form of policing; to stop or at least keep track of who is going where with what." He considered the bigger ramifications. "We'd need to ensure quarantine to prevent pathogens—" Nicholai started.

David interrupted. "The portal neutralises any pathogens."

"It does?" Nicholai sounded surprised. "Good ... Still, some form of customs, perhaps a neutral area for trade negotiations.

But how would we get them there? Can your *Skydancer* be modified to do so? I'm thinking dragging it on a cable isn't best-practice."

"I have plans in mind." David took a deep breath.

"Forgive me, but as I hear all this, I truly wonder why I'm here." Reindet sighed. He put the tablet down and reached for his wine glass and took a long drink. "Everything you say goes over my head. I feel woefully inadequate – these concepts are still new to me. Let's not forget, I've just come from a world where the wheel was the most advanced form of technology."

"There's always the option for an implant," the Prime suggested. "But that's something to be discussed another time."

"Since all the homeworlds will have representatives at this transition station, and thereby become the hub of interstellar negotiations ... Would it not also be the ideal place for an embassy?" David supposed.

"It would save duplication." Nicholai nodded.

Reindet started to chuckle. "You wanted this all along, to establish a staging area for all the homeworlds."

David shook his head. "What I want is inconsequential. A logical scenario based on what we know was put forward, and with the input of both of your experiences, this developed into an outcome we all contributed to." He topped up his wine and that of his guests, letting the concept of the proposal mellow for a few minutes.

"Which leads us to something else we need to discuss," David said.

The Prime scrolled his tablet to the next item on his agenda. "I have Tranquillity Base virtual tour as next."

"Forgive me. Something else, now that the concept of a transition station has been established." David stood and walked around the room to stretch his legs. "We will need someone to run it. Someone with negotiation skills; someone used to giving orders and getting things done—"

Nicholai sat up. "Well, I suppose I could consider—"

David continued. "The logical choice would be someone

with a lifetime experience with dealing with *all* the different races; unaffected by them, their looks, cultural beliefs and differences."

And one who has proven his trust to these people in many previous negotiations over many years.

"Oh." Nicholai looked from David to Reindet.

"And I thought I was going to retire." Reindet considered. "At least Siola will be happy." He drained his glass. "I think I need to use – what do you call it here – the toilet?"

"By all means. We should all have a break. I need to grab some things for the next agenda item anyway."

After the break, David treated his guests by showing the latest work on his astrogation project. Unlike the previous time he worked on it with the help of Leonie and her psionics, David had to rely on his VR goggles.

In preparation, he had laid out three pairs on the desk. When Reindet returned, he looked at the strange contraptions. David showed him how to wear it and its function.

"What you'll see," David explained, "is like being there. To your eyes and senses, it will seem the real thing, but you won't be leaving the room."

You would be familiar with the concept, as when hroltahgs gave you updates from around Athglenn, Styx added to David's comment.

Even so, Reindet gasped in amazement once the display was activated. Despite himself, Nicholai did too.

Displayed before them was the Earth, then Sol and the solar system. The viewpoint zoomed back, the speed increasing. The solar system became a mere speck, denoted by a blinking blue dot.

As they moved much further afield, David spoke, and details flowed across the base of the image.

"With the assistance of Styx, we have managed to map the star formations pertinent to each homeworld. Enhanced by what we discovered when searching for Yarnik, my programme was then able to extrapolate that information and cross-reference it to what we now know."

A representation of the entire Milky Way galaxy was now visible. More lights blinked; red, orange, green, purple and yellow.

"The lights represent the location of each homeworld. Red is Yarnik, and is the closest. orange is Torone, green is Praven, purple is Masevalon, and yellow is Thiqurian."

"Coincidently, Yarnik is 3,211.47 light-years from Earth," he told Reindet.

"And it's the closest to us? To Earth, I mean?"

"Correct."

"Thiqurian is the furthest. How far is that?" Nicholai asked.

"We are in the Orion Spur, and Thiqurian is in the Scutum-Centaurus Arm, and approximately sixty-thousand light-years."

To each of their points of view, they zoomed in to the home-worlds of each race, seeing their sun, the planetary systems orbiting it, and satellites orbiting those planets.

The image faded to black.

"Time to rest your eyes," David said. "And have a drink. I'd like to show you what's been happening on Tranquillity Base, and we'll be utilising the VR goggles again."

The men rubbed their eyes and took a few minutes to unwind, and to enjoy the wine and fruit.

David continued, "As anyone native to the towers will know, above the Earth, in an orbit much closer but similar to the moons on Yarnik, we have several man-made stations. They serve many purposes; as a go-between between Earth, our moon and Mars; it also houses quite a few research organisations. The unique and specific conditions needed to carry out experiments, research and development can be more efficiently met on such stations."

"And you have one?" Reindet asked.

"Me, no. These are very expensive to build and maintain for one individual. The income and resources of multiple towers are required for structures of this complexity and magnitude, but the towers that do contribute have tenure of a section.

"Now, just relax in your chairs while I take you through the latest project."

Reindet still gulped at some of the sights but remained silent unless he had a question.

The view was from an AI drone flying around the external gantries so the viewer could get an overall appreciation of the size. David could zoom in on any section if they wanted.

"Is this facility now fully automatic?" Nicholai asked. Even he was mesmerised by what he saw. "It's been more than ten years since I visited Tranquillity Orbital."

"Yes, with the upgrades I installed prior to starting the *Sundancer* project, and only the external section. I do have a couple of personnel to oversee the deliveries and the many other sundry aspects such a complex and remote facility necessitates."

"How many sensors are there?" Nicholai asked. He had reviewed the sensor parameters on his tablet. What they saw in 3D looked like asterisks, but a three-dimensional one – including two additional spokes radiating in all directions.

"I've got a thousand being configured now," David said. "We can roll out a thousand a week with this facility alone."

The drone zoomed along the gantry with a myriad of identical sensors in a production line. Working tirelessly around each one was a range of mech-droids – each with a specific function. On completion of one task, they would move on to the next array. This happened like clockwork.

"It isn't as complicated as it looks," David went on. "The arms are passive sensors only; the hub contains the powerpac and hardware. If a signal is picked up, a TIC will immediately jump to GA-TE."

The vid went blank. "That's it, gentlemen."

They placed their goggles on the table, wiping their eyes and blinking at the change of light.

"What's Ga-te?" Nicholai asked.

"Galactic Authority - Temporal Enforcement. I mentioned it briefly when I first told you about the *Skydancer*."

"Hmm. Has that been established already? The alliance, I mean." Nicholai scrolled through his notes.

"It's a work-in-progress. We still need to build the dome and arrange for the transport of the portals, but selecting the personnel to operate it, and those representatives from each world for the embassy can begin. I foresee the portals being on the surface within a dome and the embassy and all relevant infrastructure housed in a subterranean base below the transition dome."

"And the portals themselves won't be underground ... because the bedrock would impede the signal?"

"Correct."

"Dare I ask, what's this *tic* you mentioned?" Reindet asked.

"Temporal Incident Contact." It was clear from the blank look further information was needed. "A TIC is simply a device carrying data ... information. When a sensor registers an anomaly – an unauthorised time-jump – the TIC will be sent to HQ for processing."

"How long will the power for each sensor last?" Nicholai continued. "If there are that many over huge distances, recharging won't be easy or cheap."

"In stand-by mode, the trickle charge will keep them going for approximately a thousand years."

Nicholai turned to David, blinking rapidly. "Did you say a thousand years?"

"They're passive," he repeated. "Only illegal jumps will be actioned; registered jumps will merely be noted. The only power requirements are if and when temporal ripples are detected."

"These temporal ripples? What are they?"

David explained the pebble in the pool analogy. "But in space-time, those ripples radiate as an expanding sphere."

"How and where will they all be positioned?"

"Sensor placement will be determined by using galactic coordinates, with the galactic plane and galactic poles as references. This is nothing new. We've used it for centuries to map stars, though we are now slightly more accurate.

"The distances we're now contemplating travelling are considerably larger than anything previously foreseen. What we use currently for solar travel won't cut it on a galactic scale, the same way Earth time references will be pointless outside the solar system. There's now a requirement for a system to cope galaxy-wide, a standard for all the worlds to adopt.

"I also propose this headquarters will become the centre for all portal travel and trade; it should be regarded as the reference point for Galactic Time, in much the same as Greenwich is used as a reference point for Earth Time.

"Several smaller AI-controlled time-machines will be used to place the sensors in a five hundred light-year grid initially around each homeworld sector, expanding to the regions in between them and the headquarters."

"Five hundred light-years?" The Prime shook his head trying to get around the distances involved, considering less than a couple of months ago Mars was the furthest regular commuter distance.

"Once an unregistered jumper is detected," David continued, "several TICs from the area will immediately jump to GA-TE HQ for data transfer. The AI will compare the time-stamp of each sensor. This will then provide the exact time-space coordinates; a patrol craft will then jump immediately to that location to detain the perpetrator."

"Sounds complicated. How long will that take?"

"Virtually instantly."

"Instantly?" The Prime sounded sceptical, he nearly spilt his wine.

"Nicholai ... I don't think you've comprehended fully the true aspects of traveling through time."

The Prime faltered. "It took us around thirty minutes to travel to Yarnik."

"We are not talking about the duration of the trip; we're talking about how soon after receiving the TIC data a patrol craft will be in position."

Nicholai nodded, but failed to hide his confusion. Reindet sympathised, and drank more wine.

"Let me put it this way, using random figures. Three TICs arrive at GA-TE from region X at approximately 1200 hours; once the data from all three is calculated, we can triangulate the exact position – let's call it Y; we calculate the duration of the trip from GA-TE to Y will be forty-five minutes, the AI will program the response craft to arrive at Y at the space-time 12:00:10 hours. Regardless of the duration of the journey, they will arrive within ten-seconds after the incident."

"But if—"

"If we arrived earlier; we would inadvertently be responding to an incident that had not yet occurred; also bear in mind the time-jump ripple may produce disruptive interference patterns. These would affect the arrival conditions for the offending vessel. We can only arrive after the event."

"Do you know this? How can you be sure?"

"I analysed the flight-recorder of the *Skydancer*. They jumped from here to 2401. They were hailed by GA-TE cruisers. When they refused to comply and attempted to evade, they received several laser strikes to the tail section before jumping away. Referring back to the ripples in a pond scenario, by jumping too soon after the previous time-jump – compounded by the damage and the ship's intrinsic design faults – they were knocked off course by these ripples."

"Wait, you said they jumped fifty years to the future and hailed by GA-TE cruisers? So ... GA-TE will exist?"

"It does sound promising. Yes." David grinned.

"How is it they arrived over Yarnik and crashed near Delta?" Reindet asked.

"During my experiments, after I complete a jump and ensure it is 100% safe, I add it to the computer's nav. The last save-point is hardwired to an emergency override. If the button is pressed, the coordinates for the last jump is initiated, but with the damage and ripple effect, the displacement threw them back 155 years."

"So, you're saying you've been to Yarnik before?"

"I have, but in space only, long enough to calibrate the coordinates."

Nicholai selected more fruit and chewed thoughtfully. "How many sensors do we need?"

"We'd need to produce millions to make any significant impact. More than SciCorps can comfortably produce. This is where negotiations with other towers would be beneficial."

"We can't possibly have sufficient quantity of *jotnarium* for that many."

"Evidently, we will. However, the sensors themselves do not require it." From out of his lab-coat pocket, David produced a sphere the size of a golf ball. "This is one of the TICs I mentioned." He handed it to Nicholai.

The Prime examined it, noting the familiar dull shade.

David continued, "I'd like SciCorps to be the sole producer of the TICs; allowing other worlds and organisations to concentrate on the sensors. Mainly for security and also proprietary reasons. We can't have everyone across the galaxy with knowledge of how to build a time-machine.

"I've decommissioned the *Skydancer* due to its inherent design problems, and removed the *jotnarium* coating from her. That will be sufficient for the first six months of production."

"Well," Nicholai said after the presentation. "Though I now have a headache, it was quite insightful."

"I do get carried away, but at least you both know all of it now."

"Thanks," he said drily. "You sure that's all of it? You've not got any other project in mind yet?"

"Of course I do. Would you like to know?"

Nicholai sighed, any animosity from the trial forgotten. "Only if you can reduce it to one short sentence?"

"The design of the Transition Dome, the embassy and GATE HQ is well underway, as is the portals' relocation to Luminor."

When the men left, the droids entered to remove and clean

up. With his wineglass in hand, David strolled out to the pad for the view and fresh air; a storm was forming on the horizon.

Expanding on your explanation for sensing unauthorised time-jumps, they did not pick up on the fact a TIC would have also sensed the Skydancer's unauthorised arrival at Yarnik.

"I can only assume at some stage in the future I will somehow over-ride the report, perhaps a sub-routine in the AI to ignore the second time-jump."

Nor did you mention the seventh, larger portal, Styx stated.

"It's not even in the same galaxy! You noted the difficulty they had with comprehending what we've got now?"

I did.

"They aren't ready for that yet." Then added after a thoughtful sip. "I don't think any of us are."

36

ALEXANDER

"What's going on?" Leonie asked when she appeared rubbing her eyes. She glided to the lounge screen where David sat, tapping steadily on the keypad. "You called my link?"

"I'm checking now. I got a report last night from Tranquillity Base that Alex had left a day ago. And now someone looking like Alexander went through the portal to the hub."

It took a few moments before the screen came to life. Leonie grabbed a bite to eat and coffee for the two of them while David scrolled to the time of the incident.

"Here it is." He accepted the mug of steaming liquid. "No audio, though."

On screen, the guards manning the portal fell down. A masked figure entered the scene carrying a satchel and blaster. His build and hair were definitely similar to Alex's. Holstering the blaster, he pulled something from his satchel and tossed it through the portal, followed by another.

"What are they?"

David zoomed in and enhanced the image. "Looks like sleep grenades. That would explain all the guards collapsing here."

The figure checked his watch, then after giving the finger to the monitor, stepped through the portal. Other TowerPol officers, not realising the gas presence, ran in. They collapsed like their colleagues, sprawling to the floor. Only one, the last one to enter, had the reflexes and wherewithal to dive back and raise the alarm.

David checked his chrono. "That was three hundred-and-thirty seconds ago."

"How long until the gas disperses?" Leonie asked.

"They began venting the dome moments after the alarm. It should be clear now."

On screen, another pair of officers burst in and, seeing the dome empty, jumped into the portal in pursuit.

"We better get up there—"

"You don't want to leave this to SecForce?" David indicated the screen. Six armed and masked SecForce personnel arrived, then went into the portal.

"Common sense says yes; my gut says no. I always follow my gut."

"Then we go. Your guts have been fine so far ... more or less."

"More or less?" she queried, mocking hurt feelings. "And I suppose you want to go in your pj's?"

David looked at his clothing. "I'll get changed." He downed the mug's contents and walked back to his room.

"Thought you might." Leonie laughed. "I'll keep an eye on the screen." She kept eating and sipping her coffee.

By the time David returned in day clothes, the SecForce personnel were back, reporting to Commander Jay.

"Let's go." Leonie said.

They walked to the pad where she flew with David to the roof. The area had mostly been repaired, with the new atrium skylight installed. The Earth portal was housed in a secure dome, now used as an interplanetary port. The debate for where a permanent area should be set up could drag on for months.

She landed sedately outside the dome and they casually walked to the entrance.

"Halt. You're not permitted—" the guard started. "Yes ma'am." He marched away on some errand with his colleague.

David suppressed a smile as he entered the dome beside Leonie.

"Commander Jay," he acknowledged the officer as he turned at the disturbance.

"I assume it would be pointless to try to remove you two?" Jay didn't sound happy to see them.

"Pointless, but amusing," Leonie showed her teeth, tail flicking in anticipation.

"Never mind." Hearing his men moving in, he raised a hand to keep the soldiers from getting hurt. "You know what happened I take it?"

David recounted what they saw. "But not what happened beyond the portal."

"Alexander threw two grenades through, one was a sleep gas, the other one was concussion."

"Lunacy! Doesn't he know it's in a dome surrounded by vacuum?"

"I can't say, but he knows now."

"Where is he?"

"Unsure," Jay replied, perplexed. "The entrance to the Masevalon portal was breached—"

"Fragging idiot!" Leonie cursed. "He'd be crushed, burnt and dissolved instantly."

"That would save us having to deal with him. I think the breach was unintentional, but closest to the blast. Anyone surviving that was put to sleep with the gas."

"Are you certain it was Alex?" David asked.

"We had him ID'd shortly beforehand, but he must have had help and slipped through."

"Are there survivors?" Leonie asked.

"One TowerPol officer KIA, the other injured. There are science personnel with severe injuries and two KIA."

"And no one is there dealing with the survivors now?" Leonie watched the guards, standing idly.

"Medtechs are on the way."

"Did the blast breach the dome?" David asked.

"It did, but it was minor. Your DomeDoc sealed it in time."

"DomeDoc?" Leonie sniggered.

"Purely a marketing ploy." David blushed. "Not my idea."

"I'm going in to help the injured." Leonie started walking. As the SecForce squad blocked her path she turned to the commander with a warning look.

At a word from Jay, the squad let her through. She sensed their tension, but no hostility.

"She's a force to be reckoned with." David gave a half-apology, following her.

When he arrived, she was bent over the nearest casualty, a TowerPol officer. "That one took a blaster, point-blank." She didn't look up. "This one's alive."

"Don't overdo it," he warned.

"I'm fine." Leonie moved to the next one and applied her paw to the wound. "Enough to make sure they don't die before the medtechs arrive."

David examined the area. The dome looked intact. He noted the breach where grenade shrapnel had pierced the wall. With the shimmering surface facing the centre, all the portals were arrayed in a circle a few metres in from the wall. Each was labelled with the homeworld destination in several languages.

The infrastructure for the hub was damaged. The long-term plan was to establish a neutral area for the conduct of diplomatic and trade negotiations.

Because of the extreme atmospheric conditions, the hroltahg portal to Masevalon was in a secure enclosure. The portal to Isui-ips, the vorien homeworld, was dim.

He went to the security station and accessed the monitor, scrolling back the last ten minutes until just prior to the explosion.

Port personnel were going about their tasks when the first grenade lobbed in. It was the concussion grenade.

The vid blurred momentarily. When it came back, the personnel were lying all over the place, some still moving until the effects of the sleep grenade took over. A short time later, Alexander arrived. Disregarding the bodies on the floor, he looked around the area, checking each portal's label. As he was nearing the Isuiips portal, the two TowerPol officers stumbled in. He turned in surprise, snapping off two shots; one struck an officer, the other missed.

David looked startled; the officers were using ballistic weapons! It was difficult to see where the bullets hit.

Lying prone behind another body, the second officer fired his weapon randomly in Alexander's direction. With no cover Alex dropped to the ground and returned fire, crawling backwards towards the portal.

The *shimmering* portal!

Alexander looked in a panic, firing wildly. The officer did the same, and a lucky shot took Alexander in the shoulder. In pain or panic, Alexander stood and jumped through the portal.

A heartbeat later, the portal dimmed.

David looked up from the monitor at the vorien portal. *How long before it recharges?*

"So, what was so interesting? Did you find out where he went?" Leonie was sitting against the wall, panting.

"Did you overdo the healing again?"

"They're breathing." She shrugged. "What did the monitor show?"

"He went to Isuiips." David came over to join her, sliding down the wall. As he did so, he scanned the far wall, looking for bullet holes.

"But the portal's drained," Leonie stated the obvious.

"It is ... now."

"Ah." She nodded. "When Sussah and I first arrived on Earth, our portal did the same thing. It must have a slow charge rate, or a weak power source."

"Well, that's where he is, at least until it recharges."

"Isn't Isuiips an oceanic world? I wonder how long he can tread water?"

Medtechs appeared and began checking the casualties. One

young fellow came towards her, unsure. Leonie waved him away. He looked relieved.

David stood when Jay came through, filling him in on the later details. "There may be some flak from the other worlds; these guys were using ballistic weapons. Alex was hit in the shoulder before he fell through there." David pointed, explaining the circumstances.

The commander scowled at the report of ballistic weapons, making a note on his wrist-com. "So, it will recharge?" He was looking at the portal.

"Eventually, but I haven't the resources right now to calculate how long it will take. I wasn't certain if my repairs were successful as attempts to recharge it with powerpacs failed."

"I'll keep men here on guard – with lasers only," Jay added. "How's she doing?"

"I'm doing fine." Leonie took a deep breath, stood up and sauntered over. "And so are they, now." She pointed to the casualties. The medtechs were looking curiously between her, the casualties and their notes.

———

As seen from the hovering *Sundancer*, there was little over the atoll. Some dark patches of a lichen. A short, broadleaf seaweed around the tidal area. Near the centre of the white sandy islet stood the portal, raised on top of a set of steps carved into a rock.

"Reckon the steps are to allow for the tides?"

"It would be problematic otherwise. Look there." David pointed.

A bloody trail led down to a red patch at the base. The atoll was devoid of anything else as if swept clean by a large broom. Much further out a sizable reef ringed the islet, blocking the bulk of the waves.

Sundancer circled the atoll. The area on the other side of the portal also had steps, but the sand here was churned up, with much more blood and discolouration.

"That doesn't bode well," Leonie observed. "Are we landing?"

"No, but now I have precise coordinates, I'll send a drone to observe the time just before his arrival."

Isuiips blinked out. Twenty-minutes later they were back over the tower and landing on the designated area on the roof.

"You sure about this?" she asked, looking at the head-sized sphere, dull and drab even in full sunlight bathing the SciCorps pad. "And that will get there?"

"Absolutely. It's a fully automated drone with an AI." David showed her its specs on his tablet.

"You just love your AIs."

"That goes against Elite fetish standards."

"They have fetish standards? Never mind. I don't want to know!" She shook her head. "We couldn't have gone back ourselves? In time I mean?"

"In theory, we would slingshot away the instant our early-selves met our present-selves," he paused. "There are complications with crossing time when you already exist."

"Slingshot?"

He nodded. "Because ..."

Leonie waited. "Oh, this is one of those *because* moments when you're going to fill my head with technobabble and I'm going to get glassy-eyed and throw up?"

"Something like that. Or I can grab a bucket."

She put her paws up. "*Because* is sufficient. Thanks."

David tapped at the tablet. There was a *pop* and the sphere disappeared.

"Now we wait. Coffee?" she asked.

There was another *pop*. David stepped forward and retrieved the drone.

Mid-step, Leonie looked back. "Did it get lost? I thought you said it would work?"

"Why do you think it didn't?" David walked past with an innocent smile. "Because time-travel and all that." He winked.

"I ... Fine!" she huffed. Ears flat in annoyance, she followed.

Getting comfortable by the table, he placed the tablet for easy viewing by both, and watched the recording. The vid screen on the table stand covered the interior of the transit dome from the roof, where maintenance personnel worked on repairs. The bodies and casualties had been removed.

On the tablet, the drone appeared where the *Sundancer* was earlier and performed a circuit of the islet thirty metres out from the shimmering portal. As it did so, Alexander fell through, sliding and tumbling down the steps. He clutched his left shoulder when he came to a stop on the sand.

Slowly and silently the drone moved closer. David enlarged the hi-res image to see Alexander panting and grimacing in pain. His foot kicked the sand several times.

"Is that pain or is he having a tantrum?" Leonie wondered.

Alex started fidgeting then rolled away, standing up awkwardly, looking wide-eyed back at the ground. The drone focused on the moving figure, but the 3D allowed David to pan in on the area, seeing in detail where they blood patch was. Small crab-like critters were emerging from the sand.

As he moved about, more appeared. Soon the sand was covered in them. Alex ran up the steps and jumped through the portal, but merely landed on the other side, struggling to keep upright as he slid down the steps.

"Been there; done that," Leonie joked.

Alex stumbled to the water's edge, digging into his satchel. The crabs followed his movement. He pulled out a grenade and flung it at the thickest grouping.

"The fool's going to blow the portal if he isn't careful!"

David watched with concern.

The grenade went off, blowing sand and crab-meat in all directions. Many of the surviving crabs were stunned, but then began to consume the fresh food-sources around them when they could move.

"Notice how they ignore him now that he isn't moving?" David observed.

"That man is too agitated to keep still for long."

Alex reached for his arm again, swaying. The injury was severe, and blood freely dripped down his arm into the water. With slow, deliberate movements, he knelt in the water to wash his wound. He looked nervously back to the beach.

"I reckon he's realised vibrations and movement attract them."

Alex's shoulders slumped either in exhaustion or despair. Every now and then he looked up to see if the portal was shimmering. The crabs had settled, many digging back into a burrow. A few scuttled in search of more morsels.

"I wonder how long before the tide turns?" David zoomed back to view the reef. There was less white water, indicating the rise. "It may be several hours before the atoll is covered."

"Reminds me of the harbour in Delta," Leonie reminisced, pointing to the slight blood trail in the water. "He better hope there aren't any crocs."

"Maybe not a croc, but there *is* something."

"There's *always* something." Leonie watched, mesmerised and horrified at the same time as a dark shape approached the atoll beneath the surface.

The drone hovered and maintained the focus on the one lifesign. Again, using the AI's higher functions, David zoomed to the approaching shadow. "It's a big *something*."

Closer to the shore, a portion of the creature writhed to the surface in the shallows; several thick tentacles snaked about.

Alex, hearing the sound turned his head. While no sound was conveyed through the drone, it was obvious from his facial contortions he screamed in sheer terror. He staggered and stumbled out of the water towards the portal, reaching into his satchel, but there were no more grenades.

"That's got to suck," Leonie mused.

"It looks like a kraken ... a mythical creature similar to a giant octopus," David muttered in awe.

The monster and its writhing mass of tentacles dragged itself closer sensing the blood trail, as were the crabs now back on the surface. Laboriously, it closed in, the tips of the tentacles touching the blood-soaked sand.

Half-staggering, half-crawling he desperately made his way up the stairs. There was the merest shimmering. Reaching the white crystal structure, he barely had enough strength to climb onto it, bracing himself, one-handed.

The shimmer was too weak as he found out when he didn't disappear.

Leonie's eyes darted to the other screen; the portal on the roof mirrored the weak glow.

Back on the tablet image, Alex pulled himself upright, standing within the gateway, waiting. In a last-ditch effort, he pulled out the blaster and fired at the tentacles that squirmed closer, only managing one shot as his powerpac discharged ... at the same time the shimmer grew brighter.

"Did the portal just drain his blaster?"

David nodded slowly in consideration. "It's what the portal was doing to the pacs on Skyhome."

The creature's massive, beaked jaw widened in anticipation of a meal as two tentacles reached through and wrapped around his torso and legs to pull him closer.

Or tried to.

Alexander started to disappear through the shimmer, along with the tentacles entwining him.

Dragged towards the portal, the monster braced against the steps while trailing tentacles gripped obstacles within the water. It halted its forward momentum. The appendages within the portal strained.

Seconds dragged by with a tug-of-war spanning the galaxy. The tension increased. The portal started to shake.

A tentacle snapped. The recoil was enough to jolt the remaining tentacle free. The creature slithered back, one tentacle missing. The other gripped a torso; globs of entrails dripping to the sand.

The giant octopus retreated to the depths as it consumed its meagre meal. The crabs scavenged the fallen entrails and soon disappeared leaving the sandy islet with its gory dark stains. The recording finished.

On the other screen, a pair of crushed and misshapen legs wrapped in a tentacle splattered blood and gore across the floor. The personnel who had moved back to cautiously watch the shimmering portal fled the area, dodging the thrashing appendage.

Leonie sat, quietly, lost in her thoughts. She noticed even David was in a state of shock.

Though she had never actually met him face to face, she reviled Alex for all the pain and anguish he caused her – directly or indirectly – including the death of her mother.

"Now he's half the man he used to be," she muttered. "No medicomp's healing that."

EPILOGUE

37

2451

As the *Skydancer* slowly rotated, familiar stars began to fill the inky blackness out the viewport. The three occupants blinked rapidly as the Earth came into view. Their dizziness and pins and needles soon faded.

Brendon recovered first, and checked the console readout; 2352. He released a big sigh of relief.

"Did it work?" Alex asked.

"Yep. Just like I set the program – fifty years into our future." Brendon swivelled sideways so Alex could see the readout.

Alex leaned forward. He looked at the readout then the view. "Is that green haze ... vegetation?"

Dianah unclipped and stood to peer over their heads. "They've done a huge amount of land regeneration to get that much greenery. We *must* be in the future! Outside was a wasteland for centuries." She patted Brendon on the shoulder. "Looks like we're in the clear."

All three heads turned as one to the sudden beeping from a monitor on the left of the console.

"What the frag is that?" Alex spat.

Brendon checked the screen display. "We've got three craft moving in very fast!"

"Shift! I'll try and fly us out of here."

Brendon hastily unclipped. Alex was in the chair instantly looking at the controls, recalling his few times on a simulator.

'Illegal vessel, Earth registered name Skydancer – by the order of Galactic Authority Temporal Enforcement, you are hereby ordered to stand to. Shut down your drives and prepare for boarding.' The message blared over the speakers.

"How the frag do they know who we are already?" Alexander cursed. Still unsure of these controls, he did all he could to evade the patrol.

They felt the craft vibrate as he maxed out the drives, steering to the largest gap.

"This can't be happening!" Dianah moaned.

'I repeat, illegal vessel, Earth registered name Skydancer – by the order of Galactic Authority Temporal Enforcement, you are hereby ordered to stand to. Shut down your drives and prepare for boarding.'

"Yeah, yeah. You said that!" Alex swung the joystick hard right, then down. The *Skydancer* swung to the right and dipped suddenly as one of the attacking craft moved to intercept.

'Failure to comply will result in severe repercussions.'

"Brendon! How can—" Alex glanced across. "Open your eyes!"

"I'm sifting through David's memories ..." Brendon concentrated.

The ship jolted as they took a hit to the stern. A buzzing began as lights blinked red. An acrid odour permeated the interior.

"Whatever you do, do it now!" Alex yelled.

Brendon opened his eyes, searching the console. "That button, there." He pointed.

"Which fragging button?"

"The red one! To your right. The one I'm pointing to!"

"The panic button?" Alex sounded incredulous.

"Aren't we panicking," Dianah keened.

Cursing, Alex snapped open the clear cover with his thumb and hit it without hesitation.

The view went white. Again, they endured another ear-popping. The dizziness and pins and needles felt more intense.

The *Skydancer* ploughed into the upper atmosphere of the alien planet.

More alarms assailed their ears as Alexander fought desperately to keep the spacecraft stable. Having sustained damage before the time-jump, the controls refused to work properly.

"How did those damn cops find us so soon? How had they found us at all?" Alexander raged, flicking his black hair in irritation. "He did this on purpose! If I ever get my hands on that bastard, I'll rip his eidetic brain out of his skull."

"You mean you'd blackmail a thug to do it for you." Dianah's hazel eyes starkly contrasted with her ashen face; a white-knuckle grip on the armrests as the craft rocked from side to side.

During the turbulent descent, they had passed over a large, desert island. Vast stretches of empty water filled her view now. Such a large expanse of nothingness ... it was too much. She turned her head away from the disturbing view, fighting the nausea.

Alexander gritted his teeth as he attempted to bring the vessel's nose up. "Osbourne should've kept himself in the lab, instead of converting this space yacht into a damn time-machine!" The threatening tone of the drives mellowed from a screech into a whine.

"That's why we stole it in the first place." Brendon, sitting further back, looked just as bad as Dianah. "You got to admit though, it did work," he said loudly over the noise.

"No good if it kills us," Alexander snapped.

Looking towards Dianah, Brendon could see her concern echoed his. "I don't think it's the ship that's going to kill us," he said nervously.

"You want to try, mutant?" Alex strained at the controls. The

Skydancer would shake itself apart or ditch into the sea if another stretch of land didn't appear soon.

"Maybe if you'd switched to auto-pilot instead of trying to fly this thing yourself, we wouldn't be in this mess." She didn't normally get so vehement. Alexander's impetuousness and need to be in total control always drove a wedge between them.

"Oh, so it's my fault now?"

"Yes!" they replied in unison.

———

"Brother Niko. Brother Niko awaken! The time has come! I am sure." The young monk turned his jubilant gaze to his friend. Niko's snoring stopped for a moment, before resuming even louder.

The two monks were at their posts on the top of the monastery tower. The old monastery was built on a rocky peninsula overlooking a sweeping harbour dotted with several islands. They had a panoramic view of the southern horizon, and the coastline east and west. The strange light in the sky was coming from the far south, seeming as if emerging from the constellation of The Key, leaving a trail of incandescence.

To ward off the chill of the winter evening, Niko had brought a wineskin, much to Armad's annoyance. He knew Niko would drink most of it and then fall asleep, leaving all the watching to him. Just like before.

"Brother Niko!" Armad nudged him very firmly with his sandalled foot, rolling the reposed figure over.

"Wha?" came the groggy response from the cold, stone floor.

"Look! The Pillar of Fire be here, from out of The Key constellation as it be written. The time has come!"

Niko propped himself up on his elbows, and looked with bleary eyes in the direction his annoying partner pointed. South of them, high in the sky over the Sea of Tears, was a long streak of light.

"Nah. Is just another of those fallin' stars." He proceeded to close his eyes again.

"Waken, ye fool! I tell ye it is not a fallin' star. Observe. It be not fallin' like the others."

Cursing, Niko stood up with the aid of the roughly-hewn wall. He steadied himself and tried to focus. Unlike other falling stars, this one got brighter and brighter as it fell towards them.

"Certainly seems strange." Brother Niko, squinted, scratching his beard as he watched.

"We must let the others know!" Brother Armad eagerly reached for the hammer lying on the floor next to a large gong.

"Wait! Let us be sure this time. Remember what happened to Brothers Yallod and Frew the last time there were a false alarm?"

"Aye, but—"

"But nothin'. If it is what it is, everyone will be too excited to care if they be a little bit late in the knowin', but if they be told too soon and it isn't, well, I'm sure even ye can imagine what'll be a'happenin'… hmm?"

"I see yer point." Armad reluctantly agreed, letting the hammer slowly slip from his grasp.

"So, we wait and we watch." Niko made himself more comfortable, almost empty wineskin in hand, and joined Armad in observing the new spectacle.

The light moved erratically across the sky, as if it was out of control, like a bird in strong crosswinds. Closer and closer. They watched as it pierced the clouds. Still thousands of feet in the air, it suddenly flared up, creating a flaming streak behind it. The fireball descended rapidly, a strange whine getting louder until it became a deafening shriek.

"Great Eternix, man! What are ye waitin' for?" Niko cried out in jubilation. "Ring the gong, brother! Ring the damn gong! This be it! They 'ave finally arrived!" Niko jumped up and down, even doing a little jig before he got too dizzy and fell over.

Brother Armad struck the gong like crazy, but was not too engrossed to lose sight of the flaming descent. The fireball soared directly over their heads, causing them both to instinctively duck behind the parapet. Armad followed its path all the way until, with a mighty boom that made even the ringing of the gong seem to pale into insignificance, it crashed into the jungle a league to the north.

Enough was enough. Armad dropped the hammer and both monks headed down the ill-repaired spiral staircase inside the high tower, barely avoiding slipping on the loose steps. Already they could hear commotion and confusion echoing from the hall below. In moments they ran into the main hall.

The younger, sober monk left Niko panting by the door. His sandals slapping on the flagstone floor, Armad swiftly closed the distance to Father Estley.

"They are here!" he called out over the throng, waving his skinny arm in the general direction that the visitors had landed. "The High Ones 'av arrived, as was foreseen by the Seers!"

The statement was greeted by stunned silence. All of a sudden, the monks came at him clamouring for more information: the hissing of the reptoid seleth and feline rrells being especially harsh on the ears.

"Quiet now, brothers. Be calm. Let our Armad recount his news for us all to hear," Father Estley suggested when the noise abated.

The excited brother related what he and Niko had witnessed. Everyone then had to see for themselves, racing up the stairs, jostling each other to get a view of this historic event. The area was easily discernible in the darkness, as a few low clouds reflected the light of a great fire as they scudded overhead.

In a surprisingly short time, the monks organised a party to travel to the site where the High Ones landed. Everyone who was capable of putting one sandalled foot in front of the other wanted to go, and a feeling of desperation spread among some of the younger followers. They thought that the High Ones, the ones that would bring knowledge and power to those of the faith, were in danger of injury.

Father Estley, using all his experience and wisdom, managed to calm them, explaining that being so wise and powerful They would not be susceptible to things that would injure or maim a mere mortal.

When they arrived at the crash site in the swamp, they set up a camp on the driest piece of ground they could find. When the monks got close enough for a good look, they discovered the strange craft was glowing with heat, not burning as they first thought. The heat radiating from it caused great plumes of steam to rise from the swampy terrain. Some monks were concerned for those within, trying to approach, but the heat drove them back.

Father Estley maintained the peace by conducting prayers to the High Ones' safety, and by keeping the brothers too busy to worry about anything else. Later that morning with the aid of a heavy rain, the craft was cool enough for them to get closer but they could not decipher how to open the strange door.

A vigil was set. The monks waited and watched for the time when these foretold figures would emerge to lead them. Waiting was something they were used to, after all, they had been doing it for over forty years.

———

"What're they doing now?" Alexander's voice blared from the internal com.

Dianah had taken him to medbay as he'd received a large cut to his forehead from the impact. His arm was fractured as well, and the medicomp he was plugged into would soon finish the recommended course of treatment. Brendon was still unconscious on the floor, his great bulk having snapped his harness, and too heavy for Dianah to move alone, but she ascertained his vitals were good.

"I'm not going to look out there again!" she retorted, remembering the nausea she felt when she first laid her eyes on the scene outside. She turned the screen off as soon as she found the controls. Never had she seen so much openness. Such a vast distance, it was all so disturbing. "They're just standing around and ... I think they're *praying*."

The tower, where she'd lived all her life with over a million other citizens, was completely enclosed and self-contained. Outside was deemed unliveable by TowerGov, which strongly regulated any access. The largest open space she had ever seen was the zoo on the lowest level of the Blue Zone. It was over two hundred metres long, and one could view the one hundred and twenty levels below from the south balcony, and even safe and enclosed, it was still enough to cause stress. The many walkways spanning the void were twofold; allowing easy access and breaking up the huge space to reduce the impact of the great distance.

To look out the view port now and see such wide-open spaces made her feel ill and giddy. Outside was so ... so big!

"From how you described them," Alexander called out, "they're still very primitive. They probably think we're some kind of gods or something."

"You wish! Primitive, yes, but they didn't appear to be too barbaric."

"Can you pick up anything over the com?"

"No. I think most of the external equipment was burnt-out by either our entry or from that blast just before we jumped. She looked at the display, and said, "All I know is the air's breathable. It's twenty-five degrees Cee, and the humidity level is seventy-eight per cent."

"I noticed the generator your hairy freak-boy spoke about in the passageway looks a bit damaged. Can you see anything repairable there?"

"Brendon isn't a freak!" Dianah snapped back. "And I'm a geneticist, not a damn technician! What the hell would I know about it? Maybe Brendon can help when he comes around."

There was no response, which suited her just fine. Alexander was really irritable when he wasn't in control of a situation.

Dianah sat back on the lounge, resuming her meal. She had frantically tried to get some food from the galley, but nothing seemed to be working except the vital equipment in this command centre and the medbay. She eventually found a stash of nutri-bars in a cabinet beside the small fridge. There was nothing else to do but wait, listen to Alexander, and to check on Brendon.

Nearly recovered, Alex ripped off the medicomp apparatus. An angry red welt showed where his head had been cut. As long as he did nothing too strenuous the bone would knit well, and he adamantly refused to put his arm in a sling.

"What sort of an image are we going to give these people if they see us getting hurt so easily?" he argued, stomping into the control lounge.

"Oh, I don't know … about as good an image as seeing us crashing into the damn planet I guess." Dianah looked up. "How's the arm?"

"Fracking sore! What do you think?"

Dianah left him to sulk. Although the state-of-the-art air filtration system worked with extreme sufficiency, the air still tasted of a faint acrid odour along the passage. Moving towards the rear of the craft, she looked at the structure Alex mentioned; a smooth column of dark metal running from floor to ceiling, with a small keypad and console at waist height. Thought to be physically impossible, this was the astounding temporal generator David invented. As she said, she was not a technician, and her knowledge extended to little more than its basic function.

Entering the medbay, she checked the stasis unit containing the results of her latest genetics research, relieved the crash hadn't disturbed the phials. She had hoped there would be some way to continue her experiments after their arrival at their intended destination. The way circumstances were at the moment, if she couldn't further her experiments soon, then the genetic material would become unviable and years of research would be ruined.

She cursed Alexander again, under her breath. "Damn the man for having pulled me away from my labs!"

"Don't forget, sweetheart," Alex's voice came from the comlink, "you also had reasons to escape the tower. In fact, it was lucky I came along when I did—"

She snapped the com off with viscous twist. "And damn you for being right!"

Brendon regained consciousness about an hour later. He groggily stumbled through the ship at her insistence, and plugged into the medicomp to check his condition. The medicomp rapidly scanned and measured his vitals, detecting a large contusion to his temporal lobe, but nothing else warranted treatment. It automatically administered the appropriate medications and nanites, and as soon as his condition showed signs of improving the huge man was released.

"Okay then," Dianah said when they were all back in the control centre. "We've all had our differences. How about a truce until we know where we are and how to get out of this shit?" She looked at them in turn.

Alex made as if he was examining his arm and Brendon kept looking outside through the vid screen.

"Are the both of you going to act like adults or just a couple of kids? I'm not saying who's right or wrong, just that three minds are better than one. Hostilities may resume at a later date, when our survival isn't at stake. I won't even suggest you shake on it. We know how ludicrous that would be. How about it?"

"All right," Brendon replied flatly.

Dianah turned to Alex. Eventually he just nodded slightly. It would have to do. It was time to go out and introduce themselves. Brendon used his strength to operate the door, which had buckled slightly from the heat and impact. The three slowly emerged, Alexander and Dianah in front with heads low. Brendon, unaffected by the openness, stared curiously about.

Alexander glanced at the robed men kneeling in the mud

with heads bowed low then lowered his gaze to the ground before he suffered vertigo. "So, what the hell's this all about? Where the hell are we?" he muttered.

"More to the point," Brendon muttered, "is *when* the hell are we?"

As they spoke, one of the robed men tentatively stood up and approached. He was older, with a muddy, grey beard reaching down to his waist.

"Welcome. Welcome, Oh Lords. I am Father Estley of the Watchers from yonder monastery dedicated to the Goddess of Time, Eternix." He pointed as he spoke. "We have been four decades in waiting, and are honoured to have you finally among us. How may we serve you?"

"What language is that?" Alex asked.

Bewildered, the three looked at each other.

Dianah looked thoughtful. "I believe it may be one of those old languages of Europe. I'm not sure; I'm not a linguist either." She still refused to look higher than their muddy sandals.

"Europe! Don't be stupid," Alexander snapped. "Did you recognise any of the landmasses before we crashed? Does this look like Earth to you? There's nowhere with so much greenery!"

"No, of course not, but look at them." She managed to raise her eyes to view the closest men. "Filthy as they are, they're definitely human. We can probably make good use of some of them for my experiments. I'm curious as to how they got here."

"If they got here, then there must be a way back." Alex briefly surveyed the crowd immediately in front of them, then attempted to look above the tree line, before getting giddy with the size of outside. "Look over there." He quickly lowered his eyes again to rest on the comforting ground. "See that building? I saw it just before we crashed, on a headland near a harbour. They must've come from there. Let's see what these blokes have to say." He turned to the large man behind him. "Brendon," he smiled sweetly. "Would you go and find the translator? It may be in the locker next to where those enviro-suits are stowed." He added, when Brendon left, "It would seem they think highly of us as it is. If we play their game right, we could do well for ourselves."

"As long as I can carry on with my research, I'll do whatever needs to be done." With eyes still downcast, Dianah surveyed the swampy area immediately in front of her. "Let's get out of this stinking swamp!" Unable to hide the distaste in her voice and with nausea threatening again, she turned and walked back inside the ship.

THE BEGINNING

continued in Book 1
City of Bridges

END NOTES

Characters

Earth

Leonie: a hybrid (rrell/human) thief. Agile, black fur, violet eyes, heals fast, excellent senses, faster than average, stronger than average, 6', 160lbs

Jade: human female, Taker Guild Master, Leonie's boss and friend/mentor

Feiron: illios (shapechanger) (aka Hectr Cerrin, aka Drial)

Sussah: human, female, friends of Leonie

David (Carter) Osbourne: human, male, son of Sussah, genius, inventor of a time-

machine, founder of SciCorps

Rhiannon: human, female, wilder/mutant, seer, elder of Jenolan wilder community

Bern: human, male, wilder runner messenger from Jenolan community.

Clara: human, female, elder of Jenolan wilder community

Lana: human, female, elder of Westridge wilder community

Lerry Carter: human, male, agtech from Blue Mountain Tower, life-partner to Maz

Harrond Carter: human, male, agtech from Blue Mountain Tower, son of Maz and

Stefan Felton: human, male partner to Veronica, father of Dianah, Blue Mountains

Alexander Zodaich: human, male, (aka Lord Zander) son of Nicholai and Ivana, Blue Mountains Tower

Dianah Felton: human, female, (aka Lady Dianah) daughter of Stefan and Veronica, Blue Mountains Tower

Brendon: human, male, (aka Lord Brendon) wilder/mutant from Baraga wilder

community, unknown twin of David, Blue Mountains Tower

Sergeant Bretton: human, male, TowerPol sergeant in Blue Mountains tower

Commander Jay: human, male, TowerPol commander in Blue Mountains Tower

Captain Wester: male, TowerPol officer, Blue Mountains Tower

Drake: human, male, mercenary leader working for HelixR, owner of the *Vulture*

Blanchard: human, male, mercenary working for HelixR, crew of the *Vulture*

Yarnik

Styx: hroltahg, becomes Leonie's telepath trainer/mentor, from Reenat

Dwer: hroltahg, from White Cliffs, Qelay

Riff: hroltahg, from White Cliffs, Qelay

Philbert: human, male, Tesakian, wyvern trainer. Resides Hell's Maw

Dorn: female wyvern, green, and mate to Noldor. Leonie's telepath trainer/mentor. Resides Hell's Maw, Philbert's ride, mother to Slana and Faldo

Noldor: male wyvern, green, and mate to Dorn, Dorn's mate, sire to Slana and Faldo

Slana: young female wyvern, green, sibling to Faldo, resides Hell's Maw, Leonie's ride

Faldo: young male wyvern, green, sibling to Slana, resides Hell's Maw, Feiron's ride

Ro: human, male, Jade's 'bodyguard', plainsman from the Northern Reaches

Netoha: human, female, Ro's partner, plainswoman from the Northern Reaches

Tipp Nul Chor Tukk: glins'ool, male, high-ranking bard from Reenat

Castellan Rodrig Mikanthus: human, male, commander of the garrison and mining town, Arilaso, Lyhosa

Flin si Sloor: glins'ool male, Talon from Tana Keep, Lyhosa

Arulan Simiran: human female, lady of Arilaso, Lyhosa

Jesop Simiran: human male, lord of Arilaso, Lyhosa

Rohan: human male, Dalmellington, Gnash-ville, gnasher trainer, son of Ro and Netoha

Sarrein: human female, Dalmellington, partner to Rohan

King Reindet Moreward: human, male royal seat, Reenat

Queen Brianna Moreward: human, female royal seat, Reenat

Princess Siola Moreward: human, female, first in line to the throne, Reenat

Princess Phione Moreward: human, female, second in line to the throne, Reenat

Prince Orren Moreward: human, male royal seat, Reenat

Krre'lo: human, male, First Magus, Shaper Hall Reenat

Count Trent Covinger: human, male, cousin to Siola and Phione, Reenat

Castellan Willom Lockstrong: human, male, royal guard captain, Reenat

Larp: human, male, Taker henchman, Delta

Sam: human, male, Taker Guild master, Delta, brother to Helen

Helen: human, female, Earth Temple priestess, sister to Sam

Rickard: human, male, Wharf Inn, Delta, biological father to David

Gorle: human, male, henchman, Taker's Guild, Delta

Anja: human, female, waitress Last Resort, Delta

Mr Defuol: human, male, manager Last Resort, Delta

Tieru Jerts: illios, male, High priest for Time/Eternix, in Delta

Olekk: human, male, rebel powershaper, First Magus of Delta

Agnetta: human, female, powershaper from Reenat

Kizgra: seleth, male, powershaper from Reenat

Truskot: rrell, male, powershaper from Reenat

Kade: human, male, powershaper from Reenat

Rollos: Afiid, Rutto Jyggr, Werrg, Oueel, Pewwu, Mewwr, and Hassr from Masevalon

Adera Belaarus: human, female, Flight Leader Grey Wing, Reenat Gryphon Riders

Tholart: human, male, Grey Wing lieutenant, Reenat Gryphon Riders

Florin: human, female, Grey Wing, Reenat Gryphon Riders

Omodamos: lead gryphon, ridden by Adera, Reenat Gryphon Riders

Mandilo: gryphon, ridden by Florin, Reenat Gryphon Riders

Sme'na: human, female, rebel powershaper from Delta

Zakari: seleth, male, Ambassador, from Reenat

Indala: female, human, wyvern rider, from Tesak

Limma: wyvern, female, ridden by Indala

Rmero: hroltahg, female, in Garangoa, Tesak

Graja: human, male, villager from Kalingirga, Ertuk

Councillor Peratta: female, human, from La Trobe Tower

Councillor Nan'chu: male, human, from Carlton Towers

Lieroh: illios, female, ambassador, Blue Mountains Tower

Slarrnok: illios, male, ambassador, Blue Mountains Tower

Brother Armad: male, human, Watcher priest, pre-Delta

Brother Niko: male, human, Watcher priest, pre-Delta

Father Estley: male, human, Watcher High Priest, pre-Delta

Air/Spacecraft

Skydancer: prototype time machine, space yacht conversion, designed David Osbourne, SciCorps

Sundancer: time machine, designed David Osbourne, SciCorps

Vulture: Drake's craft, used for his mercenary tasks for HelixR

Eidolon: ex-military dreadnought pre-2300, now old pit-mine workhorse

Races of Yarnik

The bulk of the populace inhabits the Shak'aran continent, however a few groups of seleth and rrell have favoured the more arid conditions of Ghalena, a continent to the south.

humans: fair skinned, bipedal, generally head and facial hair (males), average senses, strength and speed, 4'5"-6'5", 110-230lbs

rrell: (feline): generally bipedal, fur (can run faster on all four paws), any solid colour: white, brown, grey, ginger, black, but may have dual or tri-colours (rare), whiskers, claws, keen smell, acute hearing, highly agile and dexterous, acute hearing and vision/night vision. Between 5'-6', 80-150lbs, possibly telepathic

illios: (shapeshifter): greyish blobs (natural form), potentially can form many shapes (can't change mass), average senses, telepathic immunity, regenerative ability, 1'-7' (shape-dependant), average senses

hroltahg: (rollos): very heavy/dense individual, grey to black, 100% powerful telepathy (no eyes, nose, mouth, ears), very heavy: 250-500lbs, ball-shape approx. 1'-2' diameter

seleth: (reptoid): bipedal, scales/thick skin, variations of mottled green or brown (black or white rare), 150-350lbs, 4'-5', acute smell and taste, very strong, poor reflex and speed, possibly telepathic

vorien: (mermen/women): bipedal, fine scales, any colour/combination, fins, acute smell and taste in water/poor on land, can survive on land for several hours, slow on land, fast in water, 100-300lbs, 4'-6', possibly telepathic

glins'ool: (avian): bipedal & wings feathers, fast and agile (better in the air/flying), any colour combination, 50-100lbs, 4'-6', possibly telepathic

gryphon: large, fierce flying creatures

gnasher: large, flightless birds with a temper

wyverns: indigenous to Yarnik, bipedal & wings, long necks, spiked tail, various solid colours (offspring lighter shade than parents), all telepathic, keen senses, can fly/glide all day, 2000-4000lbs, 40'-80' long (snout to tail)

l'ithnamagri: indigenous to Yarnik, giant ant-like creatures, ten legs, mandibles, black, 500-800lbs, acute smell/hearing and vibration senses, poor eyesight, very fast, very strong, telepathic/ pheromones

<u>Temples / Religious Orders</u>

The religious orders on Shak'aran are based on the eight elements:
Air, Fire, Water, Earth, Spirit, Time, Life, and Death

Woorin Temple: Woorin: God of Fire,
Opsyss Temple: Opsyss: God of Death,
Temple of Eternix: Eternix: Goddess of Time
Temple of Life: Mimmis: Goddess of Life
Air Temple: Oes'het: God of Air
Water Temple: Ler'eni: Goddess of Water
Spirit Temple: Emera: Goddess of Spirit
Temple Of Earth: Qevlir: God of Earth

Locations / Places of Interest
Yarnik

Shak'aran: major continent, includes countries: Athglenn, Lyhosa, Tesak, Fisbane, Ertuk, Gruarch, In'sha, Central Steppes, Northern Reaches, Shattered Isles

Ghalena: arid continent to the far south across the Gratharg Expanse

Delta: rogue 'city-state' trading port in southern Athglenn, at the mouth of the Urmaq River

Reenat: capital city of Athglenn, seat of the true rulers of Athglenn

Plenari: capital city of Tesak, built on and around the massive trees of the Tesakian

'The Web': poor quarter of Delta, generally for downtrodden, outcasts and misfits

Portside: western side of Delta harbour, for more prosperous traders, merchants and families

Dockside: eastern side of Delta harbour, for smaller, less prosperous traders and merchants

Indras: rural town on the North Road, half way to Qelay on the Urmaq River

Dalmellington: rural town, halfway between Hellam and Qelay, Athglenn

Hellam: rural mining town in the foothills of the Central Ranges, Athglenn

Hell's Maw: volcano in the Central Ranges, lair to wyverns

Central Ranges: vast mountain range stretching from far north coast to south coast, also called 'Spine of the World'

Qelay: major rural city in Athglenn, halfway to Reenat. Head of the Urmaq River

White Cliffs: resort especially designed to cater for hroltahgs, located in Qelay

Swangrove: small rural town north of Indras on the Urmaq River

Urmaq River: Largest river in Athglenn, from springs in Lake Urmaq to south coast

Deraz River: small tributary feeds into the Urmaq River

Vale of Dromas: a region in the centre of the continent. Fabled to be home to the original and ancient city of Dromas. Historians believe it was destroyed during a Powershaper War, which had a devastating impact on the terrain

Kalingirga: fishing village in Ertuk, location of the illios portal

Garangoa: rural mining logging community in southern Tesak

Scorian: rural mining logging community in northern Tesak

Skyhome: temporary wilder refuge on a skyland over west Shak'aran

Skylands: hundreds of these sky islands of many and varied sizes, float around the Shak'aran hundreds or thousands of feet in the sky. It is believed they are the remains of Dromas; the effects of the Powershaper War ripped the ground asunder. The unusual crystalline mantle – believed to be the source of 'power' (magic) – is repelled when drained of 'power'

Ghalena: southern continent. Very arid, mostly desert

Garangoa: Tesakian township at the foothills of the Central Ranges

Luminor & Luxor: twin moons orbiting Yarnik, believed to eclipse approx. every 100 years

Diphei: Yarnik's sun, closest star of the binary-star system, G-type star

Zastre: the other star of the binary-star system, much larger and hotter. The elliptical orbit of Diphei will bring it (and Yarnik) very close, resulting in extreme temperatures

Locations / Places of Interest
Earth

Blue Mountains Tower: a megabuilding housing over a million people, east coast of New South Wales, Australia

Atherton Tower: a megabuilding housing over half a million people, Atherton Tablelands, Far North Queensland, Australia

LA 3: a megabuilding housing over two million people, west coast of California, America

Jenolan: wilder community, New South Wales, Australia

Westridge: wilder community, New South Wales, Australia

Kanangra: wilder community, New South Wales, Australia

Burraga: wilder community, nearest badlands, New South Wales, Australia

Northcliff: wilder community, New South Wales, Australia

Badlands: area west of the mountains, most radiated region in New South Wales

Badlands Pit Mines: open mine nearest meteor impact site, New South Wales, Australia

Outpost: domed structures surrounding the vast crop fields of the towers, used by agtechs when on duty

The Home Worlds

Earth: human homeworld

Ey'ikar: glins'ool homeworld

Isuiips: vorien homeworld

Masevalon: hroltahg homeworld

Praven: seleth homeworld

Torone: illios homeworld

Thiqurian: rrell homeworld

Yarnik: l'ithnamagri and wyvern homeworld

ACKNOWLEDGMENTS

As always, nothing could be done (with any level of confidence) without my intrepid beta-readers, Peter J Aldin, Stephen Kerwin and Aaron Cordy for their perseverance and polite pointing out of my failings … all of them.

I'd also like to thank Belinda Crawford for her artwork for the series covers;
https://www.facebook.com/groups/designedbyboots/

and Barbara Holten for her editing prowess:
https://barbarajholten.com

And finally but most importantly, my wife Morag for putting up with my absent-minded rantings, and our daughter, Meredith – for putting up with me and also *her* mum for putting up with my absent-minded rantings.

ABOUT THE AUTHOR

Andre Jones made his debut appearance (unless you believe in reincarnation – in which case this is his third) in Wollongong, NSW Australia and has managed to stick around for 59 years so far.

Okay, okay … enough of the third-person stuff …

My parents were Dutch immigrants, and since I had a gloomy and challenging childhood, (and I've forgotten most of it) I immersed myself with drawing, reading and sometimes writing. As a child, I devoured the works of Enid Blyton before progressing to Tolkien, McAffrey, Asimov, Heinlein and Bradbury. As a young adult, I got happily lost in many and varied roleplaying games, including: MERP, GURPS, Harn, Skyrealms of Jorune, good old D&D *(and its many variants)* and Traveller. (I never got into these new card games) … and I also spent far too much time on video games like Skyrim (but nothing to regret).

This 'not so interesting' life led me to various occupations: Security Officer, Police Officer, Park Ranger and finally as a Petty Officer Electronics Technician in the Royal Australian Navy for 18 years *(sadly, my role-playing stopped there)*.

Currently residing in Melbourne with my lovely – and very understanding – Scottish wife and a British Shorthair cat, I'm now a Navy Veteran with the opportunity to write, roleplay, draw and potter to my heart's content.

ANDRE JONES is an emerging author of epic fantasy, urban fantasy and science fiction novels.

<u>Please consider leaving a Review</u>
Help other readers find this epic fantasy series by leaving a review on Amazon, Goodreads, or any other website. Even simple ones like a star-rating really help with a book – and an author's – success.